About the Authors

USA Today bestselling author **Catherine Mann** has books in print in more than twenty countries with Mills & Boon Desire, Mills & Boon Heroes and other imprints. A six-time RITA® finalist, she has won both a RITA® and Romantic Times Reviewer's Choice Award. Mother of four, Catherine lives in South Carolina where she enjoys kayaking, hiking with her dog and volunteering in animal rescue. FMI, visit: catherinemann.com

Lynn Raye Harris is a Southern girl, military wife, wannabe cat lady, and horse lover. She's also the *New York Times* and *USA Today* bestselling author of the *Hostile Operations Team*® Series of military romances, and twenty books about sexy billionaires for Mills & Boon. Lynn lives in Alabama with her handsome former-military husband, one fluffy princess of a cat, and a very spoiled American Saddlebred horse who enjoys bucking at random in order to keep Lynn on her toes.

With two beautiful daughters, **Lucy Ryder** has had to curb her adventurous spirit and settle down. But, because she's easily bored by routine, she's turned to writing as a creative outlet, and to romances because – 'What else is there other than chocolate?' Characterised by friends and family as a romantic cynic, Lucy can't write serious stuff to save her life. She loves creating characters who are funny, romantic and just a little cynical.

Passion in Paradise

Passion in Paradise:
Stranded and
Seduced

CATHERINE MANN

LYNN RAYE HARRIS

LUCY RYDER

MILLS & BOON

First Published in Great Britain 2022
By Mills & Boon, an imprint of HarperCollins*Publishers*, Ltd
1 London Bridge Street, London, SE1 9GF

www.harpercollins.co.uk

HarperCollins*Publishers*
1st Floor, Watermarque Building,
Ringsend Road, Dublin 4, Ireland

PASSION IN PARADISE: STRANDED AND SEDUCED © 2022 Harlequin
Enterprises ULC

His Secretary's Little Secret © 2016 Catherine Mann
The Girl Nobody Wanted © 2012 Harlequin Books S.A.
Caught in a Storm of Passion © 2016 Bev Riley

Special thanks and acknowledgement are given to Lynn Raye Harris for her contribution to *The Santina Crown* series.

ISBN: 978-0-263-30571-5

MIX
Paper from
responsible sources
FSC **FSC™ C007454**
www.fsc.org

HIS SECRETARY'S LITTLE SECRET

CATHERINE MANN

To my animal rescue pals everywhere—especially Virginia, Sharon and Tiffany. You bring such talent, joy and support to this emotional journey!

One

Portia Soto's mama always said doctors didn't grow on trees. That an exotic name couldn't make up for her plain looks. And to count her blessings if she got a proposal from a podiatrist twice her age.

Clearly, Portia's mama hadn't counted on her daughter ever sitting beneath a towering palm watching Dr. Easton Lourdes hang upside down by his knees as he tried to save an ivory-billed woodpecker. An endangered species and thus warranting the wildlife preserve veterinarian's full attention. Which was convenient, since that meant he wouldn't notice he'd totally captured Portia's.

Between the branches of the ancient black mangrove, small stars winked into her vision, the lingering violet of sunset fading into black. The moments just after sunset in the wildlife preserve were Portia's favorite. Night birds trilled overlapping tunes through the dense, steamy woods. Everything seemed somehow prettier, more lush and flamboyant in the absence of sunlight—the preserve transformed into a decadent Eden. At night, the place was a mysterious beauty, far more enticing than Portia had ever considered herself to be.

Except she didn't feel much like herself when she was around Dr. Lourdes.

To be frank, Easton was hot. Really hot. Sexy in a shaggy-haired, unconventional way. An extremely wealthy heir to a family fortune, and a genius veterinarian with a specialty in exotic animals.

He also happened to be the unsuspecting father of Portia's unborn baby, thanks to one impulsive night during a tropical storm nearly two months ago.

In the time that had passed since their unplanned hookup, she'd done her best to put their relationship back on a professional level, to safeguard her hard-won space and independence. A task that had been increasingly difficult to stick to, what with him casting steamy, pensive looks her way when he thought she wasn't aware.

But wow, was she ever aware of him. Always.

So apparently, for Portia, doctors did grow on trees. But that didn't stop the chaos overtaking her life in spite of her best efforts to carefully organize and control her world. She wanted to figure out her plan for the future before she told her onetime lover about their baby. But she was running out of time.

They'd had an impulsive encounter during the stress and fear of being in close quarters during a tropical storm. Such an atypical thing for her to do—have a one-night stand, much less a one-night stand with her boss. She'd always followed the rules, and she'd denied her attraction to Easton until the tension of that tumultuous frightful storm had led her to give in.

She'd enjoyed every moment of that night, but the next morning she'd freaked out. She'd worried about putting her much-needed job and on-site housing in jeopardy—and about how intensely being with Easton had moved her. She didn't have time for messy emotions, much less a relationship. She'd been living day to day, working to keep her head above water financially, especially since her brother had started college four years ago.

Now she had no choice but to think about the future for her child. Her need to establish her independence had to be placed on the fast track for her child's sake. She refused to let her baby have the unsure life she herself had lived through because of her parents' lack of any care or planning for their children's welfare.

The thought of the future nudged Portia into movement. A small movement, of course. It wasn't as if she could just run out of here and leave her boss without the spotlight she was holding. Her hand fell to her still smooth stomach covered by a loose T-shirt layered over trim cargo shorts—her fieldwork basics. Neatly pressed, of course.

A leaf plummeted to the ground with surprising speed. Ten more fell down from the limb above her head, reminding Portia to pay attention to the man above her.

"Can you adjust the spotlight to the left?"

"Sure, how far?"

"To the left."

Ah, nice and vague. Her favorite sort of directions. "Four inches? Twelve inches?"

"Move and I'll tell you when to stop."

"That works—" Portia checked her response. She'd been second-guessing herself more than ever since that night. Things that hadn't bothered her before now suddenly worried her.

"Stop."

Four inches. She'd moved four flipping inches. How much easier would it have been for him to say that?

She sighed. She was irritable, nauseated and her swollen breasts hurt like crazy. She needed a new bra ASAP. Under cover of the dark, she repositioned one poking end away from her tender flesh. "Can you see now?"

"Almost got it. Just have to stretch farther."

The syllables also stretched, just as she imagined his fingers were doing. Always dramatic. Which was part of his allure…

A cracking sound popped through the night. Portia looked up into the twisted web of branches, her eyes desperately trying to process the image before her. She watched Easton fall out of the black mangrove in what felt like slow motion. He was a silhouetted rush of leaves and flailing limbs, culminating in an echoing thud as he hit the ground. The chorus of nighttime birds stopped as if they too were interested in the doctor's fate.

Panic filled her veins. Her feet and hands grew numb but she pushed them into motion. Fast.

He didn't move, and from her distance, she couldn't see if his chest rose and fell. "Easton!"

His name was a plea and a command to answer all at once. His limbs were splayed out inches from the tree trunk. He'd barely missed landing on the protruding roots. From the muted light, it looked like he had barely avoided impaling himself on a decaying tree limb.

She closed in on him, crouched down to examine him. Thank the Lord, he was breathing. She felt his pulse. It was strong, but he didn't respond to her touch.

Laying a hand on his shoulder, she gently shook him. Wanting him to be okay. Needing him to be okay. The thought of him hurt sent her mind tumbling into the land of what-if? She'd become adequate at shoving the big what-ifs aside, but with the father of her future child lying unconscious, worst-case scenarios flooded her mind.

What if she didn't get to tell him about the baby? What if he was in a coma? What if…

What if his eyes—sharp blue as lapis lazuli—opened and he continued to look at her like *that*? Her wild thoughts halted as she saw his mischievous gaze trace her outline in the dark.

"I'm alright but don't let that make you move," he muttered, the right corner of his lips pulling up with sexy confidence.

His dark hair curled around his neck—twigs and branches adorning his head like the crown of some mythical forest prince. A sexy prince at that. Her hand lingered on his wrist, making her recall the night they'd spent together. The way he'd held her. She had carefully avoided his touch since they'd woken up to safety and a return to their normal working relationship—since finding out she carried his baby. Everything felt complicated.

She wanted to bolt away. Pushing her back into the neighboring Florida buttonwood tree, she swallowed hard. She didn't know how much longer she could keep her job, living in her cabana on the refuge, and hide the truth. There just wasn't time to save all the money she would need to be independent before the truth became obvious. The panic nearly made her lose her breath, but she pushed it aside as she'd been doing for weeks.

Yes, she would tell him. He deserved to know. But she wanted to get through that initial doctor's appointment first, and each day gave her more time to organize her thoughts into the best way to balance this scary turn her life had taken.

A turn of events made all the more difficult by the way her body remembered too well the explosive passion they'd shared. Even thinking about that night, with the feel and scent of him so close now, turned her inside out with want.

He rested on his back, watching her with those clear blue eyes as he stroked a loose strand of her hair. "Damn, you're a pretty woman."

"Stop. You don't mean it." Why had she said that? It was as good as asking for another compliment and she'd sworn to herself she wouldn't spend her life wrapped up in appearances as her beauty queen mother had.

His gaze held hers and refused to let go. "Don't I?"

"Maybe you do in your own way. But you're a flirt. Get your mind on business. How's the bird?"

Though the movement made him wince, he straightened, sitting up. He had managed to protect the fragile bird during his fall. Easton held it proudly as it nestled into his hand. "Not a mark on him— not from the fall, anyway. We should get back to the clinic and figure out why he's unable to fly."

"I'll drive. Unless you object, but you really shouldn't," she couldn't stop herself from babbling, "since you did just fall from a tree."

He shrugged, rising slowly to his feet. "Of course

you can drive. Why would I have a problem with your driving?"

"Most men prefer to drive." Her father always had, declaring her mother too airheaded to be trusted behind the wheel. Scrunching her nose at the memory, Portia stood, dusting off the leaves that clung to her pants.

"I'm not most men. And you're right. I did just fall out of a tree." He shed more small twigs as they made their way to the sanctuary's four-door truck.

"Then it's settled. I'll take the wheel." Driving the massive vehicle would allow her some element of control. And damn, did she need that in spades right now.

"You're a better driver than I am anyway, even when I haven't backflipped down a few limbs to land on my ass."

"Okay, seriously, I can't think of another man on the planet who would admit that." As her head moved, a strand of her normally perfectly pulled-back hair caught on her eyelash. On instinct, her hand flew upward, folding it back into her ponytail. Back to order.

He grinned roguishly. "Then they must not have my confidence."

Her eyebrows lifted. "Or arrogance."

"True." He slid into the passenger side. "You asked for an appointment with me earlier and then the emergency call came in about the ivory-billed woodpecker. We'll have some time to talk on the drive back. What did you wish to speak about?"

Telling him about her pregnancy like this? Not at all what she planned. Not at all what she would do. When she told him, it'd be in a calm setting. One of her choosing. Not in the company of a wild, injured animal. Or a wildly sexy, injured man. "This isn't the time."

"Why not? Is it that serious? If so, speak up now," he said firmly, turning to face her. Those blue eyes demanding something of her.

"Let's take care of business first." Her lips thinned into a line. Pushing him away. Her mother had depended on a man for everything and then had nothing when that man died bankrupt in prison. Portia had vowed she wouldn't let herself commit to anyone until she was certain she could stand on her two feet, debt free and independent. She wouldn't let herself think about how much harder that would be as a single mother.

His eyes narrowed and she could practically see him running through a catalog of possible topics.

"It's personal?" he asked.

"That's not what I said."

"About the night of the tropical storm six weeks ago—" A hungry smile pushed along his mouth.

Damn him for being so intuitive. He had a knack for that. All the more reason for her to be carefully guarded around him.

"Let's not speak about that now."

"You haven't wanted to speak of it since the storm. When are we ever going to talk about it? You're a determined woman, that's for certain."

She knew she couldn't delay the conversation forever, but right now her stomach was still in turmoil over his fall. And she wanted to go to her first doctor's appointment to confirm that the pregnancy was on track before turning her whole world upside down.

And yes, she was trying to think of any reason she could to delay, because once she told Easton about his baby, she would lose control of her life forever.

Dr. Easton Lourdes leaned his seat halfway back, his head still spinning. Partly from the fall, but mostly from the woman beside him and the memory of those moments he'd kept his eyes closed and just absorbed the feel of her against him. Since she'd come to work with him two years ago, he'd suspected there were fires burning behind her uptight demeanor. But hell, he'd had no idea how hot they'd blaze until that one night with her during the storm.

Portia Soto. The most organized secretary on the planet. The woman who—until recently—had kept his eccentric spirit in line. Until their night of passion during a tropical storm showed him just how wild she could be once she let down that tightly upswept hair.

But the next day, she'd gathered her long caramel-brown hair back as fiercely as ever. Tighter even.

He needed his secretary. The Lourdes Family

Wildlife Refuge was fast becoming an internationally renowned animal research and rescue center, and he was the man in charge of the science. To make the impact he wanted to make on the world, he *needed* his secretary. But he wanted Portia. And he wasn't sure how to have both.

If only he understood humans as well as he did animals. His childhood spent with rich, globe-trotting parents had exposed him to creatures around the world. He'd paid attention and taken in an understanding of animals' unspoken language. But even though he'd had the best of everything money could buy, he'd lacked much in the way of learning how to make connections with people other than his parents and his older brother. No sooner than he'd make a friend, his family would pack up and jet off to another exotic locale.

Easton cracked his neck, a crescendo of echoing pops responded in his back, the tension finally unwinding. With his neck less contracted, he positioned himself so he could watch her. Portia's gel manicured nails were still quite perfect as she gripped the pickup truck's steering wheel at a "nine and three" position that would make any driver's ed teacher proud. Her doe-brown eyes were focused, attentive to the road.

Intentional. That was how he'd describe Portia. Intentional and proper.

With all her wildness contained.

Despite her manicured look, she fit in well at

the wildlife preserve his family owned and funded. Easton brought his world-renowned skills as a veterinarian/scientist specializing in exotic animals. His brother, Xander, ran the family business and fund-raising.

And there sure as hell was a lot of fund-raising and political maneuvering involved in saving animals. Portia's calm organizational skills were an immeasurable asset on that front too, according to his brother, Xander. Easton only had to show up in a tux every few months and talk about the research he loved.

For the most part, he spent his time handling the hands-on rescue and research efforts, and Portia's efficiency helped him make that happen. He was lucky his family's wealth meant he could leave the fund-raising to his brother and get his hands dirty doing what he enjoyed most.

And he tried his damnedest to entice Portia to play in the dirt with him.

Easton's eyes slid from her face to the soft, yellow lights on the road back to the clinic. The preserve stretched for a few acres on Key Largo, a small island in the archipelago south of Florida. A necessary answer to urbanization and tourist development, Easton believed, as did his new board of directors, apparently.

He was damn lucky. He lived his dream every day. Sure, some people were able to turn passion into a paycheck, but Easton was a veterinarian at his preserve solely for passion. He recognized that he'd been blessed by his family's money. It had enabled him to follow his vocation without worrying about compensation. He didn't advertise his lack of salary because, for Easton, it didn't matter. He felt honored to work for the sole purpose of helping the animals. To do some good in this world. Money had never been a big concern for him personally, but the reality of a small refuge accountable to a board of directors meant he had to worry about things like that on occasion.

As a secretary, Portia was brilliant—organized, dedicated—exactly what a free-spirited guy like him needed. But he also wanted her, as a man, and that made working with Portia increasingly challenging.

Since he'd hired her, he'd noticed her—and then he'd immediately move his attention back to business. But now, he caught himself distracted by the pinkness of her lips, the way she straightened her ponytail when she was thinking. Over and over, he'd replayed that night in his head. In a perfect world, he could have both. His kick-ass secretary and his sexy lover, too. But Portia had made it damn clear he wasn't welcome in her bed again. She'd sent him a brief morning-after text and then ignored his messages unless they were work related.

His heart pounded as he thought of the last—and only—time they'd been together. The memory ramped him up—before he deliberately pushed it aside.

Regaining focus on the present, he surveyed her tight smile. Portia hadn't said much in the past few minutes, but as if she needed to fill the space with words, she sliced through his thoughts. "So do you think the bird broke a wing?"

He blinked, troubled at the formality of her tone. "Perhaps. I'll have to x-ray it to be certain."

"Good. I'm glad we were able to help him." Matter-of-fact as ever. All business. No hint, no trace of anything more.

She pulled the truck into the driveway of the clinic, parking it. As she turned to face him, he saw concern pass through her eyes. Had she been that worried about his fall?

His fingers ached to touch her bare skin, to explore her gentle curves. Although her breasts were more generous than he remembered. What else had he remembered wrong from their dimly lit, rushed lovemaking? The space between them dwindled, electricity sparking in the air there.

Her eyes danced, and he saw that spark take hold in her, too. The same spark from the night of the storm.

He wanted to nurture that spark into a flame.

He kissed her. God, he kissed her. Tried to rein himself in so he could savor the moment rather than risking another fast and furious encounter. He didn't want to send her running as he had before. But damn, she tasted good. Felt good. He slid his hands up to cup her face.

For an incredible moment, she seemed to kiss him back. Then everything shifted. She pulled away, her skin sickly pale.

And then she opened the door and ran. More than ran. She flat-out bolted before he could even form a syllable.

This man had a way of flipping her stomach upside down on a regular day, and now that she was pregnant, her stomach didn't seem to know which way was up.

Her ballet flats slammed, skidded against the ground. Her stomach rumbled a protesting gurgle, bile rising in the back of her throat.

She ran inside the clinic, through the side entrance and toward her office off the main reception space. She sagged back against the wall, sliding down to the floor while trying to decide if she needed to race the rest of the way to the restroom or simply stay put, calm, unmoving.

Yes, staying still was best. She drew in one deep breath after another. With each breath, she tried to focus on her immediate surroundings. At least the normally bustling clinic lacked people at this hour. All the staff and volunteers had gone home after settling the animals in for the night. Good, she'd hate to have an audience for this. Her eyes adjusted to the dim light, and she heard the creak of the door that lead to the supply closet.

Portia swallowed again, feeling unease and nausea reclaim her stomach.

A light flicked on in an adjoining office with the door open. Maureen. Easton's research assistant and sister-in-law. Like Easton, Maureen put in long hours, sacrificing sleep for the animals' sake.

She had a clipboard in her hand, and a pen tucked in her hair. Maureen must've been doing inventory. While keeping a meticulous inventory made life at the clinic run smoothly during all seasons, hurricane season made this task rise to a new level of importance. If the intensity of the tropical storm a few weeks ago was any indication of the hurricanes to come, Portia knew how vital it would be to the survival of the refuge for them to maintain plans and supplies.

But what of her own plans?

Portia took a steadying breath as Maureen noticed her and came over. Her bright red hair bouncing in curls, Maureen crouched next to Portia, green eyes searching.

"Are you okay?" Maureen's slight Irish brogue lilted.

"I'm fine. I just forgot to eat dinner and I'm lightheaded. Low blood sugar. I'll be fine."

Standing, Maureen opened a drawer in the supply room, the one where she'd stashed other sorts of emergency supplies—saltines, PowerBars and gum. "You work too hard."

Maureen tossed her a packet of crackers. To

Portia's surprise, she actually caught the wrapped package, shaking hands and all. Tearing open the wrapper, Portia stood and took her time nibbling while she searched for the right words to deflect Maureen's comment.

"I enjoy my work." Not completely true.

She was grateful for her well-paying job and the adorable one-bedroom cabana that came with it. She had a dream of becoming a teacher one day, but she needed to pay for her brother's education and save enough to finance her own—

Except that wasn't going to happen. She was out of time to fulfill her own dreams. She had to think of her brother and this baby. And even if her pay doubled, there wasn't even enough time to figure all of that out before she had to confess everything to Easton.

She hated thinking about money at all. It made her feel too much like her gold digger mother. But there were practical realities to consider.

Like getting some crackers into her stomach before she hurled.

She nibbled on the edge of a saltine. Each bite settling her stomach. For the moment, anyway.

Maureen glanced around the clinic, leaning around the corner that lead to the examination room. "Where's the doctor?"

"He's examining an injured bird we rescued." Or so she assumed. She'd left him in a bit of a hurry.

What on earth had he been thinking to kiss her like that?

More to the point, what had she been thinking to allow it to happen? To respond? Normally, she prided herself on her control. Her good sense. With Easton, it seemed, she had neither.

Maureen passed over a container of wet wipes, her bright diamond ring glittering. Recently, she'd married Easton's brother, Xander. "Here."

"What?" Portia took them, confused.

"You've got dust on your knees and on your elbows."

She looked down to check, heat flaming her cheeks as she remembered being close to Easton. Of their bodies pressed against each other on the hard ground. Not that she intended to share those details with anyone. "It's messy work out there."

As if on cue to make her cheeks flame hotter, the side door opened and she heard the long stride that was distinctly Easton's. From a distance, he glanced at her, the bird cradled against his chest in a careful but firm hold.

Maureen stepped forward. "Do you need help?"

He shook his head. "I've got this. You two carry on."

Easton headed toward the back where they did X-rays, away from other animals. His footsteps grew softer until the sound faded altogether.

Maureen turned back to her. "You seem more of the office job type. I've often wondered what made you take on this position." Blunt and honest conversation with Maureen. While normally Portia appreciated Maureen's directness, Portia didn't know if she had the stamina for this sort of exchange right now.

"The pay is more than generous and the locale is enticing."

Did that sound as lame out loud as she thought? Didn't matter. It was true. She'd needed the better-than-average pay, with housing included, to save the money she needed to pay for her brother. Her stomach did another flip and she reached for a cracker. The scents of the clinic were bothering her in a way they normally didn't—the stringent smell of antiseptic cleaner used religiously on every surface, the wood shavings lining crates, the air of live plants.

"And the pay is such because the other secretaries before you couldn't handle an eccentric boss and his unconventional hours, helping him with X-rays, the animals and fieldwork, cleaning his messy office...or they tried to put the moves on him. And yet you've put up with him even though he's clearly not your type."

Portia stiffened, biting down hard on the edge of the cracker. She chewed and swallowed before speaking. "What would my type be?"

"Did I sound presumptuous? I'm sorry if that came out wrong."

"Not at all. I'm truly curious because... Oh, never mind." The question had sounded innocent, but in a strange way, Portia began to wonder if Maureen knew, or at the very least suspected something had happened between Portia and Easton.

"I just meant I can see you with a suave, well-traveled businessman or a brilliant professor. But of course you're clearly more than capable of taking care of your own love life. Tell me about your type? Or maybe there's already a gentleman in your life?"

A gentleman in her life? Time for a stellar deflection.

Portia arched her brow and rolled her eyes. She did everything she could to visually signify that she had no connection to anyone at all. One of Portia's greatest strengths had always been hiding behind conversation.

"Tell me about your honeymoon plans." That topic ought to do it. Maureen and Xander had delayed their honeymoon trip because, after they were married, they'd realized just how deeply they cared for each other. Originally their marriage had been for convenience—he'd needed a wife to keep custody of his daughter and she'd needed citizenship—but it had since deepened into true love.

"I cannot wait, Portia. It will be hard to be away from Rose for two weeks, but she'll be staying with her grandparents."

Rose, Xander's sweet, blonde baby girl. Portia's unborn baby's cousin.

The weight of that sentiment slammed into her every fiber.

Her baby and Rose would be family. Portia's hand

settled on her stomach. She was connected to this place and this family now, no matter what.

Portia's brother was connected too, through her, even though he lived in the panhandle—in Pensacola, Florida—getting ready to enter his last year of college. He had emotional support from their aunt nearby, but the older woman barely made ends meet. She had gone above and beyond by taking the two of them in after their mother drank herself into liver failure when Portia was thirteen and her brother, Marshall, was only seven.

It was up to Portia to support her family—including this unexpected baby.

Her head started spinning with how tangled everything had become.

Maureen stepped forward, concern creasing her brow. "Are you sure you're feeling alright?"

"It was a long work day. I'm hungry and exhausted. That's all."

She needed to get herself together. Wear looser clothes if need be. Give herself a chance to verify everything was alright with the pregnancy and if it was, take the time she needed to come up with a plan for her future.

She'd worked too hard for her independence to give it up now, no matter how tempting Easton might be.

Two

What the hell was up with Portia?

When he'd stepped into the wildlife preserve's main building, he had taken note of her pale face and standoffish demeanor. Leaving her alone to talk with Maureen seemed the best option. He'd heard the two women leave a half hour later, each sending a quick farewell shout before heading out.

Easton understood that Portia regretted their impulsive encounter during the tropical storm. He'd almost started to accept that it wouldn't be leading anywhere. It was one night and no more.

But then he'd seen that look in her eyes today.

Shaking his head in bemusement, he closed the clinic door and punched in the security code before turning away into the inky dark. Night creatures spoke to him through the cover of darkness, a cooing mix of coastal birds and tropical bugs. He could identify each sound as readily as he could identify different human voices. As a young boy, Easton digested each sound the way some men committed the sounds of roaring engines to memory. He knew each voice and wanted to help ensure they all continued to speak.

He'd had offers to work at other, larger clinics in more exotic locales, but the newly named Lourdes Family Wildlife Refuge was a personal quest for him and his brother. And he liked this place he called home.

As much as he'd enjoyed his eccentric life growing up, always on the move with his globe-trotting parents, he also enjoyed waking up in the same place each morning. The Key Largo–based animal preserve blended the best of both worlds for him—the wilds and home.

Even the main house reflected that balance of barely domesticated wildness. A sprawling mansion, it stood two stories tall, complete with open balconies and an extravagant, oasis-inspired pool.

Which was where Easton was headed now. His brother, Xander, sat alone on one of the lounge chairs, a glass of bourbon neat in his hand.

Easton and his brother had always been different but close. Since their parents traveled the world with little thought of creating a home or helping their kids build friendships, he and his brother relied on each other. Even more so after their father died and their mother continued her world-traveling ways, always looking for the next adventure in each new country rather than staying in one place to connect with her children.

This house represented more than Easton's commitment to preserving animals in Key Largo. This shared space with his brother represented an attempt at familial cohesion. An attempt at proving they could grow something stable, something to be proud of. The moonlight filtered through stray clouds, peppering his walk in a play of shadow and light on the well-maintained lawn.

He didn't want to blame his parents. They deserved to live their lives as they wanted, to be themselves. And even if they hadn't been conventional parents, they had more than lived up to their commitment to feed, house and educate their children.

But as much as he didn't want to blame them, he'd found his rocky relationship with them had influenced him. He found it difficult to sustain lasting relationships with women. He'd had a series of short romances. And the only time he'd even considered the altar, she—Dana—had split up with him right before he could propose. She'd said he was too eccentric, too much of a kid at heart, for a committed relationship.

Which was ironic as hell since he'd already been looking at engagement rings.

He hadn't told her that. Dana probably would have said he wouldn't have been much of a husband, or that he wouldn't have actually bought a ring. And she probably would have been right. He knew he was eccentric, and he'd worked to find the right career to blend his passion and personality with work he cared about. He got to climb trees and play in the woods for a living. Not too shabby as a way of channeling his strengths. He'd taken what he'd inherited of his parents' quirky ways and toned them down, figuring out how to stay in one place.

None of that seemed to matter, though, when it came to figuring out how to settle down, based on his history with Dana, Laura, Naomi... Damn, he was depressing the hell out of himself.

So where did that leave him with Portia?

Once on the stone ground that surrounded the pool, he grabbed a plush lounge chair and pulled it beside Xander. Easton sat in the middle of the lounger, facing his brother. Xander's ocean-colored eyes flicked to him.

Xander had taken on the wildlife preserve in memory of his wife's passing. Reviving the then struggling refuge had been her passion.

This place meant the world to both brothers.

"What's the deal with you and Portia?" Xander's tone was blunt and businesslike—the commanding voice that won him boardroom battles left and right.

"What do you mean?" The answer came too quickly out of Easton's mouth.

"Don't play dumb with me. I was out for a walk with Rose and I saw the way you looked at Portia when you both got into the truck earlier." He sipped his bourbon, fixing Easton with the stare of an older brother.

"Why didn't you say hello or offer to help out?"

"You're trying to distract me. Not going to work. So what gives between you two?"

Easton chose his words carefully, needing to regain control of the conversation before his brother went on some matchmaking kick that would only backfire by making Portia retreat. She was prickly.

And sexy.

And not going to give him the brush-off another time. She'd been avoiding him more than ever recently and he was determined to find out the reason.

"Easton?" Xander pushed.

"She's an attractive woman." Not a lie.

"A cool woman, classic. And she's been here awhile. She's also not your type. So what changed?"

She absolutely wasn't the sort to go out with a guy like him. And yet there was chemistry between them. Crackling so tangibly he could swear he was standing in the middle of a storm with the heavens sending lightning bolts through him. She clearly felt the same way, except the next morning, once the storm had passed, she'd insisted it couldn't happen again. He'd thought if he waited patiently she would wear down.

She hadn't.

Until today. "And what would my type be?"

"You really want me to spell that out?" Xander's crooked glance almost riled Easton.

Almost. Then he reminded himself he was the chill brother normally. He was letting this business with Portia mess with his head.

"No need to spell it out. I'll get defensive and have to kick your ass."

"You can try."

Easton smiled tightly. As kids, he used to lie in wait for Xander, always trying to best him in an impromptu wrestling match. He won about half of the time, which wasn't too bad considering his older brother had shot up with height faster and Easton hadn't caught up—and passed him—until they were in high school. Now, they had exchanged the good-natured physical wrestling for well-placed banter.

Silence between the brothers lingered, allowing the chorus of nocturnal creatures to swell. Not that he minded. Easton and Xander could both get lost in their own thoughts, with neither of them rambling on with nonsensical chatter. He'd always appreciated the ability to hang out with his brother without feeling the need to fill every moment with speech.

Easton had to admit Xander was right. Easton had always dated women who were more like him, free-spirited, unconventional types.

Date?

That didn't come close to describing what had happened between him and Portia.

And maybe that was the problem. What had

stopped him from asking her out on a date? Before that night, he'd wanted to keep their relationship professional. But after they'd crossed that line... He'd been trying to talk to her about that night. But he'd never done the obvious. Ask her out to dinner...and see where things progressed from there.

He'd always been a man of action and speed. But why not take things slowly with her? He had all the time in the world.

Easton didn't know where things were heading with Portia, but he wasn't giving up. He hoped that dating was the right plan and considered asking Xander for input. Usually he and his brother told each other everything, relied on each other for support—hell, they'd been each other's only friend when they'd been traveling with their parents. Easton needed a plan. And his brother was good at plans, and Xander had far more success in the romance department.

Except right now Easton wanted to hold on to the shift in his relationship with Portia. Keep that private between the two of them. He didn't want to risk word getting out and spooking her.

Because, yes, something had changed between Easton and his brother too since Xander had married Maureen, and Easton couldn't figure out what that was. His brother had been married before and had loved his wife, mourned her deeply when she'd died. Still, Easton hadn't felt he'd lost a part of his brother then, not like now.

So yeah, he wasn't ready to share yet.

Or maybe it had nothing to do with his brother.
And everything to do with Portia.

Up until realizing she was pregnant, the most anxiety-inducing moments in Portia's life had been when she'd fretted about taking care of her brother and paying bills.

This morning had combined all of her anxieties. Her secret pregnancy coupled with arriving to work a half hour late. She'd been sick for what felt like hours and it had thrown her off schedule. Portia was never, ever late. Tardiness drove her insane. Since the morning sickness seemed to be getting significantly worse, she might have to move up her appointment with the doctor to next week. That made her stomach flip all the more since it would mean facing the uncomfortable reality of having to tell Easton.

Dr. Lourdes.

Her boss.

Damn.

Refocus. She pushed those thoughts out of her mind. Easton's schedule needed to be organized for the day. That wouldn't happen if she didn't collect herself right now. Tugging on the sleeves of her light pink cardigan, she stepped into the office, ready to do prep work for Easton's arrival.

Blinking in the harsh white light, her tumultuous stomach sank. Easton sat behind his desk, already at work.

His collar-length dark hair was slicked back, blue

eyes alert and focused on a stack of papers in front of him, full lips tightly pressed as he thought.

She drew in a sharp breath, another wave of nausea and dizziness pressing at her. He looked up from his desk, his clean-shaven face crinkled in a mixture of concern and…surprise? She realized *he* was the one all put together this morning and *she* was the one feeling scattered and disorganized.

This sudden reversal robbed her of her focus. His eyes traced over her, his head falling to the side in concern.

"Are you okay? It's just—you are never late. In fact, you arrive to everything at least fifteen minutes early." He set his pen down, eyes peering into hers.

She swallowed, her throat pressing against the top button of her off-white button-up shirt and her strand of faux pearls. Part of her wanted to lean on him, confide in him and get his support. But how? She didn't have much practice in asking for help.

"Uh." Stammering, her mind blanked. "Yeah. I just… I think I may have the stomach flu. I haven't felt this bad in ages."

She put a hand to her stomach as if to emphasize her symptoms. But really, her palm on her stomach just reminded her of the life growing inside her and how difficult telling Easton was going to be.

"I think that is going around. Maureen called out with the same symptoms. Should you go rest?"

"I'll be fine. I've got crackers and ginger ale on hand. Anyway, how's our little patient doing this morning, Doctor?" She added the last part to keep a professional distance between them.

"Walking around, even attempting to take flight. X-rays show no breaks in the wings and there are no missing feathers, so I'm guessing it's a strained muscle that will benefit from rest. Then back into the wild." He ran his hands through his hair, his athletic build accented with the movement.

"That's good to know. Your risky climb saved his— or her—life."

"His," he answered simply.

Oppressive silence settled between them. She hated this. There had been a time, not even that long ago, where conversation had felt easy and natural between them. But since the tropical storm, she'd looked for every reason to put distance between them. This morning was no different. "If you're busy with patients, then I'll get to some transcriptions."

"Actually, I'm not busy with patients. Let the transcriptions wait." His voice dropped any pretense of nonchalance. Determination entered his tone.

"Okay. But why?"

"Let's talk."

Every atom in her being revolted. Talk? How could she begin to talk to him? She wasn't ready. She needed more time.

"I don't think that's a good idea. We don't talk. We work." She fished the planner out of her oversize bag and waved it in the air.

"I think talking is an excellent idea." A small,

hungry smile passed over his lips, blue eyes shining with familiar mischief.

Why did he have to be so damn sexy?

"Please, don't make things more awkward than—"

"Go out with me on a date."

A date? With Dr. Easton Lourdes? The world slammed still. "A what?"

"A date, where two people spend time together at some entertaining venue. Tomorrow's not a work-day, so it can be afternoon or evening. I don't want to presume what you would enjoy because honestly, you're right, we haven't spoken very much. So for our date, what do you think about a wine-tasting cruise?"

She couldn't drink, not while pregnant. She winced.

"Okay," Easton said, moving from behind his desk, "from the look on your face I'll take that as a no. Concert in the park with a picnic? Go snorkel-ing? Or take a drive down to the tip of the Keys and hang out at Hemingway's old house or climb to the top of the Key West Lighthouse?"

"You're serious about wanting to go on a date?" What would she have thought if he'd made that re-quest months ago? Or if she weren't pregnant now? What if he'd made that request when she had the luxury of time to explore the possibility of feelings between them?

Except she didn't have time.

He sat on the edge of his desk, a devilish look in his eyes. "Serious as a heart attack."

She could see by his face he meant it. Totally.

He wanted to go on a date with her. She'd spent two years attracted to him while never acting on it in order to maintain her independence and now—when the last thing she should be doing was starting an affair with him—he was asking her out.

Her emotions were clouding her judgment. Their impulsive night of sex had flipped her mind upside down. Their attraction was every bit as combustible as she'd expected. It had stolen her breath, her sanity. She'd even entertained pursuing something with him. For a moment, she'd not cared one whit about her independence. But fears had assailed her the next morning. Heaven knew if he'd suggested a date then, she would have run screaming into the Everglades, never to be seen again.

Okay, maybe that was overstating things. Or maybe not.

But it did bring up the point that now, things were different. She really did need to talk to him soon and come up with a plan for their baby. Meanwhile, though, maybe she could use this time to get to know him better on a friendship level and find the best way to tell him about their "love child."

She just had to ignore the electricity that sizzled between them every time he looked at her.

"Key West," she said. "Let's take the drive to see Hemingway's house."

The romantic ride he'd planned just yesterday to Hemingway's house had somehow gone awry.

What should have been a leisurely scenic drive down the heart of the Florida Keys was getting him nowhere with Portia. He wanted her to open up to him, to reveal something about herself. But she was totally clammed up and he was on fire to know more about her. To find a way past her defenses and back into her bed. To pull her clothes off, slowly, one piece at a time and make love to her in a bed, at a leisurely pace rather than a frenzied coupling in a bathroom during a storm.

And she'd gone into her Ice Queen mode again.

Which had never overly bothered him before but was, for some reason, making him crazy now. Yes, he burned to know more about her than what she took in her coffee—although these days she seemed to enjoy water with fruit slices more than her standard brew. He needed to get her talking.

And he also needed to power his way past this slower moving traffic into a clearer stretch of road.

Checking the rearview mirror, he slid his vintage Corvette into the fast lane, getting out from behind a brake-happy minivan. As they passed the van, he noted the map sprawled out on the dash. That explained everything about the somewhat erratic driving behavior.

He used the opportunity of an open road to check out Portia, noting her slender face, porcelain skin and pointed nose. The edges of her mouth were tensed slightly. Her hair was gathered into a loose ponytail, not completely down, but definitely more casual than her usual tightly pulled-back twist. The hairstyle had led him to believe getting through to her today would be easier.

Apparently, he would have to work harder at getting her to reveal her thoughts. And work harder at restraining the urge to slide his hands through her hair until it all hung loose and flowing around her shoulders. He remembered well the feel of those silken strands gliding through his fingers as he moved inside her—

Hell, there went his concentration again.

He draped his wrist over the steering wheel and searched for just the right way to approach her. Often times the simplest ways worked best. Maybe he'd been trying too hard.

"When my brother and I were kids traveling the world with our parents, we became masters at entertaining ourselves during long flights. I'm thinking now might be a good time to resurrect one of our games."

She tipped her head toward him. "Oh really? What did you two play?"

Ah, good. She'd taken the bait.

"Our favorite was one we called Quiz Show. I was about ten when we started playing. I was determined to beat my older brother at something. He was still so much taller, but I figured since we were just a year apart, I had a fighting chance at taking him down in a battle of the minds."

"Tell me more," she said, toying with the end of her ponytail, which sent his pulse spiking again.

"We'd already been on a transcontinental flight and then had to spend ten more hours in a car. So we'd burned out on books and toys and homework. We started asking each other outrageous questions to stump each other."

The result? Two very tight brothers. He hoped to re-create that experience with Portia. To learn something about her. "Would you like to play?"

"Uh, sure. You go first, though, and I reserve the right not to answer."

"Fair enough." A natural quizmaster, he paused, thinking of his first question. One that would help them flow into more personal topics. "What do you do for fun?"

"Are you being rude?" she asked indignantly.

Well, hell. "What do you mean?"

"You said the questions were meant to stump the other person so your question could be taken as an insult."

"Damn. I didn't mean that at all. How about consider this as a new game, our rules. I meant what does Portia Soto do for fun? To unwind? Because I don't know you well and I'm trying to get to know you better." He needed more than just raw data. He wanted her quirks, her idiosyncrasies. He wanted to figure out his attraction to her. Once he did, then he could put those tumultuous dreams to rest.

Or know whether to pursue an all-out affair.

She shot him a sideways look, her ponytail swishing, the ribbon rippling in the wind. "Okay, I see what you mean. But you have to promise not to laugh at my answer."

"I would never. Unless you tell me you make to-do lists for fun. Then I might." He kept his tone casual, his grip on the leather steering wheel light.

"I may be a Post-it note princess, but that isn't my 'fun' time. No. I actually like to draw." She said the words so quietly that they were almost swept away by the wind.

"You draw?" He spared her a sidelong glance, noting the way her cheeks flushed, even beneath her oversize sunglasses.

She nodded, pony tail bobbing. "I do."

"Well, what do you like to draw?" He pressed for progress.

She took a deep breath, hand floating in the air as she made an uncharacteristically theatrical gesture that drew his attention to her elegant fingers. "Oh, you know, the usual kinds of things. Animals mostly. Lots of animals. People, too. Their faces especially. I like the small details."

"You are just full of surprises, Ms. Soto." He bet her way of noticing made her a brilliant artist. Nothing seemed to escape her gaze. He liked that about her. He was finding he liked a lot more about her than he'd realized. Apparently before now his absent-minded professor ways had made him miss things. His attention to detail wasn't as fine-tuned as hers.

Something he intended to rectify.

"Hmm. I can be... Well, how about you, *Doctor* Lourdes? What do you do for fun?"

His formal salutation felt unnatural coming from her. He knew she used it to put distance between them, but he wasn't allowing it this time. "I'm afraid to confess my favorite downtime activity is fishing."

"Really?"

In the corner of his vision, he saw her angle toward him.

"Really," he responded without hesitation. "I know some would say that goes against the conservationist, animal lifesaving oath I took, but I'm not a vegetarian and I always eat what I catch."

"It's not bungee jumping or something equally adrenaline inducing?"

"I know. I'm a letdown. I like fishing because I enjoy the quiet time to think and reflect. And I'm humbled by the way the ecosystem works—how connected everything is."

"Now who is full of surprises?" she murmured, more to herself than to him.

"My turn. What about your dreams? What do you really want to do?"

"I'm happy to be your assistant."

He shook his head. "Not what I asked."

They were only a few minutes away from the Hemingway Home and Museum, and the traffic around them increased, taillights glowing all around like a faux fire.

Portia tugged on her ponytail, thinking.

"In a perfect world? Like a money- and responsibility-free world?"

"Yep." Tall palms stretched above them, casting shadows over her face.

The bright-colored houses and tropical foliage made the island look more like a movie set than reality. Foot traffic was dense too, but the cruise ship passengers on tour for the day would be pulling out before too long and things would quiet down.

"I think I'd like to do something with art. Maybe a nonprofit for kids that focused on creativity after school. Especially for kids who don't have a strong family support system. I'd love to help them see they have the ability to create something beautiful and wonderful."

Her words touched him as he turned the corner, traffic heavier as they drew closer to the historic landmark. "That's a wonderful idea. There isn't enough of that in the world. Any particular reason you chose this need over others?"

"When I was younger, I saw a lot of kids bogged down by circumstances out of their control and they had no outlets of support. I hated that."

He could hear in her voice a more personal reason for her dream, one he felt like she wanted to share. This woman was more like the one he remembered from the night of the storm, the Portia who'd told him of her need to keep on the lights during storms as a child so her brother and her stuffed animals wouldn't be afraid. But he'd seen in her eyes that she'd craved that light and comfort then too, but even now was unwilling to admit her own need for support. Even as her standoffish ways frustrated him at times, he also couldn't help but admire her strength.

If he could keep her talking, he could win her over. What he'd do once he had her, he wasn't sure. All he knew was that he wanted her like he'd wanted no one and nothing else.

But how to tease this information out of her?

He slowed the car to a halt, the traffic in front of him growing worse.

And then the unthinkable happened, interrupting his thoughts. A crash echoed in his ears less than an instant before the car jolted forward.

They'd been rear-ended. Damn. His protective instincts went on high alert and his arm shot across in front of Portia.

Only keeping her safe mattered.

Three

Her near-electric moment with Easton ended with a resounding thud.

A minivan had rear-ended them.

Easton had flung his right arm out to protect her... and protect their unborn child. Not that he knew anything about the baby, and she wasn't any closer to being ready to tell him on this far-from-normal day.

As far as dates went, her romantic outing with Easton had been anything but typical. Yet not in the quirky up-for-whatever way that normally characterized Easton's gestures. She'd seen his protective impulses around his niece and the animals. But this was the first time Portia had been on the receiving end. If she weren't stunned—and more than a little afraid—she would think longer on how that made her feel.

His blue eyes filled with concern as his hand reached for hers, helping her step out of the car.

"I'll be fine." She waved him off, eager to get out of the Corvette and take dozens of deep breaths away from the scent of scorched rubber and brakes. "I promise, I will tell you if I feel the least need to go to the doctor."

And she would. Keeping her secret wasn't worth risking her child. Already, she could hear sirens and see cop cars, firetrucks and an EMT vehicle. She would check in with a medical tech.

"All right. I'll go give the statement to the police." He squeezed her hand quickly before walking away to check in with one of the officers.

One deep breath after another, she calmed her nerves, taking comfort in the strong breadth of Easton's shoulders. She winged a prayer of thanksgiving that he was okay, as well. This could have been so much worse than a dented fender.

In all honesty, she had been in a worse accident when she was thirteen, shortly before her mom died. Her mother had taken her to school in a little blue car. At the final turn before the school, they'd been side-swiped by a bright red pickup truck. That day, she'd needed stitches, and her mother had severely damaged her already ravaged liver. Only a few months later, her mother had died, leaving Portia and her brother alone. They'd moved from Nevada and into the house with their father's older sister in Florida.

While today's crash had only been a fender bender and there were no overt signs of damage, still, she worried. Had the crash harmed her unborn baby?

The thought brought a wave of nausea as the steady swirl of red-and-blue lights echoed in Portia's peripheral vision. How much longer until those emergency vehicles wove their way closer?

She was responsible for the life growing inside her. The life she had to protect. A little boy or little girl—

And thank goodness, one of the EMS trucks stopped on the shoulder of the road just one car up. Since there wasn't a line of others who appeared in need of emergency care, she pushed away from the light pole and moved toward the ambulance.

Smoothing her sundress in an excuse to steady her hands, she approached the younger of the two EMTs. The gold name tag read Valez.

"Uh, sir?" Stammering, she twisted her fingers together, a flush crawling across her face.

"Yes, ma'am?" Valez, a man in his midthirties with a jet-black mustache, asked, gesturing toward the back of the ambulance.

"I feel fine. But…" Oh Lord. This was the first time she would talk about her pregnancy out loud. "I'm pregnant and I just want to make sure every-thing is alright."

The rest of the sentence flew out of her mouth, the reality of her situation echoing back to her.

"You did the right thing in coming over here, ma'am. Please, sit down. We'll get you checked out. If you need additional care, we'll transport you to the nearest hospital. But let's hope that's not needed. Okay?" He lifted her wrist and began taking her pulse. "So just relax and let's talk. How far along are you?" He glanced at her while waving a hand for the other EMT to come over. The older gentleman handed Valez a bag filled with equipment.

"Umm. Well, not quite two months. But fairly close to that point." Portia's voice was a whisper, nearly covered by the sounds of car horns and conversations.

Valez's brow furrowed, reaching for his stethoscope. "And so far, your pregnancy is going well?"

"Yes."

He checked her pulse, nodding to her. "So far, your vitals seem just fine."

Deep breath out. Good. "What should I watch for?"

Handing his equipment back to the other EMT, Valez turned to face her. "There are two things you can watch for—bleeding and cramping. Based on your vitals, I think you are in the clear. Just be sure to put your feet up and try to relax."

Portia's vigorous nod sent loose tendrils of her hair out of her ponytail and into her face. Before she could respond to Valez, Easton strode toward them, concern wearing lines in his ruggedly hand-some face.

"Everything okay?"

Heart palpitating, palms sweating, she urged her tongue to find words. "Fine, I'm just fine."

He glanced at the EMT. "Is that true? She's a tough cookie who doesn't complain."

Valez nodded, holding his medical kit. "We've checked her over and everything appears fine. She knows what signs to look for."

"Signs to look for?" Easton's brow furrowed, looking confused.

Damn.

Panic pulsed in her throat. This could not be how he found out.

The two technicians exchanged glances. Valez cleared his throat. "Yes, symptoms to look for after a car accident."

"Symptoms?"

She tried to interrupt, panicked over what the tech might give away, but he nodded at her reassuringly.

"Whiplash, for example. If your neck feels stiff in the morning. Or aches from the seatbelt or from the impact if your airbag went off."

She inched away. "No airbag. Our vehicle was barely tapped, but I appreciate all the other infor-mation you provided. Truly." She spun to Easton. "We should clear out so they can check out any oth-ers who need help."

"Okay," Easton answered, giving a final wave to

the EMT. "Thank you for taking the time to be so thorough. I appreciate it."

"Just doing our job." The tech nodded to her. "Take it easy, ma'am."

Easton turned back to her, gesturing to the slightly damaged car. A deep sigh escaped his lips, though when he turned to face Portia, a smile manifested. An easygoing smile. One she wanted to give in to. She wanted to lean on him, to rely on him, but she knew that was a recipe for disaster. She had to do this on her own. The sensible thing? Cut her losses on today—on the idea of them.

He touched the top of her arm with gentle fingertips. "This is not the way I envisioned our date going, but I'm glad no one was injured. You must be starving. I know I am. Would you like indoor or outdoor dining?"

The accident shook her ability to remain calm. Though her vitals checked out, she worried about the baby. And that worry made her realize the futility of pursuing anything personal or romantic with Easton. She would always be connected to him, but she couldn't come to rely on him.

"Honestly, I would like to pick up to-go food and head home."

"I know it's a long day driving the whole way down the Keys. Would you rather we get a hotel?" he asked, rushing to add, "Separate rooms of course, if that's what you want."

"I want to go home."

Portia felt downright foolish. She needed space—a place to think. Somewhere away from Easton.

He studied her eyes for a long moment, then shrugged, "Sure, your day. Your date. But it's going to be damn good carryout."

Thoughts of the accident still shook Easton. Though small, the fender bender replayed in his mind.

Portia's scrunched brow visibly displayed her stress. Her demeanor shifted after talking to the EMT. Easton had the sinking feeling that she wasn't as fine as she let on. Or maybe the accident had spooked her as it had spooked him. She'd been initially hesitant to accept his offer of the date. Maybe she'd interpreted the accident as a sign that they had to turn back.

He fished his soda out of the cup holder and sipped on the cola. She was safe. They were both safe. The car had received some damage, but that didn't matter. Not really.

Portia, currently chowing down on carryout, appeared pale, but her color was returning by the bite. She'd chosen a hogfish sandwich, which he hadn't expected at all, even though the delicate fish had a scallop flavor he personally enjoyed. But he'd thought she would order something grilled on top of a salad, the kind of thing she'd pick up locally when she grabbed them takeout for lunch if she needed to go into town on a workday. Yet, this time she'd chosen heartier fare and downed the sandwich like a starved woman. Even alternating each bite with a conch fritter.

This glimpse of her zest for life, her savoring of the senses, made him hungry for a taste of her. He'd wanted to stop for a roadside picnic, but she'd shot down the suggestion, noting the gathering storm clouds. He had to concur. They needed to start for home.

Traffic in the northbound lane moved moderately fast, but allowed Easton to take in the scenery. Sometimes, he felt like he lived at the refuge. Not a big complaint—he loved his work, knew caring for the animals transcended a job and landed squarely in the realm of a vocation. But he often forgot what a normal day looked like.

Then again, his unconventional childhood had never really allowed for normalcy either.

Regardless, the drive reminded him of just how damn lucky he was to live in the tropical Florida Keys. People on bikes lined sidewalks. Palm trees bowed in the summer wind. Easton could make out the turquoise of the sea catching radiantly in the sunlight, the shoreline dotted with shacks that were homes and shops, colorful and scenic. The natural panoramic view was gorgeous.

But not nearly as gorgeous as the woman next to him.

Portia continued to surprise him. Intrigue him. He had a few hours until they'd be back at the refuge. Maybe he could restart their quiz game. Figure out more about her. Easton wanted to tease answers from her lips. Understand more. He could ask her about her family. He knew nothing about them. In fact, Easton didn't really know much concerning her life before she came to work for him.

He could ask her if she'd ever been close to marriage. Did she want a family of her own? What was the worst kiss she'd ever had? That could at least break the ice and make them laugh. Or he could ask why she'd been avoiding him over the last few weeks when they worked together every day, for crying out loud.

With a renewed commitment to demystifying Portia Soto, he turned his head, ready to begin the questions again.

But as he opened his mouth, he knew he couldn't continue.

Her head rested against the window, her eyes were closed and she was fast asleep. He picked up her empty food container, tossed it into the carryout bag, and decided to take comfort in the fact that she felt at ease enough to nap around him. He reached for the radio to turn on a news channel just as his phone rang, the Bluetooth kicking in automatically.

He reached to pick up fast before the tone woke her. But she only twitched once before settling back into even-paced breathing.

He spared a quick glance to the caller ID. His brother, Xander, was on the line. Easton tapped the monitor and his brother's voice filled the air.

"Hey, dude, check this out." Background noise echoed as he said, "Rose, baby girl, come back to Daddy and talk on the phone. Tell Uncle Easton what you just told Daddy."

Easton's mouth twitched. His brother was such a devoted father, and it was funny as hell watching his starched-suit, executive brother wrapped around that tiny little finger.

Easton's toddler niece babbled for a few indistinguishable sentences before she said, "Birdies, birdies."

"That's great, Rosebud." Yeah, Easton had to admit his niece was mighty damn cute. "Give the phone back to your daddy now. Love you, kiddo."

"Hey, brother," Xander's voice came back over. "That's awesome, isn't it? We have the next generation of veterinarians in our family."

"Could be, could be." His eyes flicked back to Portia. She readjusted in her seat, sleep still heavy on her brow. The warmth of the afternoon sun hit her cheekbones, making her glow with natural, sexy beauty.

Xander's baritone voice snapped Easton back into focus. "Maybe she'll add to the family portfolio with inventions the way you have."

"She'll one-up me, for sure. And how the hell did you know about that? It was supposed to be—"

Xander cut him off, a smile present in his tone. "A secret and you just invested well, I know. But one of your colleagues saw me at a wildlife preserve con-vention and thought I was you."

"Ouch." While the brothers shared the same deep blue eyes and broad-chested build, Xander's clean-cut executive look could never be confused with Easton's collar-length hair and slightly disheveled persona.

"It was a windy day. I didn't look like I'd combed my hair."

"I think I was just insulted."

"You were." A laugh rumbled in Xander's throat.

"Thanks."

"No problem. How's it going on your...what was it you were doing today?"

He was probing. Easton could hear it in his voice. Through clenched teeth Easton replied, "A profes-sional run with my assistant."

"Right." Doubt dripped from Xander's tone. Easton could practically see Xander's eyebrow raise, incredulous as always. "How's that going?"

"We'll be back by the end of the day."

"Given your wanderlust soul, something makes me doubt that," Xander teased, but the joke missed its mark. Struck a nerve in Easton.

"We will be."

"That reminds me of when Mom used to say she'd have us all back to the hotel by dinner, but instead, we'd spend the night somewhere unexpected. You've got her sense of time, you know."

Easton's jaw clenched tighter. "See you in a few hours, brother."

He hung up the phone, eyes intensely focused on the road. Wanderlust was one thing, but he still struggled to be taken seriously. To prove he could stay in one spot for a long time, be dedicated to something outside himself. That he wasn't wandering aimlessly in Neverland.

"Easton," Portia's voice jolted him out of his fog. "What did he mean by invention?"

"Oh—" he shrugged "—it's nothing."

"Clearly, it's something—" she paused to sit upright again "—if it added to your family's financial portfolio." She held up a hand. "Wait. Forget I said that."

"Why? I encouraged questions today. Quiz Show, remember? The more outrageous the better."

"Most people find it rude to ask about another person's finances."

"That's not really a secret. And as for my invention…" He shot her a sidelong glance, trying to get a read on her. Truthfully, he felt exposed, talking about this aspect of his work. This idea felt more personal than any bank balance. "It's… I created a shunt to go into the liver duct. It opens and closes in a way that enables multiple testing of a sick animal without multiple sticks."

A smile warmed her face, nose crinkling. "That's really amazing and compassionate."

Eyes back on the road. He changed lanes, sunlight

streaming into the car. "The animals I take care of, they're my kids."

"Until you have children of your own."

He shook his head. "I'm not going to have them."

"But you're so great with Rose, I never would have guessed you don't like kids." Shock entered her tone, and Portia cocked her head to the side.

"I do like them. I just don't plan to have any of my own. I'm crummy father material. Too devoted to the job. I expected you of all people to understand that."

She smiled quickly, fidgeting. What had he said wrong?

"You do work long hours," she said simply.

He needed to get this conversation back on track. Heat filled him as he remembered his reason for this little outing in the first place—to romance her—to woo her. To get her back into his bed. "We have spent many, many hours together."

And he hoped to spend many more in a nonbusiness capacity, sooner rather than later. In fact, there was no moment like the present. The accident left him wanting to seize the day. Talk of the invention nudged him to take things in a new direction with Portia.

He eased the vintage car over to the shoulder of the road and turned off the car.

Portia looked around, confused. "What are you doing? Is something wrong with the Corvette?" She fished in her purse and pulled out her phone. "I'll look up the number for auto service—"

"Portia?" He started to lean toward her.

"Yes," she answered without looking up from her phone.

"Stop talking." He cupped her face in his hands and pressed his mouth to hers.

Four

The taste of Easton tantalized her senses, intoxicating and arousing. This was what she'd been trying to forget from their passionate encounter the night of the tropical storm. A night she hadn't spoken of since then, except in vague references, but a night that had filled her dreams more often than not.

His hand palmed her back and drew her closer until they were chest to chest. Her swollen breasts were especially sensitive and felt the contact all the more acutely. With a will of their own, her fingers crawled up his hard muscled arms to grip his wide shoulders. She wriggled to get closer, her mouth opening wider to take the bold sweep and thrust of his tongue.

Warping her away from reality, the kiss unlocked Portia, electric sensations enlivening her awareness. Her normal laundry list of concerns were rinsed from her mind. Instead, she solely focused on the curve of his lips, his deepening kiss, the sweep of his tongue and the stroke of his hands. He pulled her closer, lifting her out of her seat and into his lap. Holding her in his broad arms, the scent of his amber aftershave mixing with faint sounds of ocean waves crashing to shore. Her fingers wandered into his long hair, silky beneath them and she relished every moment of making an even bigger mess of his normally tousled mane.

She'd slept with him—albeit a hurried encounter. Still, she knew the full extent of his appeal, and so she couldn't figure out why a simple kiss could turn her so inside out. Okay, not a simple kiss because nothing with Easton was ever uncomplicated.

Still, she knew the risks of getting too emotionally involved, of depending too heavily on a man. How could her body betray her so, especially after what he'd said about not wanting children? As quickly as that thought hit her she shut it down again. She'd ached to be in his arms again for so long she was a total puddle of hormones in need of an outlet.

In need of *him*.

Now.

His lips moved from her mouth to her jawline to her neck, until her head fell back to give him unfettered access as she reveled in his hungered frenzy.

Back resting against the steering wheel, she slipped slightly, the car horn wailing into the moment. Snapping her into the present. Back to the fact that they were on the side of the road and not anywhere private enough for the thoughts shooting through her mind.

As the car horn died, they both winced, a laugh emerging from Easton. He brought his hands to his face, running them through his dark thick hair. Returning to her seat, she laughed too, watching the way his hair fell back into a sexy disheveled mess.

A smile still playing on his lips, he clicked the keys into place, engine warming back up. He steered the yellow Corvette back onto the road, and she settled deeper into the plush leather seat, warmed by their shared exchange of heated breath and hotter skin even as her worries returned.

A calm silence descended, broken only by the slight rustle of tires on gradient pavement.

An unquenchable need to understand what had just happened loosed her lips. "What made you do that?"

Bright blue eyes met hers briefly before he returned his attention to the road. "Because we're dating and you look incredible and I couldn't help myself."

"Dating? This is one date. That's all I agreed to, in case you've forgotten." She felt the need to clarify, because the thought of more scared her. She couldn't risk sliding into an emotional commitment of any kind, not with her and her brother's future so uncertain, not with the secret still looming between her and Easton. This was about getting a sense of him for her child's sake. Wasn't it? Her baby had to come first.

"One date? For today. If I'm not mistaken, you enjoyed that kiss as much as I did. Deny it. I dare you."

"What is this? High school? I'm not taking a dare."

He reached for her hand, the simple gesture sending pulses of interest through her body. Her stomach flipped, phantom traces of his lips echoing along her warming skin.

Easton brought her hand to his lips, the five-o'clock shadow scratching her hand. Teasing. "Double dog dare you."

She choked on a laugh, but kept her hand in his. "That is so…silly."

"Yes, but you're smiling. That's as dazzling as kissing you." He winked and grinned. "And make no mistake, kissing you, just looking at you, is mighty damn amazing." His grin broadened.

And stole her breath.

Her guard was slipping too fast. He was clearly trying to draw her out, and he was succeeding. She needed to erect some boundaries. Fast.

"You can be too charming for your own good sometimes." Her grumble was only halfhearted, she knew. She turned to stare out her window at the dark plumes of violet-gray clouds in the distance. Chances were they would blow northward, but the unpredictability of storms in this state still made her nervous.

"You say that as if it's bad. I'm simply being honest with you."

"How about hush up and drive so we can enjoy the sunset." Tugging her hand from his grasp, Portia leaned forward, watching the sun sink behind the whitecap crests. Easton's declarations rocked her defenses and struck a nerve in her tender heart.

"Can do."

The deep, dark clouds descended on the horizon, hungrily devouring the serenity of the sunset. Rain dripped onto the roof of the Corvette, faster and faster until the drops turned into a violent barrage of water.

So much for that picture-perfect sunset.

The bad turn in the weather had literally and figuratively reduced their momentum.

Easton gripped the Corvette's steering wheel in tight hands. For the past two hours, the wall of tropical rain had brought traffic to a crawl. Red brake lights filled the road, their colors seeming to smear as the windshield wipers worked as a frenzied metronome.

While this rain didn't mount to tropical storm level, it was bad enough to back up traffic as people navigated slowly along the packed, narrow road. Many had just pulled off to the side. So many, in fact, the shoulder was lined with vehicles as tightly as the highway.

Whatever electric moment that passed between them had fizzled, fading with each pelt of the rain.

That could be due to the intensity of the storm. Portia's eyes seemed heavy with inexplicable worry.

From beneath his fingertips, he felt a tug on the low-slung Corvette's steering wheel. A result of the piling rain and flooding streets. The tug shifted them slightly to the right, toward the shoulder of the road.

Portia's hand touched his arm, a gesture of re-assurance. Her lilting voice contrasted against the harsh thunder. "This is almost as bad as the storm we drove in to rescue the Key deer that had been hit by a car."

He nodded, remembering well that night and how difficult it had been not to kiss away the tender-hearted tears she'd cried. Only the reminder that she was his secretary had kept him from acting on the moonlit impulse. "By the way, this rain is piling up and tugging on the steering—I think it might be slightly worse than the night with the Key deer."

"So more like the time we were transporting the pelican back from Pigeon Key?"

Ah, he recalled that vividly too, how her hair had lifted with the crackle of electricity from the light-ning, how his fingers had ached to stroke over the wispy, flyaway strands, how he had realized he was feeling more and more drawn to her the longer they worked together.

So many experiences, long work nights, storms, had been shared between them. And now, another storm and more experiences brewed and crackled. The night she refused to address. That seemed to echo louder than the thunder.

"I'd say so. I mean, just look outside the window, Portia. The water is building on the streets. I think a flood is imminent."

She peered out her window, lips pursing together. As lightening flashed in front of them, he recalled how electric their connection had been during the last tropical storm. The undeniable chemistry had sent them slinking into the bathroom together.

He wanted to touch her like that again. To taste her. But his thoughts were interrupted by the extreme deluge. He could barely see the taillights in front of him.

He had driven in worse when he had to, but right now he didn't have to. They didn't have to. It was more important to be safe.

After the accident earlier today, he wasn't taking any chances. He blipped on the turn signal, seeking shelter on the side of the road.

She turned to him quickly, her lush brown ponytail bouncing, her eyebrows raised. "What are you doing?"

"Pulling over. This is insane to keep driving." He didn't risk taking his eyes off the road as he steered into a tourist shop parking lot with dozens of other cars. "Any problems with that?"

"You're right. No need to risk us getting in another wreck. There are plenty of people who can take care of the animals."

"Maureen is definitely capable." He pulled into an open spot and parked the car.

"Then let's stop for the night." She leaned forward to pick up her purse from the floorboards. "I'll start searching on my phone for a hotel."

"You have to know our chances of finding two rooms open are slim to none."

"I realize that." She pulled out her cell, smiling smartly. "Luckily, you're going to be fine with sleeping on the sofa."

A tapestry of blues and oceanic greens flooded Portia's vision when the door to the honeymoon suite—the only room available on such short notice—swung open.

The Sheltered Crescent Inn sat twenty feet from the ocean, providing panoramic views of the storm. Flashes of pure white light made shadows dance across the room, revealing an array of coastal-themed decorations. Entering the room, a smile lifted Portia's lips. The decorator seemed to have stuffed every free space with conch shells, sailboats and kitchy sayings about life being better at the beach.

Shuffling over a kelp-green rug, she leaned against the solid tan couch, eyes drifting to the open door that led to a luxury bathroom, complete with a spa Jacuzzi built for two.

Fresh-cut roses stood tall in a white vase on the driftwood coffee table. This, of course, was the most expensive room in the inn, and part of her felt bad about having to stay the night here, even though she knew money was no object for him.

The other part of her desired this extra time with Easton. As if by staying in such close proximity, she'd figure out the right words to say to deliver her life-altering news.

Turning her head, she surveyed his broad shoulders, the way his dark hair curled slightly. Ruggedly handsome with those bright blue eyes. His appeal, she tried to tell herself, had not motivated her decision to stay the night with him.

A quick scan revealed a single king-size bed peeking out from the bedroom. But there was no second bed. Just the tan couch she leaned against.

Easton's voice rumbled, and she caught the scent of his spiced cologne as he moved past her to the minibar. "Can I get you something to drink? A snack?"

"Just water for me, please." She pulled her tablet from her purse, the fading, rain-drenched sun just barely reflecting off the screen. "We could work. I have my phone and tablet."

"Do you carry that with you everywhere?" he asked as he poured bottled water into two crystal goblets.

"It's a part of my life," she answered defensively. "Organization is crucial."

"Why?"

"What do you mean by that? It's a positive trait." Frowning, she tugged her ponytail tighter into the scrunchie. She'd been responsible for taking care of her brother when they lived with their mother and she'd found early on that it helped to make lists, to have everything laid out ahead of time, to leave as little as possible to chance.

The crashing of waves echoed in the room blending with the *tap-tap-tap* of the smoldering storm. The deep sounds of thunder ebbed, becoming more and more distant.

He passed her drink to her, their fingers brushing, static snapping like the lightning outside. "Crucial, though? Do you really believe it's that important to be so regimented?"

"Of course I do. It's why you hired me." She caught sight of her own reflection in the glass window. Her hair now perfectly coiffed in a ponytail, but her face bore the stamp of exhaustion she felt tugging at her more and more at the end of each day. "Why are you pushing the point now?"

"Because I can't figure you out."

"Well, the feeling is entirely mutual."

"How so? I'm an open book."

Sort of. And then not at all. "When I took this job, I expected a scientist would be more...scientific."

He clapped a hand to his broad chest. "Have I ever been anything other than effective at work?"

"It's not that. I just didn't expect such a free spirit.

Someone who doesn't own a comb and climbs trees." She couldn't hold back her teasing smile even as she knew she was playing with fire by flirting with him.

"I own a comb."

"Do you use it?" She crossed her arms, unable to resist teasing him.

He smiled crookedly, lines of amusement fanning from his eyes into his tanned face.

She nodded. "That's what I thought."

He moved toward the radio, abandoning the work space. She moved past him, his body gently skirting hers, teasing her senses and awareness. Portia's eyes narrowed, suspicious as she sat.

She had to carefully construct her walls, to keep him out of her mind. It would be easy—far too easy—to become undone by his gaze. "Easton..."

"What? We need to listen for weather alerts." He stepped away from the radio. "And I don't need a comb to organize my thoughts. As for organizing everything else, that's what I hire you for. You're stellar at your job, by the way, and I appreciate that more than I can say. I don't want to lose you over... this," he said, waving his hand between them, "either, so I've been taking things slow. But when I saw the look in your eyes after I fell out of that tree, I knew the waiting was over." The corner of his mouth pulled upward, a cocky smile in place. He looked at her hungrily.

"Oh really? This whole romance deal has been because in a weak moment I was actually worried about you?" She'd had no idea she was so transparent.

To him at least.

"Worried? I saw more than concern when you looked at me." His sidelong glance unsettled her.

And made her skin tingle with awareness.

"Easton, is that ego heavy to carry around?"

She tossed a sofa pillow at him. He easily deflected it with an arm.

"Fair enough. Does it help if I say I'm incredibly attracted to you? Because I am." He closed the distance between them, leaning on the other side of the couch. "You don't believe me?"

"I do—you're just…over the top."

"I'm honest. Is that so difficult to believe?" He touched her chin and guided her face toward his. "You're a beautiful woman. So lithe and elegant."

Rain continued to drum on the roof, a soothing sound. But his words gnawed at her. The tone was direct, straightforward, when normally he flirted. So his honest question tugged at her more, compelling her to answer straightforwardly.

"I'm comfortable in my skin, with my life, with my appearance." She brushed off his compliments, the image of her mother manifesting in her mind's eye. "I'm pleased with who I am, and where I'm going in my life."

"And well you should be."

"Thank you." She avoided his gaze, picking up

another decorative pillow and hugging this one to her stomach. "That peace was hard-won though."

"How so?" He sat next to her, confusion coating his tone.

His thigh brushed against hers and a part of her wanted to just succumb to the attraction, to avoid this discussion, to avoid the future. But his eyes probed her with undeniable curiosity.

She didn't really like discussing this. Usually made it a habit to avoid this kind of conversation. But she'd decided to share more with him, and she intended to follow through on that. "My mother was the first runner up in the Miss Nevada pageant. She was bombshell gorgeous with pinup poster curves. She'd grown up poor, making her own dresses and costumes. She found her stiletto heels for competitions at yard sales and dyed them herself. The world thought she made a fabulous match with a wealthy casino magnate in Las Vegas, my dad."

Fabulous? More like financial. Her parents had made each other miserable the minute his money dried up and he'd been sent to prison for tax evasion.

"But you may already know this," she added.

"I don't."

That came as a shock. She would have expected him to know all about her history. "You didn't have me investigated when you hired me? I would think given your family's money..."

"I did a work history check, and called your professional references, all of whom spoke of you in glowing terms. But we're not talking about work. And even if they'd told me personal details, that wouldn't have been from your perspective. I want to hear about your life. From you." His tone was genuine, but firm.

She wasn't used to being the center of attention, and she wasn't sure how she felt about it. But best to finish the story and get the sad truth about it out there and hope he wasn't the sort to judge her for her parents' actions the way others had.

Easton didn't seem the judgmental sort. She liked that about him.

She continued, "My father lost all his money when he went to jail for tax evasion. He died in jail a few months later of some strain of flu—he was a lot older than my mother."

Her dad had kids from another marriage and hadn't been much for the family scene. But he'd taken Portia to work and let her sort casino chips by color. God, she hadn't thought about that ritual of theirs until now.

She shook off the memory and moved on, eager to finish this convoluted history. "My mom…she drank herself into a liver crisis that was compounded by an injury in a car wreck. She died when I was thirteen and my brother was seven."

Portia had been crushed over her father's conviction, and she'd been devastated all over again when she realized her mother had only married for money. Taking the job working for Easton, Portia had been determined not to be drawn in by the wealth of the estate—or the man. And she'd managed to keep her distance from him for nearly two years, only to have her resolve crumble in one emotional night.

"I'm so sorry you had to lose your parents that way."

"Me, too." She shuddered, the memory wounding her all over again. "But they made their choices and paid a high price for them. My brother and I were lucky we had an aunt here in Florida who took us in so we didn't end up in the foster care system."

"You and your younger brother."

"Yes, she didn't want to be a mother that late in life. She was happily single." Her aunt, while kind-hearted, had been career minded and set in her ways. But her aunt had given them stability if not an abundance of motherly affection. "But she did her best by us."

"You brought up your brother."

"He means the world to me." She swallowed hard, then froze as a horrible thought hit her. "I hope you don't think I would ever have made a move on you to keep my job."

"No, God no. I know you better than that. You have always been a trustworthy person in the way you've handled business, the volunteers and the animals. I trust you, implicitly."

His praise and trust should make her feel good, but given the secret between them, she could barely hold back a wince of guilt.

"What happened between us that night was impulsive."

And impulsive was not her style. She didn't know how to roll with impetuous feelings. Ever since she'd become responsible for her younger brother, she had laid out a life plan. Put structure over desire because she had to. She didn't want to end up like her mother.

"But that night did happen, so why won't you speak to me?" He linked their fingers and rubbed the back of her hand against his stubbly jawline, holding her gaze as if he knew full well what that rasp against her skin did to her senses.

As if he knew full well how deeply attracted she was to him even as she sought to keep the boundaries high.

"I am speaking to you now."

"That's not what I meant and you know it." He kissed her fingers one at a time, and then lowered their clasped hands to rest on his knee. "But we can let that go for the moment. You were telling me about your mother."

"I told you already."

"You said she was first runner up for Miss Nevada. Why was that important?"

A loaded question.

Her mother had had full lips, long curly brown hair and the perfect hourglass figure. Conventionally beautiful. A fact her mom impressed upon Portia, who lacked those qualities. Her mother reminded her frequently that she was plain, average, in need of "sprucing up" with flashier clothes and makeup. Whereas her younger brother had a more classic cute kid look that her mom had insisted would make him a child television star.

Portia settled on a benign response. "She even made it into the national pageant when Miss Nevada got pregnant and married during her reign. Mom didn't crack the top tier at nationals though."

"You're still not answering my question."

A lump grew in her throat. "Some parents play favorites. My brother was her favorite."

"That's not cool. Parents should love all their kids the same."

"Maybe I misspoke a bit. She loved me. She just… liked him better."

"Why?"

She plucked at the pillow in her lap. "He was everything she wanted in a child."

"How so?"

"Charismatic. Attractive." Her brother's eyes were deep brown, his skin always easily tanned. He could have been a child model. Compared to him, Portia had been disappointing.

"You're mesmerizing and gorgeous, and most importantly, brilliant."

"You don't need to stroke my ego. I told you. I'm comfortable in my skin. I don't need a centerfold body." This conversation had to end. Now. She didn't like this level of flattery. It set her on edge.

"You're beautiful."

"Stop—"

"I mean it. I've been clear about that." He looked at her with intense curiosity, lifting a rose from the vase on the table. Easton handed it to her, a romantic peace offering of sorts.

"Well, I did look like a drowned rat that night—" She stopped short.

"So we're finally going to talk about that night." He leaped on her words, like he'd been waiting for any chance to discuss the night burned into her mind.

"I was there. I remember it well. Very well." For a moment, she imagined the feeling of his lips on hers, his hand twining in her hair and wrapping around her ponytail.

"As do I."

Five

After weeks of strained silence, Portia finally looked ready to discuss the night of the storm with him. Perhaps there would be an explanation for why she'd shut him out so completely since that night, and why she squirmed away from his compliments. Because damned if he was any closer to understanding this woman.

A knock at the door stayed her lips, causing them to shut tightly into a thin line. Easton was content to ignore the door, but she tipped her head in the direction of the continued tapping.

"Room service," Portia reminded him, starting to rise.

He'd already forgotten he'd ordered them dinner—

a bread basket, herb-crusted red snapper, jasmine rice and side salads.

He grabbed her hand, gently tugging it. "Please, sit. I'll get it." He gestured for her to return to the tan couch or go to the small dining table. "Let me do something for you for a change. You're always running around keeping my life in order."

"Thank you. I appreciate it."

Good. He hoped so, because he was doing his best to salvage something from this disaster of a date.

Easton opened the door, met by a nervous-looking woman with bright red hair. She wheeled the overburdened cart into the center of the room and cast a glance at the rain-slicked window. Another crack of thunder sounded above them, sending vibrations through the building's foundation. The food attendant winced. The lights flickered and she shot them a faltering smile. "I thought it would be an adventure to move here." She quickly unloaded the food onto the table, and a blend of spices steamed into the air. "I'm ready to go back to shoveling snow. Um, sorry to babble."

"Please, don't apologize. We understand." Portia lifted lid after lid on the tray, inhaling. He heard her stomach growl in response, a blush rising to color her cheeks.

Even in the smallest moments, Easton found her drop-dead sexy.

The attendant nodded to Easton, and set three candles on the table. "Just in case we lose power."

She took her tip and raced out of the room as if in search of the nearest transport north.

Easton pulled away the last of the covers, pleased with the results, especially considering how busy the hotel must be with the influx of guests due to the storm. "Come on, let's eat. You sound hungry after all."

"I'm going to pretend you didn't just insult my femininity." She fixed him with a dark look, but he saw the amusement in her eyes.

"Portia, your femininity has never been in question. I thought I made that abundantly clear two months ago. Unless you've forgotten about that night."

Her throat moved with a long swallow. "Of course I remember."

Good. Very good. "The rain sure sounds like that night."

He pulled out the rattan dining chair for her.

Another whack of thunder overhead. The lights strained brightly for a moment. A strange buzz erupted and the lights winked out. Easton grabbed the candles and matches, lighting the wicks. They hissed to life.

He was suddenly thankful for the lack of light. The flickering candle flame provided intimacy. Maybe the romantic date could be salvaged? Albeit in an unconventional way. But he never liked status quo anyway.

Portia bit into her roll, chewing thoughtfully. She

swallowed before responding, eyes wandering past him to the window where raindrops beat onto the storm glass. "This tropical storm's nowhere near as bad as that one."

"I know. I guess it just sounds louder since we're not in a storm shelter," Easton agreed, stabbing a piece of snapper with his fork.

"It was secluded," Portia agreed, her eyes fixed on the flame. She looked up through her lashes. "And crowded."

And that wasn't his point, but at least she was talking.

The night with Portia had been all heat and fire. One that demanded attention and kindling. A draw he hadn't felt since his teenage years when he'd fallen hard for a girl in a village his family had hung around in for a whole four months—a time that had felt like forever to him as a teen. But as always, the next move was always in the works. He'd learned a lot about starting relationships, but not too much about how to maintain them. "It's a wonder we found a place to be alone and no one noticed we were gone.

"In case you're worried about gossip, I told the others you were nervous about the tropical storm since you're from Nevada, and I was reassuring you."

"Thank you."

"I would have told you as much if you would have spoken about that night before now."

"Well, you told me now. And I'm glad you stemmed any embarrassment."

"My brother was so caught up in his newfound love for Maureen I doubt he even heard me."

"They are a beautiful, happy couple. I didn't think there was a chance your brother would find someone after his wife died. He grieved so hard for Terri." A trace of sadness edged her voice. Portia had liked Terri, and he knew she was sad for little Rose to be growing up without her mother. The loss had devastated Xander and everyone at the refuge.

"Their marriage surprised me as well, and Maureen is so different from Terri, too." In fact, Easton had been more than surprised at his brother's interest in Maureen, Easton's quirky, outgoing second-in-command. Yet somehow, Xander and Maureen managed to make it work. "But there's no doubting how he feels about her."

"That's true." Portia pulled a weak smile. A roll of thunder sounded, lightning coursing through the room, dressing her slender face in shadows. Darkness lingered in her eyes.

He moved the candle to the center of the table. "You don't look like you agree."

"I do, then and now. I was just thinking how their romance made me feel." She shrugged. "I don't know, kind of sad that night, seeing them together."

"How so?" Tilting his head to the side, he leaned on his elbows, drawing ever-so-slightly closer to her.

"My life is such a mess I didn't think I would ever feel that way about someone." Portia sighed, that weak smile intact.

Easton raised a brow, confused. "You're the least messy person I've ever met."

She chased a piece of lettuce with her fork, a frown forming on her mouth. "My parents had an awful marriage. My brother, who I all but brought up, was barely keeping his head above water in school after a diagnosis of dyslexia. My plans for my life are on hold until he finishes college, and I can help him get his loans paid down. Then I'll go back to school."

"And what about now?"

She looked at him, a quiet resignation set in her brow. Everything about her stance looked defeated. "I'm not where I expected to be at this point in my life."

"Where would you like to be?" His voice dropped an octave, becoming gentler. Serious. He wanted her to know he was interested in what she wanted. Truly captivated by her.

"In college." She held up a hand. "But let's stop with that line of discussion. I don't want to talk about it. At all."

"Portia—"

"Seriously." She took a deep breath, shutting her eyes. "No. I don't want to discuss that. Let's talk about something else."

One strike and she'd already declared him out. But he didn't give up easily or play by the rules.

With nothing left to lose, he decided to gamble. Ask the question he'd most wanted the answer to.

"Okay, how about you tell me why you didn't speak to me the day after the storm?"

"We were busy cleaning up the place." Her standard response was too calculated to be real.

"You really expect me to keep accepting that answer?" he asked with a laugh, trying to inject levity into this dark moment.

"It was worth a try." She smiled so wide her nose crinkled, then her grin faded.

"Nice. But I would really like an answer."

She tore at another piece of her bread. He watched her try to collect herself. "Okay, you're right that cleaning up after the storm just offered an excuse to keep my distance. The feelings were so intense that I worried if we repeated that night, I wouldn't be able to keep working with you." She set down her plate. "Now more than ever, I'm still not sure. And that's why we need to keep our distance."

In a flash, she'd scooped up a candle and her pink purse. The chair rocked slightly from her departure, and her footfalls were lost in the sustained rumble of thunder. Portia's hand covered the flame, bracing it from the air's assault.

Easton barely stood before she strode past the Jacuzzi and into the solitary bathroom. The door closed behind her slender back, coming into place with a definitive click.

The sound of a lock.

Damn.

He heard water rushing through pipes, and he

imagined her—a siren amid the water's steam and bubbles.

She clearly needed space, but that image tortured him. Especially after the intensity of their roadside kiss and the honest answers she'd given him.

Deep breath.
Another.
One more. She ran the bathwater, trying to calm herself with the sound, but her heart pounded and she found herself blinking back tears.

With shaking hands, she pulled her cell phone from her purse. Her tired eyes squinted at the intense light of the screen as she found her brother Marshall's contact information.

One ring. Two. He should be picking up soon, up late studying for a test he'd told her about. Portia knew he was at school. He'd opted to take a summer class at University of West Florida in Pensacola in order to finish in five years rather than sliding over into a sixth.

The ringing stopped and the light sound of music filtered through the connection.

"Hey, sis." Marshall's voice was hoarse and distracted.

She imagined his lanky frame hunched over his desk, his dirty blond hair buzzed shorter these days so he could sleep later in the morning after staying up late studying.

"Do you have friends over? If you need to go, that's okay."

"I'm studying. You know how I like white noise in the background."

"I do remember." Her brother had had a tough time in school and she'd worked hard to help him stay on track. His grades hadn't been good enough for a scholarship and it was taking him an extra year to graduate. But as long as he finished, she would be happy.

"What can I do for you, sis?"

An excellent question. She had no idea what anyone could do for her. She hadn't even really had a reason to call Marshall. "I'm just calling to let you know I'm okay since the weather is so bad here."

"Um, the weather's bad there? I really have been locked down studying. I didn't even know there was a problem. Should I be on the lookout for a tropical storm or hurricane to swing my way?"

"I don't think so. It's just heavy rain. And maybe I needed to hear my little brother's voice." She poured bubbles into the tub, watched them grow, blanketing the top level of water.

"You're the best. Really. I appreciate it."

"Marshmallow—um, you don't mind if I still call you that, do you?"

His rich laughter made her smile. She was so damn proud of him.

"No problem, sis. Just don't post it online or anything."

"I wouldn't dare." She tested the water in the tub, appreciating the warmth.

"Thanks. And hey, be careful, okay?" A note of concern darkened his voice. "You work too hard and deserve a rest. I've been thinking I should take next year off and get a job, sock away some money and give you a break. You could go on a cruise or something."

Panic iced her. She loved her brother as much as if he were her own child—she'd practically raised him, after all. Held his hand as he learned to walk, wiped his tears when he scraped his knees, helped him with his spelling words. She feared if he stopped with school he would never go back. She'd seen it happen with other students, and she especially worried for him given how hard his learning disability made things for him. "Don't even entertain the notion. You are so close to finishing. Once you have your computer science degree, you're going to be so much more hirable. Just hang in there."

"We can talk at the end of the summer."

"You're going to break my heart if you don't finish. Please, see this through."

"What about you make me a promise as well to take care of yourself?"

"I will." She would have to tell Marshall about the baby soon, but not until he'd enrolled for the fall. She didn't want to distract him from his studies any sooner than necessary.

And of course, she still had to tell Easton, too.

As soon as she had her doctor's appointment. One more week.

"Do you promise?" he pressed.

"Yes, I promise. I will relax. I went out to dinner tonight with, um, friends, and in fact, I have a bubble bath calling my name. So I should sign off. Love you."

"Love you, too."

She disconnected the call, putting the phone back in her purse, attention fully on the bath. She shimmied out of her clothes without the least thought of neatly folding them. For once, she had too much on her mind to care. The chill on her skin urged her to get beneath the blanket of warm water.

As she slid into the filling bath, her hands instinctively went to her stomach. She and Marshmallow would have a bigger family soon, a caring, close family. Another redeeming thought? This baby would offer her another chance to be a mom, this time an older and wiser one.

And what kind of father would Easton be? Involved? Distant? A playmate or educator?

She knew how he worked with a sense of fun and creativity, and she knew how he felt against her. Intensely focused on her needs and unwavering in his attention.

All of her thoughts led back to that night. The sustained thunder reminded her of the thunder from that other storm. How soothing Easton had been, how caring.

Portia inhaled deeply, listening to the sounds of the storm, watching the flame crackle to itself until her eyes grew heavy and she slipped into sleep…

Flashes of awareness entered her vision. As a non-Florida native, the power of the tropical storm terrified her. Easton's good-natured teasing shifted into pure comfort. In the storm shelter, he slid his arm around her.

That's when she felt yet again the undeniable heat between them at a time when she was too damn vulnerable. Marshall was close to failing out of college and losing hope that he could finish. She couldn't let her hard work and sacrifice be for nothing. She was scared for her brother's future. She was scared for her own future, listening to the storm rage.

Her defenses were down, and her heart was oh so vulnerable. She simply couldn't find the resolve to resist her attraction to Easton any longer. A passion she hadn't come close to feeling in her past two relationships with men, both more conventional types like her.

The attraction to Easton had burned into her with those blue-fire eyes, and before long, she wandered into the bathroom with him, first with a pointed look, then him following down the short hall to the tiny room with a simple shower stall.

They snuck in there, peeling themselves away from the others in the storm shelter.

CATHERINE MANN 91

"Portia," he said her name simply, the syllables so sexy coming from his mouth.

"No words. Just..." She couldn't find a way to express to him what she felt without giving away too much. She'd been attracted to his good looks from the start, but the physical was superficial. She'd been able to hold out, especially fearful of being seen as a gold digger like her mother.

But over time, she'd been drawn all the more by his intelligence as well as his compassion around animals. Now here they were, acting on that attraction. She didn't want to think beyond that. She reached for him.

Or he reached for her. She wasn't sure who moved first. She only knew the attraction, the passion—the craving—was entirely mutual. Their first kiss felt like one of ultimate familiarity. Like coming home. Like one of a lover who'd known her for an eternity.

She wanted more. She wanted it all, regardless of where they were or how they'd ended up here or what tomorrow could hold because she couldn't think that far into the future. She whispered her need to him and he answered in kind as he lifted her onto the sink. She felt the ripples of his honed muscles as he managed the maneuver in an effortless sweep. He was such a fascinating mix of brains and brawn, privilege and earthiness.

"You're so beautiful, so enchanting, so sexy. You've turned me inside out countless times with those take-no-bull eyes and the confident toss of your

head. I've been burning to touch your hair, to take it down and feel it," he whispered onto her skin with kisses, pressing his mouth into her flesh as his hands skimmed over her French twist. His fingers plucked at the pins and they clinked against the sink behind her one at a time as fast as her racing heart.

Her mind blurred with passion. Their hands a frenzy as they pulled up shirts. Opened pants. Touched. Explored.

Found.

The room was dimly lit and small, his body close to hers with minimal room to step back. Yet driven by need she wriggled and he positioned. And he thrust inside her.

Her head fell back, a husky moan rolling up her throat. He captured it with his mouth, then skimmed a kiss along her ear, whispering gently shhh, shhh, shhh. Reminding her of the people a short hall away.

She dug her fingernails into Easton's shoulders, rolling her hips in sync with him, meeting him move for move. Their lovemaking ignited her every nerve, leaving her feeling, for the first time in a long time, connected.

For years, Portia had carefully constructed walls, pushed people outside to remain focused on providing a good life for her brother. She still wanted that. But she also wanted more. She wanted this. She wanted Easton.

Every kiss and every thrust reminded her of how lonely she'd been for years. For her whole life even.

Each move and touch imprinted on her body and mind how exciting this was. How exciting they were together.

"Portia."

Her name sounded like a promise on his tongue, caressing her ear. Calming her senses but bringing her body to life. The beating of her heart sped up, becoming more ferocious and urgent.

And her name again. "Portia?"

No longer a promise, but a question...

Bolting upright awake, she grabbed the side of the tub and sloshed water over the sides, realizing she'd been asleep. Easton was, in fact, calling her name—but just from the other side of the door. Portia looked across the bathroom, a different and more spacious one than in her dream.

The bathwater had cooled, chilling her overheated flesh. She glanced at the door, then down to the haphazard pile of her clothes on the tile floor. Water pooled along the Saltillo squares. A lot of water. She must have splashed and thrashed during her nap in the tub leaving her clothes totally soggy...

And impossible to wear.

Easton rapped his knuckles on the door. Portia had scurried away an hour ago. In the last ten minutes, his desire to give her space ebbed, replaced by worry. He'd imagined her sick, or passed out on the floor.

"Portia? Are you okay? I'm getting worried." He called again, fingering the plush white hotel robe he held ready for her, "Portia, answer please or I'm going to need to open the door."

"I'm okay."

Finally. Thank God. The sound of her husky voice soothed him slightly.

"I'm sorry for disturbing your bath." He pressed his forehead to the door in relief, the cool wood soothing his overheated brow. "I apologize for upsetting you into bolting away earlier. I don't know what I said, but you have to know I would never deliberately hurt you."

"I'm really okay."

Still, he couldn't step away. "Are you going to spend the night in there?"

"Of course not."

"Do you plan to come out anytime soon?" He angled back and stared at the door, as if that act alone would cause it to swing open.

"I was thinking I would come back in there right after you go to sleep."

"Well, that's a problem because there's only one bathroom in here and I'm going to need to step in there before bed. Or rather before I go to sleep on the sofa."

"Oh, of course. I'm sorry about that. I'll be right out."

More rustling water sounds echoed, followed by drips of water. The lock popped open, and she stood in front of him. Damp tangled hazelnut hair, the small white towel wrapped around her, accentuating her curves.

Air pulled away from him. Damn, she was sexy. She turned him inside out in a way he remembered well from their night together but he had wondered if his memory was faulty.

He had tried his best to get answers from her. To be a gentleman. To get closer to her on a more cerebral level.

But that hadn't gotten him jack squat. He didn't understand her any more now than he ever had. But he recognized the heat between them. And damned if he didn't see that same simmering warmth reflected in her eyes.

On to Plan B.

Hungry for her touch, he reached for Portia.

Six

His lips found hers, catching her by surprise until she almost stumbled back into the bathroom.

All the tension she'd been storing in her body seemed to flood out of her as she unfolded into the moment. In the taste of his lips, the curve of his tongue. Her nerves melted, all tension over thoughts of meeting him in only a towel leaving her.

For this evening, here in this hotel honeymoon suite she could be a little foolish. Give in to the chemistry between them. Hell, she wanted him. Like with the kiss in the car, she didn't have much time to be with him, to get to know him, to explore every inch of him. Because her plan to put boundaries between them wasn't going to work. It wasn't boss and secretary time, not anymore.

She would have to find her way to a new peace with him. She would have to find a way to have him and her independence, too. And while this might seem reckless, playing it safe hadn't worked. And once the news of her pregnancy came out, her window of time to explore avenues for connecting with him would narrow. Considerably.

He sighed heavy against her, taking a step back deeper into the living area. Closer to the sprawling bed. A rush of cold air pressed against her chest and neck, a palpable absence. "I'm sorry. I didn't mean to grab for you like a caveman. I saw you in the towel and, well, damn, I couldn't think straight." He nodded past her, toward the bathroom. "I realize now your clothes are damp and hanging out to dry. You didn't have a choice but to wear the towel."

She leaned into him, the rain-fresh scent of him tempting her all the more. "If I'd wanted you to stop kissing me, I would have said so."

His eyebrows shot upward. "Really?"

"Really. I'm a mature woman. I know what I want and I am capable of speaking my mind." At least, for right now, she knew she needed his touch. All of him. Reality could wait until the sunrise.

"And what would that be? I need to hear you say what you want before I make another move."

"I want you." She stepped back, closer to the bed, unable to miss the way his eyes lingered on her long hair falling in damp and loose strands. "Right now, I want you to keep kissing me and more. I want us to explore the attraction we found that night of the tropical storm. To take it further and take our time. I wasn't planning this, but let's see where it goes."

"Well, I'm very glad to hear that since I want you, too. So damn much." He reached for her and she took another step back. He tipped his head, intensity stamped all over his face. "Are you going to drop the towel?"

"Are you going to undress for me?" Her gaze roamed over his muscled body, wanting to see and feel more of him.

"My pleasure." He began unbuttoning his shirt.

"I believe it will be mine. We didn't get to see each other before." So much of the sensations of the night had been lost to frenzy. She wanted to know every inch of him.

"No, we didn't." He tossed aside his cotton button-down, revealing the sun-bronzed chest she'd admired more than once while he'd been swimming. "I'm not arguing with you by any means, but what brought about this change of heart?"

"Do you need to know why? Can it be enough to know I want to be close to you tonight? Because I do, so very much." She gripped the towel in her fist, holding it closed as the water nearly steam dried off her warming body. "This day may not have been what we planned, but I have enjoyed being with you. I'm not ready for it to end."

"Portia…" He gritted his teeth, obviously wanting to say more.

"That's all I can give," she answered softly, honest in this much at least.

He gave in with a growl of frustration and desire. "Okay, beautiful lady, that's good enough for me tonight."

He toed off his shoes and tugged off his socks.

His hand fell to his belt buckle and then to the zipper of his khakis. He kicked his pants aside and there was nothing left between them except her towel and his boxers. His erection strained the waistband, attesting to just how much he wanted her.

The towel slid from her grip and his eyes went wide with appreciation. A step later from her—from him—and they stood chest to chest, mouths meeting.

His hand wandered to her damp hair, the movement bringing them closer. Easton kissed her, tongue exploring, urgency mounting. Her hands outlined circling swirls on his skin, enjoying the way he seemed to respond to her touch. His kiss becoming more urgent with every sweep of her fingertips.

He walked her backward toward the bed until her legs met the mattress. A gentle nudge sent her onto her back—into the downy blue duvet, pillows scattering.

She pulled back from him, eyes adjusting to the dim light, appreciating his body and the hungry look in his eyes. Portia stared up at him through her lashes, worried he might notice the changes in her body, in particular the swell of her breasts. Or would he just write off the differences to mistaken memory over time? Or perhaps to the fact that they hadn't even had the opportunity to look closely enough that night? She certainly hadn't been able to gaze her fill of him.

He leaned her back on the bed, the coolness of the cotton bedspread pressing against her skin—a stark contrast to the heat of his body. Wandering lips found her collarbone, and her hands tugged at his boxers, pulling them off. He angled on top of her.

His hand tucked between her legs, his fingers finding the damp core of her, stroking and coaxing and dipping inside. His touch slickened; he rubbed over the bud of her arousal.

Tonight was already so different from the evening of the other storm, the night they'd quickly and impulsively made love. Every kiss tonight was more deliberate, more passionate. She bit his lower lip, and he growled in response, pressing into her. She hooked her right leg around his, needing him to get closer. Her heart bolted at a maddening pace, her excitement intensifying as his hands brushed back her hair so he could kiss her neck. Her lips.

Palming his chest, she traced him with her other hand, trailing down, down, farther still until she cupped his straining need, wrapping her fingers around the length of him. A groan of pleasure hissed from between his teeth just before he pressed his lips to hers again.

He stole her breath, and she stole his right back. Their tongues met, thrusted and stroked just as their hands touched and caressed each other. Each touch brought her closer to completion and his quickening breaths between kisses told her he was equally near the edge.

She wondered when he would call a stop to this and reach for the honeymoon suite gift basket by their bed—a basket with condoms in every color imaginable. But he showed no signs of stopping.

With knowing hands, he kept touching her, pushing her toward the edge, interspersing deep kisses with roving hands. Driving her wild. He took her closer to release, then eased up, only to tease her closer again. And she reveled in tempting him in equal measure, stroking and stroking, grazing her thumb over the head of his erection. The first droplets of his impending release slicked over the tip, giving her the power to move faster, his breath speeding in time. Thank goodness. Because she didn't know how much longer she could hold back...

Bliss.

Pulse after pulse of pleasure ripped through her, and she only barely kept her wits around her enough to bring him to his release, as well. His deep groan caressed her ears bringing a fresh wave of aftershocks shimmering along her passion-sensitive nerves.

As the last tremble faded, she sagged back, gasping from the power of her orgasm. She couldn't even find the will to open her eyes just yet. She could only feel.

A rustle sounded beside her. Easton. The covers shifted as he untangled them from their feet, and then a sheet settled along her. The ceiling fan overhead sent gusts of air down to dry the perspiration along her forehead.

Easton settled beside her, and she glanced at him, rolling to her side. His arm was flung over his eyes, his chest rising and falling rapidly, each breath a hint slower but still not back to normal. She reveled in the knowledge she'd brought him the same pleasure he'd given her.

Her eyes drifted to the honeymoon suite gift basket by their bed, looking at the assortment of neon condoms. Was that glitter on them, as well? A hint of apprehension whispered through her. She wasn't ready to tell him that they didn't need condoms.

Now she just had to figure out how to deal with using glitter-covered birth control.

The moment felt like an eternity as she stared at the basket, contemplating how to proceed. Heart hammering, Portia felt her hands start to tingle, a sure sign of her anxiety.

Easton's deep blue eyes searched her face. "Come here."

He opened his arms to her.

She hesitated.

He lifted her hand and tugged her gently until

she toppled to rest against his chest. His arms folded around her and anchored her there. "Sleep."

Surprise drifted through her passion-fogged mind as she realized somehow he'd understood her hesitation even though she hadn't voiced it. "You're serious? You don't want to finish this?"

"I do. But I can tell you're not ready and I'm smart enough not to make the same mistake twice. You're too important to me."

His words touched her as intensely as any stroke against her skin.

"If you're sure?"

"I am. Very." He rubbed her bare shoulder gently. "Now rest. We'll talk more tomorrow."

He draped himself around her, encircling her in his muscled arms. Protective and gentle.

She settled into him, noting the rhythmic rise and fall of his chest. The darkness in the room covering them both, shielding them from the reality of the morning. But for right now, Portia could pretend everything was fine and normal. That having someone take care of her was exactly what she needed.

And it was damn hard to deny that this didn't feel natural.

Morning sun streaking through the shutters, Easton listened to the patter of the shower and thought of the night before when Portia had been in that same bathroom, soaking in the tub.

They'd never made it to the spa in the corner of

their bedroom, the ledge decorated with candles and champagne. But then this was a honeymoon suite, and they were not honeymooners.

He scratched his chest and kicked aside the covers. While all his plans for the evening hadn't come to fruition, he had no regrets. He'd made significant progress in his hopes of winning his way back into her bed.

Instinct told him the best move was to give her space. To pursue her carefully so as not to scare her off again. He wasn't risking this second chance to be with her. He knew too well how fast life could change, how quickly people he thought he could count on were gone. He also knew his own shortcomings in maintaining relationships for the long haul.

He swung his legs off the mattress, feet meeting the cool floor. He tugged on his boxers and reached into his pants pocket for his cell. After that storm, he should check in with Maureen and make sure the refuge hadn't suffered substantial damage. While he loved spending the night with Portia, he knew the staff and animals at the preserve counted on him.

Walking out to the balcony, he cued up Maureen's number. The Gulf Coast waters glistened in the aftermath of the storm. A few branches littered the beach and chairs were overturned, but he didn't see any major upheaval. Morning walkers and shell collectors were already on the sand, a few kids dodging waves in bathing suits and tiny life vests. Vacationers were getting back to normal. Hopefully he would get the same report from home. Maureen answered on the third ring, her voice bright and alert.

"How'd we fare with that storm last night?" Easton asked in lieu of a normal introduction.

"And good morning to you, too," Maureen teased. "We've been worse this year. Some debris, naturally. I'm mobilizing a team of volunteers for yard cleanup."

Easton sank into one of the wooden Adirondack chairs, looking out onto the sun-speckled water. "How about the animals?"

"Spooked a few of them. But no substantial damage to any of the facilities and no major injuries to speak of," Maureen said, a parrot cawing in the background. "We were lucky."

"That's great to hear. I worried about them and you guys." He inhaled deeply, the scent of ocean overpowering his senses.

"So are you transporting any animals on your way back up?" Maureen asked.

"No. This isn't exactly a business trip."

He could practically see Maureen's eyebrows raising as she responded. "Yeah. I guessed that. Easton?"

"What?"

"Be careful with Portia. I think she is going through something. She's just been off lately. At first, I thought she was worried about how Marshall was doing in college, but now I'm not so certain that's the only concern in her life."

Protectiveness crept through him, making him

want to scoop her up and handle any worries that burdened her. He *would* figure them out, damn it. "Thanks for the heads-up."

"We all care about her. She's more than an employee."

"I know. I'll talk to her today on our way back. See you soon." He ended the call, looking through the sliding glass door, Maureen's words echoing in his mind. He had noticed the same thing about Portia more than once lately.

But he'd failed to take action in helping her. He'd been so focused on his own pursuit, his own needs. Guilt stung.

Easton went back inside and practically ran into Portia. Her hair was damp and loose from her shower, but rather than a towel, this time she was dressed in her clothes from yesterday. They were wrinkled, but dry. He didn't want to rush her, especially not after he'd just made a point of deciding to give her space.

No caveman tactics today. He would take things slow.

But she looked gray, like the color had been leeched from her. Her eyes briefly met his, but she turned away to perch on the edge of the sofa as if ready to take flight.

With a doctor's eye—even if for animals rather than people—he studied her more closely. Looked into her eyes. Counted her respiration as well as her pulse throbbing along her neck. And still he was no closer to figuring out what had upset her.

He could heal any animal, identify birds by their songs, but determining what made Portia tick was proving to be much more challenging.

Noting the exhaustion on her pale face, he said the first thing that came to mind, "You've been putting off going to school because of your brother's loans. What if I told you that you don't have to wait?"

"What do you mean?"

"Plenty of bosses help pay for their employees' college education. So why not start classes now?"

"I'm not the kind of woman who will take money from a man she's seeing, much less sleeping with, and it's insulting that you think I would." Fire burned in her eyes.

And her response struck a nerve for him.

"I'm insulted you think I would offer for any reason other than wanting to help. I should have thought to learn more about you sooner, and I would have known the need." He clasped her shoulders in a gentle grip and hoped she would read the genuine concern in his eyes. "Clearly stress is wearing you down and if you're burned out then that's bad for me on many levels. As a boss and as a person who cares about you. So let me help how I can."

"No." She shook her head, lips tight.

"That's it? No?" His hands dropping to his sides, he stepped away, and paced for a moment until he caught his betraying restlessness and leaned against the doorframe, trying his best not to appear frustrated. Easton wanted the best for Portia. No strings attached. He cared about her.

"Yes." She tugged her hair scrunchie off her wrist.

"Good."

"No, I meant, no you can't help." She piled her hair into a high ponytail on the top of her head, pulling it tight. "And yes, my answer is still no."

"Would you care to expand on that?"

She sagged into a chair. "Another time?"

Every road led back to this with her—to him being shut out like last time. As if she was leaving before she even had a chance to inevitably head out the door. "Sure, but on one condition."

"What's that?"

"You won't close yourself off again and block me out completely," he said, a gentle demand. He searched her face to gauge her reaction.

Portia's eyes fluttered shut. For a moment, she didn't speak. A sigh escaped her, and she opened her eyes to stare at him. "That's not a promise to sleep together. Last night—"

"Was another impulsive moment." He completed the sentence for her, finding he actually agreed with her. Stepping closer, he continued, "I get that. Completely. That's why we didn't finish."

"Truly?" She played with her necklace, sliding the charm back and forth on the silver chain.

"Yes, Portia. Truly. I want you to have sex with me totally aware of what we're doing. Not swept away. Well, swept away, but for all the right reasons. And trust me, I do believe that will happen and in the not too distant future."

"You're mighty confident." The first hint of a smile shone in her eyes, tipping her beautiful lips and chasing away some of the strains of exhaustion.

"About what we're feeling? Yes, I am." He lifted her hand and pressed a kiss to the inside of her wrist, lingering, holding her eyes for an instant before linking their fingers and stepping back. "Now let's get dressed and hit the road. We're both going to be late for work."

The ride back to the refuge had been mostly silent. Portia organized her notes, working hard as they drove.

As she color-coded her tasks, she felt more settled. This process with her notes and highlighters provided order and grounding. Each precise stroke of the pen and marker helped erect her protective walls.

Easton hadn't pressed her during the ride, letting her work in silence while he guided the low-slung Corvette around the storm-tossed debris on the roads. He hadn't even argued when she'd bypassed breakfast and asked only for warm tea with peppermint. Although she had pretended to nibble on a cookie.

She looked up from her planner, the afternoon sun warming her skin. They were on the road to the refuge. Somehow, two hours had come and gone.

He pulled the Corvette into the driveway, parking beneath a tall royal palm tree. They unbuckled, each exiting the vehicle. When her foot touched the solid ground, Portia's nerve and resolve grew.

She wasn't normally a person of impulse but after last night, she wondered if perhaps she should tell him about the baby now after all.

"Um, Easton," she began, hesitantly, words catching in the air as Maureen bounded onto the scene.

Portia couldn't ignore the huge sense of relief over being let off the hook a little while longer. Yes, she selfishly wanted more time with Easton to explore this attraction before risking a possible confrontation when he found out about their child.

"Hey pretty lady, you're back. I have a surprise planned for us." Maureen beamed at her, wrapping Portia in a hug. "I'm stealing your assistant for the remainder of the day. And your brother wants to talk to you." Maureen laughed, pulling Portia to the door of the mansion.

"You two have fun. Portia, we'll talk more later." He waved. Heading toward the clinic.

Maureen tugged Portia into the mansion toward the spacious women's locker room. She put her hands over Portia's eyes as she led her inside.

Relaxing harp music sounded, and when Maureen removed her hands, Portia took in the transformation. The steel and oak-benched locker room had been transformed into a day spa, not just with softer lighting, candles and sparkling water, but complete with pink-draped massage tables, a table of dainty foods, and makeup/hairstylist gear.

Maureen spread her arms wide. "Surprise. I knew you would try to go back to work after the time away, so I caught up with everything at the clinic. Now we can enjoy a girls' getaway, complete with dinner and pampering. Facials and shoulder massages and even a hair trim."

Portia froze, indecision and old insecurities taking control. "I appreciate your generosity, but I'm not comfortable with a makeover."

"That's not what this is about at all. You're beautiful as you are. I meant what I said about pampering only. You work too hard."

Maureen pointed to the spread of food on the far table.

Portia pursed her lips, leery of trusting Maureen. She felt vulnerable. But the food smelled divine. The long wooden table had a mixture of breads, garlic-crusted chicken, crab legs, and angel-hair pasta with lemon butter. Portia's stomach growled in response.

Now that Portia's stomach had settled and since she hadn't eaten yet today, the meal tempted her as much as the prospect of a shoulder massage.

"You have beautiful hair. Why do you keep it pulled back? It looks almost painful."

"It isn't." She touched her ponytail self-consciously.

"I'm sorry." Maureen winced. "I shouldn't have said anything. That was rude of me. I just wondered... but it's none of my business."

"I actually have my mother's hair." Portia stepped up into the stylist chair, looking at her reflection in the mirror. She shrugged her shoulders.

"And that's not good?"

"We had our differences, many of them. In fact, we were different in every way except for our thick hair—if not the same color. I want to be my own person so I chose a different style than hers."

"Then be your own person. Take charge."

"I have." Mostly. Partly. She'd brought up Marshall. She'd provided for him, a contrast from her mother's version of caring, which involved making sure they had the right "look." Their mom's pampering of her son had been almost smothering as she paraded her little boy in front of agents in hopes of landing a child star role in a commercial or television show. Portia felt that lack of a normal childhood could have been at least as damaging as the criticism she'd received. And then after their mother's death when Portia and Marshall had gone to live with their aunt in Florida, the decidedly nonmaternal woman had used what bit of parenting instincts she had to parent the younger of the two, leaving teenage Portia to fend for herself as she navigated young adulthood.

"Okay." Maureen nodded, slicing a mix of cheeses from the assortment and sliding the samplings onto the bone china plate along with fruit and crackers. She brought it to Portia, a smile resting on her lips. "Good?"

"Looks delicious." Portia took the delicate dish,

wary of Maureen's easy acquiescence. "Just okay? You aren't going to push me to participate in some magic makeover?"

"Remember! Today is *not* about makeovers. It's about relaxation and letting our inner self shine through." Maureen plucked up a grape and popped it into her mouth.

"But you want to offer advice."

"Of course. I'm opinionated." She snorted on a laugh. "Just ask my husband. Or anyone who knows me for more than five minutes then, like you."

"Alright, then. Let it fly. I'm a canvas." She popped a cheese cracker into her mouth before setting aside the china. "Paint me."

Maureen sat back in her chair, examining Portia. "I would suggest you let your hair down and quit thinking about your mother. Embrace who you are. Your hair doesn't have to be up or completely down either. I realize you like it back from your face. So perhaps try some clips, have fun with jewelry."

"That's it? Let my hair down and pack some Be-Dazzled pins?" She was surprised, half imagining that Maureen was going to suggest a severe haircut or worse—bleach it as her mom had not-too-subtly suggested more than once.

Well, damn. She did think about her mother's criticisms too often.

"It's a start, Portia. If you could choose any dress you wanted, no holds barred, what would you choose?" She gestured wide with her hands, as if all the clothes in the world were actually in front of them.

"I thought you were supposed to be helping me pick."

"I will, if you need me, but I don't think you need anyone's guidance on this."

Portia glanced back over her shoulder, curious and a little suspicious of some mystery motive. "What's really going on here? Did Easton put you up to this?"

Or worse yet, after their night spent away, was Maureen attempting to matchmake?

"I'm just empowering you to be who you want to be." Maureen removed Portia's ponytail, letting her heavy hair fall. Grabbing a brush, she worked through her tangled air-dried locks. "Oh Lord, did I really just say that? Empowering? I sound like some kind of self-help book—you're the last woman who needs help. I just want to pamper you since you go out of your way to take care of others. And in case you're worried, the professional hairstylist will be here soon."

"It's kind of you to arrange all of this, and I don't mean to sound like an ingrate." She looked at her short, neat nails and wondered what they would look like with a bolder color, not long French tips or fake nails, but just something…fun. "I shouldn't have said what I did about my mother. I don't want to be someone who blames everyone else for my hang-ups."

Maureen set down the brush and took a chair beside her. "You're the last person I would assume that about. You are levelheaded and confident."

Portia didn't feel that way. She felt like she'd clawed her way through life to find confidence and a future for herself and her brother. To find the independence she craved. She didn't want this roaring frustration inside her. She wanted to be happy about this baby, her child. Instead, she was just...scared.

What did she know about being a mother? She hadn't had good examples. Maybe this spa day, and the time with Easton, would help her get her head on straight before her whole world changed.

The doctor's appointment was less than a week away. A relief.

And the ticking clock counting down her time to finish exploring this whole empowerment exercise. Soon she would take on the whole Lourdes family full force—and one incredibly charming veterinarian—and tell them she was carrying the next little addition.

Seven

Three hours later, Easton stood in the doorway leading to the women's locker room and braced his hands on either side to keep his footing. He'd heard from his brother that the women were getting dinner, massages and makeovers. And he'd expected some glammed up, artificial look. He'd prepared himself to say the right things on his way to kissing the artifice away. Had anticipated the moment with a raw sensuality that burned deep inside him.

However, he hadn't expected Portia's angled features to make her look downright ethereal. And the difference rocked him. He'd always found her attractive— her kindness, her stunning smile, her deep, dark eyes.

But with her hair falling around her ears…

How she sat relaxed and causal...

She knocked the air from his lungs. Literally.

Her eyes widened as she noticed his stare, a faint blush rising, swirling in her cheeks. The shadowed light catching on her slender face. Damn.

"You look stunning," Easton said, his voice hoarse as he worked to drag air into his lungs again. "And I don't just mean the hair or the makeup. There's a glow to you that's incredible."

Maureen tipped her head to the side. "A glow?"

Portia shot to her feet, dismissive of his compliment. "Thank you. All the credit goes to the makeup artist and hairstylist. I just sat still and let them work."

She walked to the drink station and fixed herself a glass of sparkling water and then dropped in a lime slice from a bowl.

Don the security guard and his wife, Jessie, floated into the room. Active fiftysomethings, they were a powerhouse volunteer couple. They donated a substantial amount of time and money to the refuge. Somehow, they'd also become surrogate grandparents to Rose, poking in and out of the house. Down-to-earth people no one would suspect actually had made billions through savvy investments in the dot-com world, getting out right before it crashed. They were a regular fixture around here, often staying late. It was never a surprise to see them wander in, and the Lourdes family could never pay them back for all they'd done for the refuge.

The dim light of the room made Jessie's spotted pullover appear like a molten mix of tan and black, making her seem like a jungle cat. Elbows hooked together, they strode over to Easton and Portia who had shrugged off her robe to reveal a formfitting mint dress. All of her curves accented, the mint color brought her pale skin to life. Teasing him, tempting him.

She brushed her fingers against his. A small gesture, sure. But he found himself itching for more. A lot more.

Jessie cooed, patting Don's stomach. "Did y'all know that we are celebrating thirty-three years of marriage next week?"

"That is amazing." Portia nodded, a smile on her lightly glossed lips.

Easton nodded absently as well, eyes fixed on her. Wanting her.

"Are you doing anything special?" Easton said after a moment, shifting his weight slightly so his body would caress Portia's. She leaned into him, like a palm tree swaying in a springtime breeze. Awareness simmered between them, a slow burn.

Don combed his fingers through his snow-gray hair. "When are you planning to ask her out on an official date?"

Portia choked on her sip of sparkling water.

Easton set his drink aside slowly and lifted an eyebrow. "When did you start up a matchmaking service?"

Don shrugged, proceeding in his typical straight-forward manner. He'd never been one to mask his thoughts or feelings. "Sorry to have put the two of you on the spot there, but it's obvious to all of us around here that the two of you are an item. So I was just wondering when you're going to start dating. Or if you already are, let the rest of us in on it so we can double date."

"Double date?" Portia squeaked, putting aside her own drink now.

Jessie reached her hand out to gently squeeze Portia's arm. She gave a quick wink. "Sure. Do you think married couples don't date anymore? If that's your idea of marriage, no wonder you've stayed single for so long."

Easton watched as color drained from Portia's face. He decided to steer the conversation to a different topic—anything to make Portia feel more comfortable and not derail his plan to win her back into his bed. "I know married couples have romance. I've seen my brother married twice, happily both times."

Jessie lowered her voice, holding a glass of sparkling wine in a relaxed grasp. "Then you two are dating and keeping it quiet?"

She asked so casually, as if she were inquiring about the weather and not asking for a piece of private, intimate information.

Easton folded his arms over his chest, frustrated that his friends could be eroding the progress he'd made toward getting Portia back into his bed. "No offense, Don, but why is this any of your business?"

"Wow, you're in a bad mood. Must be the barometric pressure drop," Don teased, still not getting the message. Easton saw Portia's spine grow rigid, the glow of earlier replaced by seething discomfort.

Jessie gave an exaggerated wink. "Or a lack of romance in your life."

Portia waved a hand. "Hello, I'm here and a part of this conversation."

Jessie turned to Portia, blinking. In faux seriousness, she asked, "So is he properly romancing you?"

Easton held up a hand. "Stop. Yes, I'm interested, very interested, in Portia. And I want to win her over, but that's for her to say and you're not helping matters."

All eyes turned to Portia.

"What?" She held up her hands defensively. "Things are complicated."

Jessie nodded. "He's your boss."

"True." Portia winced. "Thanks for reminding me."

Easton had kept his frustration under control when it was all good-natured ribbing, but now, as he watched Portia grow increasingly uncomfortable, he started to steam. He wanted to protect her from any upset, even something as innocent as this sort of thing.

Jessie shot a warning look at Easton before leaning toward Portia. "Has he made you uncomfortable with his advances? Because that wouldn't be right."

Easton bristled. Established, wealthy volunteers or not, there were lines and they were skirting close to crossing them.

Portia touched his arm lightly. "Easton hasn't done anything wrong. I made the first move on him, okay? So there. Yes, we have feelings for each other. Yes, we're attracted to each other. And yes, it was probably silly of us to think our private lives could be private in such an intimate work environment, but we really would appreciate some space to figure this out. Thank you."

She adjusted her weight and fixed them both with a commanding stare before striding out of the room. Her chin up.

He had never seen her be so assertive before. She'd become a force—like the storms that had brought them together—firm, unflinching and unapologetic.

Dazzling.

And he was stunned as hell that he wanted more than just to have her back in his bed again.

Drained, Portia sagged against the door after the men left, watching the stylist pack her gear, listening to the sounds of zippers and bottles of products clinking together before more footsteps reverberated along with the closing of a door. With the portable salon packed in bags, the room echoed.

She hadn't been in the mood for such prying questions from anyone, even friends like Don and Jessie. And the questions seemed to carry more weight, hit her more deeply, because of her pregnancy.

Her still secret pregnancy, made all the more complicated by that look in Easton's eyes when he'd seen her. She could have sworn she saw more than just passion, and that excited her and scared her all at once because heaven help them, this could not be a regular dating relationship. They didn't have the luxury.

Pressing a hand to her forehead and closing her eyes, she couldn't remember the last time she'd felt so alone. Then the warm press of another person sidled beside her, sweeping an arm around her shoulder. Portia looked over, the smell of peonies and powder lingering.

Jessie. A woman happily married for decades. A grandmother. Content with where she was in her life.

A painful sight for Portia right now.

The older woman patted Portia's shoulder. "I'm sorry, dear, we didn't mean to upset you. My man, he can be pushy, but he didn't mean any harm. We thought it was so obvious."

Portia found it easy to forgive the woman for her overreaching. Jessie showed her tender heart daily in how she sang to wounded animals as they underwent treatment. Which made her think of Easton's tender care of animals that could seriously injure him in their wounded, frantic state. He was such an intriguing, unexpected sort of person.

She looked down at her fingers twisted together in her lap. "Our feelings are that apparent?"

Maureen's brogue answered as she called from behind a changing screen, "Yes, they are. Especially this past week." She passed Portia a tissue. "I've never seen you cry before."

Portia sagged onto an oaken locker room bench. "I do have emotions."

Sitting beside her, Jessie stroked a lock of hair over Portia's shoulder. "Of course you do. You just usually keep them to yourself. But those feelings are tougher to keep inside when hormones are out of control."

Jessie gave her a pointed look that all but had Portia squirming in her chair. Her secret pregnancy wouldn't be a secret much longer if people were already guessing. Luckily, Maureen seemed oblivious. Still, the time clock was ticking down. Portia had to tell Easton. "I'm doing better now, but thank you for caring.

"Of course, dear, we're all a big family here. And I'll make sure Don lightens up on the teasing." Jessie clucked her tongue like a protective mother hen.

"Thank you. That would be helpful." Especially until Portia figured things out for her future as a mother.

With a satisfied nod, Jessie stood up. She fluffed her hair with her fingers, and started to walk away. She paused for a moment, spinning on her kitten heels to face Portia. "You really are lovely, and glowing. Take care of yourself, dear. Maureen, would you mind taking me to see my favorite little Key deer baby that has a broken leg?"

Maureen pranced out from behind the screen, her curly red hair falling midchest, contrasting with her white shift dress. Her gold accessories catching the light, making her look like some Celtic princess from centuries past.

"Of course. I have about an hour before I'm supposed to meet Xander. I'll take you to the baby deer."

She linked her arm with Jessie's and tossed Portia a wave and a wink.

Glowy.

Such an intentional and loaded word.

Did they know? Or at the very least suspect?

Before panic could fully rise in her chest, Portia's cell phone rang, sending her thoughts skittering. Looking down at the screen, she read *Marshall*.

Scrambling to answer, she clicked the green button, shoving the phone to her ear.

"Hey, sis. I haven't heard from you in a while—"

"Since last night."

"I know," he teased gently. "I was being sarcastic. You sounded, um, off last night. I wanted to follow up. You're not the only one who worries."

The weight of responsibility felt heavier than ever on her shoulders. Every decision she made could have such far-reaching repercussions. "Work has been hectic. How are you?"

"I'm good. Classes are good, grades are solid and I have good news for you."

"I could use good news." She couldn't keep a wobble of concern out of her voice. She was so confused, and for a woman used to controlling every inch of her life, that was a difficult and alien way to feel.

"Are you sure you're okay?"

Oh, nothing. Just my life being torn apart.

She wanted to say something like that—wanted to share her life-altering news with her brother. Instead, she looked at her nails, choosing to remain the strong, balanced force she always thought Marshall needed. "Yes, of course. Tell me your news?"

"I got a gig as a residence hall counselor after summer session this fall, which means free dorm and a break on tuition. There's been a last-minute opening and they asked me."

"That's fantastic." A shred of positive news. There'd be less to siphon away from her pay. The debt for his college education was worth it though. She needed to see him settled before she could make any plans for her future, however much she wanted to... She stopped thoughts of Easton short. For now. And she focused on her brother's words instead.

"I'm trying my best not to be a burden to you. I appreciate all you've done for me."

"It's my joy. I'm proud of you." She'd never told him of her own dreams to go to college. She was so afraid if he didn't complete his education now he never would. She needed to know he was secure in his future.

But she also had a child to consider. Life was so very complicated.

And she wanted to be with Easton again so damn much.

The next day, when Easton had asked her to have dinner by the pool after work, she hadn't even bothered making an excuse to decline. Clearly, hiding their mutual interest from everyone and each other was futile. In a way, that observation caused a degree of relief for Portia. There would be no sneaking around now. Fewer secrets. This would be their first date since their night in the inn. The night they'd almost slept together.

A night she couldn't get out of her mind.

After his date request, she'd rushed to her cabana to shower and change. As she slipped into a simple backless green dress, she felt a buzz hum through her body.

Apprehension coursed through her spine, filling her with a strange mixture of curiosity and desire. She fluffed her hair, opting to let it stay down like the stylist had done the day before.

Maybe there was something to all that empowerment talk Maureen had given Portia. A new hairstyle for a new chapter in her life. The small change felt like she'd made a promise to herself to be brave for her own future and not just for her brother.

Regardless of the attraction between her and Easton, Portia needed to get to know him better. The father of her unborn child. No. Wait. That was wrong.

Their unborn child.

That shared child meant they would forever be in each other's lives, even if he was a reluctant parent. She couldn't see him turning his back on his child altogether. And if he did? Then he wasn't a man worthy of either of them.

She left her little home and walked the path over to the pool by the main house. Easton had said he planned to walk her over, but coming to him gave her more of a sense of power.

Now she was glad she had done so as she had a few minutes to take in the dinner arrangements unobserved. Easton had hired a Spanish guitarist and a pianist to play sultry songs. The beautiful riffs filled the night air, making her forget for a moment that she was at his house and not in some fancy restaurant.

Glancing around the pool deck, she certainly felt like they had been transported somewhere magical. High romance. No expense spared. Globe lights were strung overhead like personal stars. The whole patio was decorated in hibiscus flowers and soft green ferns—a tropical getaway in the middle of daily life.

The house was silent and unlit. Xander, Maureen and baby Rose had left for an evening getaway.

Easton stepped through the double French doors with a bouquet of peonies in his hand and stopped short once he saw her, then he picked up his pace again.

"Portia," he called out, "I wanted to escort you over."

She met him at the stairs. "I know, but I was ready early, and I do know where you live."

"That you do." He extended his hand clasping the pink blossoms. "These are for you."

"Thank you, they're lovely." She brought the dozen buds up to her nose and inhaled the sweet fragrance.

Easton took a carafe from the wet bar and slid the flowers inside, pouring water into the makeshift vase. She was touched by the way he didn't order staff around to do his every task. He was a man with the money to pay for most anything he wanted and help for every moment of the day, and yet he lived a purposeful life.

He nodded to the flowers' placement before turning to her. "I thought about getting you candy too, but I keep seeing that basket full of edible toys back in that honeymoon suite."

Laughing, she pressed a hand to her lips and finally gave up holding back her amusement. "I'll return the vase once the peonies wilt."

She would be drying them as a keepsake for their baby. Far better to explain how she and her child's father had dated and enjoyed their time together. She couldn't bear for their child to feel like the unwanted result of an impulsive night.

Easton pulled out a chair for her at the wooden

table. The peonies added the perfect touch to their romantic dinner, no one but the server and the musicians around.

Soft wind whispered as Easton pushed in her chair, his fingertips lingering for a moment on her bare shoulders. He took his seat across from her, foot knocking playfully into hers. His ready smile illuminated by the Tiki torch that kept bugs at bay.

Easton tucked his ankle against hers. "You really do look beautiful. If I didn't think to tell you before tonight, I apologize."

"You told me."

"You didn't believe me, though, did you? There's a skepticism in your eyes that stuns me."

Portia leaned closer to him, so her words didn't strain against the melody of the guitar and piano. "Of course I realize we're attracted to each other."

He touched her chin and tipped up her face. "You are lovely, elegant and always have been. It's all I can do to keep my hands to myself at work."

"You've always been completely professional in the workplace."

"I'm a damn good actor, then." He plucked a hibiscus from a nearby arrangement, spinning the stem between his fingers.

She laughed, unfolding her napkin and placing it in her lap. These luxurious meals were a treat, but she would have to watch her fish intake for the baby. Still, her mouth watered with hunger, a welcome relief from the morning sickness that grew worse each day. "I do appreciate and respect that you've been restrained in the office."

He tucked the flower behind her ear near the jeweled pin, ramping up her awareness. Distracting her from the parmesan-and-herb-spiced yellowfin tuna that overtook her plate.

"So it's okay for me to touch you outside the office now?"

"I didn't say that, exactly."

He dragged another flower up her arm, until it rested on her cheek. "I can see something's holding you back. Am I simply not your type?"

"Why do people assume they know my type?" She shimmied away from the flower, picking up her fork and skewering one of the roasted tomatoes.

"Someone else agrees with me?" He lifted one eyebrow.

"I didn't say that."

"I know I'm eccentric." Laughing, he pointed to the decorations overhead.

"You're brilliant and a gifted veterinarian who manages to work with a wide variety of exotic animals." Portia rested her fork along the upper edge of her plate. "And, yes, you're also one eccentric tree climb away from having your own television series."

"You don't make that sound like a compliment."

"I only meant I'm reserved. Some have even called me prim—" She held up a palm. "I'm alright with that description. I know myself. But you *are* eccentric. I would expect you to be drawn to someone more flamboyant."

"Some say opposites attract. I think it's more complex than that. Attraction defies reason."

So true. But that didn't stop reason from interfering with attraction, reminding her how hard she'd fought to be independent, to build a life for herself outside of her parents' shadow. She couldn't afford to forget that in the long term.

And yet, still, she burned for this man. Unable to resist for this one moment at least, she lifted her fingers to stroke his collar-length, wild hair. The touch happened before she thought better of it. And maybe it wasn't so bad as long as she knew it was her decision. She was in control. "Relationships are based on common interests."

"What are your interests? You draw, but what else?"

"I'm your secretary."

"My assistant." He corrected her gently, placing his hand on top of hers.

"Whatever. It wasn't your place to know my hobbies."

"We've spent more time together than some people do when officially dating. I should have listened better." He thumbed the inside of her palm, a small smile tugging at his mouth.

"Is this going to be round two of Quiz Show?"

"I was just going to ask you what song you would like for me to request from the pianist."

"Something with a beach music flavor. I love to dance."

"You do?" His bold mouth twitched in a crooked smile. "See, we have something in common after all. Hold on while I place our request."

He pushed out of his chair, heading to the pianist, all elaborate arm gestures and flash. An intoxicating vision.

Returning to the table, he extended his hand. "If you've finished with your dinner, could I have this dance?"

How could she resist? Right now, she couldn't. "I would like that, very much."

"I'm honored." He bowed deeply before whisking her onto her feet to the makeshift dance floor.

Pressing against each other, she felt time strain and stop for this moment. The scent of his cologne mingled with sea breeze and salt. He sang softly in her ear, his hot words warming her inside out.

His soft eyes met hers, desire and electric sparks passing through his gaze.

No matter what the future held for her, or how he reacted to her secret, there was only one way this night could end. Together, tangled.

Eight

Dancing with Portia set him ablaze. His hands had touched the bare skin of her back peeking out from behind her breezy green sundress. After the music faded, she looked at him through shy eyes.

"Walk me home?" her voice quiet, eyes burning into him.

Easton's hand trailed alongside her right arm, enjoying the softness of her skin, the way she seemed to melt under his touch.

He leaped at the chance to lace her fingers with his, for the extra time together. His stolen sidelong glances at her increased the farther away they walked from the main mansion to her modest off-white cabana. Her shoulders, normally strained, seemed relaxed. A light breeze tossed her half up, half down hair, the moonlight illuminating soft traces of makeup that accented her slender face and beautiful pink lips. She seemed like a tall fairy—an extension of the landscape. His landscape.

Their footfalls on the white sand road looked like shooting stars in the night.

Portia had always been naturally beautiful, but he couldn't recall a time when she'd seemed so at ease and calm. The spa afternoon had brushed life back into her, making it all too obvious to him how she always did things for other people and didn't do things for herself. He wanted to pamper her. He wanted to protect her. But as she spoke of common interests and viewpoints, he wondered if he should be protecting her from himself and his vagabond spirit.

She fiddled with her keys, fishing them out of her pale yellow purse. Shifting her weight from leg to leg, he noticed how her strappy sandals pushed against her skin.

The cabana she'd been given as part of her pay had been stark and basic when she'd arrived. Now the little wooden hut glistened with peace and beauty, her stamp everywhere. Flowers of nearly every hue overflowed from boxes and pots. Lush ground cover filled in spaces with only jeweled step stones breaking their flourish. A fountain built of terracotta clay pots overflowed into a pool of fat orange fish.

She unlocked the bright yellow door, brushing her feet on the mat before stepping inside and clicking on the lights. Inside, a plump, inviting sofa, in what he'd heard Maureen call a shabby chic print, nearly filled the room. There was an artistic flair to Portia he hadn't noticed before, in spite of her telling him she enjoyed drawing. He could see her creativity in the way she'd planned her garden and how she'd refinished old pieces of furniture, end tables with swirls of color patterned into the grain and shape. Even her simple ice cream parlor table sported hand-blown glass spheres that filled a bowl like crystal-lized treats. Somehow, he knew she'd made those, with her patience, frugality and eye for beauty. Why hadn't he thought before about how she commented on the distinct hues of the birds and other creatures in the wild?

And how had he not stepped inside here before now?

He'd missed so much about her until that night of the storm when he'd been drawn to her with new eyes, the electricity in the air gathering around her like lightning bugs. Even in trying to get her back into his bed, somehow he'd missed important details. Getting to know her had been a selfish plan, but he was finding himself more captivated than he'd ever been by another person.

"Portia, your place is lovely." Like her.

She slipped her shoes off and nudged them in line beside the door with her toe. "It's nothing compared to your professionally decorated mansion."

"You have an artist's flair to you that surpasses anyone else we could have hired."

"Thank you." A blush on her cheeks, she stared lovingly at her possessions. Proud of her space and vision. Confident.

"I like the way you brought nature inside." He stepped to the walls lined with pen-and-ink sketches of Florida coast scenery and animals. "And your art. These sketches are yours?" he asked even as he saw her initials precisely in the corner of each one.

"Yes, I mentioned I like to draw." She tapped one of her sketches, an alligator winding through marsh grass, a wry smile on her face. She'd never seemed so sexy, so decisive. So sure of herself as she was in the arena of her art.

"I remember. But this is more than just doodling or drawing. This is talent, a gift." He turned back to her. "I respect the work you do for me. You keep me organized and focused in a way no one has managed before. But here, I feel like I'm keeping you from your true calling."

She looked at him thoughtfully, her love of art apparent on her face. "I'll get back to it one day as more than a hobby."

"Why one day? Plenty of college students work while enrolled. I did."

Taking his hand, she led him into the living room. She sat on the bright yellow couch in lotus position, patting the seat next to her. Inviting him closer. She leaned forward, interest and surprise knitting into her brow. "Even with your family's money?"

"Absolutely. I wanted hands-on experience." He sat too, linking fingers with her. Needing to touch her.

"That's nice to hear about you. I didn't know." Her palm rested on his knee in an unspoken promise of more to come.

This was another dance they were doing now, one he could see in the awareness in her eyes, the widening of her pupils.

"It must not have come up in your Quiz Show."

"I would have expected your life growing up, traveling the world, would have given you the opportunity for vast experiences."

"We were talking about you. And your brother. And why you refuse to let anyone help you with him," Easton said, not taking the bait to talk about himself. Portia so often deferred her interests and needs to others. He didn't want her to do that now. Not as he finally glimpsed her soul and her sparkle.

"Because I can take care of him. He's my family. He has a learning disability. He's brilliant but needs tutors. He will graduate, it's just taking five years with summers. He's even picked up a part-time job as a residence hall advisor this fall. I'm proud of how hard he's worked."

"And then it will be your turn?" He reached for her cheek, stroking it with a soft thumb. Wanting to give her all of her dreams.

She placed her hand over his, stilling the motion of his fingers, yet pressing his touch more firmly against her skin. "I thought we were coming here to make love."

"Wow, I struck a nerve, didn't I?"

She rose from the couch, headed to the kitchen as if she were considering his words. Lingering by the fridge, she cocked her head to the side and popped her hip out. "Maybe I want to start getting hands-on experience with my art right now."

"What do you mean?" His heart pushed, hammered, at the suggestion in her pose, at her yet to be articulated promise. Standing, he strode into the kitchen.

"You can be my canvas." She pulled a tub of whipped cream from the refrigerator. She lifted the lid and swirled her finger through, painting her lips before licking them clean.

He almost swallowed his tongue.

She was distracting him on purpose. Of course she was. But looking at her right now, feeling the answering heat inside him, he would gladly let her. He would find out more about why she was delaying her schooling later.

After he explored every tasty inch of her. He couldn't take his eyes off her still-damp lips. "I assume that's my cue to get undressed."

"If you want." She shrugged nonchalantly, staring at him with a certain, commanding smile.

He made a mental note to make sure her future included all the spa days she wanted. Whatever magic Maureen had worked in getting Portia to take some downtime had paid off in spades. There was a new relaxation and confidence in her.

"I want. Very much." He stepped closer, unbuttoning his shirt and tossing it aside.

She swept her finger through the dessert topping again and touched his collarbone. Her stroke was cool from the cream, and then she dipped her head, her breath warm as she said, "Ooops, I need to erase that." She swept her tongue along his skin. "I'll need to draw that over again."

"Do I get to practice my artwork on you?"

"Are you any good?"

He took the tub from her and set it on the table by the colorful glass display. "I damn well hope so."

His hands damn near shaking, he reached behind her to unzip her dress until it slid from her body to pool around her feet. She kicked it to the side. He took in the vision of her peach-colored lace bra and panty set, her breasts perfect globes calling to his hands to explore. Her eyes held his as she released the front clasp. He was quick to help her stroke free of the scrap of lace so he could "paint" a snowy cloud of whipped cream over one nipple, lave it clean before giving equal attention to the other.

Her kittenish purrs of pleasure rewarded him for his diligent effort. She cupped his face and guided him back for a kiss. The sweet taste of sugar on her tongue went straight to his senses. Before he could gather his thoughts again, they'd both stripped away their clothes in a frenzy of motion on their way to kneeling on the kitchen rug.

Taking turns, they painted each other, although his artwork was more precise than hers, Portia's more in the league of landscapes that sent her kisses all over. He focused more on her breasts, a trail down her stomach, then settled between her legs for an intense, intimate kiss. The sweetness of her had little to do with the topping and far more to do with her. Portia. This amazing woman who'd come into his life and shaken him from his superficial dating ways.

He wanted more from her. So much more.

With each stroke and circle of his tongue, her breathing grew faster. She gripped his shoulders, her nails digging half-moons into his flesh urging him to cover her body with his. He didn't hesitate.

He settled between her legs and positioned himself at the hot slick core of her. Something tugged at his mind but before he could finish the thought, Portia skimmed the arches of her feet along the backs of his calves and hooked her ankles around his waist. The arch of her hips welcomed him inside her. Where he belonged.

His head fell to rest against hers, the bliss of being joined with her so incredible it almost pushed him over the edge. He gritted his teeth to hold back his release, to make sure she found complete pleasure, everything he could give her before he indulged himself.

Stroke after stroke, thrust after thrust, he filled

her and savored her rocking motion in sync with his. They were learning each other's bodies, specifics and needs, erogenous zones. The scent of her freshly perfumed skin and some kind of massage oils along her shoulders teased his every breath.

He would drink her in if he could.

Let her know how beautiful she was. Always. No makeover needed.

She was Portia. He'd not realized why he'd pursued her so stubbornly, but this surprising woman was who he'd been waiting for. And finally he was where he wanted to be.

That thought tore away the last vestige of his restraint and sent him hurtling over the edge into a blinding orgasm. His release sent him pulsing deeper into her, faster, each pump of his body drawing a "Yes, yes, yes" from her lips until… Her back arched upward. Her head fell back, her silken hair fanned around her.

No need for them to be quiet here in her home, just the two of them. Their cries of completion twined in the way their hands did over her head. Together.

His arms gave way and he just barely caught himself on his elbows before he rolled to his side, taking her with him. He folded her against his chest, their bodies sticky with sweat and the remnant of whipped topping.

In the stillness of this cabana, he felt at peace. The rise and fall of his chest made more comfortable by the press of Portia's body against his. His fingers stroked down her side. The moment of rest as beautiful as she was.

Easton kissed her cheek before nuzzling her with his late-day beard. "What brought on this change of heart?"

Portia looked up at him through long eyelashes. "Not a change of heart. I've always wanted this. I just felt like the time was right. This is our night."

"The first of many more, I hope."

She hummed in answer and kissed him, silencing any more talk or even rational thought, for that matter.

His hammering heartbeat started to recede into normal rhythms.

"We should get clean." He said into her skin. In response, she kissed him, deeply, her tongue darting over his.

"Done so soon?" She bit his bottom lip, hand wandering down his side.

She got up, her body a dark silhouette in the streaming moonlight. Walking to the bathroom, she looked seductively over her shoulder.

He wanted her, even more than before, and he planned to have her again and again. Thank goodness he'd brought enough condoms—

A sinking feeling slammed him in the gut. Damn, damn, damn it.

He was always careful. He'd only ever forgotten one other time, the first time he'd made love to Portia and when he hadn't heard anything from her in spite of his attempts to reach out, he'd known they'd somehow been lucky.

As he followed her toward the shower, though, he snagged his pants with his wallet full of condoms to use from here on out. They could talk about the lack of birth control during those other two encounters in the morning.

Because he wasn't letting anything interfere with this night in her bed.

Bright sunlight streamed into her room, nudging sleep from her eyes. Looking out the window, she began to turn her gaze inward. To memories of last night.

Allowing Easton to come to her space had been a big step. A bold one. Portia had allowed him to glimpse her private love affair with art—the one activity that steeled her nerves, made her feel brave and resourceful. She'd channeled that creative capacity into their night, blending art with love.

She stretched fully, remembering the way their tangled bodies sought each other as if by their own volition and inclinations. Portia painted him with whipped cream, made a masterpiece of his skin and her desire. Pulled him again into the shower. Needed him.

She'd felt like wildfire last night. A rush of flame and heat so intense, one that had to burn itself out. Which was where she felt like this morning was heading. To the aftermath. He'd used condoms those last two times. She hadn't wanted to break the mood by telling him it wasn't necessary, not when she already knew they would be talking about the baby soon, likely before her doctor visit. Because it wasn't fair to keep him in the dark now that they seemed to be heading into a relationship. Once she shared the news with him, things would change between them forever.

She turned from her side to see if he was awake.

Those bright blue eyes met hers, his dark hair curling on the pillow. "Last night was incredible. *You* are incredible." He stroked his fingers through her loosened hair. "I hope you don't run in the other direction again to put distance between us. Because I want us to be together. I want to see where this is going."

"I have no intention of running." She meant that. Running with their unborn child wasn't an option. She needed to face this head-on. No matter what. She'd been running from this conversation for too long.

"That's good to know." He leaned in to kiss her, then stroked the outline of her face. "I'm sorry for losing my head last night and forgetting to protect you."

"You mean not using a condom?" Bile churned in her stomach. The conversation was already headed in the wrong direction. She wasn't ready for this conversation. Not yet.

"Yes," he nodded. "That's twice I've let you down

and I'm sorry. But I want you to know that if there are consequences, I'll be here for you."

"Consequences." The word felt clinical. Distant. Emotionally shut off. But then she hadn't wanted the conversation to get emotional. So why was she bristling? God, her emotions were a mess and she knew it had more than to do with the baby.

"Consequences. As in pregnancy," he clarified. "Unless you're on the pill?"

All of her gusto and nerve manifested into steel will to cover the hurt his words caused. Part of her did want to rely on him and make a real relationship, but now she was second-guessing herself. Yes, she needed to tell him the truth. But she didn't need his help. Didn't need him to be obligated to her. Portia always figured things out on her own, made them work for her. Even if that path wasn't the easy or conventional one. "Don't worry about me."

"Of course I will. You don't need more responsibility on your plate in addition to your brother. In fact, can we talk again about me help—"

"No." She pressed her fingers to his mouth, surprised at the depth of her remorse over realizing they didn't feel the same way about last night. He was not ready to be emotionally involved with her, not ready to be a true parent. For a moment, she'd wanted to do all of this with him by her side, and she swallowed back the fantasy of being able to parent with him. "Can you stop talking about money and responsibilities and consequences? I know you don't want children. You've made that clear."

"As I recall, I said I don't think I'll be a good father and that I wasn't ready to start a family. Now that I think back I'm not sure exactly what I said." He scratched the back of his head. "You may have noticed but my thoughts get jumbled around you."

"You said you don't want children. I remember your words, and I would think a man of your education level would know what he's saying." Anger edged out her more tender emotions as she lobbed the words at him.

He reeled back under her attack, then he sat up, grasping her hand. "I'm not trying to pick a fight, Portia, although it's clear I've upset you. I'm sorry for that."

Portia tugged her hand from his. Distance. She had to put some space between them. And quell the rising tide of nausea building in her stomach. "Please, stop apologizing. I'm an adult. I'm equally responsible for what happens between us when we have sex."

"I'm trying to be honorable. Would you prefer I was a jerk?" His sincere blue eyes punctured her, calming her for a moment.

"Of course not." She shook her head, eyes stinging with unshed tears. The world pressed on her shoulders, pinning her to this moment.

"Then let me be a gentleman."

"Gentle is good."

The words stalled on her lips, heart growing heavy as nausea took over her body in full force.

He reached out to touch her, but she bolted from his fingertips. Running to the bathroom, door closing behind her.

Her bare thighs pressed into the tile floor as she held the porcelain toilet. Two types of illness bore upon her. One from the increasing intensity of morning sickness. That sickness she could manage—that one had an end in sight.

But her heartsickness over the lost chance to be with Easton in a real relationship?

She'd parented her brother and never felt this solitude—instead she'd taken comfort from her friends. Heaven knew she had friends and support here at the refuge.

Yet none of them were Easton. The abyss of her loneliness stretched in front of her as she heaved the contents of her stomach into the toilet.

Consequences.

The word sliced through her mind. She just wanted to curl up on the cool tile floor and not move for seven more months.

What was it about him that sent Portia running to lock herself away from him?

Easton sat on the edge of her bed, scanning the room. Everything seemed to have a definitive place. Bright, cheery colors served to accent the plain white walls. Her poppy-orange bedspread added warmth and comfort to the room.

She didn't have a lot of figurines or knickknacks, he noted. A small, skinny faux marble table sat in the corner, holding a bouquet of fresh-cut flowers.

Next to him on her nightstand, he noticed a small sketchbook, the spine worn from constant use. The visible signs of wear seemed at odds with the rest of Portia's room.

Glancing at the still-closed door, he decided to pick up the black leather-bound book. Leafing through the pages, he found himself transported.

Portia's floral sketches that hung in the hallway were beautiful. But the sketches in the notebook were stunning. Haunting, imbued with reality. She'd sketched different animals from the refuge, her images playing with shading and line structure.

He was no art aficionado, but Easton knew enough to realize Portia's raw talent. He felt a renewed dedication to getting her into an art program. She'd been self-taught. If she had resources, a mentor and time…she could be downright fantastic.

He replaced the sketchbook back on the nightstand, continuing his survey of the room. The top of her dresser housed a framed picture of her and Marshall, a gold-leafed copy of fairy tales and a ring dish where a pearl necklace coiled.

He picked up the book of fairy tales, reminding himself Portia needed her space. The door was still shut, but when they'd been at the inn, she had taken a bath and come out of that experience more relaxed.

Surely this morning was the same thing. He tried to convince himself of that.

But as time passed, seconds turning into minutes and then a full half hour without any sound other than the bathroom sink running and running, he began to worry. He hadn't heard the bathwater start, and he feared she was perhaps crying.

He walked toward the bathroom door and as he drew closer he realized…she was throwing up. Retching. Again and again. Worry overtook him and he knocked firmly on the door.

"Portia, let me help you. Do you have food poisoning?"

A long pause echoed, then he heard the sound of the sink turning off and the sound of what he thought was her head resting against the door panel.

"Easton, I don't have food poisoning. I have… *consequences*."

Her words churned in his mind and settled. Hard.

He'd discussed the possibility of pregnancy with her but he'd been speaking hypothetically. This wasn't hypothetical. This was reality.

A baby.

His.

Inside her.

The sideswiped feeling stung along his skin much like a sunburn. But soon it eased enough for other feelings to flood through. Frustration that she hadn't told him before. That she had only decided to share it with him now that they were separated by a bathroom door and there was no way she could hide the pregnancy's effects. But at the forefront of all those thoughts? But at the forefront of all those emotions?

Possessiveness.

This child and Portia were now his responsibility. They were both officially a part of the Lourdes family circle. Given her independent streak, which was a mile wide, he could already envision her shutting him out.

He'd just figured out he wanted to create something real with her. No way in hell was he letting her walk away. He would keep her and their child, using whatever means necessary.

Nine

Portia pressed her head to the cool panel of the wooden bathroom door and waited for Easton's response to her poorly timed announcement. This was not what she'd envisioned when she organized the talking points for this conversation. She'd meant to roll out the pertinent details in a logical sequence. Warn him that she was prepared to take on this responsibility by herself. Assure him his child was in good hands with her.

Instead? She'd blurted out the truth in the harshest of terms possible.

Her heart pounded in her chest, slamming against her ribs that already ached from her extended bought of nausea. She could barely stay on her feet she felt so weak, a new low in her battle with pregnancy symptoms. She just wanted to crawl back in bed and hug her pillow until the birth.

With every day that passed, the morning sickness grew worse. Although after today, she didn't know how it could be worse other than lasting all day long. Heaven forbid.

Should she call the doctor to move up her appointment date? Or...no. It was already Tuesday and her appointment was at the end of the week. Besides, she'd heard the old wives' tale that the worse the nausea the stronger the pregnancy. An upset stomach meant there were more hormones pumping through the system from her body's change. But she didn't have any scientific proof for that and couldn't risk her child based on internet articles.

She drew in deep breath after deep breath, wishing her little haven of a bathroom could be the place of peace it normally was. The old-fashioned claw foot tub had a Parisian-themed shower curtain hung from the ceiling, the whole room decorated in cream, mauve and gray. She'd painted a shadowesque chandelier on the wall with tiny rhinestone studs in the place of lightbulbs, a touch of whimsy that made her smile most days.

Rhinestones couldn't touch this nausea.

Hanging her head, her toes curled into the plush bath mat. She'd been so excited when she had come to the refuge and taken this job two years ago. The exotic locale had called to an adventurous side of herself she'd never indulged. This tiny house had been an unexpected bonus, a treat, a space to call her own since up to then she'd lived in Pensacola, close to her aunt's place, sharing an apartment with her brother. But the pay bump here had enabled her to head out on her own, and the timing had been right for her brother to spread his wings, too.

She had her own space, and now she needed to make the responsible choices that went with that freedom. Definitely she would give her doctor's office a call to see if her symptoms warranted an ER visit this weekend. They must have a twenty-four-hour service or a nurse on call to answer questions. She would not work over the weekend so she could take care of herself until that appointment on Monday. She would place the call as soon as she dealt with her baby's father on the other side of the door.

Heaven help her. She'd screwed up this announcement so badly.

"Portia?"

The low rumble of his voice pierced the bathroom door. She couldn't detect how he'd received her declaration about the baby. He'd told her he didn't want children…but the reality was, he was already a father. If he was half the man she thought he was, he would step up in some way. She'd seen him with his niece, and he was tender. Loving. She knew he would be as kind to his own child.

If she'd misjudged him, however, she could and would be a loving mother. She could take care of herself and her child. Her baby would be loved, not judged.

She swallowed hard, then took her time brushing her teeth, all the while bracing herself to face Easton. She splashed cold water on her face and toweled off.

Willing her hands to steady, she pulled open the door. Bright rays of sunshine washed over Easton, who stood, slightly disheveled, in crisp blue boxers.

Tugging on her oversized T-shirt, she really looked at him, taking in his muscled chest and abdomen. Sexy blue eyes filled with concern. His sleep-tousled hair perfectly accenting his sun-bronzed skin. Easton, the eccentric, wealthy doctor.

And the handsome father of her child.

What an exciting affair and romance they could have had if she'd only had the bravery to grasp this chance sooner. If she'd followed her instincts, which had shouted that they were both attracted to each other. Instead, she'd waited until it flamed out of control, and she had been too caught up in the moment to exercise her normal wealth of good sense. Knowing him better now, she wondered if his sense of honor had kept him from making the first move on an employee before the first storm that had brought them together.

"You're pregnant," he said, clasping her shoulders in broad, calloused hands. "With my baby."

"Yes." She resisted the urge to lean into him, to soak up the warmth of his body. "This isn't how I wanted to tell you, but yes, I am. Nearly two months along. I took seven pregnancy tests that first week I was so…stunned." Shocked. Scared. "They all came back positive. I called my doctor and she said to start prenatal vitamins, and we made an appointment for my first visit with an obstetrician. I go at the end of the week."

"Just a few days away." His voice was quiet, as if processing. He had to be feeling even more overwhelmed than she was. She'd had more time with the news.

She chewed on her lip before responding. "I was waiting until then to tell you."

"So you did plan to tell me," he said as he sat, causing fabric ripples on the bright comforter.

"Yes, God yes. Of course. What did you think I would do?" All she'd done was make plans since she had first discovered the news. Planned how to tell him. How to deal with a new addition to her family. She had a bullet list of baby needs. A monthly plan of action a mile long.

He shook his head, blinking rapidly, no words forming on his lips. After a small breath, he pressed on, "I wasn't thinking much of anything since I've had less than five minutes to absorb the news. I don't even know if you're planning to have the baby."

"I just said as much didn't I?" Heat built in her cheeks, hands growing numb.

"Not really." He grabbed her hand, studied her features. Her stomach gurgled an involuntary response and an aggressive wave of nausea threatened her again. "Portia? Are you okay?"

The scent of their lovemaking clung to the sheets. She wanted to crawl in the bed and press her head into her cool pillow and simply sleep the day away.

Another roll of nausea knocked into her along with a wave of dizziness. She fumbled for the edge of the mattress, gripping it.

Anchoring herself, she twisted the comforter in her fist. "Yes, I'm having my baby, and I plan on keeping him or her."

"My baby, too," he reminded her quietly, firmly. "I want you to put your feet up." Standing, he cleared a space for her on the bed, fluffing pillows before gently sliding his hands under her arms to prop her at one end. He also set an empty small trashcan nearby diplomatically. "In case you're feeling ill again, you can use this rather than getting up. Is this typical for how long your nausea is lasting each day?"

He went into doctor mode. She could see it in the patient way he asked her the question. Feel it in the touch he brushed on her forehead, surreptitiously checking to see if she ran a fever.

As his longtime assistant, she knew he was assessing her symptoms while trying to keep her at ease. Just like a sick deer. Or a surly monkey. How flattering.

"*Our* baby," she reminded him, remembering his possessive words. "And the nausea's gotten worse this week."

Her stomach churned again, bile rising in her throat. With a deep breath in, she tried to settle herself.

"Yes, ours, which gives me a say in the child's life." He took her wrist in one hand, his thumb squared over the pulse that she guessed was sporadic at best.

She felt like crap.

"I'm glad to hear you feel that way." She wanted to keep up her end of the conversation, tell him she didn't need his veterinarian care for her very human baby. Except she appreciated the way he tugged the blankets over her. Mopped a cloth on her forehead.

When had he gotten a damp cloth? Nerves pulled tighter inside her, making her head spin faster. She was glad he wanted to be a part of their child's life, but she could also feel her control of the situation slipping away.

"Portia, I would never abandon my child."

Determination and something Portia thought looked like hurt passed over his features, finding purchase in the tension of his expression.

"I know that." Yet while she knew Easton was kind, she hadn't been sure how he would respond to the news based on how quickly he'd bailed on old relationships. "Yet you've admitted to feeling ambivalent about parenthood. You've purposely steered clear of meaningful relationships and you climb around in trees like a mash-up of Peter Pan and Tarzan."

"I'm not sure I like that analogy at all." He knelt in front of her, taking her hands in his, meeting her gaze with such earnest urgency in those mesmerizing blue depths. "But right now, the important thing is to make sure our child is healthy and thriving. Do you think you could hold down some water or ginger ale?"

She tried to answer but his concern for their baby—for her—touched her heart, and the more emotional she became, the more her stomach misbehaved. She was already so weak from morning sickness that she simply couldn't face another bout.

"I could try." She said it only to make the medical professional in him happy.

The thought of putting anything to her lips made her queasy. But this conversation was important in setting the tone for the rest of her and her baby's lives. She'd done such a poor job telling him about her pregnancy and now was her chance to set boundaries. Assure him she would be okay on her own.

Portia could hear Easton speaking, but the words grew softer as her head swirled. She worked to steady her focus by grounding herself in the beauty of his eyes, the rough velvet of his voice.

"Portia? Portia are you listening?"

"Yes, of course," she said softly, her vision growing fuzzy around the edges.

"Then what do you think?" he squeezed her hands.

He sounded so distant, fading by the moment.

"Easton?" She struggled to make sense of his words. "Think about what?"

Her fingertips seemed to lose contact with the

comforter, sending her into a widening spiral. Nothing made sense. She tried to reach out for his hand. For the bed. For anything, really. But her vision sputtered, growing foggier as she tried to figure out what she thought about the proposal. No use.

More nausea, more dizziness, the room giving way like some scene out of *Alice in Wonderland.*

She fainted, her world swallowed by the unknown.

An hour later, sitting dumbstruck and numb in the ER waiting room, Easton stared hard at the window to the outside world as if he could somehow get himself and Portia back to that familiar reality. Not that staring helped. He barely registered the sway of palm trees or the glimpses of the ocean.

His thoughts kept turning inward, replaying the morning's events. Portia telling him she was pregnant, growing paler and disoriented. Portia fainting suddenly on her bed, scaring the living hell out of him.

Typically, Easton was the sort of man people liked to have around in emergencies.

When he was a teenager, he and his brother had hiked up a hill in Virginia. Their parents had let them have free range that afternoon. Easton had pushed them to explore. But as they neared the top of the hill, Xander lost his footing, tumbled down, falling on the rocks and trees, breaking his right arm in three places. Even then, Easton possessed a doctor's cool hand for dealing with injury and illness. He helped his brother to his feet, and calmly transported them both to a hospital. Fear never pushed at him once.

But today when Portia had been nonresponsive... he'd felt fear wrap icy hands around his heart and mind. The ride over to the hospital became a blur. She'd gone straight into a wheelchair, unable to stand without swaying. Seeing his beyond-competent Portia so incapacitated leveled him.

The staff's urgent and worried care revealed just how fragile and ragged she'd become. Why the hell hadn't he made sense of her symptoms earlier in the week? Maureen had told him something was off. He knew something was off.

And yet he'd ignored all those signs, too damn focused on his own goals. He was a first-class ass. By the time he'd handed her over to the hospital staff, her pale skin had felt so clammy.

The cackle of a loose parrot from outside snapped him back to the ER waiting room. He stood, wanting to be in the exam room with Portia. To do something, anything, to help her. Instead, he was out here. He sat back down, back pressing into the hard plastic of a lime-green chair. Across from him, he watched an older couple in their sixties talk in hushed tones.

The man's swollen ankle was propped up on a stool. His wife stroked his arm, love shining in her eyes along with a hint of irritation. Over what?

Not that it mattered. Easton just grasped for distractions.

Two seats away, a small girl cried intermittently.

Her mom stroked her hair, cooed to her. Soothing the toddler. No father in sight.

Easton's heart seized. He wouldn't be that way with his child—an absentee father. If everything was okay.

Everything had to be okay.

Worry pushed into his thoughts again. He felt shock stiffen his joints. What if something terrible was happening to Portia right now? He clenched his hands into fists, squeezing. Trying to get a grip on the situation.

He'd been upset with her that she hadn't said anything to him before this morning. He wasn't sure what would happen with them. Her news had changed everything. But more than anything else, he wanted her to be okay.

A swoosh of the automatic doors sounded, letting in a blast of muggy heat from the outdoors an instant before a familiar voice called out to him.

Xander.

His brother had arrived, two cups of coffee in hand along with a bag of something.

"Easton? What's going on? I heard you were rushing Portia to the hospital."

"Who told you that?" Easton asked, surprised to see his brother huffing and puffing in front of him.

Xander snorted and passed over a large cup of aromatic java. "Do you think anything's a secret with all those volunteers around?" He held out the bag. "Want a doughnut?"

Clearly some things were secret since his brother made no mention of what ailed Portia. Still, Easton got the point. "No, thank you. The coffee's just what I need though. Thanks." He took a bracing drink of the nutty brew, then set the cup on his knee. "Portia's pregnant."

"What?" His brother blinked, surprise coloring his face. All that boardroom bravado gone. Xander dropped into a seat beside Easton, setting the bag and his coffee on the steel end table. "I'm...confused. Surprised. Details?"

"She's pregnant, and the baby's mine." Easton took another sip of the strong coffee. Too bad they didn't serve IV caffeine around this place.

"Congratulations, brother." Xander clapped him on the shoulder once, twice. "I assume you're happy— but hell, wait." Worry crept into his voice. "Why is she here?"

"Her morning sickness is out of control. They have her hooked up to IVs since she's dehydrated."

"All during the pregnancy with Rose, Terri battled that. You remember."

"Sort of, yes." A memory of his niece after Terri died wandered across his mind. He'd taken her to the beach, built towering sandcastles for her. Easton told her stories of magical lands and talking animals. His flair for theatrics making her squeal with sharp giggles of uncontrollable laughter. He'd always thought his role as über-involved uncle would quell any parenting needs. Easton was crazy about his niece. But then Xander remarried Maureen and Rose didn't need him as much anymore.

For a few weeks, the lack of time with his niece had been strange. He felt like a castaway from that family unit.

But with Portia...

New possibilities leaped before him. He wanted Portia—he sincerely wanted to marry her. And he wanted to be there for their baby. To do whatever it took to be a good husband and father.

Because, damn it all, they would be a family. He wouldn't be relegated to the sidelines. He knew what it felt like to be an afterthought in his parents' lives. He wouldn't let his child entertain so much as a hint of a notion that that could be true.

He might not have planned on being a father, but he would figure out how to do this. He would be there for the baby and for Portia.

Xander angled forward, elbows on his knees. "You should be in there with her."

"They're going to let me join her soon. We're not married so I don't have a spouse's rights."

"You look shell-shocked."

"I only found out about the baby this morning." Easton combed his fingers through his hair, likely doing more harm than good. "I'm still...adjusting to the news."

Adjusting didn't even begin to cover it. He'd been set on romancing Portia, taking her out on dates, winning her back into his bed. He hadn't thought beyond that. He didn't do long-term relationships well. At all. His history spoke to that.

But now the baby—and yes, the power of his growing feelings for Portia—flipped his world upside down. He needed to think. To process. And figure out how to become someone she could depend on.

"Is she planning to have the baby?" Xander whispered, eyes darting around the emergency room.

"Yes, of course." He'd been so relieved when she had reassured him on that score. Of the million questions he had for her when he'd heard the news, that one had been the most important and she'd put his mind at ease.

"Then congratulations, brother. You're about to embark on the most amazing experience of your life." Xander slapped Easton's shoulders again.

"Thanks." He meant it. Still, he had worries and doubts.

His brother had embraced parenthood full-on. But he had always been better with personal relationships, too. He'd taken time to build something with Terri before they married and had Rose. Easton, on the other hand?

Every woman he had ever dated had been disappointed with his brand of interpersonal skills. Before, it hadn't bothered him. Much. But for Portia? He wanted to be better.

Xander leaned away, astute eyes locked on Easton. "You don't look happy."

"I'm just concerned about Portia right now." He

wasn't ready to talk about his concerns and explain what a mess he'd made of things by not pursuing Portia outright after the tropical storm. He'd wanted her then, had played in his mind a million ways to angle for another night together, yet he had stopped short of acting on those thoughts. Now he wondered what had held him back. Whatever it was had made his life a helluva lot more complicated.

"Of course you're concerned about her and the baby. I understand. I'm sorry. What can I do?"

"I appreciate your coming here. You could have just called though, you know." He hated distracting his brother with personal matters. He didn't like burdening him or taking him away from his family.

"We're brothers. I was worried. You would have done the same thing if the positions were reversed."

"Truth." He nodded, meaning it all the way to his soul. His brother was his best friend, always had been. "You're right about that."

"And besides, you must have forgotten your damn phone again and didn't answer when I tried to reach you." Xander cast a sidelong glance his way, eyebrows knitting in faux annoyance.

Easton welcomed the ribbing, needing to share a laugh with his brother now more than ever. His laugh tangled up with his brother's, rumbling in the waiting room as a doctor in green scrubs stepped through one of the endless row of doors.

"Easton Lourdes?" the tall silver-haired doctor called, clipboard in hand.

Easton rose from his chair, lungs tight as he nodded.

The doctor waved a hand, motioning for him to follow. "You can see Ms. Soto now."

Portia kept her arm preternaturally still, glancing at the IV needle. Though she knew she could move her arm slightly, she felt like it needed to stay still as she processed the events of the morning.

She clenched her jaw as she looked at the ultrasound. A tiny bean-like figure was displayed on the screen. Her baby. The future frightened her slightly—or it had until the doctor came in with the ultrasound monitor. She watched her child move, become real before her eyes.

Looking around the sterile white room, she knew she needed to plan. To figure out what direction she'd take. Her fingers itched for pen and paper…to make checklists and doodle storks.

The medicine she'd been given worked wonders. For the first time in weeks, she didn't feel sick to her stomach in the morning. That alone stabilized her.

The thin door that led from her room to the rest of the ER allowed muffled sounds to pass through the light wood. Sounds of machines beeping, a small child crying, a cart rattling down the hall. Adjusting her weight, the paper crackled beneath her, bringing her back to the stillness of her room.

The blue cotton hospital gown allowed air to kiss her back and neck, the coolness refreshing her as she leaned forward, letting her paper-shoed feet dangle off the edge. She tested her balance and found the floor didn't wobble or spin anymore.

At the sound of a quick knock, Portia raised her head and called, "Yes?"

"It's me." Easton's deep voice filtered through.

Nerves tingled but her stomach remained steady. She reached for the blanket and draped it over her shoulders and wrapped it around her protectively. "Yes, come in."

The door clicked open an instant before a wide hand swept back the privacy curtain. His broad shoulders and chest in a refuge-branded polo shirt filled her vision, blocking out the rest of the world. He shoved his hands in his jeans pockets. "How are you feeling?"

"Better, much better. The fluids help and they gave me something for nausea."

"So you're, um, both okay?" Concern furrowed deep in his brow, and for the first time since they'd met, he seemed unsure.

"Yes, we are." Lifting her left hand, she pointed to the ultrasound machine behind him. The image of the baby—*their* baby—was frozen in black and white on the screen. "You can see here. That bean is your child."

He turned to face the ultrasound machine, the profile of his face in her direct line of vision.

Portia watched the way his eyes squinted and refocused, almost as if his identity as a doctor disappeared, leaving behind a man in awe. Of course, she was aware he could read this ultrasound from a medical standpoint—note nuances, explain away the shape.

The man in front of her clearly did not process the image from such a technical angle. Instead, his lips, though pressed together, curled upward in a faint smile. His cheeks softened. She couldn't get over the expression of awe on his face. The possessiveness and pride etched into his stance. Looking at him now, she began to realize all his talk about not wanting to be a father was false or delusional. He'd already become attached. This baby wasn't just hers anymore.

And her baby's father was a man of money and power. She couldn't help but remember how his brother, Xander, had used that wealth and power to ensure he maintained full custody of his daughter after his first wife died. Portia had applauded his efforts, since in that case, his former in-laws had strange ideas about what a child needed to be happy.

But the incident worried her now as it occurred to her Easton had the same kinds of resources at his disposal. He'd admitted he had never invested in a long-term relationship. What if he got tired of Portia but wanted more time with his child?

Easton eyed her, his rich dark hair falling in waves, catching the cold, sterile hospital room lights. "You're absolutely sure you're alright?"

"The hormones are really something else." She swiped away those worries, telling herself she was being ridiculous.

"Can I get you something to make you more comfortable?" He gestured around the room. He was trying, she could see that. "Like a pillow or another blanket?"

"Once the meds kick in a little more, how about an ice cream sundae, loaded with peanuts, bananas, cherries and fudge sauce?" Her taste buds shouted yes, but she still wasn't confident her stomach would cooperate. All the same, it felt good to dream that soon she could indulge all these cravings.

"Done. The freezer will be packed with options before we get home."

Home?

His home and hers were not in the same place, not really. Nothing was settled yet between them.

"I'm joking. Soon though, hopefully." She put her hand on her stomach, staring back to the ultrasound. To her future. "I just would like to have my simple, uncomplicated life back."

"That isn't going to happen."

"I know." She nodded, eyes drifting to the IV bag filled with fluid. Knowing that this was one of those defining moments—a moment she'd like to sketch or paint when she could.

"And I'm committed to being a part of my child's life." His voice carried such fierce determination, hinting at the kind of father he'd be.

The kind of father she *hoped* he would be.

"You're so good with Rose. You'll make a wonderful father. You're more prepared than I am."

He had a way of taking unexpected things in stride, a trait she'd always envied. His wanderlust soul necessitated quick readjustments. Portia felt like his personality prepared him differently for the trials of parenthood.

"I don't agree. You have brought up your brother. You help care for the animals. You have a great knack with the kids that come to visit the refuge. You'll be a great mom." He laced his fingers with hers, showing his sincerity in the strength of his touch. "But let me be clear, you won't have to parent alone. We'll be here for each other."

"So many details to work out." Her mind reeled. Now that he knew…well, she'd have to make all sorts of new plans. And backup plans.

"But we don't have to work them out now."

She chewed her bottom lip, confused. "How can we not?"

"Can you put the need for organization on hold for a while and let us live in the moment? We have months. Let's take things one step at a time."

"What's the first step?" She found comfort in breaking tasks into smaller portions, everything falling into neat categories and checkable boxes. She knew enough about Easton to know he didn't think so linearly. An intense curiosity burned in her as she waited for him to explain.

"First?" He stroked a thumb across the back of her hand before his blue eyes met hers. "Will you marry me, Portia? Make a real family for our child?"

Marry him?

Portia swallowed, an eternity passing between them. Words scattered from her mind, leaving her to only stare at him. What on earth was he thinking to jump into marriage so quickly? Sure, they appeared to be compatible, and maybe the relationship could go somewhere, but how could she know where for sure. They'd only had two dates!

Frustration bubbled up that he wasn't taking her concerns seriously. Their focus needed to be on parenting. Not romance. Not right now. She needed to protect her independence more than ever, for her child. Because heaven help her, she was starting to care for Easton—too much.

And didn't that thought cause the room to spin again?

"You're not going to pass out again are you?" he teased, tipping her chin up gently with one knuckle.

"No." She shook her head. Now more than ever, she needed her wits about her to withstand the will of Easton Lourdes. He might be eccentric, but he was a man accustomed to getting what he wanted. "I'm just not ready to make that kind of commitment. We have so much more to plan out."

"Fine, then. You're a planner. We'll plan." He stepped closer, wrapping his arms around her. "But just so we're clear, this time that you're taking to plan? I'm going to be using everything in my arsenal to convince you to marry me."

Ten

Two days later, deep, dark clouds encroached on the late-afternoon summer sky with threatening force. Tropical Storm Elliot rumbled in the distance, a menace that, if the forecasters were correct, would pass them by, turn into the Gulf of Mexico and eventually head toward Louisiana.

Sure, the outer bands of the storm would dump water on them with some degree of severity. But that weather shared more in common with a tropical depression—a resounding difference in destructive capacity.

Still, Easton wasn't taking any chances with the lives of the animals and people he cared about. He'd begun to organize the volunteer staff into small task forces—everyone charged with securing different aspects of the refuge. Just to be safe.

And, truth be told, he felt like he needed to keep busy while he waited for Portia to give him an answer about his proposal. Easton threw himself full force into storm preparations.

Hoisting a bag of bird seed onto his shoulders, he made his way around the atrium, opening the feeders with practiced ease. A brightly colored, talkative macaw cackled, landing on a tree limb overhead.

Easton poured the seed into the dispenser, his eyes trailing to the window where he saw volunteers scurry across the yard securing loose objects, checking shutters.

"Here we go," he said to himself. The macaw cocked its head, stretching wings wide and displaying the red underside.

"We go. We go. We go." The macaw's shrill voice made Easton laugh lightly.

"That's right. You sit tight during this storm," he told the bird as he made his way to the door of the atrium, surveying the flutter of wings. Antsy. All the animals were.

Then again, animals had a way of knowing things about storms that seemed to escape the notice of humans. Judging by their unease, Easton couldn't help but wonder if this storm would turn into something stronger than predicted. It'd been a few years since Key Largo had taken substantial storm damage, something he'd been incredibly thankful for.

But as a Florida native, he knew that luck only lasted for so long.

Exiting the clinic, Easton noticed bright red hair against an increasingly gray backdrop. Maureen and his brother worked across the yard by the main mansion, checking the storm shutters. Rose bounced and waved from a navy blue carry pack on Xander's back. Her little blond curls rustled in the wind, streaming behind the toddler's face. Her expression lit up in a smile—too young to realize the severity of the situation.

His niece's peal of laughter carried on the wind, causing a wide grin to take over Easton's face. He felt it warming his eyes. She blew him a kiss, which he caught in the air. With theatrical flair, he pretended it took two hands to hold the kiss, wrestling with it. She clapped her hands, watching intently. Easton pulled his hands to his heart, patting lightly on his chest. Rose loved this game they played. He'd started this ritual a few days ago with her.

With the uncertainty brewing around the fate of his relationship with Portia, Easton felt desperate to fortify the connection with his niece.

Growing up, Xander and Easton had been well traveled, following his parents on adrenaline-fused adventures. Adventures that made him feel like the world had magic in it. When their father died in a mountain climbing accident, his mother had been like a ball that suddenly lost its tether. She skidded and skirted out of Easton's life. She'd simply checked out, a bohemian spirit that refused to settle. Another lost connection, another kick in the gut.

And Portia? Would he have to add her name to the list of the lost?

He didn't have the chance to dwell too long on that thought. There she was—barely released from the hospital, taking an active role in storm preparation. A protective desire stirred in him, drawing him to her. Making his way past volunteers carrying a kayak to one of the storage sheds, he approached her.

With the wind whipping violently, her hair loosed from her ponytail. She looked wild, fierce—a part of the stormscape. A force all her own.

She directed a group of volunteers carrying emergency supplies of water and canned food for the storm shelter. He'd arrived by her side by the time the last member of the volunteer supply train had disappeared into the house.

Portia turned, knocking into him, her pointed features pensive but relaxed. Starting to walk, she held a clipboard in her right hand filled with a page-long checklist.

He loved that about her. *Loved?* The word caught him up short. He wasn't the kind of guy who thought that way emotionally, just that reason had ended more relationships than he could count.

He'd known Portia for two years—professionally, sure, but still a long time. Longer than most nonfamily relationships. He would have used words such as *liked. Adored. Admired.* But *loved*? He wasn't sure what to do with that word.

Easton shook off the tangent and said, "While you're deciding whether or not to marry me, let me help you."

"Help me?" She blinked at him, confused. She held up the clipboard as if to show him everything was under control.

He shook his head, holding up a hand. "Financially. You need to rest more. Put your feet up. Especially until you get the morning sickness under control. Let me pay for your brother's college and yours."

"Are you aware there's a storm brewing?" Her eyebrows shot heavenward with confusion. "I'm sure you have as much to do as I do. And furthermore…" She shook her head. "Why would you do that?"

"To ease your stress. I won't miss the money." Money was the least of his concerns. He wanted her well cared for. She worked so damn hard for everyone. She would never even think to put her needs first.

"You want to keep me closer because of the baby. You want to put me in your debt." She met his gaze measure for measure, but her shift from foot to foot relayed her nerves.

"Of course I do. But I also want the chance for us to parent together. You and I both want what's best for all of us."

Her eyes narrowed, challenging him. "Don't play games."

Easton bristled, stopping in his tracks. He could be a lot of things—eccentric, stubborn. But he'd never been one to play games with people. He respected other living beings too much for that. "Think of the money as child support. This is what I should do, and it's what I want to do."

"You're not going to try to take the baby from me?"

The question shocked him silent for a moment. He'd proposed after all. He wanted to be a team. To tackle this together. "No. Hell, you're going to be an amazing mother. If anything, I'm worried about what kind of father I'll be. Surely you are too, after what I said about not wanting children."

Her eyebrows pinched together and she hung her head, watching their steps along the path as if thinking. "I've thought more about that, especially since our time in the emergency room, and I've decided you don't give yourself enough credit. I've seen you here with the animals. You have a tender, nurturing side to you whether you want to admit it or not."

Nurturing? "There's a difference between baby animals and human babies."

His words were practically lost to a roll of thunder. Rain, hard and determined, came pelting down on them. On instinct, his hand found hers and he gestured toward the barn on the far end of the property.

She nodded in understanding, tucking the clipboard under her arm.

He pulled her forward in a brisk jog, making for the entrance of the teal-colored barn. Wind nipped at their backs, surprisingly chilly.

"How so?" she yelled as they picked up the pace, her fingers gripping his tightly.

He strained to hear her as they made their way to the barn. "There just is."

"Well, that's not very scientific," she said smartly. "I think nature kicks in either way."

And speaking of nature. He really needed to check on the animals in the barn, particularly the pregnant Key deer with a wounded hoof.

Around them, palm trees bowed to the ferocity of the wind, lightning sizzling around them like a sporadic camera flash.

They crossed the threshold into the barn. Portia closed the door, sealing out the weather.

"I'll check on Ginger Snap," she said, pressing a hand on his shoulder. He nodded, fumbling in his pocket to call his brother for a storm update.

Portia gave a small smile, heading to the pregnant deer they'd rescued a few weeks ago. Ginger Snap had a nasty cut on her right hind leg that he'd stitched. But before she could be released back to the wild, the deer needed to recuperate.

"Um…Easton?" Portia's voice interrupted his phone scrolling. He noted the urgency in her tone and jogged over to the stall door.

Ginger Snap was in labor.

"I think we're going to have to stay with her," Portia said, setting her clipboard down. No script for this.

Hell. She was right. He couldn't leave the injured deer, but his heart felt heavy. Conflicted. He wanted Portia to be in the safest place in the refuge. While the barn was up to current hurricane code, he would have felt better if she were in the storm shelter.

"Give me a second." He queued up Xander's number and pressed Call.

Two rings in and Xander's deep voice pulsed through the speakers.

"Where are you?" his older brother demanded.

"In the barn with Ginger Snap," he said, watching the deer pant heavily.

"You better stay there. Trees are falling. Debris is flying. Tropical Storm Elliot just got upgraded to Hurricane Elliot and it has turned to us. We're going to take a direct hit sometime in the next hour, brother."

Damn. The increased strength meant it was too risky to move Portia and her unborn baby.

"Thanks for the update. Stay in touch and stay safe."

Xander's voice sounded garbled. "You, too—" The connection winked out, lost to static.

"Are you ready for your first hurricane?" Easton asked, shoving his phone into his back jeans pocket as he turned to face Portia. Her face paled, eyes widening as she looked around the barn.

He pressed on. "We'll ride out the storm. We're in a safe place with plenty of supplies."

"If I didn't know you better, I would think you stirred up this storm to get me alone." Her lips twisted in a smile, spunk invigorating her. She looked at the office area in the barn—a small sofa, desk and bathroom. There certainly were worse places to be trapped. "I'm not sharing a bed with you just because we're trapped here."

"Of course you're not." He clapped a hand over his chest. "I'm going to be a total gentleman and give you the office sofa—since there isn't a bed here."

"You're being too nice. I'll feel bad if you sleep on the floor."

"I'm not going to be sleeping. There's a hurricane."

"Well, yes, there's a hurricane, so what exactly do you think you can do to hold that back? You're not a superhero."

"Good point. Although I guess I'll have to return my special hurricane cape."

A smile slipped between her teeth, then a giggle, followed by a full laugh as the tension eased from the room after their mad dash readying for the storm. Lord, he liked the sound of her laugh.

"That's better." He skimmed his hand along her arm, static easing back into the air again as awareness stirred. "You are right that we should both relax."

Her smile faded. "You make it so difficult to resist you."

He wished she didn't say that like it was such a bad thing. But he would work with what he could to persuade her. He sure as hell hoped nature would do its job for the deer. And for him and Portia.

Because the stakes were too high to consider failure.

Rain thumped and beat against the tin roof, the wind loud like the train Portia had ridden as a teenager when she went to live with her aunt. The breathy whistle of the wind felt unnatural—a sound that deeply unsettled Portia to her core.

For six hours, the storm raged, tossing debris into the metal-cased doors. It had made Ginger Snap's delivery stressful.

The tan deer's eyes had widened at the extreme noise, stress beyond labor pains visible in her deep brown eyes. So expressive.

But Easton had helped Ginger Snap. Spoke to her in calming tones, his voice seeming to have a mesmerizing effect on the doe. A beautiful fawn they'd named Cinnamon had been born about an hour ago.

So much excitement and stimulus over the last six hours had left Portia tired. She'd made sure to chug water, to stay hydrated. If she fell ill during the storm due to dehydration again, the options were limited.

Her medication had been tucked away in the storm shelter. She felt fine though—and especially attentive to her body and her baby's health.

After she and Easton both washed in the small bathroom, bodies skirting and pressing against each other, they'd gathered an impromptu storm picnic. She ate like she hadn't in days, surprised by her own hunger.

Portia stretched out on a checkered blanket on the floor of the barn. Her body curved around the scattered snack plates—grapes, cheese, crackers. Easton stroked her hair, staring at the stall door.

She looked back at him. "I still can't believe I got to see that doe being born." The memory of the scene made her heart swell. Easton's practiced hands, his nurturing soul emerged in full force. Confirming what she already knew to be true about him. His parental instincts had been honed and developed by years of veterinarian care, his compassion ringing true.

"Cinnamon's a fighter. She's storm born. That's good luck and it means she's resilient." He smiled down at Portia, his tanned face warm and so blindingly handsome.

For a moment, she wondered if there was any truth to the superstition about being born in a storm. Portia had been born in the middle of a blizzard. Good or bad?

Gathering her head into his lap, his hands massaged her shoulders. Invigorating her senses and soothing her unease about the storm. "How do you feel? Any troubles with the nausea?"

Portia leaned into his touch, his fingers releasing the ache in her muscles. Her eyes fluttered shut. "All's well. The food's amazing and the ginger ale really works. The midwife who stopped by before I left the hospital had some great suggestions. I wish I'd thought to reach out for help sooner."

"You don't have to do this alone. I'm here for you and our baby." He leaned close to her, folding his body to whisper in her ear.

"I do appreciate your saying that. And thank you for giving me space on the marriage proposal. I need time to adjust, we both do." It'd been two days since she'd been proposed to and hospitalized for extreme dehydration. Two days hadn't supplied her with enough time to make a life-altering commitment. She needed to weigh the pros and cons to arrive at the most logical course of action. She'd lived her whole life preparing to be independent. Now Easton was asking her to depend on him. She wasn't sure she knew how.

"The news is already spreading and I can't control other people's reactions."

The reactions of other people bothered her less and less. Her primary concern remained the health of her child. "Let's deal with one day at a time. For a free spirit, you're sure trying to think fifty steps ahead."

"Then let's focus on the moment," he said, pushing ever so slightly deeper into the knot in her right shoulder.

She melted into his touch, how his strong but intuitive hands knew just how to knead away the tension of the past two months. His thumbs found and worked loose a knot below her shoulder blade, then he stroked lower along her back.

And she knew—she just knew—she wanted, needed, more from this elemental moment alone with him. So beautiful in its secluded simplicity with the whole of nature at work around them, as tumultuous as her feelings for this man. She wasn't used to such a lack of control over her emotions, but right now, she reveled in it.

Angling nearer, Portia tipped her face up for a kiss, her emotions close to the surface after all they'd experienced together today. She palmed his chest, his heartbeat firm and accelerating against her touch. Her arms slid upward and around his neck, deepening the kiss, and with a hard groan he rolled her onto her back until they both stretched out on the quilt. The scent of the laundry detergent teased her nose along with the sweet musk of fresh hay. Clean and earthy and elemental all at once.

Easing her refuge-branded T-shirt off, she tossed it aside and met his eyes boldly, inviting. And as his eyes lit with fire, he didn't hesitate to unhook her bra and reveal her body to his hungry eyes. He stroked her skin, pulled away her shoes and jeans, touching and kissing and igniting her until her head thrashed on the thick quilt and she whispered pleas for him to get naked now, damn it.

A sigh of relief shuddered through him and he tossed away his clothes in a haphazard pile, his eyes staying linked with hers. Peering deep into her with fierceness.

Even in the muted glow of the barn's backup lights, she could still make out the definitions of his tanned, muscled body. Every fiber of her being screamed a possessive *mine*.

And yes, she saw how his eyes caressed all of her with clear appreciation, arousal. Desire. She'd never felt more beautiful, and truth be told, it had more to do with the way he touched her than with any look in his eyes.

Easton kissed along her neck to her ear, nibbling her earlobe and whispering, "Are you sure you feel okay? You were just in the hospital—"

Her fingers went to his sensual lips. "I'm fine, and the doctor cleared me for all activity short of bungee jumping."

"Well, then that's good for us since bungee jumping is nowhere on my agenda." He grazed kisses along her jawline back to her lips again. "But if you need to stop at any time, just say the word."

"Trust me, I will. Our baby means the world to me."

Easton's hand trailed down her side to her stomach, his eyes focused on her pale skin as he rested his hand there. A small, awestruck smile tugging at his mouth. "To me, as well."

Her heart softened at his words, and she reached for him, pulling him back over her, determined to take everything from this time together that she could.

The storm raged outside, but she and Easton were safe here together. But she knew too well the real world and worries couldn't stay at bay forever.

That marriage proposal still loomed between them, and she was no closer to feeling comfortable saying yes.

Sleep eluded him, but that was probably for the best. After they'd made love, they'd dressed and curled up on the blanket together. Portia fell asleep in an instant.

He wondered if his brother was safe or if the storm was letting up anytime soon. He'd tried to call Xander, but the cell phone reception was crap due to the storm.

They were in the oversize stall with Ginger Snap and her baby. It was the safest interior room in the barn. He watched as the deer tried to nurse her fawn, struggling to get the action right.

He picked up a piece of hay, rubbed it between his fingers and crooned softly, "You can do this, Ginger Snap. I know it's not easy, girl, but you can do it. You can be a good parent to your baby. You know what to do."

The momma deer flicked her ears toward Easton.

"I'm sorry we're not in the clinic, girl, but I'm here with you. Portia's here with you, too."

Oh Lord. Portia. He turned his gaze back to where she slept. Watched her chest rise and fall, the soft sounds of her steady breath reassuring him.

He could spend an eternity with her. And damn, but that rocked his world. And settled his footing all over again. He'd never found any woman he felt this way about, and he knew he never would again. She was...Portia.

His mind drifted back to their lovemaking and the spark between them. Incredible—like nothing he'd experienced before. He wanted to win her, to make her stay. Every moment without an answer to his proposal made him feel like she was a step closer to bolting out of his life forever.

Easton snapped the piece of hay, smiling at the deer. "And we care about you. You're not alone in this parenting. We won't let anything happen to you. We'll stay here with you all the way through. Although it's going to be a long night, I'm afraid. Care to answer? Because I could use some help on my end with being a parent."

Cinnamon started to nurse, which seemed to calm Ginger Snap. Her head rested on the barn floor as she appeared to relax, her stressed breathing becoming easier.

"You look like you don't even need my assistance right now after all. But then you deer have been having young on your own without the father around. So maybe you could tell me something about why Portia is being so stubborn about marrying me? Or hell, even talking about it?"

He watched Ginger Snap settle even more, her ears flicking attentively to Easton. The doe's eyes were deep and dark. But mostly, he noticed how calm she looked now. He tilted his head, laying a hand on the ground.

Portia stirred beside him, tossing slightly in her sleep.

He waited for her to settle before continuing, "Sure, you and she can do this on your own. But she doesn't have to. If she could just accept how much I care about her. I'm not going to leave her. I'm not like my parents. I'm steady. I've found a way to have adventures right here at home. I'm not…leaving…"

Portia moved restlessly again, stretching, then yawning as she woke. She sat up slowly, carefully, and smiled ever so slightly before pushing her tousled hair from her face. She removed a scrunchie from around her wrist and piled her hair high on her head. With bleary eyes, she reached for the water bottle, popped off the cap and took a sip.

Easton eyed her, worried. "Are you feeling alright?"

She took another sip, waited, then nodded. "All seems well." She picked up a cracker and nibbled it, as well. "Here's the real test though."

He moved closer, cautioning, "Take it slow."

"I will. Morning's close and I know what that usually means." She rolled her eyes and stayed still, waiting.

"No need to do anything other than rest." Damn crummy time for a hurricane. A sense of helplessness kicked over him even as he knew there was nothing he could do to battle Mother Nature's forces outside the barn door.

The winds sounded softer but he suspected that was merely the eye of the storm.

He stroked along her arm. "Have you given any more thought to my proposal?"

She held up the cracker in the muted light, scrutinizing it. She shook her head dismissively. "Can we talk about that later, please?"

Ginger Snap gave a huff.

"I know I said we had time to work on this during the pregnancy, but I'm wondering if that's a copout. We're good together. We've known each other for two years. We get along well, and the chemistry between us is incredible, beyond incredible. I've never felt this much for anyone else. Can you deny you feel the same?"

He meant it. Never had a relationship been more real to him. He'd ended other relationships quickly because he'd known they would not work out. He'd already spent more time with Portia than he had with any other woman. And even if he and she hadn't been romantically involved, he knew her.

Wanted her.

Couldn't let her go.

He wanted to provide for her. For their child. He knew he could make this work between them if she stayed and didn't bolt. How ironic was that? He'd been the king of leaving and now he could well be on the receiving end.

It scared the hell out of him. And also made him all the more determined.

"All of what you mentioned is good for dating or an affair. But it's not enough for a marriage." She set the cracker down, picked up the water again. Swirled it around as she stared at him.

"Why not?"

She put aside the water bottle. "Because it's not love. We can have everything in sync, all the chemistry in the world and without love, we won't last. That will be so much worse for our child. We have to get this right."

Ah, there it was. Portia's need for absolute perfection bubbling to the surface. That need had held her back in the past. It kept her from pursuing something if every aspect wasn't perfectly hammered down, all boxes checked. She'd waited for the perfect time to go to college too, but she'd been so busy planning, she'd never gotten around to just doing it.

"My mother and father loved each other and it didn't make them attentive parents," he snapped the truth, frustration growing. "Hell, they flat-out lost us in foreign countries more times than we can count. Most kids travel and learn words in other languages like *where's the bathroom* or *I'm hungry.* We learned *take me to the embassy.*"

She cupped his face in a gentle, caring hand. "Easton, I am so sorry. That had to have been terrifying for you and your brother and it's not right, not at all. But you also have to know that as much as you act like the absentminded doctor socially, when it comes to responsibility you are always one hundred percent there for your patients. You tell yourself you're an eccentric like your parents because that keeps you from risking your heart."

"Like you're using your brother's education as an excuse to keep from living your life?" he asked quietly.

"I'm taking care of him." Her lips went tight.

"He's an adult." Easton pointed out, reaching for her hand. "He can take care of himself. It's your turn to have a life. Marry me."

She snatched her hand away, anger brewing in her eyes, making him feel like the storm had jumped inside the barn. "I don't want to be your obligation and I don't want some marriage of convenience."

"My brother and Maureen married for convenience and it's worked out well for them. No one can deny that. Portia, I care about you."

"I realize that. You're a good man. But I don't want to depend on anyone. And if I did, it would be a man who loves me wholeheartedly. I deserve that."

"And you'll have everything as my wife."

"Everything?" Her head fell back in frustration and she sighed before she looked back at him. "You're missing the point altogether."

"And what is the point?"

"You've been thinking differently since you saw those glitter condoms in the honeymoon suite. Seriously. Glitter. Rubbers. Is that any reason to get married?" Scarlet hues rose high in her cheeks, anguish mounting in her voice.

Damage control. Easton needed to calm her. "The lack of condoms—glitter or otherwise—is how this happened. Plenty of people have gotten married for fewer reasons."

"This is not funny."

"Trust me, I'm not laughing."

"This is no way to start a life together. I don't even think I can continue to work here."

His temper rose, the weight of her words surprising him. "What the hell?"

"Don't swear at me!"

He pinched the bridge of his nose and closed his eyes. "I'm trying to figure out what's going on in that mind of yours."

"I'm the logical one. This makes perfect sense."

"Not from where I'm standing. Maybe it has something to do with pregnancy hormones—"

"Don't. Don't you dare suggest I'm illogical because I'm pregnant." Tears welled, hovering in the corners of her eyes even as those same eyes spit fire and back-off vibes. "I know how I feel and what I want from life. I want my child to be happy and I want to stand on my own two feet."

"We're both parents now. We need to make compromises."

"Oh, you really need to be quiet." She shot to her feet. Her voice reaching new heights, causing Ginger Snap to bleat. "I am not some kind of compromise. I will never be anyone's second-best disappointment ever again. I deserve better."

Head held high, she headed out. Hand on the barn's wide double door, she hesitated. Rain still came down in sheets, but the hurricane's eye could hold.

A massive crack sounded, like a tree splitting, and Easton bolted to his feet, racing to Portia. He snagged her in his arms and rolled under a low-lying support beam just as a falling tree pierced the barn.

Eleven

The barn warped beneath the weight of the tree, groaning—a sickening sound of metal buckling. A small hole opened like a wound, allowing a throaty chorus of hurricane force wind to enter the safe space of the barn and rain to drip on the floor.

Another groan. The tree sank lower, its branches scraping, cracking, filling the main part of the barn.

Portia wriggled beneath Easton, craning her head to look. In the wind whipping through the hole in the roof, he couldn't tell if she was injured or not. Her eyes were wide as she stared at the impending catastrophe a few feet away from where she lay pinned to the floor.

If the roof gave way. No. He corrected himself—

when the roof gave way—she would be in the trajectory of the crash if he didn't get them out right now. He would have to worry about any possible bruises later. The situation was too urgent.

He pulled her close and rolled to the stall with Ginger Snap. His muscles screamed at him to move faster. He barely registered the unnatural coldness of the wind swirling inside, tearing at him, working against him. He tried to communicate with Portia, but his shout was lost to the roar and the howl.

Their fight didn't matter now. The only thing that mattered to Easton was keeping her safe. He kept moving, shielding Portia's soft body, pressing on through the invisible wall of wind filled with grit and twigs. Heaven forbid if a larger branch should come their way. He willed their bodies to move as one, shoving them both to the far left side, toward Ginger Snap and her newborn baby, who cowered in the corner. The two deer cried and bleated in unison, fear rampant in those deep, dark, knowing eyes.

Finally, Easton found a solid wall under a reinforced steel beam, the other corner of the stall and the reason he'd chosen this spot in the first place. He pressed Portia against the wooden planks of the side, rain drifting in through the branches and pooling on the floor. Rain still hammered outside, beating the roof and the ground. He kept his back to the storm just as the tree crashed the rest of the way into the barn. Sliced the metal clear open as wind and sky flooded them with the unnatural sounds of raw power.

Thick, sideways rain pelted inside, and the shifting tree brought a scream from Portia. He hugged her closer. The oak moved one last time, settling, in a surreal way almost sealing off the elements beyond.

For now.

Heart hammering in his chest, Easton's body pressed against hers. He counted them lucky to have been out of the fall zone of the tree.

Easton felt her inhale sharply, holding her breath for a long time. Noted the ragged pace of her heart as she loosed the breath. The release of air seemed to rival the strength of the storm.

She leaned into him. To Easton, it seemed as though her body might melt into his. He felt the tension in her stance, the fear in her skin. Despite the near-deadly experience, he felt strangely calm as her light floral perfume wafted by him. A glimpse of normalcy.

How he wanted to protect her against all threats and hardships. Weather. Health. Finances. All of it.

Portia's messy ponytail tickled his nose, reminding him of gentler times with this sexy woman. Of being in a bed—a true bed with her.

He inhaled deeply, steeling himself against the pelting rain as he dared a look behind him to survey the damage.

The structure of the barn was intact—they wouldn't have to demolish the building. But the barn had received substantial damage from Hurricane Elliot.

But all of that could wait. Portia softened beneath his touch. She reached her slender hand for his, entwining their fingers. He squeezed tightly and then dropped her hand. Thunder and wind assaulted their senses, but they were close enough for Easton to reassure his pounding heart that Portia hadn't been hurt.

In a bellowing voice while checking her over with careful hands, Easton asked, "Are you alright?"

"Yes, yes, I'm fine." She wriggled under him. "More importantly, how are you? You're the one who put himself in harm's way."

"Not a mark on me. But I need to secure that area where the tree came in with some tarps or the whole place could flood by the time the hurricane passes."

He looked back over his shoulder, mentally planning and strategizing what needed to happen.

She chewed on her lip, eyes trailing to the damage. With a vigorous shake of her head, she pressed up. "I'll help."

A snort escaped him before he thought better of it. He appreciated her resilience, her willingness to pitch in and help out. But being knocked around by hurricane-force winds and soaking to the bone? Not an option. "Like hell. Be still and try to stay calm for your sake and for our baby. I don't want you doing anything until you've been checked over."

Her spine went straight and rigid. "I'm careful."

His jaw went tight and he couldn't resist snapping. "Careful? Like when you tried to run out into a hurricane?"

Her eyes filled with tears, and she pressed a hand to her mouth. "You're right. I wasn't thinking. Oh God, how could I have been so reckless?"

His anger dimmed in the face of her tears, and heaven knew, he didn't want to upset her more.

He clasped her fingers, trying to soothe her. "And that's why, for the baby's sake, I'm sure you'll sit over there and watch Ginger Snap and Cinnamon. We can argue until we're both soaked or you can let me get to work."

She nodded, a mixture of annoyance and defeat in the thin line her lips formed. But she didn't argue. Instead, she grabbed the quilt from the floor and walked slowly to the deer, hands extended.

Easton heard her talk to the deer. Reassuring them everything would be alright. She sat in the hay next to them, eyes fixed on the fawn.

Easton moved quickly to the small office, grabbing a tarp from the supply closet. Scouring the shelves, he located nails and a hammer from behind a stack of toilet paper.

Knowing that he didn't have much time to make an effective barrier, his limbs sang to life. He hammered a tarp wall, reminding himself the entire time that he needed to make sure Portia stayed safe. He wouldn't have her catching her death out here.

With the help of a ladder and some rope, he got

to work, using the grommets on the tarp to stretch it in some places and using nails to secure it in others. In a few places, he nailed the thing to the fallen tree, but in the end, he did a decent job protecting them from the rain.

The blue tarp wall wasn't going to win him any construction awards, but as he stepped back to survey his handiwork, he knew it'd do its job. Nothing more, nothing less.

Putting away his tools, Easton found a clean T-shirt in the barn office. He toweled off his head and walked back to the stall where he'd left Portia and the deer. He stopped in his tracks.

Like some woodland fairy, Portia was wrapped in a quilt, fast asleep. Her head cradled by her arm, which rested on Ginger Snap's rump with Cinnamon curled between them.

She'd been wiped out. That much was clear.

But something else gnawed at his consciousness as he looked at the strange scene in front of him.

For the last several years, he'd been convinced that because Terri and Xander had joined the efforts of the refuge and set up shop here that he'd been at the core of a family. He'd been more convinced after Terri passed away, leaving Easton to help with baby Rose.

He was happy here, sure. He'd enjoyed the rewards and benefits of a family without any of the investment or risk. That'd been his role.

But as he stared at Portia, watched her sleep nestled up next to a deer, he began to realize that wasn't the role he wanted. He'd been playing it safe for too long, keeping his relationships light and easy until he'd reached this point where he didn't even know how to have a deep and meaningful one. All that was about to change, however. Because Easton didn't want a sideline role anymore. He wanted something lasting, with the strong, sweetly fierce woman in front of him.

This Peter Pan wannabe was ready to leave Neverland. To follow his Wendy.

He didn't just care about Portia. He loved her.

Marrying her wasn't about the baby. It was about building a life with her, forever. And he'd sabotaged his proposal by not recognizing her most vulnerable of insecurities. He'd made her feel like an obligation rather than a precious treasure.

No wonder she'd tried to storm out of here.

He'd minced his words, convinced her that their circumstance as parents were the reason he'd wanted to pursue a relationship with her.

That formulation had been completely wrong. He loved her enthusiasm for logic and how that balanced her artistic soul. Easton loved the way they balanced each other. His love for her coursed through his veins. He didn't know why he hadn't recognized it before.

He loved her. Not for her secretarial skills. Not as a valuable employee. He loved Portia for all that she was—sacrificing, kind, artsy and wildly sexy. All of her.

Now he had to persuade her to say yes.

So after a crash in the barn and another five hours trapped in said barn, Portia had weathered her first Category 3 hurricane. Now, in the strangely bright morning sun, she sat on a kitchen barstool watching the cleanup effort through an open window, cooled by a fan running off a generator. She should have gone to the doctor by now, but that had been rescheduled due to the storm.

Both Easton and Xander refused to let her help. The ER scare and the stress of the storm had them both convinced she needed to rest. To stay away from any form of physical labor.

So here she sat on a stool in the kitchen looking out the window. And looking. And looking. Just as she'd been stuck in the barn unable to act. Sure, she'd slept. But even when she was awake, Easton wouldn't talk to her or let her exert herself in any way, physically or emotionally. As if her emotions weren't already in a turmoil regardless. Thank goodness one of the volunteers was a nurse and had checked her out or she would be in an overrun ER right now. And Portia had to admit to a massive sense of relief that Easton and their baby were okay.

And thank heaven there were no casualties, human or animal. All damage had been structural, which could be repaired with time.

She propped her chin on her elbow. She felt like a true Floridian now, down to a leveled house. Her small white cabana hadn't been a match for Elliot's relentless winds and storm surge. The majority of her belongings were probably floating to a distant shore, displaced.

Like she felt. Out of sorts.

At least not everything had been lost. Some photo albums and sketchbooks she'd tucked away in her closet remained. Some clothes, too. But there was so much damage.

Every line of sight and perspective revealed more destruction. Debris littered the lawn, pieces of people's lives from yards away. A Jet Ski, pieces of a dock, even a window air-conditioning unit. She could barely see the presence of light green grass.

She'd been through snowstorms before, when traveling with her parents, but there was a crystallized beauty after a blizzard. People holed up with hot cocoa in front of the fire. This kind of destruction and loss after the hurricane humbled her. Made her feel small and fragile. Made her question her need not to rely on anyone.

But so did being confined to the main house while other people worked to make the place habitable again. Volunteers picked up debris, moving branches and pieces of buildings with military precision. Or, she thought, a laugh pushing at her lips, with ant-like precision—moving things so much larger than the human body.

Maureen kept Portia company, pouring her a glass of water. Maureen's red curls fell in her face, making her look wild. "Anything else for you, love?"

Picking up the orange-tinted glass, Portia shook her head. "Not unless you can sneak me outside so I can be useful to somebody."

Maureen put a hand on Portia's shoulder, shaking her head. "Everyone just wants to make sure you are okay. And you are being useful. Honestly. Taking care of yourself is useful to all of us. We care about you, you know."

Portia had grown to appreciate her friend's blunt honesty. She simply nodded.

From across the kitchen counter, Portia's phone rang, vibrating like mad.

Maureen glanced at the caller ID. "It's your brother. I'll leave you to it." She gave Portia a side hug before disappearing into the house, her footfalls echoing until they were silent.

She slid over to answer the phone, steadying herself.

"I've been so worried about you," Marshall said by way of greeting.

Portia traced the ridge of the glass with a light fingertip, staring nowhere in particular. "Well, hello to you, too."

"I feel like when one sibling goes through a crazy hurricane unexpectedly, hello falls a bit short. Are you okay?"

Was she okay? Again, she didn't know how to answer that.

"Of course I am. I'm not going to lie, Marshmallow. The hurricane was the most intense thing I've ever witnessed. But I am okay. Everything here is just fine."

"You just…" Marshall trailed off. "You just don't sound like yourself. I can come see you, take a job in Key Largo and help you out."

The words knifed Portia in the chest.

"Absolutely not." Portia took a sip of her water, deciding not to tell him about her destroyed cabana. He didn't need to be worried by that. Hell, that would send him on a plane within the hour.

She pressed on. "Finish school and then kick butt. That's what would make me happiest."

He paused, sighing. "Fine. But I'm coming to see you this weekend."

She stuttered. "That's really un—"

He interrupted her. "No, it is necessary."

"Okay," she found herself saying. "Yes, please. I would like to see you. I, um, need to see you. I've missed you."

"I miss you, too. See you soon, sis. Love you."

Portia looked back outside at the chaos. "Love you, too."

He hung up, leaving Portia to her swirling thoughts about letting others into her life, accepting help and comfort. She couldn't hide from the truth. She needed other people as much as they needed her.

The realization settled inside her with a depth that went beyond just the physical implications of a hurricane, and made her question all the times she'd pushed offers of help away. She'd denied people the chance to give back the way she gave to others.

And why?

To protect herself from rejection? To give herself control over her world after a tumultuous childhood? Maybe. Probably. The whys didn't matter so much. What mattered was changing, becoming less rigid in her views and broadening her scope, letting love into her life as well as giving it.

She saw Easton from a distance. She would know his walk, his stance anywhere, even if he wore a tuxedo rather than his regular cargo pants, boots and T-shirt. Or nothing at all. Her heart squeezed with emotion.

She couldn't hide from the truth anymore. She'd fallen totally and irrevocably in love with him. Chances were, she'd loved him for a very long time and hadn't allowed herself to admit it to herself because her feelings weren't logical.

Love wasn't logical. It wasn't based on looks. Or a checklist. Or criteria. Feelings couldn't be stacked into a neat, orderly pile. Her emotions were messy and tangled and to hell with independence.

Her soul hurt so much because she loved him, completely and irrationally. Her feelings didn't make sense and they weren't supposed to. This was about leading with her heart rather than her brain. She'd worked so hard not to be like her mother, Portia had missed the whole point. Her mother hadn't really loved anyone but herself. All of her mother's relationships were based on—checklists and criteria. Portia may not have looked like her mother, but in a sad way, she'd fallen into the same trap.

How sad was that? Tragic actually.

Hopefully she wasn't too late to change things and build a future with Easton and their baby. A future built on love.

As Easton drew nearer, he caught her stare through the window. In his arms, he carried stacks of her artwork. He raised them above his head, a smile forming on his face.

But not on hers. She knew this gesture was a kind of peace offering, and oh how she wanted to accept it. But sadness blanketed her, pulling her heart into a plummet.

Because as deeply, completely and passionately as she loved him, she now understood her own self-worth.

She'd always wanted to be independent. Well, this was her test. She owed it to herself and to her child to stand up for herself. As soon as the cleanup was completed, she would demand the fullhearted commitment from Easton they all deserved.

A week later, fading sunlight washed the bruised but recovering refuge in orange hues. As Easton scanned the outside patio tables, he could barely believe that a week ago, the place had been torn apart by Hurricane Elliot.

The substantial damage to the barn and clinic had been repaired. Both Xander and Easton spared no expense, contracting the quickest, best construction companies in southwest Florida to bring the structures back up to tip-top shape.

As he looked around the gala fund-raiser tonight, he could see all of that hastened hard work paying off. Manicured grass, well-maintained buildings. Normalcy.

Which was exactly what he needed to show the collection of celebrities, politicians and socialites that bustled from table to table with champagne glasses in hand.

A snazzy pianist set up on a pop-up wooden dance floor, string lights winking on overhead, creating an illusion of stars brought down to earth. The pianist's notes mingled with the jazz singer whose sultry alto voice spit out lyrics from crooners of another more elegant age.

The brothers had agreed this event would be black-tie and impressive. They needed to be out in public view to fully demonstrate their success as an organization for the reopening of the refuge. So the Lourdes brothers had pooled their connections, hired a decorator and thrown a major event together in five days' time. Impressive, even for them.

As he watched the black-tie affair unfold in his

backyard, Easton felt proud of the roots he'd laid down here. The roots he hoped to add to tonight.

The Serenade to Starlight signified the official reopening of the wildlife refuge. This event allowed them to renew their presence in the public eye, something completely essential for maintaining their facilities and the care of the animals.

The whole place seemed to twinkle in cool silver lights and accent pieces. The guest list consisted of A-list types from Miami, South Florida and the Keys. A few prominent West Coast starlets had flown in as well, lured by the promise of positive press coverage for their philanthropic efforts. Of course, the brothers made sure the volunteers could attend, too. The refuge depended on their time, effort and grit. They deserved to enjoy this evening.

Still, a moment of pride and joy turned to apprehension as Easton scanned the crowd, zipping past the women in cocktail dresses. Skipping over the heads of the politicians with cigars and whiskeys on the rocks. He spotted Maureen facilitating media coverage. Xander shaking hands with one of their big donors.

There was only one person is this crowd of people he really wanted to see, however. And that was Portia.

Since the storm, they hadn't had a moment alone. Despite living in the mansion together—under the same roof—she'd kept her distance. Their conversations had been short, quiet. An air of pensive distraction painted her face and actions all week, but he'd wanted to give her time to collect her thoughts and recover from the storm.

Some time where he wasn't pressuring her about marriage.

And she'd retreated totally.

A lesser man, one not dedicated to wooing the love of his life, might have turned tail and given up. But Easton had never been that kind of man. His bones didn't allow him to quit. He knew when to use his theatrical, eccentric, romantic heart. He'd laid down a plan to win her over. Moreover, he'd determined a way to prove how important she was to him.

Then, he spied her through the crowd.

His heart hammered, breath catching in his throat.

Portia rested a slender hand on one of the cocktail tables set up by the massive pool. Her hair was piled on her head, but not in her normal ponytail. Instead, her hazelnut hair was swept into an Audrey Hepburn bun. A slinky peach ball gown clung to her curves, suggesting her natural grace.

Damn. She was sexy.

She moved and the peach-colored dress shimmered in the lights as she leaned to talk to her brother, Marshall, who'd decided to visit for a week. That was another reason Easton had wanted to give Portia space. He knew she needed to spend time with her brother.

But tonight, it was Easton's turn. And he had to get to her.

His brother clapped him on the shoulder, a small glass of bourbon neat in his opposite hand. Easton's open stare at Portia interrupted, he turned to face his brother.

Xander winked at him, understanding what was going on.

Jessie flanked Xander, a vision in glittering silver sequins. She absently straightened Don's bow tie as she spoke. "You boys have completely outdone yourselves."

Sipping his bourbon before answering, Xander nodded. "We just wanted to express our appreciation for the hard work of the volunteers."

"We wouldn't be here without all of you," Easton added, his eyes watching the governor. A few feet away, the man paused. He stooped down, a smile on his wide, tanned face as he took a bright pink carnation that Rose offered him. She clapped when the governor stuck the flower behind his ear. Rose waved goodbye to the official when Maureen scooped her up, heading toward her husband.

Rose's bright eyes lit up when she noticed Easton. She bounced in her sunset-yellow smock dress, blond curls catching in the light summer breeze, twisting over the green wreath crown in her hair.

Rose looked over at her uncle and blew a kiss. Easton caught it in the air and pressed it into his heart. And in that moment he knew he would continue the ritual with his own daughter one day. Because yes, while he couldn't explain why, he knew without question that his and Portia's child was a girl.

A daughter. A son would be great, too. But he already could envision his and Portia's little girl in his heart's eye. And she was incredible.

The pianist and jazz singer faded, their set coming to an end. Elle Viento, a famous singer-songwriter, was up next. The brothers had flown her in from her vacation house in Destin, Florida, to sing.

Her guitar and soft vocals rippled through the crowd, giving the guests a small pause. Even Harvey Fink the movie star stopped to watch Elle play.

The gorgeous night needed to stay this way. Just a bit longer. Just until Easton could make his way to Portia.

Don interrupted Easton's thoughts. "I'll bring you another drink, dear," he told his wife, kissing her on the cheek before disappearing to the bar. Jessie looked like a schoolgirl, her eyes glowing.

"So, Easton, how is Portia? Things settling between you two?" Jessie asked in her matter-of-fact way.

He exchanged a glance with Maureen. "She's fine. And we're pregnant."

Easton wasn't concerned with hiding that truth. He loved Portia, and didn't care who knew what anymore. All that mattered was proving himself to her.

Jessie's hand went to her chest, eyes wide. "Pregnant?" Her tone questioning, prying.

Maureen nodded, saving Easton from answering

every single nosy question. "Yes and she is doing well. Glowing and excited."

But Easton wasn't going to let Jessie think he needed shielding from the invasive questions. He was more than ready to declare himself.

"And I have every intention of romancing her for a very, very long time. I love that woman." Every fiber of his being sung that revelation.

Maureen's grin spread like wildfire to Xander and Jessie. She playfully shoved his arm. "Now, there's the magic word. Go get her, Doctor."

Easton winked, setting out to find Portia. He strode over to her, resting a hand on the cocktail table.

Marshall welcomed Easton with a big, toothy grin. The young man's square features contrasting with Portia's slender, angled ones. The sibling resemblance came in their slender height and inquisitive brown eyes. Easton had learned to size people up quickly after all the moving around he'd done in his childhood, and Marshall was a good kid, really bright. Easton understood why Portia sacrificed so much for him.

Easton cupped Marshall's shoulder.

"Do you mind if I steal your sister for a while?"

Marshall smiled, but pinned Easton with a serious look far beyond his years. "As long as you take good care of her."

"I promise, on my honor." He thrust out his hand

for the young man to shake. He hoped Marshall would soon be his brother if all went according to plan.

Marshall nodded, his dirty blond hair flopping on his forehead. He turned his attention to a young soap opera star in a bright green dress with a vee neck open to her navel.

Laughing, Easton turned away, focusing his full attention on the only woman at this event who mattered to him. Portia. He ducked his head to whisper in her ear. "I think it's time we talk."

"Right now?" She glanced up at him, her eyes scanning his as if she were looking for something.

"We've put it off long enough, don't you think?" He touched her elbow. "Come on, I have something in the barn I would really like you to see."

She chewed her glossy bottom lip for an instant before nodding. "Yes, of course. I'd thought perhaps we should talk after the property cleanup and celebration, but there's no need delaying."

He took her hand in his, leading them beneath the twinkling paper lanterns toward the barn. The rustle of music and cocktail conversation faded the closer they got to the newly rebuilt structure, repainted teal just like the old one.

Easton placed his hands over Portia's eyes. "No peeking," he teased, nudging the door open with his foot.

They crossed the threshold, lights activated by their movement.

"And now." He took his hands back, letting her see the barn.

Framed pieces of her salvaged art work decorated the barn. Some paintings hung from the rafters and were surrounded with shimmery lights. Billowing flower stalks in sunset-colored pots lined the barn, leading toward a stall at the end of the row.

Ginger Snap poked her head out, ears moving. Portia stepped forward, eyes going from piece to piece and then to the fawn Cinnamon who stood tall beside her mother on spindly legs.

Atop a pile of fresh hay, Easton had laid a brilliant white-and-gold quilt at the far end of the barn. Then he'd covered the blanket with a tray of bright, tropical fruit and crackers. Two champagne glasses flanked an ornate bottle of sparkling water.

Easels lined the path to the blanket. He took her hand, led her to the picnic.

Bright pink calligraphy scrawled across the first canvas: You're Beautiful.

She moved on to the second, a smile lighting her eyes as brightly as the strands of twinkling bulbs illuminating the barn: You Drive Me Crazy—And I Like it.

At the next canvas, her fingers went to her lips, her gaze wide: Easton Loves Portia More Than Life.

Her hand slid away from her mouth, her fingers trembling as she traced the two words on the final message: Marry me.

Tears filled her eyes, one, then another sliding down her cheeks.

"Hormones?" he asked.

"So much more," she answered. "Easton, you are...so charming. And so ridiculously handsome."

Delicate hands stroked his tuxedo lapel, moved to his face. His heart was barely contained in his chest as he looked at her, reading the supreme tug of emotions in her eyes.

He needed that emotion to be love. His whole soul sang his love for her. If she left...he couldn't even finish the thought. Her absence would devastate him.

Easton dropped to one knee and pulled out a ring box from his back pocket. He popped it open, letting the lights bring the solitaire diamond to life.

Portia's hands went to her mouth, tears streaming down her face.

"I love you. I never thought I would find a woman who would make me want to settle down and figure out how to really be in a relationship. But then I met you and everything changed. Portia, you are the kindest, most self-sacrificing person I've ever known. I want to spend the rest of my life deserving you. Will you marry me?"

She clasped her hands to her chest. "Yes. Yes. Yes, Easton."

Relief swept away the buzz of nervousness he'd refused to acknowledge until that moment.

He stood up sweeping her into a hug, kissing her deeply.

"I love you so much, too." She said as he slipped the ring onto her finger. A perfect fit—as they were for each other.

"No worries about me being Peter Pan and Tarzan combined?" he half joked, unable to keep from worrying. He needed her to believe in him.

"I'm thinking I may have prejudged you. You're more like Dr. Dolittle and Louis Pasteur. A doctor, scientist, tenderhearted veterinarian and amazing man."

He pulled her into him, touching her cheek. "God, I do love you, Portia, and while you've mentioned my dating history, I've never said those words to any woman before. I mean it."

"I know you do. You're a man of honor." She pressed her hand to his cheek, the facets in her diamond engagement ring refracting all those little lights into a prism around them.

"So you know I mean every word of this. I love you, with everything that's inside me. I wish I could explain why. I just know that I do—"

She pressed her fingertips to his mouth. "You don't have to explain. I get it."

"You do?"

"I understand what it means to feel something completely irrational and yet very real. Because I'm in love with you, too. In my head I understand we complement each other, our strengths play well to each other. Yet that doesn't matter because I've met other people who fit that criteria and they didn't come close to moving me the way you do with just a look."

"A look?" He eye-stroked her, taking his time.

"Yes, a look." She sidled closer, her body pressed to his. "But I have a little secret for you."

"What would that be?"

"A touch is even better," she whispered in his ear.

He prided himself on being an intelligent man, her very own Louis Pasteur, after all. Although a hint of Tarzan could come in handy every now and again.

He swept an arm behind her knees and lifted her against his chest, sinking with her onto the thick quilt he'd placed there with just this hope in mind.

The hope of celebrating their engagement, their future and their love.

* * * * *

THE GIRL NOBODY WANTED

LYNN RAYE HARRIS

For my in-laws, Larry and Joyce Harris. Fifty years together is quite an accomplishment. You are proof that love can last forever. I'm so happy you're a part of my life, and I love you both.

CHAPTER ONE

ANNA CONSTANTINIDES stood at the edge of the gathered crowd and hoped the serene countenance she'd practiced before the mirror for the past week was holding up. Tonight was, without doubt, the most humiliating night of her life. Her fiancé—correction, former fiancé—was marrying another woman.

It would not have been so bad, perhaps, if her fiancé wasn't Prince Alessandro, heir to the Santina throne. She should have been his queen, yet she was currently the jilted bride.

A fact the media took great delight in reporting.

Again and again and *again.* She'd hardly had a peaceful moment since Alex had dumped her so publicly and humiliatingly for another woman. He hadn't even had the courtesy to inform her personally. No, he'd let her find out in the pages of the tabloids. Simply *mortifying.*

The pity she'd had to endure. The knowing looks— even, surprisingly, a hint of censure. As if it were *her* fault somehow. As if she were the one who'd been caught kissing another man while engaged to someone else, as Alex had been photographed with Allegra Jackson.

Anna wanted nothing less than to be at his engagement party tonight, but she'd had no choice. "Anna," her mother had said when she'd refused, "you must. Protocol demands it."

"I don't give a damn about protocol," she'd replied. And she hadn't. Why, when she'd dedicated her life to protocol and duty and been so spectacularly punished for it?

Her mother took her hands. "Sweetheart, do it for me. Queen Zoe is my oldest and dearest friend. I know she would be disappointed if we were not there to support her."

Support *her?* Anna had wanted to laugh, to shout, to rail against the unfairness of life—but she had not. Ultimately, she had done precisely what her mother asked because, for pity's sake, she felt *guilty.*

Anna stiffened her spine as the king began to toast the happy couple. But she lifted her glass of champagne along with everyone else, and prepared to drink to the health and happiness of Alex and Allegra, the woman who'd turned her preordained life upside down.

At least, thank goodness, she could be certain there were no photographers present tonight. They would be waiting outside the palace gates, naturally, but for now she was safe.

And yet she still had to smile, had to pretend she wasn't dying from embarrassment. She would have to endure the stories, the photos, the quotes from anonymous "friends" who claimed she was holding up well, or that she was fragile, or that her heart had shattered into a million pieces.

Anna sipped her champagne on cue. Only an hour more, and she was out of here. Back to the hotel where she would crawl into her bed and pull the covers over her head. The toast ended, and then the ensemble began to play a waltz. Anna slipped her barely touched glass onto a passing waiter's tray and turned toward the doors to the terrace. If she could escape for just a few moments, she could endure the next hour with a great deal more fortitude.

"Anna," a woman called. "I've been looking for you."

Anna gritted her teeth and turned toward Graziana Ricci, the Amanti foreign minister's wife. The woman sashayed toward her, a bright smile pasted on her cosmetically enhanced face. But it wasn't Signora Ricci who captured Anna's attention. It was the man beside her.

An Englishman, she assumed, as there were so many who had descended upon Santina recently.

He was tall, dressed in a bespoke tuxedo like nearly every other man in the room, and quite striking. Handsome, in a boyish way that somehow wasn't boyish at all. No, it was devilish, as if he knew the temptation he offered merely by existing. Eyes the color of roast coffee glittered in a face that had been carved by Michelangelo. Somehow, the look in those eyes dared her to envision him naked atop a pedestal.

Anna shook herself. Perhaps he was a work of art, but he had not been carved by Michelangelo. How silly.

But he could have been. His face was a study in angles sculpted for the sole purpose of making the owner appear sinfully irresistible to the female of the species. Sharply defined cheeks, a blade-straight nose, firm sensual lips and a small cleft at the base of his chin that deepened when he smiled.

And when he turned that smile on her, her heart skipped a beat.

Several beats.

The picture that filled her mind at that moment was decidedly uncharacteristic of her. She had absolutely no desire to kiss this man, no matter what her mind conjured up. It was stress, pure and simple.

As were the skipped beats. *Stress.*

The man smiled and winked, and Anna very deliberately looked away. *Honestly, what was wrong with her?*

"Anna, this is Leo Jackson," Signora Ricci said, and Anna instantly stiffened. The other woman didn't notice as she giggled, hugging his arm to her surgically enhanced body. *Shameless hussy.* "Leo is Allegra's brother."

As if he could be anyone else.

"How nice," Anna said frostily, her heart careening out of control with anger and helpless frustration. Allegra's brother. As if his sister ruining her life weren't enough, she now had to be faced with another Jackson when she quite simply wished them all to hell. Which wasn't very polite or charitable of her, she knew, but it was how she felt right now. "Welcome to Santina, Mr. Jackson. If you will excuse me, I was just on my way to…to an appointment."

It was a lie and her face flamed the instant she said it. Not because she cared that she'd lied, but because Leo Jackson arched one perfect eyebrow as if he knew she wanted to escape him. His lips quirked, and the flame inside her burned hotter.

But was it embarrassment or something else?

Embarrassment, she decided firmly. There could certainly be no other reason for it. If not for his sister, she wouldn't be in this predicament now. She wouldn't be standing here enduring the humiliation of hundreds of eyes surreptitiously turning upon her every time Alex leaned in close to his new fiancée and whispered something in her ear.

"I'm sorry to hear that, Anna," Leo said, using her given name as if he had every right in the world. Arrogant man! But her skin prickled with heat at the way her name sounded when he said it. Soft, sexy, alluring. Not boring Anna, but beautiful, exciting Anna.

"Nevertheless," she said, standing as straight and tall as she could. "It is the case."

What was wrong with her? Why was she being fanciful? She was simply Anna. And that's precisely who she wanted to be. Anna was safe, predictable, quietly elegant. She was not bold or brassy. Nothing like Signora Ricci, thank heavens.

Signora Ricci's mouth turned down in an exaggerated frown. "This will not take but a moment. I had hoped you could show Leo around Amanti tomorrow. He is thinking of building a luxury hotel."

Anna glanced at Leo Jackson. There was something dark and intense behind those eyes, no matter that one corner of his mouth turned up in a mocking grin. A fire began to burn low in her belly. She might be the tourist ambassador to the neighboring island of Amanti, but that didn't mean she had to personally show this man the sights.

It wasn't safe. *He* wasn't safe. She felt it in her bones.

Besides, his sister had stolen her future, and even if that wasn't his fault, she couldn't forget it if she were forced to spend time with him. No, she wanted nothing to do with this man—with *anyone* named Jackson.

"I'm afraid that's not possible, Signora Ricci. I have other things to attend to. I can arrange for someone else—"

The other woman scoffed. "What is more important than Amanti's economy? This would be good for us, yes? And you are the best for the job. What else do you have to do now that you have no wedding to prepare for?"

Anna swallowed her tongue as bitter acid scoured her throat. If she weren't a dignified person, a calm and controlled person, she might just strangle Graziana Ricci where she stood.

But no, Anna Constantinides had more dignity than that. She'd been raised to be serene, to be a perfect queen. She would not break because one woman dared to insult her on a day when she'd already been insulted by her ex-fiancé and the overwhelming media coverage of his new engagement. She was strong. She could handle this.

"If tomorrow doesn't work," Leo interjected, "the next day surely will." He pulled a card from his pocket and held it out. "My personal number. Call me when you are available."

Anna accepted the card because to do otherwise would be rude. His fingers brushed hers, and a tongue of fire sizzled along her nerve endings. She snatched her hand back, certain she'd find her skin blackened where he'd touched her. Graziana Ricci had turned away, distracted by an elderly matron who gesticulated wildly about something.

"I'm not sure when that will be, Mr. Jackson. It might truly be better for someone else to take you."

"And yet you are the tourist ambassador," he said with a hint of steel underlying the polite veneer in his tone. "Unless, of course, you do not like me for some reason?"

Anna swallowed. "I don't know you. How could I possibly dislike you?"

His gaze cut toward the front of the room where Alex and Allegra were currently standing close together and talking in hushed tones. "How indeed?"

Anna thrust her chin out. It was bad enough she had to endure this night, but for this man to know how she felt? It was insupportable. "Tell me about this hotel you propose to build," she said. "How will this help Amanti?"

His gaze slid down her body, heat trailing behind it. *Dangerous,* a voice whispered.

He took his time meeting her eyes again. "Have you not heard of the Leonidas Group?"

She was proud of herself for not showing her surprise. If the Leonidas Group wanted to build a hotel on Amanti, that could be a very good thing. "Of course I have. They own some of the most luxurious hotels in the world and cater to the wealthiest of clients. Do you work for them, Mr. Jackson?"

His laughter was rich, rolling from him in golden tones that vibrated through her. "I own the Leonidas Group, Anna."

Again with her name, and again with the prickle of awareness skimming along her nerve endings. "How fortunate for Amanti," she said, because she could think of nothing else to say. She felt like a fool for missing the *Leo* in *Leonidas,* though it wasn't an immediately obvious connection. But if he owned the Leonidas Group, he must be very wealthy indeed.

He leaned in closer. "Perhaps you will change your mind about tomorrow, then."

Heat coiled tightly inside her. His voice was a delicious rumble in her ear, though she tried not to notice precisely how delicious. She was tired, that was all. He was just a man, and men were fickle. Unpredictable. Dishonorable.

She closed her eyes, her heart thrumming steadily. It was uncharitable to think of Alex that way, and yet she couldn't help it. He'd made a promise, damn him!

"I will have to check my calendar," she said coolly.

His smile made her heart skip a beat. Too, too charming. Perhaps his sister was equally as charming. Perhaps that's how she'd stolen Alex away.

"And yet, when you wake up and see the morning papers, you will no doubt wish yourself far from Santina."

A current of dread slid through her, icy fingers scraping her soul. The papers. They would be filled with news of Alex and Allegra tomorrow—and she would be mentioned side by side with them. The poor jilted bride. The faithful girl who'd been stood up by a prince. Sad little heiress, no longer a queen-in-waiting.

Anna's throat constricted. She absolutely did not want

to be here tomorrow. And he was giving her a way out, though she would have to endure his company. But which was worse? The media frenzy, or Leo Jackson?

If she took him to Amanti, they wouldn't escape the attention entirely, but at least they would be out of Alex and Allegra's proximity. Perhaps the press might not think her so sad and distraught if she were seen going about her duties.

"I've just remembered," she said, proud that she managed to sound so cold and detached. Professional. "My appointment isn't for tomorrow after all. I keep getting my days mixed up. It's for the next day."

"Is that so?" Leo said, his gaze slipping over her once more. There was heat and promise in that voice, and a hint of possession, as well. It infuriated her—and intrigued her.

"If you wish to tour Amanti," she said crisply, already partially regretting the impulse that had her choosing him over tomorrow's papers, "we can leave around nine in the morning."

"Nine?" he mocked. "I doubt I'll have slept off tonight's debaucheries by then."

Anna felt her ears going hot. She refused to picture *any* debauchery. "Nine o'clock, Mr. Jackson. Or not at all."

"You drive a hard bargain, darling," he drawled, as if he weren't in the least bit dangerous to her sense of well-being. "But we'll do it your way."

Before she knew what he was about, he caught her hand and pressed a kiss to the back of it. Her skin tingled as his warm breath washed over her, his beautiful lips skimming so lightly over her flesh. She couldn't suppress the small shudder that racked her body or the ache of sensation that made her crave more of his touch.

Leo Jackson looked up, his gaze sharp. Too sharp. As if he'd seen through to the core of her and knew what she'd been thinking. That devilish grin was back as his coffee-colored eyes glittered with heat. "Tomorrow, darling," he said. "I look forward to it."

Anna pulled her hand away, tried very hard to ignore the pulsing throb in her belly, between her legs. "I'm not your darling, Mr. Jackson."

He winked. "Not yet. But let's see what tomorrow brings, shall we?"

After a restless night, Anna rose early the next morning, and then showered and dressed with care. She was the tourist ambassador to Amanti, not a woman going on a date, so she chose a fashionable skirt and blazer. She paired the gray suit with a red silk camisole—her one nod to color—her pearls, and gray suede pumps. She wrapped her long dark hair in a neat knot and secured it with pins. Then she slipped on mascara and lip gloss before walking over to the cheval glass and studying her reflection from head to toe.

She looked professional, competent. Precisely the way she wanted to appear. She absolutely did not care whether Leo Jackson found her attractive or not.

Liar.

Anna frowned at herself. She wasn't unattractive; she was professional. And she intended to stay that way. If she could control nothing else about these chaotic past few weeks, she could at least control her image. And this was the image she wanted to project. Serenity in the face of turmoil. Grace under fire. A calm port in the storm.

Anna patted her hair one last time before she whirled away from the mirror, found her handbag and cell phone, checked her calendar to make sure she'd taken care of everything and left her room at precisely twenty to nine. Her room was two floors up from Leo Jackson's room, but first she took an elevator down to the dining room and grabbed a quick cup of coffee and a whole-grain muffin before going back up to Leo's floor. At three minutes to nine, she knocked on his door.

Nothing happened. Anna frowned as she listened for movement behind the door. She checked her watch, studied the sweep of the second hand across the mother-of-pearl face. At nine o'clock precisely, she knocked again. "Mr. Jackson?" she said, pressing her face close to the door in order not to wake any of the other late-sleeping guests in nearby rooms. "Are you in there?"

Two minutes later, when she'd knocked yet again—louder this time, because she was getting very annoyed—the door jerked open.

Anna's stomach flipped at the sight of Leo Jackson in all his bad-boy glory. Heavens above, why did this man have to be so compelling? She should feel nothing for him but contempt. Not only had his family wrecked her perfect life, but he was also not the sort of man a proper lady should ever get involved with.

Yet heat bloomed in her cheeks as she thought of his comment last night about debauchery. Because that's precisely what he looked like—as if he'd spent the night in some lucky woman's bed, debauching her thoroughly.

Before she could control herself, Anna thought that *she* wanted to be debauched. Thoroughly. Repeatedly.

If she could have slapped her palms to her cheeks in horror, she would have done so. She most definitely did *not* want to be debauched—and certainly not by this rogue.

"Hello, darling," Leo said casually, his sensual lips twisting in that arrogant grin that had featured so prominently in her thoughts last night while she'd tossed and turned in her bed. And yet, in the moment before he'd spoken, she'd sensed something behind that playboy demeanor, something tightly leashed in and controlled.

A sleek, dangerous beast on a tether.

"Mr. Jackson," she replied coolly, hoping he couldn't see the thrum of her pulse in her throat. "We had an appointment at nine, I believe."

He ran a hand through his dark hair. His eyes gleamed with interest as his gaze slipped over her. He had a day's growth of beard on his face—and she'd never seen anything sexier in her life.

Neither, it seemed, had some other woman. Or, heaven forbid, *women.* Yes, she definitely could see Leo Jackson taking more than one woman home with him at a time.

Oh, dear... The images in her head were definitely not safe for public consumption.

But he stood in the door, looking so dissolute and sexy in his tuxedo from last night she couldn't form a coherent thought as she studied him. The beast was concealed once more, so that she found herself wondering if she'd imagined it. But she had not, she was certain. He was smooth and magnificent—and not quite what he seemed to be at first glance.

His jacket hung open and his shirt was unbuttoned. The tie and studs were gone, probably tucked into a pocket. A bright smudge of pink was smeared across the pristine white of his collar. Lipstick, she realized with a jolt. And not the color Graziana Ricci had been wearing.

She was positive, looking at him, that he'd not spent the night in his own bed. In fact, she was pretty sure he hadn't slept at all. She tried not to think of what he'd been doing instead—or whom he'd been doing it with.

While she had lain awake thinking about this man, he'd forgotten all about her. Clearly, as his lack of readiness and his delay in answering the door indicated. She only hoped her cheeks weren't scarlet. What if he had a woman in there right now?

"I—I can come back later," she blurted. "If you're, um, busy."

"Not at all," he said smoothly, wrapping a hand around her elbow and pulling her into the room. She caught her heel and stumbled to a halt in the small foyer of his suite, her hands automatically bracing against his chest as she nearly lost her balance.

"Sorry about that, darling," he said, his arms enveloping her. His broad hands were on her back, her waist, searing into her like a flaming-hot brand. Her heart skittered. She had an impression of a sleeping lion rearing its head and sniffing the air for prey.

"I don't think you're sorry at all," she bit out, and then stifled a gasp when she realized what she'd said. No matter how she felt about Leo Jackson, it wasn't permissible to be rude. She'd spent a lifetime learning the art of diplomacy, a skill she would have needed as Queen of Santina one day. And she'd just failed miserably, hadn't she?

No wonder Alex had left her. Except, how was Allegra Jackson any better suited to be a queen, considering how scandalously her family had behaved last night?

If appearances were any indication, *this* particular Jackson had behaved very badly indeed.

Leo laughed, the fingers of one hand caressing the furrow of her spine through her clothing. Oh, if he kept doing that… Heat and light flared inside her, slid through her limbs until she wanted to mold herself to him like a second skin. His body was hard against hers, hot. It disconcerted her, and thrilled her. How could she react to this man so soon after Alex had turned her world upside down?

"Since you've landed in my arms, perhaps I'm not sorry," he said.

No man had ever held her so close. Not even Alex. She'd learned to dance with men, to conduct herself with poise and grace, and she'd been in a man's embrace before. But not this kind of embrace. This hot, needy, sensual embrace that was, on the surface, not improper at all.

Except for how it made her feel. Oh, yes, she felt quite improper when Leo Jackson had his arms around her. As if she wanted to feel skin against skin, mouth against mouth. As if she wanted to burn up in his arms and see what it felt like.

Ridiculous, since she didn't even know him. The stress of the past few weeks had obviously affected her brain.

Anna disentangled herself from his embrace and took a step back. She tugged on the bottom of her jacket to straighten it. Then she patted her hair, happy that no stray wisps had escaped the confinement of her knot.

Leo shook his head as he studied her with an expression of bemusement on his face. "Afraid of what you might feel if you let yourself go, darling?"

Fire burst through her, making twin spots rise in her cheeks. "Stop calling me *darling*," she said firmly. "And stop trying to seduce me, Mr. Jackson. It won't work."

She wouldn't *let* it work.

The gleam in his eyes was predatory. Feral. Exciting. *Dangerous.*

"Really? Not feeling the least bit angry about your fiancé and my sister? Not aching to put it all behind you with a few pleasurable hours?"

Anna lifted her chin. He'd seen right through her, hadn't he? "Actually, that sounds quite lovely. But first I'll need to find someone to spend those hours with."

"I'm wounded," he said lightly, though something in his expression made her take a step back.

"I doubt that," she replied crisply. "You'll have moved on to the next woman on your list without a moment's regret, I'm certain. We are all interchangeable to you."

Was that irritation flaring in his dark eyes? Anger?

Or pain? It shocked her enough that she couldn't decide. But then it was gone so quickly she began to wonder if she'd imagined it. Did she want him to have a conscience so it would make this strange attraction to him more bearable?

Probably.

Still, her outburst went against everything she'd ever been taught. She was out of her depth lately, stressed and furious and hurt. She had to govern herself better. "Forget I said that. It was rude."

"And you can't stand being rude, can you, Anna?" His voice caressed her name exactly as she'd imagined it last night, while lying awake in her bed.

"It's not the way I was raised," she said primly. Then she glanced at her watch, because the air felt suddenly thick and hot and she didn't know what else to do. "We're running late, Mr. Jackson. Our boat is at the dock. We were supposed to leave five minutes ago."

"Heaven forbid we are late. But you can cancel the boat. The tour will go much faster if we take my plane."

Anna blinked. "Plane? Amanti is only twenty-five miles away by sea. The boat will have us there in under an hour, and then we can hire a car to take us around the island."

His expression was patient but firm. "I need to see the coast. We'll fly around the island first, and then land and have a tour, yes?"

Anna reached for her pearls, comforting herself with the solid feel of them between her fingers. He was overriding all her plans. It was too much like what had happened to her life lately, and it made her nervous. Uncertain. Damn, how she hated that feeling.

"But I've already arranged things," she said firmly, attempting to regain control of the situation. "There is no need for you to put yourself out, Mr. Jackson."

He reached for her again, put his hands on either side of her shoulders and bent until his gorgeous eyes were on a level with hers. Her heart flipped. "Arrangements can be changed, Anna. And you really need to call me Leo."

She darted her tongue over her lower lip. "I'd prefer to keep this professional, if you don't mind."

"I do mind," he said, his eyes darkening.

Anna tried not to let the warm, spicy scent of him wrap around her senses. But he was too close, and he smelled so good, and her stomach was knotting with tension at his proximity. He confused her. She ached in ways she never had before, and she wanted things she'd once looked upon with quiet acceptance. She'd expected to be intimate with Alex, of course. She hadn't expected to find out she wanted that intimacy with a kind of earthy sensuality that was completely foreign to her nature.

But not with Alex.

With this man. With Leo.

"Keep looking at me that way, and we won't go anywhere," he murmured, his voice a lovely growl in his throat. She imagined him growling against her skin, his body twining intimately with hers, and swallowed hard.

It was shocking to be thinking these thoughts. And so very, *very* titillating.

She might be a virgin, but she wasn't stupid. She was modern enough to have read a few books on sex. She'd even managed to watch a video, the memory of which had her heart hurtling forward. The way the man had put his head between the woman's legs and—

"Anna," Leo groaned. "Stop."

Anna shook herself. What was wrong with her? Baiting a lion in his den? Was she insane?

"Really, I have no idea what you're talking about Mr.—Leo. You have a very dirty mind."

His sharp bark of laughter was not quite what she expected. He let her go abruptly, and her skin tingled through her clothes where he'd so recently touched her. "I think if this tour stands a chance of getting off the ground, I'd better change."

"That would be wise," she said primly.

She stood in the foyer, uncertain whether to follow or stay where she was. In the end, she decided to stay. She could hear him moving around, hear a soft curse as a door opened and shut again. She looked at her reflection in the mirror, blushed anew at her heightened color. Leo Jackson brought out the worst in her.

She was just beginning to worry about how long she'd been standing there when he reappeared. A jolt of surprise went through her at the sight of him. She didn't know what she'd expected, but his casual attire had not quite been it.

He wore a long-sleeved navy shirt, unbuttoned midchest, with a white T-shirt beneath. Half the shirt was tucked into faded, ripped jeans. The other half hung free in a kind of casual slouch that proclaimed this man didn't care about rules.

But the truth was that he looked utterly gorgeous. The height of Bohemian fashion, while she stood there in her prim suit and felt frumpy. Stuffy. Oh, the suit was expensive, but it was staid. Safe and boring. A generation too old for her, perhaps. The stylist had tried to get her to go with a shorter hem, a nipped-in waist, but she'd refused.

She was regretting it at the moment.

"Ready, my love?" he asked, and her heart skipped a beat.

"Only if you stop calling me names," she said, her jaw

aching with the effort it took to be polite as she forced the words out.

He grinned, and her heart melted. Damn it. Damn *him*. "I can try, sweet Anna."

Somehow, that was even worse.

CHAPTER TWO

IT WAS a glorious morning in Santina. The sun was shining brightly in the sky and the turquoise water of the Mediterranean sparkled like diamonds beneath it. Anna buckled her seat belt and tried to calm the racing of her heart as their plane began to taxi toward the runway.

Leo was flying. She hadn't quite expected that. When he'd said they would take his plane, she'd assumed he had a flight crew. Which he did, but he'd given them the day off to see the sights.

"Don't you need help?" she'd asked.

"It's a small plane," he'd replied. "Certified for one pilot. I left the 737 at home this time."

"It seems like a lot of trouble to go to for a short trip."

He smiled at her, and her heart turned over. "Relax, Anna. They wouldn't let me take off if I wasn't licensed."

She had to admit that he'd done a thorough check of the plane before they'd gone anywhere. He'd spent time looking at the instruments, walking around the craft, going over a checklist. Finally, when he'd deemed everything to be okay, he'd communicated with the tower.

And now they were turning onto the runway, the plane braking only momentarily while Leo said something else to the tower. Someone gave him the go-ahead, and then the plane was shooting down the runway. Anna bit her lip to stifle the laughter that wanted to break free at that very moment.

She loved everything about taking off. The charge down the runway, the plane lifting into the air, the ground falling away and her stomach going with it. She loved the way they soared into the sky with the landscape below getting smaller and smaller. She could see the rocky outcrop on which the palace was built, the faded terra-cotta roofs of the city, the glint of sunlight on glass and metal.

She slumped into her seat, a strange sense of relief pouring over her. She was leaving it all behind. She was free, at least for the next few hours, and her heart felt suddenly light.

She turned to look out Leo's side and caught him glancing at her. Her stomach flipped.

"Happy?" he asked, and she wondered how he knew. She hadn't given it away. She hadn't laughed, or smiled, or reacted at all. She knew because she'd practiced it for so many years. It was essential, as a queen, to be tranquil. To hide your feelings behind a mask of cool efficiency. She was good at it.

Usually.

"I don't, um, feel happy or sad," she said, stumbling in the middle and hoping he hadn't noticed.

"Liar," he shot at her. But he grinned when he said it, and a current of warmth washed over her. "I've an idea, sweet Anna."

She pointedly ignored his use of her name and the epithet he'd attached to it. "What is this idea?"

The hot, intense look he gave her had the power to melt her insides. He looked at her like he owned her, and it made little sparks fly around inside her like a racquetball bouncing off the walls of the court.

"Let's fly to Sicily. We can spend the day there, eating pasta, viewing the volcano—" one eyebrow arched, his voice dropping an octave before he said the next two words "—making love. We'll return to Amanti tonight and tour tomorrow."

Anna felt her face go red even as her heart rate notched up. "Impossible," she said.

"And why is that? Because you don't like me? You don't need to like me, Anna, for what I have in mind."

She needed a fan turned on her body full blast. "I have no feelings about you at all, Mr. Jackson."

"Really? I find that difficult to believe."

"I don't see why you should."

"Because I am a Jackson, perhaps?"

She crossed her arms and gazed out the window. Below, the ocean rolled in all directions. "I could hardly hold you responsible for what your sister has done."

He seemed to hesitate for a moment. "Whatever she has done," he said softly, "she has not done it alone."

Anna's heart burned. "No, you are quite correct. It takes two, as the saying goes."

"Indeed. Just imagine what the two of us could do together in Sicily." His voice was seductive, full of promise.

"We're going to Amanti. Now," she said firmly.

"Are you sure? I'm quite worth the side trip, I assure you."

"Good heavens, you are vain," she said, her heart racing at the thought of doing something so insane, so out of the ordinary. "No. No, no, *no*."

But a part of her wanted to say yes. She wanted to be the woman she'd never been allowed to be. She wanted to break free of her suits and her pearls and spend one glorious, hot, naked day with a man. She wanted to know what it felt like to let a man like Leo have his wicked way with her.

No, she told herself quite firmly, *she did not.*

But why not? Everything she'd prepared for, every-thing she'd thought her life was going to be, had disap-peared in the blink of an eye. She was a virgin who'd never even kissed a man because she'd been saving herself for Alex Santina. Alex, who'd never kissed her properly. He'd brushed his lips across her cheek, once over her mouth, but the contact had been so light and perfunctory that she had no idea what it truly felt like to kiss a man.

And Leo wanted to take her to Sicily and make love to her. She shivered with excitement. It was preposterous, and she wasn't going to say yes, but the idea was rather thrill-ing in an illicit way that had her sex tightening in response.

A static voice came over the headset then, and she jumped in surprise at the sudden sound slicing across her thoughts. She couldn't hear what the voice said, but Leo replied. And then he was pulling on the controls and they were climbing higher and faster.

"What?" she said, her heart thudding for a different reason now. "What is it?"

"Nothing," he replied. "Some unexpected turbulence. We're climbing to avoid it."

"Why did you ask me to go to Sicily? You've filed a flight plan. You can't just change it."

Leo flashed her another of those smiles that did things to her insides. "We aren't a commercial aircraft, darling. I can change it if I wish. Haven't you heard I'm eccentric that way?"

"I've heard nothing at all about you," she said with a sniff. It was only partially true. Last night, when she'd gotten back to her room, she'd done an internet search on Leo Jackson.

"Excellent. So you won't have made up your mind about me yet."

"Oh, I'm sure I have."

"Have you now? And what have you decided?"

Anna studied his profile. Leo Jackson was handsome and wealthy, and reputed to be intense in both his business dealings and personal relationships. He was also a serial womanizer who'd spent the past several years living in the United States, dating Hollywood starlets and supermodels and, on one memorable occasion, a gorgeous actress who was at least twenty years his senior. Of all the women he'd been linked with, that was the only one that had ever seemed to be somewhat serious.

There was no indication about what had ended the relationship, but it was definitely over. The actress had recently married someone else and adopted a baby with him.

"I think you can't be trusted," she said softly.

"Ah. What a shame."

"But you don't deny it."

He shook his head. "That depends on how you define *trust*. Will I seduce you in spite of your denials that you're attracted to me? Possibly. Will I lie to you and leave you heartbroken? Never. Because I will tell you up front that it's not wise to have expectations beyond the physical. We can have a good time, but we aren't getting married."

Anna crossed her legs. Had she really thought going to Sicily with him might be thrilling? "Why would you assume that a woman might have expectations about you? Are you truly that fabulous that no one can resist you? Honestly, I've never met anyone so arrogant as you. Not everyone thinks you're irresistible, you know."

"But you do."

Surely her face was bright red. From anger, not embarrassment, she told herself. "I do not. I don't even like you."

He laughed as if she'd admitted something she shouldn't

have. "And here I thought you didn't have any feelings at all about me."

"I'm rapidly changing my mind."

The look he gave her jolted her to her core. Dark, sensual, breathtakingly intense. "We could have fun in Sicily, Anna. Hot, decadent, pleasurable fun."

Her heart was thrumming. "Please stop saying *we. We* aren't doing anything together, Mr. Jackson."

He laughed again. "Back to that? Have you ever considered, sweet Anna, that perhaps it's time you let your hair down a bit? Time to let go of that buttoned-up perfection you try so hard to project and have some fun?"

Anna clenched her hands into fists in her lap. He didn't know her, didn't know what he was saying. He was simply guessing, because that's what men like him did. They got beneath your skin and made you desire them, made you think they understood you when in fact they only understood how to lower your defenses. It was a parlor trick, the kind of thing bogus fortune tellers did every day at the carnival.

She might not be experienced, but she wasn't stupid.

"You're grabbing at straws," she said calmly. "I am well aware I'm not perfect. And I like the way I'm dressed."

"It's not a bad way to dress if you're chairing a board meeting," he said. "But it's not your true style."

"I don't think you have the first clue about my style."

"I'm not sure you do, either," he said. "But we could start with naked and go from there."

Heat flared in her core, impossible heat. Her limbs were jelly whenever he mentioned the word *naked.* She was in danger of turning into a slack-jawed nitwit if he kept it up. "Do you ever quit?"

"I do," he said. "But I don't think we've reached that point yet."

Anna groaned. It was uncharacteristic of her, but she couldn't help it. "Why are you torturing me? Why can't we just fly to Amanti, view the coast and go back to Santina?"

Leo looked at her, his expression suddenly very serious. "Do you really want to go back to Santina? Is that where you want to be today?"

She turned to look out the window. The sea spread in all directions, as far as the eye could see. It was hard to believe they could be in the Mediterranean and it could still feel so remote. As if they were the only two people in the world. There were no boats out here, no other planes, nothing but the blue sky, the bright sun and dazzling water.

She was alone with him, and while he frustrated her, he also made her feel things she'd not felt before: attractive, alive, interesting. She wasn't quite ready to give that up yet.

"No," she said softly. And then she turned to face him, her jaw hardening. "No, I don't want to go back."

Leo wasn't sure why, but he wanted her. She was quite possibly the most uptight woman he'd ever met, but for some reason that intrigued him. Like now, when she sat there beside him and tried to look stony. He wasn't sure she realized it, but stony didn't really work when you had wide jade-green eyes that showed every ounce of hurt you were feeling, whether you wanted them to or not.

And Anna was hurting. He'd seen her across the room last night, looking so isolated and alone, and he'd wanted to know who she was. Graziana Ricci had laughed dismissively. "Oh, that's Anna Constantinides. The jilted bride."

The jilted bride. He'd watched her closely then, wondering what she must be feeling as she listened to the toasts to Prince Alessandro and Allegra. She'd looked so cool, so bored, so perfect and untouchable dressed all in icy white—but then her fingers had strayed to the pearl necklace she wore, and he'd noticed they were trembling. When she'd turned toward him, the light from the chandeliers caught her just right and he'd realized she was on the verge of tears.

Shimmering tears she never once let fall.

She'd been a beautiful ice queen in the center of that gathering, the most regal and elegant of them all—and he'd wanted to see if he could melt the ice surrounding her heart. Leo lived for challenges, and Anna Constantinides was a challenge. It wasn't simply that he wanted to seduce her. He wanted to make her laugh, wanted to see her eyes light up with pleasure.

Anyone who'd seen the newspapers, who'd read those ugly headlines and even uglier stories, would know she was suffering. It made him think of another time, another woman, who had also been deeply hurt by what the papers had said about her. His mother had kept the articles from when her affair with Bobby had been splashed through the papers. He'd found them in her personal documents when he was eighteen. She'd been dead for eight years by then.

Until that moment, he'd thought the most devastating thing she'd had in her possession had been the positive paternity test naming Bobby Jackson as his father—a fact Bobby had denied until the test was brought out in court after Leo's mother's death—but the articles had given Leo a whole new level of understanding about what had happened between his parents.

Though Bobby had raised him from the age of ten onward, their relationship could never be termed ordinary. Bobby didn't seem to know how to be a father, either to Leo or his siblings. He tried, but he was more of a dotty uncle than anything.

After Leo found the articles and confronted his father, their relationship had soured. Soon after that, he'd gone to the States to forge his way in business. He'd wanted to prove he didn't need Bobby, or the Jackson name, to succeed. He'd built the Leonidas Group from the ground up, and he'd made more money than Bobby had ever earned, even at the height of his football career.

Since Leo had returned to London recently, he'd been trying damn hard to forge a new relationship with his father. Though it wasn't perfect, they were finally learning to let go of the past and be friends.

Just then, Anna glanced down at her slim gold watch and turned sharply toward him as she realized how long they'd been flying. "Are we lost? Because we should have been there by now."

Leo flexed his fingers on the controls. "We aren't lost, darling. I thought it might be nice to fly for a little while."

He found flying soothing, especially when he wanted to think.

But Anna was used to structure. Her mouth opened. Closed. Opened again. "But why?" she blurted. "There is much to see on Amanti!"

He glanced over at her. Such an uptight woman. He found himself wanting to unpin her hair and see how long it might be. And he definitely wanted to get her out of that bland suit. Grey. Why was the woman wearing grey? The red of her shirt was the only spot of color in her drab outfit. Didn't she know she should be dressed all in red? In vibrant, sassy colors that made the green of her eyes stand out even more than they already did?

She was utterly beautiful, and trying so hard to hide that beauty. He found himself wanting to know why.

"And do you really want to be on Amanti today?" he asked coolly.

Her eyes were wide, her expression haunted. He didn't have to explain what he meant. The newspapers and tabloids couldn't seem to leave the story of Prince Alessandro's surprise engagement alone, especially since he'd picked Allegra Jackson—of those *scandalous* Jacksons—as his bride.

Anna couldn't help but be dragged into the publicity. She was the antithesis of his family, and probably far more suited to being a royal bride by virtue of her lack of scandalous relations.

Which also meant she was the perfect sacrificial lamb for the roasting fires of the papers that dogged the Santinas' every move.

The press loved every minute of her humiliation. Each story that featured Alessandro and Allegra's forbidden love also featured Anna. She endured it with quiet dignity, but Leo wondered how close she was getting to breaking. She was only human after all. It couldn't be easy to see her former fiancé with Allegra.

"I can't hide forever," she said, drawing herself up regally, shuttering her hurt behind her lowered lashes. "The press will have their fun until they tire of the story. If I run away or hide from the world, it will be a thousand times worse."

Her fingers strayed to her neck, caught at her pearls. "No, I have to endure it until it goes away."

Leo swore. He wanted to protect her, and he wanted to shake her at the same time. "It's acceptable to be angry, Anna. And it's acceptable to want to escape."

"I never said I wasn't angry," she snapped before closing her eyes again and saying something in what he assumed was her native Greek. When she trained those green eyes on him again, they were as placid as a secluded lake. She was good. Very good. But he could see the fire she couldn't quite hide in the depths of that gaze. And it pulled at him more than it ought.

"These things pass," she said. "And now we must go to Amanti and begin our tour. The last thing I need is for the press to think I'm off being promiscuous with you."

"Perhaps you need a little promiscuity in your life," he replied, very aware he was being self-serving as he said it. "A little fun that's about you, not about others or what they expect from you."

"You're only saying this because it would suit *your* purposes if I agreed with you. Stop trying to seduce me, Mr. Jackson. It won't work."

It was close to the mark, and inexplicably it made him angry. Except that he wasn't quite sure if it was her or himself he was angry with. He definitely wanted her. She intrigued him. She didn't seem to care who he was or what he offered her—and that made him think of something else, something he'd not let himself consider before. "Were you in love with him?"

Anna spluttered. He loved ruffling her cool, though he hoped the answer was no. For some reason, he needed it to be no.

"That's none of your business! We hardly know each other, Mr. Jackson," she said, her entire body stiff with outrage. Her long fingers gripped the arm of the seat. Her nails were manicured and neat, and there was a pale line on her left ring finger where her engagement ring had once sat. He imagined those elegant fingers playing his body like a fine instrument, and nearly groaned.

Since when was he interested in prim little schoolteachers anyway? Not that Anna was a schoolteacher—she was far too well bred and rich to have an actual job—but she reminded him of one. The kind of teacher who wore buttoned-up suits to work and lacy knickers beneath. Whether she realized it or not, the woman seethed with pent-up sexuality.

Whoever got her to let her hair down and give in to her sensual nature would be one lucky man. He pictured Anna in a bed, her naked body lying against red sheets, those full kissable lips open and eager as he lowered himself onto her and captured her mouth with his own.

Suddenly, flying was getting damned uncomfortable. Leo forced himself to think of something unsexy—like Graziana Ricci's collagen-plumped lips smeared in cherry-red lipstick—and hoped his body would take the hint.

"How can we possibly get to know each other," he said, "if you keep retreating behind that starched formality every time I ask you a question?"

"We don't need to know each other. I'm taking you to Amanti so you can decide whether or not you want to build a hotel there. Beyond that, I'm sure we'll never see each other again. Now, if you will please take us *to* Amanti, we can get on with the tour."

Leo shot her a glance. She was prickly as hell and completely fascinating. "You don't like it when your plans get changed, do you? You're very much a list girl."

Her head whipped around. "A list girl? What, pray tell, is that?"

"You make lists. You like a long list of things to do and then you check them off one by one. There's no room for spontaneity on your lists." He made a checkmark in the air. "Woke up early, check. Ate breakfast, check."

"There's nothing wrong with being organized, Mr. Jackson," she said. He could hear the starch in her voice, the outrage she tried to keep hidden. She was trying to keep him at a distance, and he wouldn't allow it.

"If you call me Mr. Jackson one more time," he growled, "I'll keep flying until we reach Sicily."

"You wouldn't."

Her arms folded over her prim grey suit, her chin thrusting forward in challenge. Clearly, Anna Constantinides didn't know him very well. No matter how successful he'd become, he'd never shaken that raw, edgy side of his personality that liked to push barriers to their limit. No doubt it came from trying to fit into the Jackson household when he'd been young and motherless and uncertain of his place in their lives. He'd pushed and rebelled, certain his father would throw him out, but Bobby had never wavered in his acceptance once he'd stepped up and admitted paternity.

"I would, in fact," Leo replied. "I've got nothing to lose."

Her jaw clenched tight and he felt suddenly wrong for phrasing it that way. She had everything to lose, or so she thought. A trip to Sicily with him would be devastating in Anna's world. Because she was already the focus of attention and she couldn't fathom drawing yet more. Never mind that if she were only to behave as if she didn't care, the media would soon leave her alone. He knew from experience that they liked nothing better than a victim—and Anna was a perfect victim right now.

"I don't want to go to Sicily, Leo. I want to go to Amanti."

"Tell the truth, Anna. You don't want to do that, either. But you've committed to it and so you want to get there without giving the media anything else to speculate about."

She made a frustrated noise. "Yes. This is precisely the truth. If I could run to Sicily or Egypt or Timbuktu and not have to endure another moment of this shame, I would do it. But I can't run, Leo. I have to carry on as always and wait for the scandal to pass."

It was perhaps the most honest thing she'd said yet. But he wanted more. "Tell me this, then. If you could have an affair, no consequences, no one the wiser, would you do so?"

She didn't say anything for the longest time. "I...I..."

But whatever she was about to say was lost as a light on the instrument panel flashed on. A tight knot formed in Leo's stomach as he turned his focus to the plane. He'd checked everything before they'd left Santa Maria, and everything had been fine. He wouldn't have taken off otherwise.

But something had changed in the half hour since.

CHAPTER THREE

The plane shuddered and Anna's heart leaped. Whatever she'd been about to say was forgotten as she took in Leo's sudden concentration. "What's happening?"

He didn't look at her. "We're losing fuel pressure," he said as he did something with the switches. The plane shuddered again, and the engine made a high-pitched whining noise that sent her heart into her throat.

"What does that mean?" Because she needed to know, precisely, what he was saying to her. It didn't sound good, and she didn't like the sensation of being out of control. Whatever happened, she was in a plane with Leo, high above the Mediterranean, and there was nothing she could do to fix the problem.

But that didn't mean she intended to sit quietly and hope for the best.

"It means there's a problem in the fuel line. We need to land before we run out of gas."

"Land? Where?" She scanned the horizon, saw nothing but water for kilometers. Her stomach churned. "Leo, there's nothing out here."

He checked the GPS, his long fingers flexing against the controls. "We're too far from Amanti," he finally said, concentrating on the screen. "But there's another island a few miles distant."

Another island? She didn't know what it could be, but she began to pray fervently that they would make it there. The plane bucked again, the engine sputtering before smoothing out once more. Anna gripped her seat, her fingers pressing into the leather so hard that they ached.

"Are we going to die?"

"No." His answer was swift, sure, and she took comfort in it. But doubts began to creep in. What if he was wrong? What if he was only trying to keep her calm? She couldn't abide that. She had to know.

"Tell me the truth, Leo," she finally said, unable to stand it a moment longer. "Please."

Leo's dark eyes glinted with determination as he looked over at her. How could her heart flip at the look on his face when this was serious? How could heat blossom between her thighs at a moment like this?

Because she had regrets, that's why. Because she'd saved herself for years for a husband who had cast her aside before they'd ever even wed. Now that she might die, she fervently wished she'd experienced passion, even if it had just been for one night.

Leo stared at her so intently that she could almost forget where they were, what was happening. For a moment, she could almost wish they'd had that day in Sicily.

"If we can find this island, we'll be fine," Leo said shortly.

She wanted to believe him, but she couldn't simply accept it without question. "But what if there's nowhere to land?"

"There's definitely somewhere to land," he said. "Look around you."

There was nothing but blue as far as the eye could see. She gasped as she finally took his meaning. "The sea?"

"Yes. Now put on your life jacket, and grab that orange backpack from where it's stowed behind my seat."

"But, Leo," she said, panic rising inside her as she thought of them marooned at sea. Assuming they survived the impact. *Oh, God.*

"Anna, trust me," he said firmly. "Get the pack. Get your life jacket."

"What about you?"

"Grab mine, too. I can't put it on yet, but I will."

Anna unbuckled her seat belt and found the life jackets. She clipped hers on with shaky fingers, and then grabbed the heavy orange pack he'd told her to get and brought everything back to her seat. Leo was saying something into the headset, but he didn't appear to be getting an answer.

"No," he said when she started to sit down again. "Sit in one of the seats behind me. It'll be safer on impact."

Anna hesitated only a moment before sinking into the seat beside him and buckling her seat belt. "I want to be here with you," she said. "I insist on it."

She didn't expect him to laugh, but he did. A short, sharp bark of laughter that stole into her soul and made her feel good, if only for a moment. "Dragon lady," he said, and her heart skipped again. At a time like this, how did he make her feel as if she were formidable? As if she mattered? How did he cut through the pain and anger and make her feel important again?

"There it is," Leo said, and she squinted into the distance, searching the horizon. A small gray bump rose up from the sea, growing bigger the closer they got. There were many small islands out here, some of which were inhabited and some not. Any hope she'd had this might be one of the inhabited ones faded quickly when she saw the size of the island.

It was long, narrow and rocky, with a green area at one end and a white sandy beach on one side.

"There's nowhere to land," she said.

"I'm taking us down," he replied. "It might be rough."

That was the only warning he gave her as he pointed the nose down and began his descent. Anna's stomach twisted as the plane dropped in the sky. Sweat broke out on her forehead, between her breasts. Her heart went into free fall as the sea grew bigger and bigger with every passing minute.

The engine sputtered and whined, and Leo's hands were white on the controls. But the plane continued to descend in a controlled manner. Anna grasped her pearls in her fingers, twisted hard and then chided herself for doing so. This was no time to break them. They'd been her grandmother's, the only link she had left to the woman she'd most admired. She would not destroy them.

"Leo," she said helplessly as they sank lower in the sky. She reached for him, put her hand on his shoulder, squeezed. She hoped she was imparting strength, courage, but she had the feeling he didn't need any of those things. No, it was she who needed them and Leo who provided them to her.

She could do nothing but sit there and watch powerlessly as the island got bigger. But the sea was bigger still, so big and azure that it filled her vision from all sides. She focused on the island. There were a few trees, she noted, a wooded copse that might provide shelter—and might have fresh water if the rain had a place to collect. Assuming it rained.

If only they survived the plunge into the sea. *First things first, Anna.* She was so used to planning that she couldn't help herself, when in fact there was nothing to plan if they didn't make it out alive.

"Brace for landing," Leo said as he took the plane dangerously close to the island. Anna closed her eyes at the last minute and gripped her seat for dear life. So many feelings went through her at once that she couldn't process them all. Fear, regret, anger, sadness, love, passion…

Anna's head snapped back as the plane shuddered into the water with a bone-jarring splash. It glided along the surface before coming to an abrupt stop that would have jerked her forward in the seat if not for the belt holding her tightly in place. There was a surreal moment of complete silence as the craft pitched and rolled with the waves. Anna's stomach lodged in her throat. How would they ever escape with the motion throwing them around so much? Once the seat belt was off, two steps forward would turn into four steps back.

"There's not much time," Leo said as he unbuckled his seat belt and flung his door open.

"Your jacket," she said, thrusting it toward him with a shaking hand as she unlocked her seat belt with the other. He took it and threw it out the door, then grabbed her and hauled her toward him. She barely had time to register all the sensations that rocked her as she was pressed against his hard body before she dropped into the sea.

The water was shocking, not because it was too cold, but because it was wet when she'd been so dry. The life preserver kept her from going under, but water still splashed over her head, soaking her. Anna spluttered and began to tread water as Leo landed beside her, the orange pack slung over one shoulder.

"Your life jacket," she said. It was floating just out of reach and she made a grab for it.

"I don't need it." His hair was slicked back from his head, his expression grim and determined.

"Leo," she began.

"I'm fine, Anna. Can you swim to the island?"

She turned and looked at the shore only a few meters distant. "Of course," she said crisply, her heart beating like crazy in her chest as she began to process what had happened. They'd crashed. In the Mediterranean. She couldn't quite wrap her mind around it, and yet the plane bobbed in the water nearby. The scent of salt mingling with jet fuel invaded her senses.

"We need to go now," he said. "Before we get soaked in fuel."

Leo began to stroke toward the island. She followed, easily crossing the distance before stumbling to her knees onto the shore beside him. Her hair was still in its rigid knot, but a few wisps had fallen free and snaked around her neck like tentacles. Her makeup was probably streaked and—

Oh, she'd forgotten her purse! She turned and started wading back into the water when strong arms caught her from behind.

"Where are you going?"

"My purse," she said. "My phone, my identification—"

"It's too late," he growled in her ear.

"But it's not." She pointed. The plane was still on top of the water, though the nose had begun to sink. It wouldn't take her a trifle to get out there and back again.

"It's too dangerous, Anna. Even if the plane wasn't sinking, the remaining fuel is leaching from it. Besides, was there anything irreplaceable in your purse?"

She wanted to tell him yes, of course there was. Instead, Anna slumped in his grip. "No, nothing irreplaceable." Just her lip gloss, her hand sanitizer, her headache tablets and her phone with its calendar of all her events.

Events that were sadly lacking lately. Invitations had dried up since Alex had jilted her.

She stifled a hysterical laugh. They'd crashed in the Mediterranean and she was concerned about her calendar? She needed to be thinking about survival, not social engagements.

Leo held her hard against him. She slowly became aware of his heat, of the solidity of his body where it pressed into hers. They were both soaking wet, dripping onto the sand, and she wondered for a moment why the water didn't sizzle and steam.

Anna put her hand on his where it gripped her beneath the life vest. She wanted to smooth her fingers along his skin, wanted to feel the shape of his hand, the ridges of his knuckles, but instead she loosened his grip and stepped away from him. When she turned, he was looking at her with a kind of laser intensity that made her gut clench in reaction.

Liquid heat flooded her body, her bones. Shakily, she undid the clasp on the vest and shrugged it off. She needed something to do, something that didn't involve looking at Leo.

His shirt was plastered to his chest, delineating every ridge and curve of smooth muscle. She hadn't been able to tell from the tuxedo last night, but Leo was in spectacular shape. His father had once been a famous footballer, she recalled, and Leo looked as if he'd spent quite a bit of time on the field himself. He had the leanly muscled form of an athlete.

"We need to find shelter," he said, and a hard knot formed right below her breastbone. They were stranded, alone, with nothing and no one to help them get home again.

"You were able to tell someone what happened, right?" she said. "They'll be looking for us soon."

His expression remained flat. "We were out of radio

range. I activated the emergency beacon on the plane. They'll know approximately where we went down, but it may take some time since they won't be looking for us yet."

She turned back toward the plane. "If I had my mobile phone…"

"Doesn't matter," he said. "There are no cell towers out here. You'd need a satellite phone to make a call."

"So we're stuck."

"For the time being," he replied, hefting the orange pack onto his shoulder again.

"How long will we be here, Leo?"

He shrugged. "I really don't know. Which is why we need to find shelter."

"What about food? Water? How will we survive if we don't have water?"

He gave her a long look. "We have enough water for a couple of days, if we ration it. Everything's in this pack."

Anna blinked. "You have water?"

"It's an emergency survival kit, darling. There's a bit of everything. Dried food, matches, fuel, blankets—enough to survive a few days in the wild."

He turned and started walking toward the other end of the island where she'd seen the copse of trees. Anna scrambled after him. Her feet were bare since she'd lost her shoes in the sea. She felt a momentary pang for the beautiful suede pumps that were no doubt at the bottom of the Med by now, but it was truly the least of her worries.

Part of the going was rocky, but Anna climbed after Leo and never said a word when the rocks sliced into her feet. She fell behind, but she did not call out. Why should she? He couldn't disappear. The island was small and she knew where they were headed. But Leo glanced over his shoulder at one point, stopping when she wasn't right behind him.

He frowned as she approached, his gaze on her feet. "You've lost your shoes."

"They wouldn't have been much use anyway," she said. "They were five-inch platforms."

Her one concession to impracticality.

He closed the distance between them, and then hooked an arm behind her knees and lifted her into his arms before she realized his plan.

"Leo, put me down!"

His face was close to hers. Too close. Oh, heavens. She wanted to tilt her head back, wanted to nuzzle her face into the crook of his neck and breathe in his scent. And then she wanted to lick him.

Heat flashed through her. The hot Mediterranean sun beat down on them from above, but it wasn't the sun that made her skin prickle or her core melt.

"Once we're over the rocks," he said. "I don't want you cutting your feet."

"Too late," she replied.

His coffee-colored eyes were so beautiful as he stared down at her. There was heat in them, and something darker and more intense. Something so elemental it frightened her. "You should have told me sooner."

"You have the pack," she said, dropping her gaze. Her heart hammered in her breast. Why did he affect her so much? He was completely, utterly wrong for her. He was the kind of man she should definitely avoid, and yet he thrilled her in ways she'd never expected.

He's thrilling because he's dangerous, a voice whispered. *Bad boys are always thrilling.*

"You barely weigh more than the pack does," he said. "If it gets too much for me, I'll put one of you down. Honest."

He winked on that last, and began striding toward the trees again. Anna clung to him, ashamed, miserable, grateful and oddly excited. She had to wrap her arms around his neck, had to press her face in close to his. His fingers splayed over her rib cage, dangerously close to her breast, and she held her breath for a long moment.

Would he touch her there? Did she want him to? What would she say if he did?

But they reached a sandy area and he set her down again. She tried not to be disappointed as he strode away. The sand felt good on her feet, warm on top and cool if she dug her toes down. She scrambled after Leo, catching him right as he reached the trees.

It was cooler here, and the ground was flat and somewhat sandy. Leo kept walking until he found a spot he liked, and then he set the pack down and opened it. Anna watched in amazement as he pulled out a variety of items—heavy-duty plastic sheeting with grommets, a knife and rope—before he stood and began to peel the wet shirt from his body.

If she'd thought the navy shirt molded his chest, she'd had no idea what molding meant until he stood there in a wet T-shirt and jeans. But then he yanked the T-shirt off and his chest was bare and tanned. Her gaze dropped, halted in surprise. He had a dragon tattoo low on his abdomen—

Anna gulped. And turned away. Automatically she reached for her pearls, relieved they were still there as her fingers toyed with them.

"Do I make you nervous?" Leo asked from behind her. She could hear the laughter in his voice. Deliberately she turned, dropping her hand away from her neck. *Calm, cool.*

"Of course not," she said.

He winked. "Good. Because I'm afraid the jeans are next, darling. Can't abide wet clothing."

Anna held her breath as his long fingers flicked open

the button of his jeans. She couldn't have looked away if her life depended on it. Tanned fingers slipped between the waistband and his skin, and then he was pushing the jeans down. Her heart kicked up as his hip bones appeared, and then the elastic waist of his underwear. Armani, she thought crazily. It said so on the band.

But she forgot all about it as the jeans slid down his long, strong legs, revealing tanned skin and acres of muscle. Anna couldn't breathe. Her lungs simply wouldn't fill. Had she ever seen a man as beautiful, as strong and lean and muscled, as this one?

Could this day be any more surreal? Just a few minutes ago, they'd been fully clothed strangers. And now they were marooned together and Leo was stripping out of his clothing.

"Keep staring, darling, and the show is bound to get more interesting," Leo said, his voice a growling purr that slid over her nerve endings and made her shudder.

"I've seen naked men before," she said with a sniff. "You can't shock me."

It was only a small lie: the naked man she'd seen had been on a video, not standing before her looking so vibrant and sexy that she physically hurt from looking at him. Leo wasn't wearing any less than a man might wear while swimming, and yet her insides were twisting and squeezing in a way they never had at the sight of a random man in a Speedo at the pool.

"Is that so?" he asked.

"Definitely." But her limbs felt weak.

Leo shook his head, laughing softly. "Come along then, Anna. Get out of your wet things and help me set up this shelter."

Astonishment riveted her to the spot. He wanted her to remove her clothes? She'd not thought of it before, but now it seemed as if her soaked suit clung to her uncomfortably. Her skin felt cool and clammy under the fabric, though Leo's had looked hot and silky when he'd removed his clothing.

Leo strode over to her and began to gently push her jacket from her shoulders. "Come on, Anna, it's all right. You've had a shock. Let's get you out of these wet things. I'll put everything in the sun and it'll be dry again in no time. You can armor yourself behind your buttoned-up clothing quite soon, I promise."

"There's nothing wrong with my clothes," she protested, though she let him tug her jacket down her arms.

"Nothing at all," he agreed.

"Then why did you say it?" She stepped away from him as the jacket fell free and crossed her arms over her breasts. How could she possibly take off her camisole and skirt? How could she stand before him in her bra and panties?

Leo sighed. "Because you're beautiful, Anna. Your clothes should show how beautiful you are, not hide it."

"I'm not hiding anything," she protested, her heart throbbing at the compliment. "My suit is professional, conservative. There's nothing wrong with that."

"No. But I don't think it's really you."

He'd said that to her earlier, and it was no less irritating now. "How can you conceivably think such a thing? We hardly know each other, Mr. Jackson."

She was proud of herself for sounding frosty, though her insides were sizzling hot. Leo was a stunning man and he was standing before her in nothing but a pair of black briefs with a white waistband. He had a dragon tattoo she oddly wanted to press her mouth to. And he'd just told her she was beautiful.

But she knew he didn't mean it—or he did mean it, but the same as he meant it when he'd told whichever woman he'd spent the night with last night that she was beautiful, too. Leo was a playboy, the kind of man who was pretty to look at—and probably amazing to spend the night with—but who had absolutely no intentions beyond a night of pleasure.

He was a glorious, beautiful creature designed for one thing only: to ruin the women he took to his bed. Not ruin in the old-fashioned sense, but ruin in the sense that she couldn't imagine how they ever found another lover to satisfy them once they'd had a taste of him.

Leo snorted. "And when you don't retreat behind clothing, you retreat behind stiff formality. I think we've crossed some sort of barrier that prohibits us from using the terms *mister* and *miss,* don't you?"

"Not at all. Politeness is always acceptable." It was what she'd been taught. Always be gracious, even when you were aching inside. A lady smiled through adversity. A lady didn't let anyone see when she was hurting. A lady never complained.

His snort turned into full-blown laughter. A hot current of mortification blazed through her at the sound. Why did she say such silly things? Why did she open herself up to his amusement? Leo was the kind of man who said and did what he wanted, and damn the consequences. He couldn't understand her world, couldn't understand why she had to behave stoically and graciously in the face of humiliation.

"Politeness?" he said. "I'm almost naked, darling. And if no one arrives in the next few hours to rescue us, we'll be sharing body heat under a blanket tonight. We've moved far beyond polite, don't you think?"

CHAPTER FOUR

ANNA'S heart pounded in her chest. Leo had an edge that both compelled her and frightened her. And when he talked of sharing a blanket—sharing body heat—she began to shiver deep inside.

"If you don't want to be naked when we share that heat, I suggest you take those clothes off and let them dry in the sun."

She didn't want to do so, and yet she knew she had little choice. It was either that or sit in the sun with her clothes on and risk a severe sunburn while she waited for everything to dry. Since her teeth were beginning to chatter, her only option was removal.

Jerkily, her fingers found her zipper and tugged it down. And then she was peeling the skirt from her body, tossing it aside, daring him to say a word as she did so. She almost lost her courage when it came time to remove the camisole, but she told herself it was the same as wearing a bikini—so she peeled the wet camisole upward and shrugged it off.

She looked up then, met Leo's gaze. Realized he hadn't moved since she'd begun to strip. He was staring at her, his dark eyes gleaming hotly. There was something dangerous in his stare, something too intense to fathom. She was perversely happy she'd put on a matching bra and panty set today. They were lacy, pink and not too revealing. *It's a bikini,* she told herself. *A bikini.*

Except that Leo wasn't looking at her like she was wearing a bikini. No, he was looking at her with far more heat and intimacy than if she were dressed in a swimming costume. No man had ever looked at her quite like that before. It was...thrilling. And nerve-racking.

Anna wrapped her arms around her body self-consciously and walked past him to where the pack lay. "Are we building this shelter or not?" she asked crisply, kneeling beside the heavy plastic sheeting. She had to do something, or make an even bigger fool of herself.

She heard him move, and then he reached down and lifted her gently.

"You're cold," he said. And then he pulled her into his embrace, her bare skin coming into heart-stopping contact with his as he pressed her against him, breast to belly to hip.

Her first instinct was to push away, to put as much distance between them as possible, but he was warm and dry and not the least bit clammy. His heat flowed into her, warmed her cold limbs.

But it was more than that, she realized.

It was sexual heat, embarrassment and longing all rolled into one. Her skin prickled at his nearness. Leo chafed his hands along her arms, her back. For him it was practical while for her...

What an amateur she was! What a pitiful, clueless amateur.

Anna turned her head slightly, breathed in the scent of his skin where her head was pressed to his chest. He smelled like salt, but under that he smelled like soap and spice. She wanted to lick him.

Anna closed her eyes. What was with this constant urge to lick him? Was he an ice cream cone? A lollipop?

Need washed through her, made her knees weak. Thankfully Leo was holding her close, or she'd surely sink to the ground. One hand touched her head, rubbed softly—but no, he wasn't rubbing, he was finding the pins of her knot and pulling them free.

Her hair tumbled loose and she gasped. Automatically she reached up with one hand, wanting to smooth it back into place. But it was a bedraggled rope hanging down her back. No amount of smoothing would help at this point.

She tilted her head back to look up at Leo. His eyes danced with mischief. And something else. Something hot and intense that frightened her as much as it intrigued her. He was a hard man, a ruthless man when he wanted something. She could see that in him, behind the smiles and winks, behind the *darlings*. This was a man who conquered, who took everything and left nothing behind. Would he take her if she allowed it? Would there be anything left when he was done?

Anna shivered again, and not from cold this time. "Why did you do that?" she asked.

"Because your hair will dry faster if you take it down."

Oddly, disappointment spiraled inside her. Part of her had hoped he would say he'd done it because he wanted to see her hair, but of course he was being practical. And yet his eyes darkened, his nostrils flaring as he looked down at her.

His gaze dropped to her lips and her heartbeat slowed to a crawl. He was going to kiss her. She wanted him to kiss her, wanted it almost more than she wanted her next breath. She wanted to feel the heat, the sizzle, the storm of this man's kiss.

But not like this. A thread of panic unwound in her

brain. She didn't want her first real kiss to be an afterthought. For him, it was like breathing. For her, it was everything she'd never had.

"No," she said softly as he dipped his head toward hers, her throat aching as she forced the word out.

Leo stopped, straightened. He looked frustrated. Annoyed.

"I've never," she began, trying to explain. "Never…"

She couldn't say it, couldn't admit the shame of never having been kissed. She was twenty-eight years old. She'd been waiting her whole life for a man who had thought less than nothing about rejecting her at the last possible moment. She'd spent years preparing for a wedding that wasn't ever going to happen. Saving herself for a man who didn't want her.

Anger blazed to life like a bonfire. And sadness. She'd missed so much, hadn't she?

"Never what, Anna?"

Her stomach churned. She dropped her head, closed her eyes. "I've never kissed a man before," she said, her voice a husky whisper. Shame clawed into her, singed her with its icy sting. She was a woman who'd never been kissed, who'd never been loved. She was a woman who should have had all those things, and far sooner than now.

Leo went very, very still. She could feel the incredible control he exercised, the restraint, the sudden hum of tension in his body as he stood so still and held her close. "Alessandro never…?"

She shook her head, unable to speak the word. It was humiliating. As if the stories in the papers weren't enough to make her want to hide her head in the sand forever, the secret knowledge that she'd never been kissed properly, never desired, was infinitely worse.

Leo's strong fingers cupped her jaw, tilted her head up.

What she saw in his face made her heart squeeze tight. "He was a fool, Anna. Do you understand me? A bloody fool."

And then he pressed his lips to her forehead, gently, sweetly, and she drew in a soft breath laced with tears. A sob hovered in her throat, but she would not let it escape. She barely knew this man, and here she was pressed against him, hot skin to hot skin, her deepest secrets spilling out as if the dam behind which she kept them had suddenly sprung a leak.

Her fingers curled against the hard plane of his chest. He was so warm, so vibrant and alive. She'd never been so close to a man, never felt the things she was feeling right now.

A dagger of need sliced into her. Her sex ached with want. Her nipples were sensitive points against the lace of her bra. Her breasts tingled. She wanted Leo to touch her everywhere. To show her what it meant to make love.

His body was hard against hers. Some parts were harder than others, she realized. His hips pressed into her, his erection unmistakable where it thrust against her belly. A hot, hollow feeling bloomed in her core. If she were an experienced woman, if she'd done this before and knew what she was doing, she'd run her hands over his torso and slide them beneath the waistband of his sexy, sexy underwear.

But she was a virgin, a stupid, insecure virgin, and she was afraid of what she'd never actually done. Afraid of unleashing something she couldn't control, of losing her reason and sanity.

She ached and she wanted and she stood very still while Leo kissed her forehead. And then he took a step back, setting her away from him. His eyes were hotter than she'd ever seen them, and his body...

Oh, heavens, his body was beautiful, his muscles so

tense and perfect, his erection now straining against the confines of the briefs.

"Leo…" She didn't know what to say, what to do. She wanted him to do it for her.

But he turned away. "Let's fix this shelter," he said gruffly.

Leo was out of his depth and he wasn't accustomed to it. His usual relationships were simple affairs involving women who knew what they were getting into when they dated him. He was typically monogamous, but serial. His affairs lasted days or weeks or, in some cases, months.

There was no falling in love, no happily ever afters. He didn't believe in them anyway. He'd grown up in Bobby Jackson's household, where his father's relationships with women were anything but normal. Women were the revolving door of Bobby's life. Leo figured it was possible to love one woman forever, but not for a Jackson male. The closest he'd come to a stable relationship was with Jessica Monroe, and that had ended in disaster when she'd wanted more than he could give.

Marriage and children were not for him, and he wouldn't be like Bobby and attempt to do something he was genetically doomed to fail at. The least he could do was spare his nonexistent children the shame of having a Jackson for a father.

Dear God, Anna. She was innocent and incredibly sexy, though she didn't seem to realize it, and Leo wanted her so badly he was having a tough time keeping his body from reacting. He could *not* have her. He reminded himself forcefully of that fact as he glanced over at her. She was too innocent to engage in a torrid affair—to *know* that it was simply an affair.

If he made love to her, she'd want forever. She'd thought

that's what she was getting from Prince Alessandro, and she'd happily ordered her life with that end in mind. How could she reformat her thinking simply to gratify Leo's baser urges?

She couldn't, and he wouldn't touch her no matter how he ached.

They'd set up the shelter and he'd gone to lay their clothes in the sun to dry. For once, he prayed they'd be dressed again very soon. Not that he didn't appreciate a gorgeous woman in her underwear, but Anna was so innocent that he felt like a jackass for ogling her. For wanting her.

And he definitely, definitely wanted her. He wanted to fill his hands with her lushness, wanted to slip that lacy pink bra from her shoulders and cup his hands around the mounds of her breasts. He wanted to see the tight points of those nipples he'd felt pressing into him, and then he wanted to fill his senses with her. He wanted to skim his mouth along the sweet skin of her belly and slide her panties from her hips before opening her delicate femininity to his gaze and sliding his tongue along the wet seam of her sex.

He wanted to make Anna come, wanted her to scream his name. He wanted to give her everything she'd missed out on, and he wanted to brand her as his when he did so.

But he couldn't do it. It wasn't fair to her. She was vulnerable and hurting and he couldn't take advantage of her. When he'd thought she was simply an uptight woman who'd been jilted by her fiancé, he'd imagined a bit of sexual fun was exactly what she needed to take her mind off her troubles.

He might be bad, but he wasn't so bad as to seduce an innocent virgin who'd never been kissed before. He had a conscience, no matter if it had often been reported otherwise.

"How long do you think it will take them to find us?" Anna asked, cutting into his thoughts.

He looked over at her and almost wished he hadn't as his gut twisted with longing. Her hair was long, brunette, and she'd finger combed it before it had dried into a tousled, thick mane that suited her far more than her sleek chignons did. He wanted to run his hands through that hair, wanted to bury his fingers in it and tilt her head back while he plundered her mouth with his own.

His body responded in spite of himself, the blood pooling in his groin, filling him. *Ah, damn.* What, was he sixteen again? Unable to exercise even a little bit of control?

Except it wasn't a little control where Anna was concerned, it was a lot. Especially when he could see the raw need shimmering in her eyes.

Leo shrugged casually when he felt anything but casual. "I doubt they'll be looking for us for hours yet."

She frowned. "I was afraid you'd say that."

"We'll be fine, darling," he said lightly. "We have food, water, shelter. All the necessities."

She turned her head away, her hair falling over her shoulder and seemingly caressing one gorgeous breast. He was jealous of her hair at that moment. "That's not what worries me."

It took him a moment to figure out what she meant. At first he thought she meant she was worried to be alone with him, but then he realized it was something far more significant in Anna's world. Something far more insidious. It wasn't being alone with him so much as the perception that being alone with him would create.

"Anna, you can't live your life in fear of what the tabloids will say."

She turned back to him then, her jade-green eyes flashing. "What do you know of it? You're a man, a veritable *god* for all your exploits. I've had nothing but humiliation from them. If they know I'm out here, alone, with you—"

Leo resisted the urge to swear, but barely. "Do you plan to live your entire life by the numbers? Do you think that if only you are good enough, they'll leave you alone?"

She gaped at him. Angry. Fearful. "I…I…"

He wanted to punch something. For her. He wanted her to fight back, wanted her to not give a damn—and he knew he couldn't make her do it. That was his style, not hers. Had his mother given a damn? She must have, since she'd saved the articles. And yet she'd survived it, just as he'd survived the attention later, after her death.

"It doesn't work that way, Anna. Whatever sells magazines or papers is what works. You—and Alessandro and Allegra—are the flavor of the moment. You will *always* be the poor little bride who lost her groom on the eve of the wedding. Always. It's up to you to choose how you deal with it."

She swallowed hard. "How?"

How? It seemed absurd that he was being asked to give advice on dealing with the press since he'd never much cared one way or the other what they'd said about him—since growing up anyway—but he could see she was serious. That she believed he had the answer since his family were in fact a tabloid staple. Thanks to his father.

Bobby didn't care what the press said, so long as they said *something*. His greatest fear, Leo thought, was becoming irrelevant. So long as the media were printing stories, Bobby felt he was doing something right. Even when he'd been in the papers for the wrong reasons—affairs, fights, money trouble, refusing to acknowledge his ten-year-old son until the courts shoved a paternity test in his face. Bobby mined it all and emerged from a pile of excrement smelling like roses.

And yet that wouldn't work for Anna. She didn't want or need the attention. She didn't crave it.

Leo drew in a breath. He told her the only thing he knew how to tell her. "By being happy. By living your life. By refusing to adhere to some standard you believe some anonymous *they* want from you. You're Anna Constantinides and you're free to be your own person. Screw the press and screw whatever you thought you were supposed to do with your life. The truth, sweet Anna, is that nothing you thought you were going to be is possible any longer."

Her eyes flashed with pain and fury. "I know that."

Leo clenched his fists at his sides to keep from pulling her to him and wrapping her in his embrace. Why did he feel such a strong urge to protect this woman? He wanted her, but that wasn't anything unusual for him. But to shelter her from pain? That was a completely new bit of territory he'd broken, and he still wasn't quite sure how to deal with it.

It must be because of his mother, because he'd never forgotten how she must have kept those articles year after year. Had she reread them? Or had she stashed them away and never looked at them again? He would never know. But he couldn't stand the idea of Anna brooding over what the press said for years to come.

"Then do what you want, Anna," he told her fiercely, trying to impart strength. "Stop trying to please whomever you think it is you must please. Be the dragon lady I know you can be."

She dropped her gaze, studied her feet. Or so it seemed. "My mother is Queen Zoe's best friend. Did you know that?"

He did not. And it made the whole thing seem uglier somehow. "No."

"They've been planning this wedding since we were

children. Hoping to unite our families. I have always been Alex's bride, even when I was a six-year-old playing with dolls. It was predestined."

The thought made him angry. Not because he was suddenly judgmental of the way royals ordered their lives, but because someone had told a little girl that this was her destiny and none other would do. She'd never been allowed to choose for herself, never been allowed to grow other than to grow into Prince Alessandro's wife. Everything she'd done had been in preparation for that life. He could see that now.

And it had all come to nothing because Alessandro had met Allegra. Leo loved his sister and wished her all the happiness in the world, but at the moment he was more than furious with Alessandro, a man who'd thought nothing of abandoning his bride-to-be. And he was furious with the Santinas and Constantinideses.

"They were wrong to do that to you, Anna." *All* of them, he silently added. "You should have been allowed to choose for yourself."

She blew out a breath as she combed her fingers through her hair. It was an impossibly sexy gesture. He didn't think she realized it. In fact, he knew she didn't. His groin tightened painfully.

"Perhaps. But it's what I was raised to do. Our mothers planned it when we were toddlers. I've never known quite why, except that I believe my mother and Queen Zoe seemed to think it was the perfect way to ensure the purity of the Santina dynasty."

"The purity? Isn't your father Greek?"

"Yes, but my mother is from Santina originally. Though I don't believe that is the sort of purity they had in mind. It is more of a tradition thing. Someone from another country might not...suit the Santina expectations. They are, as you may have noticed, quite conservative in their thinking. Very traditional. For my parents, it was an honor to have me chosen as the future queen."

"And it never occurred to you to object," he stated.

She shrugged. "Why would it? That was no doubt part of the plan. A girl raised to be a bride, a queen, would not question it, would she?" She shook her head. "Changing everything now—doing what I want to do, as you put it— is a bit like being marooned here with you. Not at all what I expected."

"And did you expect to be here in your knickers?" he teased, though he did not feel like laughing. "What a singular experience, sweet Anna. Think what you will be able to tell your grandchildren."

She looked up sharply, and he wanted to bite his tongue off. Now was not the time to mention progeny to the woman who'd thought she would bear the heir to the throne of Santina some day.

"I think," she said very softly, "that I'll simply see how today goes before I start thinking of the future."

Leo leaned back against a tree trunk and watched her. She was so elegant, so graceful, even in her underwear. She *should* have been a queen. She was the right woman to be a queen. Anger buzzed in his veins like an electrical pulse.

She'd accepted her fate so easily, resigned herself to being a king-in-waiting's future bride. And he suddenly wanted to know if it's what she would have chosen for herself.

"Did you love him, Anna?"

Green eyes brimming with emotion gazed at him steadily. The desire hovering beneath the surface of his psyche flared to life again, its heat scorching and painful. Because it would not be fulfilled. Because he couldn't allow it to be fulfilled.

But Anna pulled at him. Her eyes, her skin, her dark, beautiful hair. Her presence. The wounded woman beneath the buttoned-up suits and dainty femininity drew him in a way that continually surprised him.

He didn't want or need anyone. And yet he wanted *her*. He always got what he wanted because he never gave up until he won. But this time was different. This time, he had to walk away instead of conquer.

"You asked me that already," she said softly. But she didn't look away, didn't dissemble in the way she'd done only a few hours ago.

"And you didn't answer," he replied.

She bit her bottom lip and a shot of lust bolted straight to his groin. *He* wanted to bite that lip. She looked so damn demure in her lacy pink underwear and pearls. Had he ever experienced such a crazy situation in his life? Marooned with a virgin on a deserted island. A virgin who had his libido slipping into overdrive and his body humming with suppressed sexual tension.

"I was," she finally said. "Or I thought I was. When you spend your entire life preparing to marry one person, you start to believe you might love him."

It was an answer, and not an answer. He found it strangely frustrating. "What do you feel now that he's marrying my sister? What bothers you more, the fact you've lost him or the fact the media won't let you forget it?"

She seemed to think about it for a moment before answering. "I thought those feelings were all tangled together, but maybe they aren't. Because I don't hate Allegra, and I don't hate that Alex is marrying her. I hate what it's done to me, how I feel knowing I've wasted so much time preparing for something that won't ever happen."

She shot to her feet then and Leo thought she looked like an Amazon. A petite Amazon, but a fiery one nonetheless. She looked as if she could chew nails for breakfast. He wanted to laugh. Anna was fiery, passionate. She locked it away beneath her suits and her pearls but the woman was a warrior in her soul. A dragon lady.

Her eyes flashed fire. And then she swore long and loud in Greek. Leo leaned back and watched it all happen, amazed and aroused by the display of so much passion. Hell, if she weren't a virgin, they'd burn up together. She'd know what she was getting into and he wouldn't feel in the least bit guilty for taking advantage of her passionate nature.

"I am tired of being the last person everyone thinks about," she said. "I'm tired of doing what's expected of me, of trying so hard to be the best at whatever task I'm given. I'm tired of keeping quiet and bearing it all with a serene smile. I'm tired of following a list of rules that have been drummed into me since I was old enough to talk, and I'm tired of—" here she pressed both hands to her chest "—and I'm tired of being a cold, frigid person that no man wants to touch passionately. I want passion, Leo. I want love and heat and sex. I want it all. And I want it *now*."

CHAPTER FIVE

ANNA's body was on fire. With fury, with lust, with so many feelings that she couldn't contain them all. He was right, damn him. She didn't really love Alex. She'd thought she had, but she was far angrier over the way she was being portrayed in the media than she was over the fact she would never be the Queen of Santina.

And she was angry with her parents, with the Santinas, because she felt like she'd let them all down by failing to capture Alex's heart when it had never been hers to capture. Not that they'd said anything or chastised her for it, but she felt that way nevertheless. She knew what their hopes had been. Their dreams.

And it was all lying in ruins now.

Alex had never given her a reason to think he loved her, never given her anything beyond the courtesy she'd deserved as his fiancée. He'd never led her to believe there would be love between them.

She'd filled in the blanks on her own. She'd taken his quiet acceptance of their arranged marriage as tacit approval of her and of their future together.

She'd been so blind, so dumb. So damn obedient.

She was through being obedient.

She was through doing what everyone expected.

She was *through*.

Leo was still leaning back against the tree trunk, though he looked anything but casual in that moment. He was watching her with interest. Hot, sharp interest. As if she were a dessert he wanted to devour. As if she were a cold drink of water on a hot day. As if she were a lifeline in a stormy sea.

She was none of those things, but she thrilled to that heated look on his handsome face. She had never, ever been looked at like that before. No man had ever made her tingle like this, or made her limbs soften and ache. She was jumpy, itchy, her skin stretched too tight to contain everything she felt. She would burst with it if she didn't do something soon.

But what? She'd told him she wanted heat and sex and passion right now—and she did, but she was also scared of it. Scared to take the leap and crash and burn instead of soar. It was not like her to leap without a solid plan, without a safety net. It went against everything she'd ever thought about herself.

"Anna," Leo said, his voice edgy and taut.

And she knew then, before she'd even made up her mind about what happened next, he was refusing her. Without another word, without anything else passing between them, she *knew* he was rejecting her. Leo didn't want her. Alex didn't want her. She wasn't desirable, in spite of the way Leo had held her earlier, his body hardening against hers. It had been an illusion, a reaction brought about by proximity and not a true craving.

And the way he'd looked at her just now? Clearly, she was no good at reading the meaning behind his expression. She'd been wrong. Wrong, wrong, wrong.

A fresh wave of humiliation washed over her. Was she truly that clueless? Truly that blind?

Tears of frustration, tears of anger, filled her. And she

would rather do anything else than cry in front of this man. She would gut fish for a living before she would let him know how shattered she was by his rejection.

"I can't do this," he said, and the tears pressed hard against her eyes, demanding release. "I can't take advantage of what you offer, no matter how much I might want to."

"Don't," she bit out, her voice sharper than she'd ever allowed it to be. "For goodness' sake, don't lie to me."

His expression grew stormy. "You think I'm lying about this?"

She laughed, the sound harsh and bitter. "Of course you are! I know who you are, Leo! I have eyes! I saw you this morning—you hadn't even been to bed when I knocked on the door, or at least not to your own bed. When you want a woman, you take her, especially if she offers herself to you." She wrapped her arms around her torso and tilted her chin up. Her lip was trembling badly. "I must conclude then that you do not want *me.*"

He swore. "Dammit, you are dense," he grated. "I'm trying to be decent—"

"I don't want you to be decent!" she yelled. "I don't want you *thinking* for me or *telling* me what to do. I'm sick of that, sick of everyone thinking they know what I need more than I do!"

"You're acting on impulse," he growled. "And that's not like you. For pity's sake, *think.* I'm not what you want."

"How dare you," she threw at him. "How absolutely dare you? You're the one who has badgered me since the first moment we met about being my own person, about doing my own thing, about being too uptight and buttoned up and…and…rigid."

"Anna…"

"No," she yelled. "No!" It was too much suddenly. She

turned blindly, before the angry tears that hovered on the edge spilled free, and fled toward the sea. It was only a short distance before she was leaping off a small cliff and into the cool blue water. The tiny cuts on her feet burned anew, but she ignored the pain. She'd treated them with antiseptic from Leo's survival kit earlier, and this didn't burn any worse than that had.

She dove down, down, down, testing her lungs, letting them ache before she turned and kicked hard toward the surface. The sun filtered down into the depths, making the water above ripple and sparkle. It was so quiet down here, so peaceful. She could stay down here forever if only it were possible. Down in the depths of the ocean where pain couldn't touch her. Where no one pointed a finger and laughed at her. Where she wasn't pitiful, but isolated from pity.

She kicked again, realizing she'd gone somewhat deeper than she'd first thought she had. The surface wasn't too far, and she wasn't worried about reaching it, but nonetheless a pair of strong arms enclosed around her body and yanked her skyward.

"Are you insane?" Leo demanded when they breeched the surface together. Anna gulped air, the hot burn of it expanding in her lungs. If felt so good to breathe after she'd denied herself for so long. Almost like learning to live when you'd denied yourself the very basics of life— like passion and love and sexual heat.

Anna threw her head back and laughed. This was what it was like to be alive. This…this—rebellion. Yes, by God, *rebellion.* She'd never rebelled in her life, never questioned her fate or her teaching. She'd done everything they asked, been everything they'd told her to be—

And it hadn't been good enough. She'd failed at the one task they'd set for her.

And she didn't care. Dammit, she didn't care! It was liberating not to care.

"Anna!" Leo cried, gripping her shoulders and shaking her hard. They treaded water together, their limbs brushing each other. Each brush was like the stroke of a tiny flame against her skin. His body was hard against hers, his skin hot where the water was cool. He was so very alive, so vibrant, so large and real and *here*.

She wanted to live in the moment for once in her life, wanted to forget about the past, the future, and just *be*.

"Let me go, Leo!" she cried. Because she didn't want to be held against him like this, didn't want the shame of knowing how badly she'd embarrassed herself with him. She'd had enough embarrassment to last her a lifetime. If he let her go, she could float on her back and laugh up at the sun and tell herself she didn't care about anything at all. Not anymore.

"Why did you do that?" Leo demanded. "You could have hurt yourself!"

She slicked her hair back from her face, tilted her chin up defiantly. "Because I *wanted* to. Because I never do what I want. Because I always do what everyone else wants. Now," she said, her jaw tightening. "Let. Me. Go."

Leo's fingers dug into her ribs. It was exciting, thrilling. "Do you have any idea how beautiful you are when you're angry?" he growled.

Her heart skipped a beat. Her stomach clenched tight. "No, don't you dare say that," she lashed out. "You don't want me. You said so."

"I never said that," he grated. "Never. What I don't want is to take advantage of you."

Anna laughed recklessly. "How can you take advantage of me if it's what I want?"

His dark eyes flashed. His hair was slicked to his head,

molding the fine shape of his skull. His face was hard, handsome, perfectly beautiful. How had she ever, ever thought Alex handsome when Leo was in the world?

"You aren't thinking like yourself," he said. "You're reacting to everything that's happened. Taking what you offer wouldn't be fair. Have you forgotten that only this morning you refused me?"

Her cheeks burned. No, she hadn't forgotten—but everything had changed in the space of a few hours. She was tired of being staid, boring Anna. She was ready to be—if only for a little while—exciting Anna who did what she wanted and didn't regret it.

"God, you are arrogant," she breathed. "So certain you know what's right for me. For the world, I'll bet. But you don't, Leo! I will decide what's best for me. From now on, I'll decide. Isn't that what you said? What you told me to do? How can you turn around now and say I'm wrong?"

His expression hardened. His fingers burned into her. His skin was on fire. Her core flooded with heat, her nipples hardening as he brought her closer. They'd drifted toward the rocks, the gray smooth rocks that she'd dived over in her flight. Nearby was a long strip of white sandy beach.

"This is different," he grated.

"Why? Because I'm a virgin? Because you're worried I'll want something from you that you can't give me?"

He looked stunned for a moment, and she knew she'd hit home. It hurt in a way, and it was also liberating. Yes, Leo Jackson, notorious playboy, was afraid that the jilted bride was looking for a replacement husband. How terribly insulting.

It made her feel bold, wild. Reckless in a way she'd never been. She lifted her legs and wrapped them around his torso. His eyes glittered, something very dangerous springing to life in their depths. "You're playing with fire, sweet Anna."

"Maybe I want to get burned." It was the most irresponsible thing she'd ever said, and she felt so free saying it. Defiant.

Leo brought her closer then, his hips flexing against her. Her breath caught, a tiny current of cold fear threatening to douse her in reality. She was indeed playing with fire.

Because he was hard, the ridge of his impressive erection riding against the thin layer of her panties. Anna nearly swallowed her tongue. What was she doing? Was she really so brave? Was she ready for this? Could she abandon herself for a few hours on this island and then go back to Santina—and Amanti—as if nothing had ever happened?

Maybe.

Or maybe not.

But she was determined to find out. They could have died when the plane crashed into the sea. She would have died without knowing passion. That thought more than any other spurred her forward.

"I'm trying to protect you," Leo said, his voice strained and taut. "I'm no good, Anna. I won't offer you forever. You have to know that."

She thought of him this morning in his tux with the pink lipstick on the collar. He was a playboy, a rogue, a man for whom pleasure was a supreme goal. He winked and smiled and charmed, and women fell into his bed.

But maybe that's why he was the right man for this. He knew what he was doing. She was wildly attracted to him. When they were rescued, they would go their separate ways and she could concentrate on building her life anew. With whomever she wanted. However she wanted.

She was free for the first time in her life. Free to make

her own choice. And though it was one of the most frightening things she'd ever done, she was choosing Leo. For now.

"Who said anything about forever? I'm asking you for your body, nothing else."

His expression was tortured, even while the flames in the depths of his eyes leaped higher. "Anna," he said gruffly as she flexed her hips against him. Sensation streaked through her at the contact. Oh, if she just kept flexing her hips and rubbing herself against him…

He gripped her waist in his broad hands, and she realized he'd moved them toward the beach and could stand on the bottom now. "You'll regret it," he said. "Today, you might want me, but tomorrow you'll be sorry you gave yourself away to someone who doesn't deserve it. Save yourself for a man who loves you, Anna."

Anna threw her head back and blasted the air with a few choice words in Greek. "Stop trying to save me from myself," she finally said. "I'm a grown woman and it's past time I did what I wanted to do. I've been saving myself for one particular man for years. And it's caused me nothing but grief!"

Leo closed his eyes and muttered a curse. And then he was moving with her, taking them up the beach until he laid her down in the wet sand and came down on top of her. A sliver of excitement ricocheted through her as his body pressed into hers. She tilted her hips up, her sex aching with need as sweet sensation hummed inside her.

"Heaven help me, I can't say no," he told her. "I'm selfish, Anna, and I want what you're offering me. Remember that later."

"I don't care," she whispered.

Leo's eyes were dark, hot and full of promise. Anna was afraid—of course she was!—but she was also ready to live. To do something wholly for herself without regard to what anyone else thought or believed.

He propped himself on an elbow, one hand coming up to stroke the wet skin between her breasts. Water beaded in the trail he left behind. And then he was cupping her jaw, tilting her head back, his head lowering so slowly she thought she might scream.

"I'm going to kiss you, Anna. The way you should have been kissed long before now."

Her eyes fluttered closed, and then Leo's mouth was on hers, his lips full and warm against her own. Anna's heart beat hard as he kissed her. It was a soft kiss, a lovely kiss. Everything she could have hoped for in her first real kiss.

And yet she knew there was more, knew that a kiss could grow wild and needy, and she wanted that. Wanted Leo to kiss her like he was starved for her. She moved beneath him, and he made a noise in his throat that sounded so sexy she wanted to melt.

"Patience," he said against her mouth.

"No," she breathed.

He laughed, and then his tongue touched the seam of her lips. She opened to him, her arms drifting up to wrap around his neck as his tongue plunged into her mouth and tangled with her own.

He tasted like salt and mint and his mouth was hot compared to the coolness of the water. Kissing Leo was a revelation, an unveiling of worlds she'd known existed but had never experienced for herself.

So *this* was what kissing was about. How could your body ache so much from the fusing of mouths? How could you feel so hot and unsettled simply from that one act? How could you want so much more than you'd ever wanted before? How could you feel as if you *needed* more or you would die?

Leo's hand left her jaw, slid down her neck until his fingers spanned her breast. Her nipples were tight points, and he made that sound she loved when he realized it. His thumb teased across her aroused flesh, sending little spikes of pleasure shooting through her body. If she were that sensitive when he touched her through the fabric, what would happen when he removed her bra?

His arousal pressed against her, creating the most delicious sensation whenever either of them moved. She wanted more of that feeling, more of the sensation of spiraling out of control. She wanted it before she started to think too much, before she started to remind herself of all the reasons she shouldn't do this. She was determined to be brave, to do her own thing, but a lifetime of habits didn't cease with one decision.

The kiss grew hotter, Leo demanding more from her, and she answered him eagerly, drinking his kisses as if they were water in the desert. He peeled her bra away from one breast, and then he was kneading her nipple between his thumb and forefinger while she gasped and arched into the caress.

He broke the kiss and bent to her breast, sucking her tight nipple between his lips. The desire was explosive. Every tug of his mouth created an answering spike of pleasure in her sex.

The surf gently rolled in, covering their lower bodies on every wave, but Anna didn't care if it covered her head so long as Leo never stopped what he was doing. She realized she was clasping him to her, her fingers buried in his lush, dark hair. He peeled the cup from her other breast and sucked that nipple, too, his fingers taking over where his mouth left off on the breast he'd abandoned.

"Leo," she gasped as she tilted her head back in the sand. The sky above was so bright, so blue. The sun was sinking toward the horizon, and dusk wasn't too far away now. No one had come for them—and she was perversely glad.

Abruptly, Leo stood and reached out for her. "Not here," he said.

She took his hand and let him pull her up and lead her toward the shelter. There, he pressed her down onto the survival blanket he'd laid out earlier. The blanket was silver, made of thin thermal sheeting, and Leo paused for a moment, grinning.

"What?" she said, her heart pounding recklessly.

"Gives new meaning to 'served up on a platter.'"

She looked at him quizzically.

"The blanket is silver, like a serving platter. And you are delectable." He came down on top of her, hovering above her body without quite touching her. "And I am a *very* lucky man."

"Leo, please," she said as his mouth dipped to her throat. She wanted more. She wanted more now. Before she let her brain take over and ruin everything.

"All in good time, sweet Anna. But first, I need you to know you can stop this at any time." He gazed down at her, his expression grave, serious, and her heart turned over in her chest. "Just say no, and I'll stop. Got it?"

Anna nodded. She didn't want to say no, and yet she had to acknowledge that she was uncertain enough of herself to possibly do so. Knowing she could was a huge relief.

He bent to kiss her again, his hand burrowing behind her back. A moment later, she felt her bra snap free. For a brief moment she wanted to hug the fabric to her body, to keep herself hidden, but as Leo tugged it up her arms and off, she let go. His remarkable eyes were so dark, so hot, as his gaze slipped over her.

"You are too perfect for words," he said, before he claimed her mouth again.

By slow degrees his kisses grew more heated, more demanding, his tongue sliding against hers in a rhythm that sent pleasure spiking inside her body, inside the aching core of her sex. The fire burned brighter, hotter with every kiss.

She'd never felt like this, never felt this combination of heat and pain that filled her and made her desperate for relief. When would that relief happen? When would he enter her body and take her over the edge?

She craved it. Feared it. Needed it.

But Leo was in no hurry. He worked his way down her body, kissing her skin, licking her the way she'd wanted to lick him, while she squirmed and gasped. Every touch was a revelation. Every stroke of his fingers and tongue on her body only spiraled the need higher until she was ready to beg him.

"Leo," she said urgently.

"Patience, Anna," he said against her skin, the vibration of his voice humming into the deepest recesses of her soul. "I promise you won't regret it."

His mouth trailed over her abdomen, his tongue dipping into her belly button, and then he was sliding her panties from her hips and pushing her legs open for his view. She made a sound of protest, sudden embarrassment scorching her from the inside out. She'd never opened herself to a man, never experienced that moment when his eyes darkened and his jaw hardened—and then his gaze shot to hers, a question in his gorgeous eyes.

"Shall I stop?" he said, and she knew it wasn't an easy thing for him to ask. He sounded tense, edgy. Cautious. And her heart melted.

He looked so beautiful hovering over her, his jaw shadowed with stubble, his dark eyes glittering hot. His erection strained against the fabric of his briefs and she found herself staring at that part of him, wondering how badly this might hurt the first time.

She wouldn't lie to him. "I want to stop," she said softly. His muscles tensed. She knew in that moment he would stand, would walk away and leave her alone if it was what she truly wanted. "But I want to continue even more."

"Oh, Anna," he groaned. And then he bent and kissed her again, his fingers slipping into the slick heat between her legs, his thumb sliding across her clitoris. Sensation crashed through her. She'd done this for herself, of course, but it was different when he was doing it to her. More intense somehow.

His long fingers shaped her sex, caressed every part of it—the plump outer lips, the delicate inner lips, the tiny ridge at the center where all her pleasure was focused. He stroked her again and again, concentrating all his effort on her most sensitive flesh.

Until she came apart with a cry, her body stiffening in his embrace, her legs shaking with the strength of her release.

She moaned, long and loud, and Leo drank her soft moans into his mouth until she stilled.

"Good?"

She closed her eyes, turned her head into her arm and nodded once. Heat flooded her, but was it the heat of her passion or the heat of embarrassment? She didn't know, and she wasn't entirely sure she cared.

Leo toyed with the pearls which still hung around her neck. "It gets better, Anna."

And then he slid down her body and touched his tongue to her sex. "Leo!"

He pushed her legs open, took her with his mouth. She

was shocked, and not shocked. She'd watched that video, watched the woman's face as her lover had done exactly this.

It was bliss. Sheer, heart-stopping bliss. Every nerve ending she had was focusing on that one spot, gathering tighter and tighter until she wasn't certain she could take another moment of this sweet torture.

Leo gave her no quarter. He was relentless, flicking his tongue over her still-sensitive skin, licking and sucking her until the tension built so, so impossibly high—

"Leo!" she cried, shattering beneath him, her body shuddering and shuddering until she lay on the blanket, her limbs melting, her body limp. She thought that if she never moved again, if she died here and now, she would be happy.

Her body was dissolving, floating in a void, and yet she still felt restless and unsatisfied beneath the haze of pleasure. As if she hadn't quite felt everything she could feel yet.

Leo got up and walked away. The glorious heat of him, the flame and passion, was gone. Stunned, she rose up on her elbows, watched him as he stood with his back to her. He didn't move, other than to rake a hand through his hair. Confusion raced through her.

"Leo?"

"We can't go any further," he told her, not turning to look at her. "We can't risk getting you pregnant."

Anna blinked. And then she got to her feet. She was conscious of her nudity, but the sun was sinking low enough that it was darker beneath the trees. And she felt so very, very naughty right now. Confident and beautiful.

Boldly, she went over to stand behind him. She couldn't help but admire his body. He was so very gorgeous, so perfectly made. The muscles in his back bunched and stretched as he pulled his hand through his hair again. She wanted to trace every ridge and swell of him, wanted to spend hours learning his texture.

Leo was so sexy. So male.

So honorable.

Honorable? Not a word she would have associated with Leo before today.

She put a tentative hand on his strong biceps, felt the knot of warm muscle tense beneath her fingertips. Felt the sizzle of current that passed between them. It was odd, this feeling, and yet she was beginning to get used to it. She'd never felt that sizzle with Alex, but maybe that's because she'd always been so rigid around him. So controlled and cool.

She wasn't cool with Leo. Not now anyway.

"It's okay," she said, her heart thudding like mad. "I started the Pill six months ago."

CHAPTER SIX

Leo turned to look at her. His expression was taut, controlled.

She shrugged self-consciously. "I wanted to know Alex a bit better before we had children. I—I know it was my duty, but I wasn't quite ready yet."

It was a small rebellion, but after all these years of waiting and preparing, she wasn't going to get pregnant in the first month and then let Alex walk out of her life. She'd wanted more time. She'd needed to know him better, needed to know who she was as his wife. She'd felt illicit when she'd gone to her doctor to ask for birth control, but she'd always intended to tell Alex she was taking the Pill when they wed. She hadn't meant it to be a secret—but it no longer mattered, did it?

Leo put his hands on her shoulders, breathed out hard. Those clever hands slid down her forearms, leaving a trail of fire as they went. Simply from a caress.

"You plan everything to the letter, don't you?"

She swallowed. "I am a bit obsessive about the details," she said somewhat lightly. But deep down she cringed, waiting for his censure.

Instead, he laughed, a deep sexy sound that thrilled her. "Anna, you are something else."

She tried to frown. "I'm not sure I want to be something else. I want to be interesting. Desirable. Not something else entirely."

He drew her to him. "Oh, you are definitely interesting and desirable. The other was a compliment. I can't remember the last time—"

He stopped speaking abruptly, and she reached up to slide her palm against his face. She couldn't help it. She wanted to touch him. "Can't remember the last time what?"

He shook his head. "Nothing. It's nothing."

And then he was scooping her up and taking her back to the blanket beneath the shelter, laying her down gently, kissing her again and again. The fires in her body stoked higher with every touch of his lips against hers. Leo was still wearing his briefs, and she arched against him in frustration.

"You should know," he said softly against her earlobe as he nibbled her there. "I am healthy. You have nothing to fear. I am always cautious with my…liaisons."

Liaisons. The word lodged in her brain, refused to fade away. She knew Leo had many lovers, knew she was only a *liaison.* This was temporary. It was here, now, a celebration of survival. They would be rescued eventually, she was certain, and they would go back to their lives.

A pang of something pierced her but she dared not examine it.

"Now, Leo," she said as her eyes filled with ridiculous tears. "Please, now."

Before she changed her mind. Before the fears she'd buried down deep escaped the Pandora's box of her soul. Before boring Anna took over again.

He shrugged out of his briefs, and then she felt him— the hot, hard head of him at her entrance. "Anna," he said, his voice strangled with the control he exercised. "Are you certain?"

She couldn't think. Couldn't speak. Her pulse drummed in her throat, her ears, even the soles of her feet. She was certain, certain…

She pulled his head down to hers and thrust her tongue into his mouth. He moaned softly—and then he moved, thrusting into her body. There was a slight moment of pain before he broke through the barrier, but then he was inside her fully.

Their bodies were joined together more intimately than she'd ever imagined. It was odd to feel a man so deep inside her, to feel the throb of his pulse as he held himself very still and kissed her softly.

"Are you okay?" he asked.

Anna wrapped her legs around his hips, knowing instinctively that's what she was supposed to do. "Yes," she breathed. "Oh, yes."

The pain was nothing compared to the pleasure. Finally, she'd done something for herself—she'd made a decision and done what she felt was right for her, not what anyone else wanted her to do. It was exhilarating. So damn exhilarating.

Leo began to move, slowly at first and then more quickly as she caught his rhythm and rose up to meet him over and over again. Her heart swelled with feelings she didn't want to examine, and her body caught the edge of the wave and began to soar further and faster as Leo made love to her.

She had no idea what to expect, but she hadn't quite expected this. This perfect joining of bodies, this sharp edge of feeling, this physical pleasure beyond anything she'd imagined before. She was molten, glowing, burning hotter and hotter with every stroke of his body into hers.

And then she reached the peak of sensation, caught herself on the edge of the precipice, held herself suspended there for what seemed an eternity of the most exquisite pleasure/pain she'd ever known as her body kindled. She was a flash fire, a firecracker waiting to explode.

And then she did explode, soaring over the edge, free-falling into nothingness as Leo took one stiff nipple into his mouth and suckled hard.

She was aware of Leo following her, of his body pumping into hers harder and faster, of him stiffening and groaning as he spilled inside her.

He swore, hot words that made her sex clench around him. His breathing was hard, but so was hers. He touched his forehead to hers, being very careful not to crush her beneath him.

"That was amazing," he said. "*You* are amazing."

He was still inside her, still hard, and she tilted her hips slightly, wondering if she would feel anything now that it was over. His breath hissed in.

"You want to kill me, don't you?" he said, and she could hear the laugh in his voice.

"Definitely not," she said, feeling more powerful than she ever had before. "I'm not quite finished with you yet."

He did laugh then.

The sun went down and Leo built a small fire near their shelter. They had a lantern for later, but the fire was enough light for now. After he fanned the flames to life, Leo dragged dried food packets out of the survival kit and they had a picnic. They had also gotten dressed again, their clothes having dried in the sun.

Anna was rather disappointed to sit by the fire with Leo and not be looking at his bare chest, but it was cooler at night and the clothes were definitely needed. She hugged her stiffened jacket around her and glanced over at Leo. Firelight caressed the planes of his face, shadowing his cheeks and the cleft in his chin. Sitting here now, like this, she couldn't believe they'd made love only a short while ago.

She was in some ways a different person than she had been this morning. Oh, not fundamentally different. She was still a nitpicky perfectionist and she still had a desire for order and neatness. Anna sighed. She was also still afraid of looking like a fool in the press, and she still wished she could run away until everything blew over and she ceased being the jilted bride.

But at least she could now say she'd experienced passion. And, oh, what passion. The memory of it made heat flare to life deep in her belly. Leo had initiated her into a world she'd never known. He'd turned her inside out and made her into a raw, needy creature who'd craved his touch.

So much so that she'd begged him to make love to her again soon after the first time. This time, however, he'd rolled onto his back and let her take the lead. She'd been shy at first, afraid, but then she'd discovered how powerful it made her feel when she controlled the pace. Leo was so in charge of his emotions, his reactions—but at one point his head fell back and his eyes closed and he swallowed hard. And that was the moment when triumph swelled in her veins, when she felt her feminine power fully.

Leo looked up then, caught her staring at him. Her first instinct was to glance away, pretend she hadn't been looking, but he smiled and her insides melted. It was so easy being with him like this. Being out here with no one watching, with no fear of prying eyes and lying voices.

Did they even know she was missing yet? Was anyone curious? They knew she'd gone with Leo, so what were they thinking?

Anna frowned. She was pretty sure she knew what they were thinking.

And they weren't wrong, were they? Which was beside the point, because she couldn't really afford for the press to get wind of such an idea. If she was humiliated now, what would happen if they decided to report that she'd spent the night alone on an island with a famous playboy overnight?

"Regrets, Anna?" His voice sliced into her thoughts.

She shook her head. "You?"

"One. That we didn't have a bed."

She shrugged. "I don't mind."

He looked so serious. "You deserved a bed. Flowers, candles, dinner and hours of kissing first."

She shivered in delight. What would it have been like to go on a real date with Leo? To be wined and dined and made love to in a soft bed with fluffy covers they could snuggle into afterward. "Is that how you usually go about it?"

He frowned then, and she wished she hadn't said it quite like that. Jealous, possessive. A clingy virgin. *Former* virgin.

"I did try to warn you," he said mildly, and yet she got the impression he wasn't in the least bit relaxed when he said it.

She was *not* jealous. Not at all.

It was simply her competitive side coming out, the part of her that always had to be the best at everything. The part that planned and made charts and notes and calendars and felt triumphant when everything came off exactly as she'd envisioned.

There was no chart for this, no plan that would see her through. This thing with Leo simply *was*.

She waved a hand airily, as if it were a trifle. They both knew it was not.

"Forget I said that."

He blew out a breath, and she got the distinct impression he was disappointed. In her. "I wasn't with a woman last night, Anna. I was working on a business deal. When you found me this morning, I'd never actually gone to bed."

Anna's heart pounded. She imagined him at his computer all night. And then, because she couldn't quite help it, she imagined him with a woman, some svelte gorgeous thing who wrapped herself around him and wouldn't let go. She called it being real with herself, when in fact it hurt more than it should.

She knew all about wrapping herself around Leo. She wanted to do it again. She was greedy where he was concerned. She felt such a sense of urgency, as if she needed to experience everything she could in this one night. Before her real life intruded.

"There was lipstick on your collar," she told him matter-of-factly. "Not that I care, of course."

He frowned as he thought about it. Then his expression cleared. "Ah, that would be from the drunk woman who launched herself at me in the men's room of the hotel last night."

Anna blinked, scandalized. She may have acted with complete and utter abandon today, but she was too much of a lady ever to make a fool of herself in public. At least, not on purpose. "And what were you doing that she followed you into the men's room?"

Leo shook his head and laughed. "Mistaken identity. She was after another fellow, who'd ducked into a stall to hide."

Anna couldn't stifle a giggle. Odd, since she was not ordinarily the giggling sort. "And what happened when she, um, attacked you? Did he come out of hiding?"

"No, the bastard. Fortunately, she passed out before she did too much damage."

"And then what?"

"I carried her to the lobby and informed the staff they would need to see her to her room."

"Oh, my," Anna breathed. "You are quite the white knight."

"I do what I can," he said, that cocky grin of his making her heart twist. For the first time, she thought the grin might actually be genuine and not a part of the armor he wore to hide the darkness within.

"But, Anna," he went on, turning serious. "You don't have to worry about me embarrassing you. When we're back on Santina, we'll do everything properly. I won't see anyone else while we're together."

Her blood beat in her ears. A current of dread uncoiled in her veins. She didn't want to think about Santina, didn't want to think about what would happen when they returned. It was another world, another life, and she didn't want it intruding on her happiness right now. She couldn't think of them there, couldn't imagine him taking her on a date, much less coming home with her for sex.

No, when they got to Santina, it was over. It had to be. Anguish threatened to eat her from the inside out. She wanted to rage that it wasn't fair, that she'd only now allowed herself to be free, but she knew that the fishbowl of her life wouldn't permit her to see Leo once they left the island. She was brave out here where no one could see them. But when she reached home again?

"Let's not talk about that yet," she whispered, gazing into the fire and watching the flames leap and dance. She didn't want to give him up, and yet she had to. For both their sakes. He was Allegra Jackson's brother. What would the media have to say about a romance between the jilted bride and the brother of the new bride? She shuddered to think about it.

It would shame the Santinas. Her parents. And she couldn't do that to them, could she? Not after everything else. They'd counted on her to unite their houses, and she'd failed.

Her parents would be astonished if they could see her now. Horrified. Her mother had often told her when she was a little girl that her impulsiveness would be her downfall if she weren't careful. So she'd always been careful.

Until today.

Leo put a finger under her chin, forced her to look at him. "Why shouldn't we? I want to see you again, Anna. Not just here, not only like this."

She put her hand on his, gloried in the feel of his skin against hers. A current passed between them, left her aching with renewed want. How much longer did they have together?

"I'm not ready to talk about it. I don't want to spoil anything."

He looked perplexed. "Spoil anything? I'm trying to tell you that I want to see you when we get back. How is that spoiling anything? I *want* to see you, Anna, for as long as we enjoy each other. I thought you'd be delighted."

"Leo, please." She turned her head to the side, pressed a kiss into his palm. He smelled like the smoke from the fire, warm and woodsy, and she closed her eyes to breathe him in deep.

His hand snaked behind her head, drew her toward him. He looked angry, but he was planning to kiss her anyway. A little thrill leaped to life in her belly.

His lips touched hers, softly, lightly. She strained toward him, wanting more, but he withheld himself from her.

"We *will* talk about this," he growled.

"Yes," she breathed, her heart aching. "But not tonight. Please. I don't want to talk about anything tonight. I just want to *feel*."

His breath was warm against her skin as his lips skimmed her jaw. "Fine. Tomorrow, then."

"Thank you."

His voice was a purr against the column of her throat, her jaw. "What do you want from me tonight, sweet Anna?"

Anna hesitated only a moment before she put her hand on his groin, shocking herself with the bold maneuver. But he was hard, ready, and she shivered with anticipation. She ran her fingers along the bulge of his erection, enjoyed it when he sucked in his breath. "You have to ask?"

He smiled against her lips. "I like this side of you," he said, though his voice still contained a note of anger. "It's such a contrast to the buttoned-up side. Rather like a naughty librarian."

A thrill washed through her. "And do you like naughty librarians, Mr. Jackson?"

He kissed her until she couldn't think. "I might."

"What do you do with naughty librarians?" she asked breathlessly, leaning toward him.

"Ah, wouldn't you like to know?"

"I would. I most definitely would."

His hand spread across her thigh, slid upward beneath the hem of her skirt while she held her breath in anticipation. "You enjoy playing with fire, don't you, Anna?" His fingers found her, stroked her over the thin lace of her panties. "But what happens when you get too close to the flame?"

"Show me," she said on a moan. "I want you to show me."

He did. Thoroughly, completely, devastatingly.

CHAPTER SEVEN

THEY slept entangled in each other's arms, waking when the morning light streamed through the trees and pierced the veil of sleep. They ate food from the packets again, and then Leo took a signal mirror and went out into the sun to send blinding flashes into the sky at regular intervals.

Afterward, they stripped down and went for a swim. Anna could hardly believe she was skinny-dipping with a man, but Leo made her laugh so much when they were together that it all seemed perfectly normal. Who needed schedules or protocol or social engagements when they had this?

And then they made love in a shadowed cove with the water flowing over them and the sun dappling their naked bodies through the rock. Anna had never felt so free or so happy as she did when she was with Leo. He moved inside her so expertly, so beautifully, taking her to the peak again and again before they collapsed to catch their breath. She fell asleep on the beach with Leo holding her close.

"How long was I asleep?" Anna asked when she woke and looked up into his handsome face. He'd been watching her, and she blushed to think that she'd probably snored or looked decidedly unsexy while she'd been sleeping.

"Not long. Twenty minutes or so."

She stretched and yawned. She felt so decadent, so hedonistic. She wasn't wearing a stitch of clothing, and she didn't care. She'd even taken her treasured pearls off, tucking them away with her clothing beneath the shelter. She felt like another woman, lying on the beach with her lover, her body sated, and slightly sore, from his amazing love-making. Part of her never wanted to go home again.

"Do you think they'll find us today?" she asked. She almost hoped they didn't, and yet a change of clothing and a hot shower would be welcome. A hot shower with Leo.

No, she couldn't think like that.

He traced a finger over her lips. It was a light caress, nonsexual, and yet her core flooded with renewed heat and moisture. What a revelation it was to be a woman with appetites.

"I don't know," he said. "I hope so. But we have to accept the possibility no one has yet raised the alarm."

"I imagine they would have, since we did not return last night."

He simply looked at her with that combination of sultry and naughty he was so very good at. "You're with me, Anna. No one will be surprised we didn't return."

"Ah," she said, realizing what he meant. That he was Leo Jackson, famous Casanova, and she was a woman who most certainly had been unable to resist his fabled charm. A sliver of helpless anger filtered through her.

And yet it was the truth, wasn't it? She had been unable to resist, like countless other women in his life. In spite of the fact he'd said he wanted to see her when they returned to Santina, she was still only temporary in his life. He wanted her until he tired of her. She was merely another in the parade of women who'd graced his bed.

She'd known it, but it was the one thing she could not be in the real world. The reason this had to end here, on the island, and not later.

"Perhaps now is a good time to talk about what happens when we get back," he said, as if he sensed her turmoil. His dark gaze was so serious and intent as he hovered over her on one elbow.

Anna swallowed, a pang of uneasiness twisting in her stomach. "There's nothing to talk about."

"Nothing at all?" he pressed.

She sighed. "Oh, Leo, you know it won't work."

"Why not? You're a single woman, I'm a single man. Who says we can't see each other?"

She pushed herself upright, turned to look at him. "I can't, Leo. There are...expectations."

He was beginning to look angry. She could see the heat flare to life in his gaze, but it wasn't the kind of heat she liked. It was dark, piercing, scouring her senses. "Expectations? Meaning, I suppose, that I am not quite good enough for those lofty expectations?"

"That's not what I said." The sun had moved higher in the sky now, and the light that had dappled them before was now a strong shaft of sunlight creeping into their cove. Leo's body was golden, hard and lean and perfect. The dragon on his abdomen was fierce, snorting flames that fanned across his hip bone and groin. She'd wanted to trace the line of the dragon with her tongue, but had not been brave enough to do so.

Now, she reached out and traced it with a finger. His muscles clenched beneath her touch. "Where did you get that?"

He caught her hand. "You keep trying to distract me, Anna."

She peered at him from behind lowered lashes. "Is it working?"

"Hardly. Now tell me why we can't see each other on Santina or Amanti or wherever in hell we choose. You aren't marrying Prince Alessandro now. You can do what you want with your life."

She shivered to think so, and yet she knew she had to be careful. She might have been carefree on this island, but she could not afford to be so when they returned. The press would have a field day with this, if they knew, and she refused to be the target of their humiliation any longer. Leo might not be affected by bad press, but she had to live her life the way she always had or be annihilated by it.

"I need time, Leo. I can't just start dating and having affairs. I can't do that to my parents or to the Santinas. Don't you realize what the coverage would be like if we were to start dating? Especially since we seem to have skipped the date part and gone straight to sleeping together? Are you willing to drop me at my door every night with a chaste kiss?"

His eyes flashed. "You are giving them far more power over you than you should." He swore then, shocking words that sounded so coarse and angry coming from his lips. "Why do you care what the headlines say? Don't you know that the true secret to getting them to leave you alone is to do whatever in the hell you want to do? They want a *victim,* Anna—and you have made yourself into a perfect victim."

His words sliced into her, carved themselves into her soul. It hurt. "My reputation—"

"Your reputation," he ground out, "is ruined. You've spent the night on this island alone with me. Once your precious newspapers figure that out, and they will, the headlines about us will make everything up until now seem like a flattering portrayal. You have to show them you don't give a damn what they think."

Her heart throbbed at the anger in his voice. Not only that, but she feared he was right about her reputation. She just had to hope their disappearance together was kept quiet. "It's easy for you, Leo. No one cares that you've slept with your thousandth woman or broken some poor model's heart. They cheer you, applaud you, think you are clever and handsome and fun. But I was supposed to be a queen. They will not be so forgiving of me."

He got to his feet, his body simmering with tension as he looked down at her. "And why do you think you need anyone's forgiveness? You aren't going to *be* a queen, Anna. It's time you stopped acting like you were."

No one came for them that day. Leo signaled with the mirror at regular intervals, but nothing happened. He was tense, angry, and he wasn't quite sure why. It should be so easy, shouldn't it? A beautiful woman who wanted to have hot sex with him and then go their separate ways without any commitment?

He should be ecstatic. It was, after all, his usual modus operandi. He should be buried in her soft, tight body right now, making her moan and scream his name. He should do it as often as they could both tolerate, right up until the minute their rescue arrived. He should, and yet he couldn't.

He was irritated, and that wasn't quite like him. He should be congratulating himself on a lucky escape, but instead he was brooding because the virgin he'd recently bedded only wanted him for sex. And only while they were marooned together.

Pure irony, wasn't it?

He'd never considered that she wouldn't want to see him once they were rescued. No, he'd actually been worried that in spite of her heated pronouncements otherwise, she *would* want more from him. He knew her kind—wide-eyed, idealistic and inexperienced. A sure recipe for disaster in his book.

She was *supposed* to be the kind of woman who wanted

forever. She was supposed to want children, a house, a normal family life that included walks in the park, trips to family vacation destinations and a barking dog that tracked mud into the house and shook its wet fur all over the furnishings.

She was supposed to want all the things he didn't, and he was supposed to be the one who pulled back.

But it wasn't happening quite that way, and it disconcerted him more than it should.

He had to admit, the more he thought about it, that it was probably for the best if they didn't see each other again. Less messy for them both if they made a clean break here on the island. If they didn't, Allegra would quite possibly be unhappy with him for dating her husband-to-be's former fiancée. Not that he typically allowed his sister to have a say in his personal life, but for once it would touch her directly.

Because, yes, the press would have a field day with the news. Anna wouldn't like that at all. Neither, he suspected, would Allegra.

The sun dropped behind the horizon and the temperature cooled as storm clouds moved in. They'd hardly spoken in hours when Leo offered Anna another food packet and some water. She looked up at him with those wide green eyes and a jolt of electricity hit him in the gut.

Sex. It was all he could think about when he looked at her, all he wanted.

And all she wanted, if the way she looked at him was any indication. Like she was starving for something other than food.

He forced himself to turn away. Lightning flashed across the sky in the distance, turning the clouds pink before winking out again. The weather wasn't threatening, but it would probably rain later. Which was a good thing. They were almost out of water, and he'd be able to collect some in the makeshift reservoir he'd created out of plastic sheeting and rocks.

He sat down and they ate in silence as the surf crashed against the beach nearby. It was peaceful out here in a way. So different from his life in London or Los Angeles. There, he was always on the go, always seeking new business opportunities for the Leonidas Group. He traveled and he dated and he moved on to new challenges on a regular basis. Always looking for the next thrill, the next high. It was what he wanted, what he craved.

Anna glanced over at him. He looked up instinctually, as if they were connected on some level he didn't yet understand, and met her gaze. She dropped her chin, stared at the ground.

And then she fixed him with a look. "What did you want to be when you were a child, Leo?"

He didn't attempt to hide the surprise that must have shown on his face. "Where did this come from?"

She shrugged a pretty shoulder. "I'm tired of the silence. And I want to know," she said, pushing her hair from her face. It was thick hair, long and heavy, and he loved wrapping his hands in it while they made love. When she was on top, her hair flowed around them, curtaining them in their own cocoon. Her green eyes watched him carefully. Coolly, as if she expected rejection and had dared to ask anyway.

He thought about denying her, but strangely he didn't want to. Not yet anyway. "I wanted to be a professional footballer, like my father. His career didn't last long, but the perks did."

"The perks?"

"Women," he said without hesitation, and then felt bad for saying it when she dropped her gaze and swallowed.

He'd done it because he was still angry with her, but he wasn't proud of himself for it.

"So why didn't you?" she asked, pressing on.

He finished the packet of dried food and crumpled the foil. What was the point in being an ass? They barely knew each other. They'd had sex—fabulous sex—but they weren't lovers in the usual sense. And they weren't going to be. She'd made that clear.

And Leo Jackson didn't beg.

He didn't need to. Or want to. When they got back to Santina, there would be no shortage of women who wanted his attention. That was the life he was accustomed to, the life he adored. One woman, no matter how sexy, how desirable, wasn't going to change that.

He leaned back on his elbows. "I decided I could make more money catering to the exclusive tastes of the rich and famous. So I did."

"The Leonidas Group."

He could hear the question in her statement.

"Leonidas is my name," he said. He'd hated his name as a child, never understood why his mother had saddled him with something so unwieldy. He'd thought it was because she'd been an heiress and socialite with pretensions beyond her station in life. It wasn't until he was much older that he'd begun to understand she'd wanted him to be strong and brave and fearless.

"Leonidas was a hero king of Sparta," Anna said. "A very brave man."

Leo knew the story by rote. "He led the Greek forces in the Battle of Thermopylae. And he died defending the cause. I prefer to live to fight another day."

"Very sensible of you."

"What about you, Anna?" he asked, wanting to talk about her instead. He didn't like talking about himself. It took him into territory he didn't wish to explore, at least not tonight. He was, quite simply, a man who knew his limitations and hid them behind a strong will to succeed and a wealth of cocky charm he'd inherited from his father. He had no wish to discuss it with her. Or anyone.

But he did want to know what made her tick, who she was in truth. She'd given him glimpses of it last night, today. When she'd been naked beneath him, naked on top of him, surrounding him. She was a passionate woman beneath the uptight exterior. He hated to see that exterior return, and yet he knew it would when their rescue arrived. It was as natural to her as breathing.

"What did you want to be when you were a child? Or was queen your only choice?"

She shook her head. "Oh, no, definitely not. I thought I wanted to be a veterinarian. But then I realized there would be blood, so that idea went away. After that, I wanted to be a celebrity chef for a while. And of course there was the ballerina dream."

"And the princess dream, I imagine."

She tensed. "Of course there was the princess dream. But that one was supposed to come true." She shrugged, yet he knew how difficult it was for her to let the idea be lowered into the ground. "But that is life, yes?"

"Life is many things," Leo said. "Some of them disappointing, some of them frustrating and some of them blissfully happy."

She looked pensive. "Have you ever been blissfully happy?"

He'd opened himself up for that one. "I suppose that depends on how you define happy. But yes, I'd say I have."

If she asked him to name the times, he wasn't sure he could. All he knew was that he must have been very happy at one time or another. He'd lived a hedonistic life. He'd had fun. How could he not have been happy?

He had it all. He had plenty of money and plenty of women. Who needed more?

Anna sighed, the curtain of her hair falling over her forehead as she dipped her chin toward her chest. "I think I'm still waiting for that."

A sharp sensation bloomed in his gut. "Don't wait for it. Make it happen."

She looked up at him, her eyes wide and gleaming in the light of the fire. "I'm trying," she said. "I…" She hesitated before continuing. "It's not that I don't want to see you when we get home again. But I can't. Not yet."

A shaft of lightning lit up the sky, a crack of thunder following hard on its heels. Electricity sizzled in the air. He could smell the sulfur, could feel the bite of it in his throat. It tasted like anger.

"And how long do you think it will take, Anna? One month? Two? Six? A year?"

She swallowed. "I—I don't know."

"Then perhaps you're right," he said tightly. "Perhaps it's best we say goodbye now."

"I knew you'd say that."

Anger whipped through him. "What did you expect me to say? That I'd be happy to wait until you're no longer scared of the media?"

She swallowed. "That's not fair, Leo."

"Nothing ever is," he replied.

The storm broke around midnight. Water poured down onto the plastic sheeting of their makeshift shelter, waking Anna from a deep sleep. Beside her, Leo lay still, one arm propped behind his head as he stared at the roof above their heads. She felt a pang of longing, but shoved it down deep and tried to ignore it. She and Leo were through. And it was best that way.

They lay together beneath the blanket for warmth, but there was no warmth between them. Not any longer.

The thought made a lump form in her throat, a hard heavy knot she couldn't swallow. Tomorrow, perhaps, they would be rescued. And she might never see him again. He was a man of the world, and she was a woman without purpose. She would soon return to her home on Amanti and lock herself away until she could face the world again.

Without Leo. The thought hurt. Crazy.

"Leo," she said—choked, really—and he turned his head toward her. She couldn't stop herself from reaching out and touching his jaw, running her fingers into the silk of his hair.

He stiffened. She expected him to reject her, to push her away, but after a moment he groaned, as if he, too, were unable to stay strong in the face of this overwhelming need.

He caught her hand and pressed a kiss into her palm. Heat flooded her in great waves, softening her limbs, making the ache sharper. He gathered her to him, pulled her into his heat and hardness.

"I want you, Anna. Dammit, I still want you."

"Yes," she breathed. "Oh, yes."

The rain pounded against the sheeting, dripping off the sides, marooning them in a small dry place that became their island within an island. They didn't speak as they stripped and made love. Instead, they spoke in kisses, in touches, in the long luxurious glide of his body into hers. The storm raged around them, between them. Leo managed to take her angrily and tenderly at the same time, and she answered him in kind, their bodies tangling and battling and straining and melting again and again.

When it was over, they collapsed together and slept the

night away until they awoke to a bright blue sky, a clean ocean breeze…

…and a boat anchored offshore.

CHAPTER EIGHT

PREGNANT.

Anna stared at the test stick in her fingers, her entire body going hot and cold and numb all at once. She was pregnant. With Leo's child. How had it happened? How could it *possibly* have happened?

She blinked and fell back against the bathroom counter. Oh, God.

No. *No, no, no*.

It had been a month since they'd been rescued from the island. A month since she'd last seen him. As soon as they'd reached Santina, he'd left again. It had broken her heart, but it's what she'd wanted. What she'd insisted on.

She'd returned to her home on Amanti and hidden herself away, waiting for the media attention to die down.

And it had. There'd been a little bit of a stir over their plane crash and subsequent rescue by Santina's coast guard—but then nothing. Alex and Allegra, and their various siblings, had proven far more interesting to the collective conscious lately, thank goodness.

Leo had gone his merry way, she'd gone hers, and the press had turned their attention to the more flamboyant members of the Jackson family—and even some of the Santinas—and the fallout from the clash of families at the engagement party.

But now…*this.* Oh, God, *this.*

She'd missed Leo. She'd missed his touch, his laugh, his arrogant and cocky grin. She'd missed the feel of his body sliding into hers, the exquisite pleasure he'd given her for two days on that island. She'd missed swimming with him naked, and she'd missed lying beneath a makeshift shelter and making love during a raging storm.

She'd missed everything about being with Leo. But she'd pushed him away, shoved him from her life without so much as a backward glance. It was her fault he was gone.

She looked at the test again, hoping that she'd read it wrong, that the answer had changed somehow. It had not. And she had to tell Leo. He had a right to know. She considered, for one brief moment, terminating the pregnancy.

But she didn't want to. Already, though it frightened her, she loved the idea of a child that was part her and part Leo. How could she not? She'd felt so adrift recently, but now she felt as if she had a renewed purpose, a reason to be the best person she could be. She would stop feeling sorry for herself and she would teach this baby everything she knew. Her baby would have the freedom to be whatever he or she wanted to be.

From this moment forward, Anna would protect her baby at all costs.

She put the test stick in a drawer. As she was turning away, she caught sight of her reflection in the mirror and stopped short. She looked tired, drawn. Her skin was golden, her eyes bright, but there was a strain in her expression that hadn't been there before. She ran a hand over her cheeks, her forehead. There were circles under her eyes. She'd been so, so tired lately.

Now she knew why she couldn't drag herself out of bed in the morning.

A baby. Leo's baby.

She had to call him. But no, she couldn't just ring him up and deliver news like that over the phone, could she? She had to see him. She had to find out where he was and go to him. She hadn't allowed herself to search for information about him, afraid of what she might find, but now she had no choice.

Anna left the bathroom and went into her huge walk-in closet to retrieve her suitcase. Wherever Leo was, she would find him. And she would tell him personally that he was going to be a father. Her heart leaped at the thought of seeing him again.

But her stomach twisted. She was nervous, stunned. What if he had a girlfriend? What if he didn't want to see her or, worse, didn't care about her news? What then?

Anna tossed a folded sweater set into the suitcase. She couldn't think like that. She simply couldn't. If she did, she'd lose her nerve. And she couldn't lose her nerve. In the not too distant future, she would begin to show. How could she face the media then? How could she shame her parents that way after everything else they'd been through? She would *not* be a laughingstock over this, nor would she allow them to be.

This baby meant too much to her, and she wouldn't allow anyone to make her feel ashamed. But she knew that if she was going to protect her child, she needed Leo.

It only took a matter of hours to make the arrangements, and then she was on her way to London. A check of the newspapers had revealed a photo of Leo just last night in a restaurant with a group of businessmen.

He hadn't been with a woman, and that gave her hope. In fact, when she dared to skim the tabloids from the month since he'd returned to London, she found not one mention of him with another woman. Perhaps he'd missed her just a little bit. Perhaps, she thought crazily, he'd even been waiting for her to call him, to tell him she was ready to see him again. The thought gave her courage.

When her plane touched down at Heathrow, it was raining heavily. Anna stood in the chilly London air and hailed a cab to take her to her hotel. It was no mistake she'd chosen a Leonidas Group property. The Crescent Hotel was located in Mayfair, a stunning Victorian-era building that had been renovated and turned into the kind of luxury hotel Leo was famous for.

The address was exclusive, the rooms exquisite, and her reception had been beyond compare. But all she could think about was the owner of the hotel and what he would say when she told him her news.

She stood at the window and gazed out over the view of Hyde Park long after the porter had delivered her luggage. The park was green, but the sky was gray and leaden. Black cabs crawled through the busy streets along with red double-decker buses and cars of all description. It was insane compared to Amanti, and she felt a pang for home. Amanti was modern and busy, but not as busy as London. This city teemed with people going about their hectic lives. Lives she didn't understand.

She felt very small and very lost as she watched the city slide by on the streets below. But she had no time to be lost. She had to find Leo.

His offices weren't very far, so she donned her raincoat and umbrella and followed her phone's GPS directions until she stood outside the tall glass building that housed the Leonidas Group's London headquarters. It had been a bit of a walk from her hotel, but the exercise felt good.

She'd gotten wet during her walk, regardless of the umbrella, and she felt a bit bedraggled and cold, but she would not turn back now. She stood outside the building, staring at the door and trying to gather the courage that had melted on her walk. People streamed by on the sidewalk, oblivious to her torment. The smoky glass of the Leonidas building looked so imposing suddenly, like a black gaping hole into which she would disappear should she be brave enough to enter.

A car pulled up to the curb as Anna stood there, undecided. A moment later, a uniformed driver emerged with an umbrella. He walked past her to the door of the building and waited only a minute before the door swung open and a man came out.

Anna's heart kicked up. A tall, dark-haired man in an expensive suit exited the building. A man she would know anywhere, even were she blindfolded.

A man who was not alone. A fresh chill stole through Anna, rooting her to the spot. The woman with Leo was small, blonde, and clung to his arm as if she'd never let go. She turned her face up to him, smiled, her even white teeth flashing in the semidarkness that was falling on the city.

A hot slice of something passed through Anna then. She almost turned away, almost slunk into the night and back to the hotel. Except she thought of the baby growing inside her—Leo's baby—and courage blazed into her veins again.

"Leo," she said as he passed by.

He ground to a stop as if he'd run into a brick wall. Turned to her, his dark eyes as hot and intense as she remembered them. The woman with him frowned.

"Anna?"

Anna pushed the umbrella back so that her face was no longer shadowed. She was not as beautiful as the woman at his side, not as polished or…as dry, she thought wryly.

"Yes, it's me."

Leo disentangled himself from his companion and came

over to her. He was as hard and handsome as always, and her heart skipped a beat at his nearness.

He did not, she noticed, look very friendly as he gazed down at her. She drank in his scent, that unique combination of subtle spice and man that was Leo. She even thought she could smell a tinge of the ocean, of the salt spray against his sun-warmed skin. It took her back so forcefully that she nearly crumpled on the sidewalk in front of him.

He reached out to steady her, and she realized that she'd nearly crumpled in truth, not merely in her head.

"Are you well?" he demanded.

She shook her head, unable to answer for fear of blurting it out right there on the dark street.

Leo swore softly. And then he was gathering her against him, one arm firmly around her, barking orders to his driver and the woman who stood so forlornly under the driver's umbrella. The door to the limo opened, and then Anna was ushered inside the warm interior and Leo slid in beside her. The woman also joined them, Anna noted sourly.

The driver's door shut with a thud and the car sat motionless, idling in the night.

"What are you doing here, Anna?" Leo asked. His voice was hard, cold, unlike the man she'd known on the island. The man who, a moment ago, had gathered her close and put her into the car. For a moment she'd been thrown back to another time. To the tenderness and passion that had flared between them.

She shivered, a long ripple that slid down her spine and over her skin on icy little feet.

"I need to talk to you," she said, turning her head to look out at the traffic on the street. She could not look at him, or she would crumble. She would blubber everything, regardless of the woman who sat across from them, radiating disapproval and anger.

And that she could not do.

Leo pressed a button and gave his driver instructions, and then they were moving. The woman sat on the seat opposite, arms folded over her ample breasts, jaw set stubbornly as she glared at Anna. Not a business associate, then.

"It's private," Anna added, just in case Leo expected her to say anything with his girlfriend present.

"I gathered," he said shortly.

"Leo," the woman said—whined, really. "You promised you'd take me dancing tonight."

Anna could sense Leo's irritation, even if she couldn't see the expression on his face. "The plan has changed, Donna," he said crisply.

Oddly enough, Anna felt a burst of sympathy for Donna, who seemed to shrink in on herself with Leo's words. It wasn't her fault after all. Donna didn't say another word as the car moved through the city, finally coming to a halt somewhere residential. The door swung open and Leo turned to Anna. "I'll be right back."

He exited the vehicle, held out his hand for Donna, who took it and scooted out the door. Anna could hear raised voices on the sidewalk. Her skin burned, indignation a hot flush beneath the surface.

Leo had been dating. While she'd shut herself away in Amanti and tried to get over their two days on the island, he'd moved blissfully onward, compelled by the strong sensuality that she knew was as much a part of him as breathing.

Had he done the things to Donna that he'd done to her?

Anger was a cyclone inside her, whirling through her with a force that threatened to split her apart at the seams.

It made no sense, since she'd known what he was—*since she'd pushed him away*—but it was true nonetheless.

Leo returned to the car and the door closed behind him. Anna suddenly felt as if she would burst with the fury she felt. It welled inside her with the force of a nuclear reaction. She'd missed him, missed what they'd had, and he'd been with another woman.

She knew it was her fault, knew she'd pushed him away, and yet she couldn't help what happened next, as if it were a chain reaction that had begun the instant he'd walked out of his building with another woman on his arm.

She slapped him.

His head snapped back, the sound like a thunderclap in the quiet car. And then he was glaring at her. She felt wild, dazed, and she lashed out again, an angry sound escaping her as she did so.

This time he caught her wrist in an iron grip. Anna growled, swung with the other hand. It made no sense, but she couldn't stop. He caught that wrist, too, pinned her hard against the seat. And then he was pushing her back, stretching over top of her, pinning her against the seat with his lean, hard-muscled body.

"Did you think I'd be waiting for you, Anna? Is that why you're angry?"

"Let me go," she said, her voice as cold as she could make it. And yet a part of her thrilled at his touch. Her core softened, her body aching for his possession once more. Liquid heat flooded her sex.

He was so close. Too close. His breath fanned across her cheek. "I'm afraid not, darling. I'd rather like to keep my head attached to my shoulders."

Her breath hissed in as he moved against her, so warm and hard and familiar. Anna closed her eyes as a sob built inside her chest. She couldn't want him, not like this. How could she let herself feel this way? How could she want him inside her again, possessing her, making her his in a way no man ever had before? One month since they'd been together, and he'd forgotten her so easily.

What did you expect? You pushed him away.

Anna bit down on the angry tears that threatened to spill free. She'd done what was necessary, and she'd thought of him almost nonstop since. He clearly hadn't had the same problem.

She started to struggle, her body twisting beneath him. A sob broke free as he deflected the knee she'd aimed at his balls.

"Dammit, what is the matter with you?" he growled.

"You," she choked out. "You're a bastard."

She could feel the leashed violence in him. "I am, in fact," he said coldly. "But I doubt my birth is what you've come to discuss."

She lay against the seat, her body trembling beneath his, his heat soaking into her, warming her. Perversely, she wanted to turn her face into his neck, wanted to nibble the skin there.

She would not.

"What do you want, Anna?" Leo demanded. "Why did you come here?"

It was all wrong. Everything she'd wanted to say, wanted to tell him. This wasn't the way it was supposed to happen. He was supposed to be happy to see her again. He was supposed to want her, and she was supposed to be the strong one, the one who pushed him away. As she'd done on the island. She was supposed to tell him in a dignified tone that she was expecting his child.

He was supposed to be grateful she'd returned to his life.

Grateful?

Heavens above, this man was anything but happy to see her. He would be anything but grateful. How could she tell him?

How could she not?

"Not like this," she said. Whimpered, actually.

His grip on her wrists tightened until she nearly cried out in pain, but he released her and shoved back away from her. Then he was pushing his hand through his hair and cursing softly.

Anna sat up. Straightened her damp trousers. Fiddled with the cuffs of her raincoat. All the while breathing deeply, telling herself she would not cry. She'd survived Alex Santina—she could certainly survive Leo! Alex hadn't meant anything to her, but his betrayal had been far more humiliating.

Leo was the man she'd given herself to, the man she'd bared her soul to—and the man she'd pushed from her life. Could she blame him for being so angry with her, so cold?

"Where are you staying?" he demanded in clipped tones.

"The Crescent," she shot back.

"Ah," he said.

Heat flared to life inside her. "And what is wrong with that?"

"Nothing," he said a moment later. He gave instructions to the driver and the car slipped into traffic again.

They rode in silence for some time, until the feelings knotting in her belly demanded release. "It didn't take you very long, did it?"

His head swung toward her. "I beg your pardon?"

"You know what I mean, Leo. The woman. Donna. Is she the first?"

She could feel him stiffen beside her. "If I recall correctly, you're the one who said a relationship between us was impossible."

Shame roiled inside her. "You know why."

"I know why you believed it to be true. Have you changed your mind, sweet Anna? Is that why you're here?"

Her skin prickled at the name he used. He'd called her that on the island, and while she knew it had first been done in jest, it had come to mean so much more in the two days they'd shared.

It meant nothing now.

How had she let this happen? How had she lost her sense of right and wrong in so brief a time on the island? She'd been weak, and she'd allowed him inside the walls she'd erected. She'd wanted to be close to someone, and he'd offered her that. She'd known better, but she'd been weak.

"No," she breathed, unable to say anything else.

But it was a lie. Because she needed him if she were to have this baby and keep scandal from raining down on her head—their heads—like hellfire. She would endure whatever she had to endure for herself, but for her baby she would fight tooth and nail to provide the happiest, safest environment possible. And she needed Leo to help her do it.

"Then what is there to say?" he demanded. "Surely you have not come all this way to see if I have moved on with my life."

Anna folded her arms over her breasts. Her body was trembling, but whether from anger or cold she wasn't certain. "Which wasn't so very hard to do, was it?"

Yes, it stung, and yes, she knew she had no right to be hurt. It didn't change the way she felt seeing him with another woman, however. She'd felt as if someone had reached inside her and ripped her heart from her body. It stunned her, and worried her.

Leo swore. She didn't blame him. "You can't have it both ways, Anna. You might sit in your cold lonely house and congratulate yourself on avoiding another scandal, but you can't expect others to do the same."

"I don't," she said softly.

They traveled in silence for several minutes, the air as crisp and electrical as if a lightning strike had occurred in the center of the car. Anna's throat hurt from the giant lump that wouldn't let her speak the words she needed to say. Leo didn't make it easy on her, either. He sat with his fingers drumming the armrest, his face turned away from her to look out the window. He was so remote, so distant, and she didn't know how to breach that distance. How to say what she had to say.

She'd had no trouble breaching the distance between them on the island, but they'd been stripped to their barest elements there, incapable of erecting the walls that now separated them from each other. These walls were seemingly insurmountable, and yet she had to find a way.

The car pulled to a halt beneath a bright red awning, and she realized they'd reached the Crescent Hotel. Her heartbeat sped up as the uniformed doorman came down the stairs and reached for the car door.

Leo turned to her, his eyes glittering, his jaw hard. He looked so cold and remote, so untouchable, and her stomach knotted in panic.

"Unless you have something you wish to say, I'll say good-night now."

"So you can return to Donna?" she lashed out.

"You assured me this was the way you wanted it, Anna."

Where had he gone, that man who'd been so fierce and tender on the island? In spite of her wish to be strong, a single tear slid down her cheek.

"Something has changed," she said, pushing the words past her aching throat.

He clenched the fingers of one hand in his lap. She sensed that he had grown very, very still. Waiting for her to continue. Waiting for that moment when she would speak the words that would change everything. Did he know what it was? Did he suspect? Or did he simply think she was crazy?

The door swung open, the sounds from the street suddenly louder. The scent of some kind of food on the wind—an Indian curry, perhaps—skated inside the car, made her press a sudden hand to her mouth.

"Anna?" He still sounded cold and distant compared to the island—and yet his hard veneer seemed to crack just a shade.

It wasn't much, but it was enough to give her the sliver of courage she needed. Her heart thudded, her stomach twisting in fear. She rubbed damp palms along the fine weave of her trench coat.

And then the words fell from her mouth as if they'd been hovering there all along.

"I'm pregnant, Leo."

CHAPTER NINE

HE HADN'T heard her correctly. Surely he hadn't. The world seemed to slow, the sounds from outside the car distorting in his ears like he was on a carnival ride. Leo could only focus on her, on her tired face and huge eyes. Her long hair was twisted up high on her head, as always, and she wore the pearls she'd had on the island. Her white raincoat stood out starkly in the dark interior of the car, contrasted with the black V-neck sweater and trousers she wore.

No color, as usual. Anna didn't like color.

"How?" he asked, his voice colder than he wanted it to be. Shocked.

She looked away. Shrugged. "I don't know. I—I was on the Pill, but of course I didn't have it for the two days we were marooned." Her chin dropped to her chest. "I might have messed up the dosage after we returned."

She fingered her pearls, a nervous gesture he knew all too well.

Leo could only blink. A current of ice flowed through him, freezing him to the spot. A baby. His baby. He had no doubt the baby was his. No doubt.

But he couldn't be a father. He was the last person in the world fit to be a father. What if he was too much like Bobby? What if he didn't know what to do when this tiny being came into the world and needed him?

Panic threaded through the ice, melting his immobility. He exited the car smoothly and held out his hand for her. After a brief hesitation, she slipped her fingers into his palm. Fresh sensation rocked him at the touch of her skin on his.

She didn't say anything as he led her inside the hotel and over to the brass-and-wood lift. "Which room?" he asked as the lift operator waited patiently.

"Five-oh-four," she said quietly.

The lift began to move, its speed belying its age as they reached the fifth floor very quickly. "Here you are, Mr. Jackson," the operator said.

Leo took a bank note from his breast pocket and shoved it into the man's hand, uncaring how much it was for, and escorted Anna down the hall to her room. She fished the key card from her pocket, and then he opened the door and let her pass through before he closed it behind him and took a deep breath.

Pregnant.

A lamp burned in the suite, illuminating the sitting area. The room was furnished with the finest antiques, the best silks, the latest electronics—but Leo could focus on none of those things. All he could see was the woman standing across from him. Her raincoat was still buttoned up, her hands shoved in the pockets. Her eyes said she was tired, worn, wary.

Fury burned through him. She was afraid of him? Of *him?* After all they'd been through together?

"You have confirmed this pregnancy?" he said. It wasn't the first time a woman had claimed to be having his baby, though it was the first time he thought it was true.

Her head snapped up, her chin thrusting forward defiantly. "I only took the test this morning. It was positive."

"You have not been to a doctor?"

She shook her head. "I...I panicked. I had to see you."

"And what is your plan now, Anna? What do you want from me?" He knew he sounded callous and cruel, but he couldn't seem to quite wrap his head around the fact he'd fathered a child. An innocent child who deserved far better than Leo could give. "If you are considering terminating the pregnancy, I won't interfere," he added.

Her jaw dropped, her eyes growing wide. She clutched a hand over her stomach, and he felt like an ass.

"I'm not," she said firmly. "I want this baby."

"Why?" He didn't mean to be cruel, but he had to know. His mother had been a single parent up until her death. He'd often wondered if she would have chosen differently if she'd realized how difficult it would be.

"Because I do. Because I'm not without means, and because I'm not so selfish as to deny this baby a chance at life when I have so much to give."

"It won't be easy," he said. "You have to know that."

She looked determined. Fiery. *Dragon lady.*

"I am well aware."

Leo walked over to the stocked liquor cabinet and poured two fingers of Scotch. He needed something to calm the rat-a-tat-tat of his heart, something to ease the jangle of shock coursing through him. *Pregnant.*

He'd always been so cautious. No doubt it was because of the circumstances of his birth—something he swore he would never do to his own child. Leo hadn't even known, until he was ten years old and motherless, that he actually *had* a father.

He lifted the crystal tumbler. The first sip of liquid scalded his throat, his gut. He welcomed it. Needed it. Craved it.

"I will support you and the child, of course," he said, turning back to her. Because he would not abandon his child. He would do the best he could, though he had no idea just yet what his best was.

"We don't need your support," she shot back, head held high. He knew she was still offended that he'd said he wouldn't stand in the way of a termination. But he'd had no idea what else to say. He didn't know how to be a father. In fact, he didn't know what he felt about anything at this moment. "Money is not the issue."

"No, of course not," he said. Anna came from money, and she had an inheritance of her own—rather like his mother had had. But his mother's money hadn't protected her in the end. She'd still died alone, and she'd left him to the care of a father he'd never known existed until she was gone. What a shock that had been, going from one household to another in a matter of weeks. From one loving parent to the other who was a stranger.

Leo knew in his mind where this conversation was leading, where he had to take it, and yet part of him resisted doing so. He sipped the Scotch as if he were savoring the last moments of his freedom.

"I need something else from you," she said, her accent growing heavier with the emotion she was feeling. "Something other than money."

He thought for one terrifying moment that she would sink to her knees and beg, but of course she didn't. This was Anna.

She lifted her head higher, if that were possible, her eyes gleaming with determination. With fire. A bolt of desire shot through him, reminded him forcefully of why he'd wanted her in the first place.

"And what is that, sweet Anna?" But he already knew what she would say before she said it. Because he knew her. Knew what drove her.

The words fell from her lips exactly as he expected they would. "I need your name."

He didn't speak, and she wondered if he'd heard her. He looked so distant, so detached. And so gorgeously male she wanted to weep. He wore a dark suit, custom fit, of course. He wore no tie, but a deep blue shirt open at the neck. He looked like the ladies' man he was, she thought bitterly. His dark hair was combed back from his face, the ends curling up over his collar in sexy little waves she wanted to touch. His perfect face was serious, troubled. Not at all the carefree playboy he was reputed to be.

He cradled the crystal tumbler in one hand, stared at the contents before turning it up and draining it. "Are you asking me to marry you, sweet Anna?" he said, his voice deceptively mild.

Anna swallowed. "Yes." Because it was the best way, the only way, to protect their child. She'd thought about it a lot on the flight today, and she'd known it was right. "But don't fear I mean to tie you down," she continued. "The marriage will be temporary."

One dark eyebrow arched. "Temporary?"

She could hear the ice in his voice, the disdain, but she hurried on anyway. "It makes the most sense. We marry to give our child a name." She licked her lips. "To prevent any scandal…and—and then we divorce after the baby is born. The perfect solution."

"Of course," he said coolly.

She twisted her fingers together in front of her, realized it made her seem uncertain. She made a deliberate effort to stop. To remove her trench coat calmly and lay it across the back of a leather chair. To sink onto the overstuffed couch and lean back against the cushions. To tilt her head up to watch him with what she hoped was a competent and serene expression on her face.

"I'm glad you see it my way," she said.

He set the tumbler down on the bar, stalked across the room like a caged lion suddenly unleashed. "Did I say that?" His voice was so sharp it could cut glass. Cold. Full of thinly veiled rage.

Anna shivered involuntarily. She was tired, and her heart slammed against her ribs. She hadn't eaten a thing all day. She wanted to curl up and go to sleep for hours, and she wanted to wake up and have Leo by her side. Smiling down at her as he brushed the hair from her face and kissed her. Just like on the island.

"You have an alternative plan?" she asked. She sounded so businesslike when in fact she wasn't businesslike at all. Her insides were clenching tight and a tiny muscle in her throat began to throb.

"You've not really thought this through, have you, Anna?"

"I did," she said. "I considered alternatives. This is the best choice."

"For whom?"

She blinked, momentarily disconcerted by the question. "F-for us. For our child. Would you have him or her born under a cloud of scandal?"

A muscle in his cheek flexed. "I think, darling, you are the only one who cares about that. There are worse ways to begin life."

Anna pressed a hand to her belly self-consciously. A current of anger whipped up like a mini dust storm inside her. "You know why it's important to me!"

Hot tears pressed against her eyes. The insanity had calmed a bit since Alex had jilted her over a month ago now, but she knew she was still an object of interest. If she gave the press something scandalous to report, she'd be back in the headlines in what she'd once heard referred to as a New York minute. Which she took to mean blindingly fast.

Leo was still remote and cool. "I know why it's important to you. I simply don't understand why you care. And I don't think you've thought this completely through, Anna."

She sniffed. "Then tell me what I've forgotten."

He came over and put a hand on the couch on either side of her head, trapping her in the circle of his arms. She would have ducked away, but she wouldn't let him know how much he still affected her. Not after Donna. Let him think she was unmoved by him.

Anna tilted her head back while he bent until his face was only inches from hers. She could see the bulge of muscle in his upper arms, the stretch of expensive fabric across his chest. The blue shirt gaped open, revealing tanned skin that had once pressed so sensually against her own.

"You're here, with me, in one of my hotel rooms. You jumped on a plane, without warning, and flew to London to be with me. You had no prior plans to come, you simply leaped without thinking."

"It wasn't like that," she gasped—and yet she knew very well that it was. From the moment she'd seen the two pink lines on the test, she hadn't been thinking clearly. Coherently. She'd simply known she had to see Leo, had to tell him what they'd created together.

"And yet that's what it looks like. If we marry—and I assume you want it to happen quickly—what do you think your precious media will say then? They will put two and two together, don't you think?"

Anna dropped her gaze from his. "It's possible." And then, because she couldn't help herself, she reached up and cupped his face in both hands, her fingers shaking as she spread them over the blades of his cheekbones. She thought he shuddered at her touch, but she couldn't be sure. She didn't have time to be sure. "But, Leo, it won't matter once we marry. It will be nothing more than speculation, and our baby will be safe."

His gaze dropped to her mouth, his lashes dipping over the hot gleam in those dark eyes. A shot of pure lust hurtled to her core. In spite of being tired, in spite of being pregnant, in spite of the pain and anger of seeing him again, her body wanted his. Ached for his.

It was outrageous—and inevitable, she realized. Hadn't she secretly gloried in the idea she would soon be at his side on the long trip to London?

A healthy dose of self-disgust filled her. Was she truly that weak and susceptible? She let her hands fall away from his face. He pushed upright again, the moment broken in ways she didn't understand. What had there been to break?

And yet, looking at the hard angry glint in his gaze, she knew there had been something after all. Regret sliced deep, but she pushed it away. She had no time to puzzle it out. She needed to convince him to marry her and let the rest sort itself out later.

"I should send you home," he said. "Back to your miserable existence."

"But you won't." She was confident he wouldn't. She didn't know why, but she just knew he would *not* send her away. She could feel it in the way he looked at her, in the recognition that flowed between them. They were in this together, like it or not.

He shook his head slowly. "No, I won't. I'll do something far worse."

Her heart skipped a beat. What could be worse than going home to face the media frenzy alone? But she didn't speak. She simply waited.

"I'll marry you, Anna," Leo said softly. "But not on your terms, darling."

Fear spiked, twisting her stomach. "I—I didn't think I offered terms. I simply said it would be temporary."

His smile managed to both chill her and thrill her at the same time. "Temporary implies this would be a false marriage. A pretend marriage. And I won't pretend, Anna. I'm not going to. So if you want this marriage, then know you'll be sharing my bed and my life for as long as it lasts."

Horror seeped into her bones. "But that—" She stopped, swallowed. This was not at all what she'd imagined. She'd imagined a nice, tidy little arrangement that gave her baby a name and had them acting together toward one purpose. Naively, she'd even thought that after a couple of weeks together, they could live apart the majority of the time. Certainly Leo's schedule as a busy entrepreneur would make that possible.

But this…oh, heavens. "That's blackmail," she said, her throat constricting around the words. "You know I have no choice but to accept whatever conditions you attach."

His gaze glittered. "You always have a choice."

Not if she wanted to protect her baby. "Why are you doing this? Why can't we just be civil about it? I've not asked for much from you. Just that you do the right thing and help me protect our child from the scandal that will surely break if I remain unwed." Her voice had risen until she was practically shouting.

Leo was unmoved. He stared at her coldly. "Are you quite finished?"

"For the moment," she said defiantly. Damn him for making her so emotional! Damn him for standing there and looking so unruffled, so cold, while she was a mess of feelings and insecurities. Nothing touched him.

"Have you ever considered," he said, "that perhaps you

are more worried about yourself than you are about the child? Do you honestly believe that it will matter in five years—or ten or twenty—whether or not you were married when you gave birth? Do you think a child cares more for your marital status than whether or not he has a happy and safe home to grow up in?"

Anna swallowed as a tiny sliver of doubt pricked her. There was something in his voice that cut deep. *Was* she more concerned about herself? Was she too afraid to face the fire alone?

"Leo, I—"

He held up a hand, silencing her. "We will marry, Anna. But on my terms. If you can't live with those terms, you *do* have a choice. If you don't make that choice, then don't blame me for your own cowardice."

By the time Leo made it back to his temporary lodgings—Bobby's Knightsbridge apartment—the shock of what had happened tonight was pressing hard against the confines of his head, making his temples throb. He'd gone from bachelor to expectant father in the space of a breath, and now he was getting married.

Married. The second thing he felt completely unqualified to do, fatherhood being the first. And he'd not started this marriage-to-be off on quite the right footing, had he? But he'd been so bloody angry with her, with her plans and schemes. She was having his child and she still thought of him as an accessory. A temporary inconvenience. A sperm donor she only needed for a short while to stave off scandal.

It infuriated him. And yes, it hurt deep down on a level that surprised him. He knew he wasn't fit to be a father, thanks to his genetic material, but she only assumed it to be true. And only on the barest of evidence.

Leo stepped into the private elevator that awaited him. He wasn't accustomed to not being in control of the situation. *He* was the one who made decisions, who made things happen. He wasn't an accessory, and he damn sure wasn't going to be an ornamental husband simply to please her.

Because the one thing he'd realized tonight when she'd landed so forcefully back into his life was that he still wanted her. One brief touch of her skin against his on the street, the scent of her sweet perfume filling his nostrils, and he'd been harder than stone. She'd managed in two seconds what no woman since he'd left the island had managed at all. If he was going to be married to her, then dammit, he was going to enjoy it.

Leo froze as the elevator doors opened onto the foyer of the apartment.

The television blared from the living area, which meant that Bobby had stopped by again. Bobby often let himself in when Leo wasn't home. Since he'd returned to London, his father had come around a lot, almost as if he'd missed Leo over the years. Their relationship had never been much of a father-son relationship, but one of the things Leo had been determined to do when he returned to London was put his anger at his father behind him.

It wasn't always easy, but it was getting easier with time.

Leo had intended to stay in one of his hotels until he found the right place to buy, but Bobby had insisted he stay in the apartment since Bobby rarely used it anymore. Leo had wanted to refuse, but one look at the hopeful expression on his father's face and he'd been unable to do it.

"He's missed you, Leo," Allegra had said.

"Did he say that?" Leo had practically snapped.

His sister had shook her head. She was the good girl in the family, the sweet one who tried to keep peace between them all. "Not in so many words. But he did. He's talked of nothing else since you said you were coming back again."

Leo sighed. Bobby wasn't a bad man; he was simply an impulsive and irresponsible one.

The last person Leo felt like dealing with tonight was Bobby, but he threw his jacket across a chair and headed into the lounge anyway. Bobby was watching a football game and drinking a beer, shouting when his favorite player made a particularly tricky shot. The ball missed the net and Bobby swore.

"Hey, Leo," he said, looking up when the shadow of Leo's form fell across the room.

Leo shoved both hands into his pockets. "Dad."

"Something wrong, boy?" Bobby asked, muting the television as he gazed up at Leo. Somehow, Leo wasn't surprised his turmoil was showing. He *was* surprised that Bobby asked about it, however.

Yes, he wanted to say. *Help me figure this out. Tell me something useful.*

"Nothing I can't handle," he replied instead. He'd learned long ago not to count on Bobby for advice. Bobby meant well, but he had no clue. Like when he'd stood up at Allegra's engagement party and congratulated her on landing a wealthy prince. That had certainly *not* been his finest moment.

Bobby shrugged. "You always were a smart kid. Got that from your mother. I'm right proud of you, you know."

Leo felt a twinge of hurt at the mention of his mother. Bobby had long ago apologized for the way he'd left Leo's mother to raise him alone, but it still hurt sometimes when Bobby mentioned her. "Yeah. Thanks."

His father looked up again, his forehead creasing. "You want me to go?"

He did—and he didn't. "Not if you don't want to."

Bobby leaned back on the couch and took another sip of beer. "Chantelle's having some damn girls' night thing at home and I didn't want to be around for it. Women can be diabolical when they congregate in packs, let me tell you."

Leo went into the kitchen and grabbed a beer of his own before returning and sitting across from Bobby. The game continued unabated, Bobby cursing and cheering depending on who was down at the time.

Leo drank his beer, feeling sour. Why hadn't he just told Bobby to go? Having his father here was like having a college frat brother staying over. You had something in common, you knew you did, but you couldn't for the life of you see what it was.

"Why did you get married?" Leo asked during a lull in the game.

Bobby hit the mute button and swiveled to look at him like he'd grown another head. "Which time?"

"Any of them," Leo said shortly.

Bobby blew out a breath. "Seemed like the thing to do, I guess."

"Were you ever in love?"

Bobby's face split into a grin. "Every single time, my boy."

Leo felt a pang in his gut. "How is that possible?"

His father shrugged. "It just is. What's this about?"

Leo leaned his head back on the seat, closed his eyes. What did it matter? It would be in the papers before too much longer anyway. "I'm getting married," he said shortly.

"You don't sound happy about it."

"I don't know how to feel."

"Is she pregnant?"

"Yeah."

Bobby made a sucking sound with his teeth. "It's the

right thing to do, then. You'll figure it out." Then he stood and put a hand on Leo's shoulder. "It'll work itself out, son."

"I'm sure it will," Leo said, oddly regretful that his father had nothing else to say. Bobby squeezed, almost as if he wanted to say something else, but then his hand fell away and Leo heard his footsteps retreating across the floor.

A few moments later the elevator doors whisked closed, and Leo knew that Bobby was gone. He took out his mobile phone and stared at the face for a long while before he brought up his contacts. He had to let Allegra know before she read about it in the papers. But he couldn't stand to talk to another person tonight, so instead he typed out a message.

Getting married. To Anna Constantinides. Just wanted you to know. Papers will have a field day.

He lay the phone down for barely a moment when it buzzed again.

Wow! I take it more happened on that island than you let on. Congratulations. I think. J Oh, Leo. Please tell me you're happy.

Leo hesitated only a moment before he typed the answer he knew Allegra needed to hear, whether it was true or not.

Don't worry, A. I'm happy.

CHAPTER TEN

ANNA slept pretty well, considering all the stress of the day before. She awoke late, ordered breakfast in her room and dressed hurriedly in navy trousers and a cream blouse with tiny buttons that went almost to her throat. She left the last few unbuttoned so she could wear her pearls, and brushed her hair into a long, thick ponytail fastened loosely at the base of her neck. It was a departure from the usual updo, but it felt like the thing to do today.

She put the brush down and sighed at her reflection. She should be happy. Leo had said he would marry her. Their baby would be safe from scandal. And yet what he'd said to her last night still ate at her. Did she want to be married for the baby's sake or for her own?

She'd thought she was doing this for the baby, but a tiny part of her nagged that she wasn't. That Leo was right and it was herself she feared for. Was she truly that much of a coward?

She thought of the headlines the day after the photo of Alex kissing Allegra Jackson had first appeared in the paper. She'd been stunned by the report that he'd bought an engagement ring for this woman when it was she who had been wearing the official ring.

And then the reporters had started calling her every hour of the day and night, wanting a quote, wanting to catch her in an unguarded moment. Wanting to humiliate her even more than she already had been. She'd gone into seclusion on Amanti and prayed for the storm to pass. It hadn't, though the attention had lessened somewhat as the press focused more and more on Alex and Allegra's whirlwind romance.

Even her crash with Leo had only garnered a bit of attention, more for the spectacular circumstances of the crash and rescue than because she'd been alone with a notorious playboy. She'd been surprised by that, but she'd taken it for the rare gift it was.

But when she married Leo, when her secret was out, it would all change. She only hoped the storm would pass quickly, and she'd be free to live her life out from under the microscope of the media.

At precisely a quarter to eleven, Leo arrived as promised. Her heart turned over again at the sight of him. He wore a charcoal suit with a maroon shirt unbuttoned at the neck. It was stylish and daring and fit Leo to perfection. She envied him the ability to get away with color and still look so powerful and masculine. He made her seem dull in comparison, but perhaps it was the truth. She was dull.

And she wanted to keep it that way. She'd had enough color in the form of media attention to last her a lifetime. Shame flickered to life inside her.

Have you ever considered that perhaps you are more worried for yourself than you are for the child?

"I've made an appointment with one of the city's top obstetricians," Leo said to her. "We'll need to be going if we're to make it on time."

"Is that necessary?" she asked, gripping the door frame. "I feel perfectly fine. And I'd prefer to find someone on Amanti after we're married."

Leo frowned. "I'm not sure how you envision this wedding happening, Anna, but it won't happen today. And it won't happen on Amanti. We are marrying here. And we're staying here."

"I can't stay in London," she said automatically, her pulse throbbing. "I'm the Tourist Ambassador to Amanti. I have things to do. A home, family—"

"So go back to Amanti," Leo said tightly.

She squeezed her fingers on the door frame until her knuckles were white. "I can't do that."

"Then we have an appointment to keep, don't we?" He turned without waiting for an answer and strode down the hall toward the elevator. Fuming, she grabbed her purse and a light jacket and followed him. They took the elevator down to the ground floor and emerged in the bright sunshine of a clear London day. A minute later they were in his limousine, crawling through traffic like everyone else.

"I didn't come here to stay," she said coolly, though her pulse beat erratically beneath her skin.

Leo swung his head around to look at her. "You expect me to leave my business and move to Amanti because you wish it?"

"No. But surely we can work something out."

"What is it you suggest?" he asked.

Anna shrugged. "I could go back to Amanti after we're married. You could visit from time to time—"

"Out of the question," he said. "Did you not hear a thing I said to you last night?"

Her ears felt hot. "I heard you."

"Then you'll know that we're staying here. For the time being."

"Why?" she burst out. "You don't really want this marriage, or me, so why make it any harder than it needs to be?"

His gaze was so very cool. Unemotional. And yet she

thought she saw a glimmer of heat behind those dark coffee eyes. "How do you know what I want, sweet Anna?"

She dropped her head, stared at the purse she clutched in her lap. "I don't want you to pretend, Leo. I know this isn't easy for you, and I appreciate that you're willing to help me—"

He made a noise that brought her head up. His expression, she noted, was patently furious. "You act as if this were an immaculate conception. I believe it takes two to make a baby."

"I know that," she said quietly.

"Then stop attributing motives to me that are designed to make you feel superior."

His words stung. "That's not it at all," she snapped. "But I have eyes, Leo, and I can sense when someone is unhappy. You'd rather be waking up this morning with the lovely Donna, not taking me to the doctor, so don't *you* pretend you're offended by anything I have to say. You'd rather this baby didn't exist, and you'd rather I was back on Amanti and nothing more than a memory."

He leaned toward her, his jaw set in a hard line. "If you're always this charming, it's no wonder Prince Alessandro found my sister more appealing."

Her skin prickled with heat as a sharp pain daggered into her. "Are you always this cruel?"

"That depends," he said. "Are you always this self-righteous?"

She stared at him for a long moment, locked in battle—but she suddenly felt so defeated, as if life had conspired to knock her down at precisely the moment when she was already at her lowest. Anna put her face in her hands, breathed deeply.

"I'm trying to do the right thing," she said, her voice coming out muffled and weak. Which made her angry.

She wasn't weak, dammit! She was strong, as strong as she needed to be to protect her child.

She dropped her hands, thrust her chin up. She would not cower before him.

"There's the dragon lady," he murmured. "If only you would bring her out to play when the press dares to mock you."

"It's an impossible battle to win," she said with a haughty sniff. "And I'd rather save my energy for other things."

The flame she'd seen in his gaze earlier flared to life again. "Yes, perhaps that's a good idea after all."

Anna felt herself coloring. *Cool. She must be cool.*

She might not be a queen-in-training any longer, but she hadn't spent years learning to be serene and unflappable for nothing. She held her head high, determined to be professional and businesslike. "How soon can we be married?"

Leo chuckled. "Eager, are we?"

Even the roots of her hair felt hot. Anna folded her trembling hands over her purse. "I'm eager to move on with the plan," she said. "Before I start to show."

"It will take at least two weeks, possibly three."

She felt her jaw drop. "Three weeks?"

"I'll do what I can, but two weeks is the minimum time needed. You won't be showing by then."

"We could go to Amanti," she said practically. "The wait time is seven days."

Leo shook his head. "That's hardly worth the trip, Anna. Besides, I can't leave my business at the moment."

"You left your business to go to Santina for the engagement party," she said.

"Yes, and I lost several days, most especially when we crashed on the island. Being out of touch with my board of directors for two days during negotiations for a property in Brazil was a bit, shall we say, chaotic."

She didn't like the delay, but what else could she do? She already knew that once the baby was born, everyone would count backward. What did two—or three—weeks at this point matter?

She turned her head away from him. The limo had ground to a halt near Marble Arch, and happy tourists took photos and gawked at the white structure. They looked so carefree it made her ache. When had she ever been that carefree?

On the island, a voice whispered.

Except it wasn't *quite* true, was it? She'd definitely had cares—would they be rescued, what would the press say and so on—but she'd felt more like a different person there than she ever had before. A person without so many worries. A person who could swim naked with a gorgeous man and make uninhibited love on a secluded beach.

Anna clenched her fingers around her purse strap. She could still see him naked, his golden body so hard and perfect in the Mediterranean sun. Leo was flawlessly made, tall and lean and muscular in all the right places. He'd smiled on the island. Made her laugh. Made her moan and beg and shudder.

It had meant so much to her, she realized. Too much. While he'd returned to London and continued as he'd always done, she'd thought of him endlessly.

Despair flickered around the edges of her soul, but she refused to let it in. So she'd lost one man she'd been promised to and another she'd given herself to. So what? Others had it worse, didn't they?

And she had a baby on the way. There were new, more important worries to contend with.

In spite of the traffic, they arrived at the obstetrician's office located in a quiet Georgian town house on a side street a few minutes before the scheduled appointment.

Leo exited the car first before reaching in for her, glancing up and down the street as he did so.

Anna's heart lodged in her throat as she sat on the edge of the seat with one leg poised over the pavement. "Do you see anyone?"

"No," he said curtly. "But it doesn't hurt to be on guard."

No, it certainly didn't. She didn't know how long it would take the press to discover her whereabouts, but she didn't imagine it would be long considering the way Leo's family always seemed to appear in the tabloids.

She joined him on the street, clutching his arm as she put her heel in a grate and nearly lost her balance. Leo held her hard against him, steadying her with an arm around her body as they came together breast to belly to hip.

It was the first time she'd been so close to him since the island, and she swallowed, her hands pressing against his chest for balance. They stood that way for a long moment, Leo gazing down at her as she stared back at him, her entire body humming with his nearness. His eyes dropped to her mouth.

Anna held her breath, surprised at how desperately she suddenly wanted him to kiss her. His fingers skated along her jaw, and her eyes drifted closed. His mouth claimed hers oh-so-lightly that she almost wondered if he'd meant it to happen.

Her heart beat like a trapped bird, her body straining toward his. She wanted the kiss to be hotter, harder, more intense—and yet it was perfect just like this. So achingly sweet and tender.

He lifted his head, and then set her away from him as he took her hand and led her into the doctor's office.

Eight weeks pregnant. It didn't seem possible, and yet the technician explained that the math had to do with the day of her last menstrual cycle and not the date of conception. Anna stared at the tiny bean on the screen as tears filled her eyes. She was really, truly expecting a baby. Leo's baby. She turned her head to look at him. He sat beside her, his gaze riveted to the screen. She reached for him without thought and his fingers closed around hers, squeezing softly.

For the briefest of moments, she thought it might be all right. That everything would turn out okay. Together, they would protect this child. Love this child. But then the technician turned on the Doppler and the sound of the baby's heart filled the room. It beat so fast that Anna thought there must be something wrong.

"The heartbeat is perfectly normal, Mrs. Jackson," the technician said in response to her cry.

"I'm not—" She stopped, swallowed. She felt so guilty, as if the technician would know that she wasn't actually Leo's wife yet.

Leo had filled out the paperwork and she hadn't bothered to check it. She'd answered the questions while he ticked off boxes. It reminded her, forcefully, that this was simply an arrangement. They would not be raising their child together, or at least not in the traditional sense. Leo didn't love her. A wave of depression washed over her at the knowledge.

"That is, thank you," she said smoothly. "I'm relieved to know it."

The remainder of the appointment was routine. The doctor asked questions, prescribed antinausea medication, told her when she would need to consider taking a birthing class and informed her when the next visit should be and what would happen then.

And then she was back in the car with Leo and they were pulling away from the curb, leaving Dr. Clemens's office behind. Anna chewed the inside of her lip. There was a pain in her chest, right beneath her breastbone, that wouldn't go away. Not a physical pain, but an emotional one.

What kind of mess had she gotten herself into? What had made her think she could barrel into Leo's life and ask him to marry her for the sake of the baby? What had made her think she could do it and remain untouched? Sitting in that room with him just now, his hand wrapped around hers while they listened to their baby's heart, had been one of the most significant moments of her life. How could she feel this way and not acknowledge that at least some of it was due to him?

"How are you feeling?" Leo asked.

How was she feeling? Lost, confused, alone. Uncertain. But she blinked away the moisture in her eyes and turned to him. "I'm fine."

He smiled for once, a rakish grin that had her heart turning over. Did he have to be charming when she was trying to keep her emotional distance? Why couldn't he keep snarling and frowning?

"It was a bit overwhelming," he admitted, and the breath squeezed in her lungs.

"Definitely." She smiled back, though the corners of it trembled. She hoped he didn't notice. "I have a feeling it's going to stay that way for quite some time yet."

He sighed, his expression troubled. "I think you're right."

She bit her lip, glanced away. It hurt to see him look like that. As if everything in his life had made perfect sense until she arrived in it. "I'm sorry, Leo."

He looked surprised. "For what?"

She took a deep breath, her heart burning. "For everything. If I'd been stronger on the island—"

"Stop," he said, his voice suddenly rough and edgy. "I was there, Anna. I know what happened as well as you do. And I was every bit as much involved in the decision process that got us to this point. Stop trying to insinuate it's solely your failure that created this situation."

"I didn't mean…" But she did, didn't she? She meant that he was simply a man, a rogue, acting on adrenaline and hormones and that she was the one who should have been smart enough and moral enough to put a stop to the sexual heat between them before it got out of hand. By inference, she was accusing him of thinking with his penis.

Of not thinking at all.

He was insulted, and rightfully so. Anna toyed with her pearls out of habit. Would she ever know the right things to say to this man? A lifetime of etiquette training, and she still couldn't manage to be diplomatic when it counted most. She was not the cool, serene woman she'd always thought she was. What a joke to think she could have been a queen when she could barely govern her emotions when it counted most.

"You're right," she told him. "I'm sorry for suggesting I was the only one who should have been in control."

"I know you think you're supposed to be in perfect control of yourself every minute of every day, but that's not the way it works, Anna. You're human. You're allowed to make mistakes."

She dropped her gaze. "I know that." And even if she didn't, she was learning that mistakes were not completely avoidable.

"I'm not quite sure you do. You live by your calendar and all that bloody training you did to be Alessandro's wife. You think that rigidly controlling every moment of every day will keep you from faltering."

"No one wants to be made a fool of," she said in defense.

And yet it felt like such a weak defense now. She'd been made a fool of more in the past month than she ever had in her life, and she was still here. Still kicking.

"Of course not. But it's only when you care so much that anyone has the power to do that kind of harm."

"That's easy for you to say," she snapped, feeling pinned in from all sides. How could you *not* care when people said the most awful things about you? Printing lies to sell papers without a care for the truth? *She* knew what they said wasn't true, but not everyone did. And it hurt to see censure or pity in the eyes of those around her.

He had no idea what she'd been through, what she would go through if anyone found out she was pregnant before she was ready for them to do so. Santina and Amanti were far more conservative than the world Leo inhabited.

"When have you ever been the subject of negative attention? When has anyone ever said anything less than glowing about you?" she demanded.

He looked at her so steadily that she felt the need to drop her gaze from his. She wouldn't, however. She would hold steady and be brave, no matter what he was about to say. And she was suddenly certain, whatever it was, that she wasn't going to like it.

Once more, she'd blundered. She knew it in her bones.

"Before I was born, sweet Anna." His smile was smooth, polished. "My father had an affair with my mother while he was still married. He was at the height of his football career then, and quite the cad. When news of her pregnancy hit the papers, his first wife divorced him. He denied he was my father, of course. It was all the rage for weeks. You can look it up online if you're curious."

He sounded distant, detached, but she knew it had to bother him still. The way he spoke so carefully, his voice devoid of emotion. His expression sadly mocking. As if to say, *See, it's not so bad. I survived.*

"But you're a Jackson now," she pressed, because she didn't know what else to say. Her palms were damp, her skin prickling with heat. *Keep digging yourself a hole, Anna.*

"Yes. Another tabloid adventure when I was ten. My mother died in a drunk-driving accident, and I inherited not only her money, but also the DNA test she'd had done to prove paternity. After a stint in court, Bobby finally decided to do the right thing."

Her heart throbbed for the boy he'd been. He'd lost a parent who loved him and had then been forced onto another one who had tried to deny him. How terrible would that have been for him? "That must have been difficult," she managed.

He shrugged as if it were nothing. "It was a long time ago. I've moved beyond it now."

"But that doesn't change the hurt." How could it? How could you ever forget that someone hadn't wanted you? She'd grown up in a household where she was cherished, the beautiful, talented, bright daughter. And yet she hurt because she'd failed her parents, failed the King and Queen of Santina. Because Alex hadn't wanted her.

"You really are a sensitive creature, aren't you?" Leo asked. "You've lived your life in a bubble and you've been terrified to step outside it. But now you have, Anna, and you have a choice. Be brave, face it head-on, or crumple and let them defeat you. They *will* find out about the pregnancy. You can't keep a secret like this in our circles. Are you prepared for it?"

She sucked air into her lungs. Was she? Because she knew he was right. She'd come here knowing all the while it was a secret that wouldn't remain hidden for long.

"That's why I'm here, Leo. I'm trying to prepare for it in the only way I know how."

"Then I hope, when the news breaks, you aren't hurt by it."

"If I am, I'll get over it. I've had a lot of practice recently." She said it to be brave, but inside she quaked.

He took her chin in his fingers, held her steady, their gazes locking. "You are a dragon lady, Anna. The fiercest, strongest, bravest woman I know. You survived a plane crash, two days on a deserted island and more bad press than any one person should have to endure. And you've done it all with grace and dignity. You will survive this, too."

His words pierced her to her soul. No one had ever, *ever* called her fierce or strong or brave. Competent, organized, pretty—yes. But fierce?

"It's my intention," she said softly.

"Excellent."

He tilted her chin up, and then leaned in and kissed her. The touch of his mouth was a pleasurable shock. His lips were hot against hers, his mouth infinitely more demanding than it had been on the street in front of Dr. Clemens's office. Anna melted into the kiss, though she told herself she should be more reserved with him. More careful. The only person who could get hurt in this situation was her.

Leo was nothing if not famous for his exploits with women. What meant the world to her was simply passing time to him.

But, like it or not, she felt something for him. She'd known it for the past month, though she'd denied it to herself over and over. Leo made her feel things that Alex never had. She felt beautiful, alive. Wanted, needed. Perhaps they were false sensations, but they were wonderful while they lasted. While she believed them.

His tongue slid across the seam of her lips and she opened to him, unable to stop the little moan that escaped her when their tongues met. He was the only man she'd ever kissed. And she didn't feel deprived by that fact. No other man could kiss her like this, she was certain. No other man could make her feel hot and achy and itchy and wonderful all at once.

Leo pulled her closer, the warmth of his body sinking into her flesh. He tilted her head back to give him better access, one hand cupping her jaw while the other slid to her waist. The touch of his fingers burned into her, through the fabric of her shirt and jacket.

He was her Kryptonite, weakening her until she couldn't resist.

"I've missed this," he said. "Missed you."

"Leo, I—"

He kissed her again, and she lost whatever she wanted to say. But her mind raced ahead, took her back to last night, when she'd first seen him walking out of the Leonidas Group headquarters building. He hadn't seemed to miss her at all then. He'd been so utterly self-assured when he'd strolled out of that building with a woman on his arm.

She pushed against his chest, lightly but firmly, and he leaned back, gazing at her through heavy-lidded eyes. Sensuality was as natural to him as breathing, she thought. She wanted to pull him back to her, forget her confused thoughts and lose herself in the promise those dark eyes made to her.

But she couldn't. "Last night, you were with Donna. If I hadn't come along…"

He blew out a frustrated breath. And then he looked down his fine nose at her. "You do realize that I am quite capable of going without sex for more than a day or so, right? Perhaps even weeks at a time. Being seen with a woman does not equate to having gone to bed with that woman."

She felt a stab of guilt. Once more, she was accusing him of thinking with his penis. A tiny, jealous—yes, jealous—corner of her insisted it must be true. He was Leo Jackson, lover of women, serial breaker of hearts.

"But you were planning on it."

"Probably," he said unapologetically. "But not for another week or two at least. Perhaps longer."

Anna sniffed, both chastened and irritated at once. "Then I'm sorry I ruined your plans."

Leo smiled, a sharp predatory smile that made a tingle start in her toes and work its way deep into her core.

"I'm not," he said. "I've a new plan I like much, much better."

CHAPTER ELEVEN

THE next few days were a whirlwind of appointments and appearances. Photographers had started to show up whenever Leo and Anna appeared in public together. He'd told her to expect it, but she still cringed every time. Inwardly, of course. Outwardly, she smiled and posed and tried to look ecstatically happy.

The headlines screamed at her each morning: *Jilted Bride of Santina's Crown Prince in Torrid Love Affair with Notorious Playboy; "I Had No Idea Anna Was in Love with Leo Jackson," Shocked Friend Says; Love Blooms Between Marooned Couple—But Were They Really Marooned, Or Was it Planned?; Crown Prince Alessandro Calls Anna— Come Back to Me, He Begs.* And the worst one of all: *How Long Will Lucky Leo Last This Time?*

Anna crumpled the morning tabloids and made a noise of disgust. He looked at her over the cup of coffee he'd poured from the silver service sitting nearby.

"It's ridiculous how they make these things up!"

"Surely you aren't surprised."

She ran a hand over the back of her neck, rubbed absently. "No, of course not. But it infuriates me anyway. You'd think they have nothing better to do."

"You did insist," he said. Yes, she had insisted on seeing the papers. When she'd sent the order to the front desk originally, Leo had come barreling in soon after, grumbling at her that it wasn't a good idea. She would get upset and that couldn't be good for the baby.

When she'd pointed out that she'd be more upset *not* knowing, he'd relented, albeit reluctantly.

Now, Leo got to his feet and came over to where she stood near the window, looking out over Hyde Park. The sun was shining today, and people strolled along the sidewalks and sat on park benches. Pigeons congregated around a man throwing something onto the ground. A red double-decker bus glided by on the street below, the top open and filled with tourists craning their necks and aiming their cameras.

Leo's hands settled on the back of her neck, and then he began to rub. Anna bit her lip to stop the moan that wanted to escape. It felt so good to have his hands on her. She wasn't quite sure if it was soothing in the way he intended it to be or titillating.

"You're tense," he murmured against her ear, and an electrical zap of energy shot down her spine, gathering in her core. Leo hadn't touched her since that kiss in the car, other than perfunctory touches for the cameras. She'd thought then that he'd wanted to make love to her again, that he intended to seduce her into his bed. It had excited her and frightened her at the same time.

But he'd done nothing since, and she'd been humming with frustration. It was better this way, she told herself. Better because this marriage would be temporary. Leo must have decided it, too, because he'd not pursued the issue when surely he must have known how easy it would be to send her over the edge. She was a mass of sensation waiting to happen. A collection of tinder anticipating the match.

"I keep expecting something worse," she said, her skin

tingling wherever he touched. His fingers were sure as he kneaded her shoulders and neck.

"Something worse than Lucky Leo?" She could hear the smile in his voice, but she wasn't nearly as amused as he was.

Finally, something to focus on that would distract her from the sensation of his hands on her skin. "That is a rather disgusting name, considering how you earned it."

"By bedding six lingerie models simultaneously."

"It's not funny, Leo," she said, turning to look up at him.

His smile didn't fade. "Perhaps not. But what you desperately want to know, sweet Anna, is if it's true."

She dropped her gaze from his, a jealous fire flaring to life in her belly. *Jealous?* "You couldn't be more wrong," she said haughtily. "It's a vile exaggeration anyway."

His laugh was soft, deep, pulling at something elemental inside her. "Slightly. There were only four of them."

Anna stepped away from him, certain her cheeks were flaming scarlet by now. Leo with four women. Leo, naked and surrounded by *four* women. She didn't want to imagine it. A hot, sharp dagger of anger pierced through her heart. She wanted to choke someone. Four someones. "I said I didn't want to know."

"I'm only telling you the truth, Anna. Why keep secrets when we're about to be married?"

She wrapped her arms around herself. *Because this isn't real! Because it's a game to you!* The words swelled against the back of her throat, aching to escape, making it hard to breathe for the barest of moments. But she swallowed them back, refusing to let them out. "I don't see any need to confess deep dark secrets. This is an *arrangement,* not a true marriage."

He was still smiling, but she could see the hard glint in his eyes. As if she'd angered him. Or insulted him.

"Yes, of course. How could I have forgotten? You only need me to help you get through this difficulty, and then it's back to Amanti where you can play the proper lady. Though perhaps a slightly tarnished one, since you will have been married to me."

A throb of guilt beat a new tempo in her veins. "That's not fair," she said. "You twist my meaning."

The hard look was still there. "Do I? From the first, you've impressed upon me the importance of your reputation. Your status as the *ex*-bride-to-be of a future king." He tsked. "This must be so embarrassing for you, Anna. You've lain down with a mongrel and come home with fleas."

She flung away from him. He twisted everything she said, made her seem so awful and shallow when she was only trying to be fair to them both. To who they were as people. They didn't know each other well, it was true, but she knew what he was. What he'd always been. He'd never denied it, and now he was angry with her over it?

"You act so wounded! But tell me the truth, Leo—did you really want to be a husband and father? Is that what you see yourself doing? Because if so, why didn't you marry Jessica Monroe?"

He didn't react, and yet she knew the name had affected him. The air had changed between them when she'd uttered the name of the woman he'd been linked with in L.A. Grown heavier, thicker, tenser. She waited for him to speak, both fearing and needing to hear his answer.

When he did, his voice was cool. Detached. Clinical. "Jessica and I came to a mutual decision."

But Anna wasn't letting it go that easily. "And then she married some other man six months later and adopted a baby."

"We had different goals."

"Is that what it's called?" Bitterness churned in her belly. How could he not admit the truth when it was right there for everyone to see? He'd lived his life in front of the tabloids, sleeping with and casting off women with the kind of frequency with which most men changed their shirts. *Leo Jackson* and *family man* were not words ever used together in the same breath.

He'd practically said as much to her on the island.

"My relationship with Jessica Monroe has nothing to do with my relationship with you," he said tightly. She had the distinct impression that he was leashing some deep anger—or hurt?—within him. It gave her pause, but only for a moment. "*We* are getting married, and we have a child on the way."

"I've not forgotten it, I assure you," she said crisply, the blood beating in her temples, her throat. Something was going on between them that she didn't quite understand, and it infuriated her. Bothered her. How could she engage in conversation with him and still not quite know what either of them meant by the words they said? It was like going through a carnival fun house and not knowing what to expect around the next corner. "But I still don't believe it's your first choice of occupation."

He was going out of his mind with desire for her. Leo was still furious at their conversation of that morning, but he'd shaken it off as best he could and had taken her out to look at potential homes. He'd been putting the task on the back burner since he'd been so busy lately, but once Anna had arrived with her proposal of marriage, there was no getting past the fact it was high time to find a place and buy it.

Now, they were touring a two-level exclusive flat in a period building in Knightsbridge. Anna had grilled the estate agent on the amenities and led the way through the

five-hundred-square-meter property. The agent had finally retired to the walkway out front to smoke a cigarette
and make phone calls while he waited for them to finish.

Anna stood in the center of one of the upper bedrooms,
staring at nothing that Leo could see. He took a moment
to admire her form. She was, as always, buttoned up tight
in a cream sweater set and gray skirt with, surprisingly,
platform heels that made her legs so long and sexy. The
pearls were a fixture around her neck, of course. She was
playing with them, as she always did when she was upset
or nervous or simply concentrating on something.

Her long dark hair was loose today, and he ached to
thrust his fingers into the heavy mass as he took her body
for his pleasure. Anna never wore her hair loose. The effect was about to kill him. He'd never been as achingly
aroused as he had been for the past hour, watching her bare
legs and round bottom as he followed her through the flat.

There was also, he had to admit, a simmering brew
of despair and anger mixed in with the arousal. She was
convinced he had nothing to offer in the way of being a
husband or father. He wasn't sure he did either, but it was
damned depressing to think of her leaving him once the
baby was born. He'd been thinking about it all morning,
and found himself surprisingly affected by it. He wanted
to punch something. He wanted to rage and howl and ex-
pend a great deal of energy by doing *something* that re-
quired him to push himself to physical extremes.

Base-jumping. Mountain climbing. Extreme hiking
across the Sahara.

Barring that, he wanted to lock Anna up and never let
her out of his sight.

It was true that he didn't know the first thing about
babies. They terrified him. So tiny and delicate and depen-
dent on adults to take care of their needs. What if he was

terrible at it? What if letting Anna go back to Amanti to raise their baby was the best choice for all of them?

And yet the thought of Anna and his child leaving him to his previous life of empty sex and meaningless relationships made him feel strangely forlorn. What if Anna met someone else and married him? That man would become his child's father, and Leo would have no business in their lives whatsoever.

Something deep and elemental inside him responded with a resounding, *No!*

"I'm not sure, Leo," Anna finally said, cutting into his thoughts as she turned to him in the empty room. Her voice echoed down from the high ceilings.

"Not sure of what?"

"It's gorgeous, but I'm not sure it's you. I see you in a penthouse somewhere, with sleek modern furnishings and a city view."

A flicker of annoyance slid across his soul. "It's not about me, Anna. It's about us. You will have to live here, too."

She dropped her gaze from his, and a current of anger and misery flared to life inside him, scorching him with the force of a thousand burning suns. And yet, could he blame her for thinking what she did? For thinking he was incapable of being what she wanted and needed him to be?

He'd made a second career out of being the kind of man women didn't say no to. He'd never met a woman he couldn't charm straight out of her knickers, and he'd never hidden that fact. Nor had he hidden the fact he wasn't the settling-down type. He'd never thought he would want to. The idea that he might after all gave him pause.

"Jessica wanted to get married. I didn't."

Anna's head snapped up, her jade-green eyes wide. He didn't know why he'd said it since it confirmed everything she thought about him, but he felt compelled to continue. He loved it when she looked at him, he realized. There was a little kick, right beneath his ribs, every time.

"She had a grown daughter, but she wanted a new baby. The roles in Hollywood were drying up for an actress her age. I believed she was latching on to the idea of marriage and a baby as a new challenge in life. She believed I was wrong. The split was mutual."

"Did you love her?" she asked, and he sensed that it cost her something to ask it.

Leo blew out a breath. The answer would do him no credit, but he wouldn't lie. "No."

She blinked. "No? Just like that, no?"

"If I'd loved her, would I have let her go? Or would I have done everything in my power to make her happy?"

"I see," she said.

He didn't think she saw anything. He and Jessica were similar in personality. Neither of them demanded anything from the other. They'd had a good time together. Love had never entered into the equation, for either one of them.

But then the arguments had begun. Small at first, escalating later as Jessica Monroe, once prized for her face and body, had started to weary of the fight for new roles. He'd never quite understood, as she remained to this day one of the sexiest women he'd ever known. But Hollywood was fickle, and that fickleness had driven Jessica to want more from him than he was willing to give.

Ironic that he now stood here with a woman who was not only pregnant with his child, but that he'd also agreed to marry.

He closed the distance between them suddenly. She took a step back, but he caught her and pulled her to him. He didn't know why he had to hold her, but he did. He needed to feel her soft, warm body against his. Needed to know she was real, that their baby was real. He'd never quite known his place in life, never understood where he fit in in the Jackson family. He was the odd man out, the one who'd come in from the outside and tried to belong. Well, maybe Angel knew that feeling, too, but it was different—her father hadn't denied she was his and refused to have anything to do with her. She wasn't a Jackson by blood. He was, though he wasn't sure it had ever meant anything to him.

Anna put her hands on his chest as he caught her close, her head tilting back. She did not try to escape. In fact, he felt a tremor run through her. That faint vibration that let him know she was not unaffected. That she still wanted him as much as he wanted her.

Oh, she'd been good at pretending she did not—but only when he didn't touch her. When he touched her, he knew. And he wasn't prepared to show her any mercy. Not any longer.

"Do you ever think about it?" he asked. "Those two days on the island when there was nothing but sand and sea and *us?* You and me, naked beneath the hot sun?"

Her eyes were green pools of mystery. And warmth, he realized. Warmth for him. She usually hid it, but she wasn't doing a good job at the moment. It gave him hope, though for what he wasn't quite certain.

"I've thought of it," she admitted, her cheeks flushing as she spoke. Such lovely, lovely color, he mused. "How could I not?"

A low throb of arousal pulsed at the base of his spine. He wanted to take her here, now, in the middle of this room with the estate agent outside and the bright London sunshine streaming through the tall paned windows. "Then why are we merely thinking about it," he murmured, "when we could experience it again? In a bed this time, sweet Anna, with all the romance and tenderness you deserve."

"I—I'm not sure that's a good idea," she said, her gaze dropping to study her fingers where they rested on his shirt.

"How can it be a bad idea? You burn for me, Anna. You want me."

"That doesn't mean it's a good idea."

"Doesn't mean it's a bad idea, either," he told her, dipping his head to skim his lips along her jaw. She tilted her head back, her fingers clutching him. His body was stone. Hot, hard stone.

"Leo…"

"We're marrying, Anna," he said, trying not to make it sound like begging. Was he begging? An interesting thought, really. But he would, at this moment, do anything to get her naked and beneath him again. A singular thought. "Shouldn't we see if this could work between us before we assume it will not?"

Before she could answer, he heard a door open and shut, and he knew the estate agent had returned. Anna took advantage of his distraction to disengage from his embrace. But it wasn't a rejection. That much he knew. She tucked a strand of her hair behind her ear and folded her arms over her body. It wasn't a defensive gesture so much as a protective one.

Triumph surged in his bones. She would be his again. Soon.

Tonight.

CHAPTER TWELVE

A TRIO of boxes arrived within a couple of hours after she'd returned to the hotel. Anna directed the porter to place them on a table. Once she'd given him a tip and he'd gone, she turned her attention to the pretty white boxes tied in red ribbon. A card was on the top of the smallest one.

Wear these tonight. Eight o'clock for dinner.

She opened the smallest one first. A pair of slender designer heels with crystal studs on the straps made her heart kick with excitement. She'd never hidden the fact she loved beautiful shoes. Just because she wore conservative clothes didn't mean she needed to wear ugly shoes. That would be a sin against nature.

Next was a box with an electric-blue lacy thong and a matching strapless bra that made a tendril of heat uncoil in her belly. Leo wanted her to wear these tonight because he hoped to see her in them. She wasn't so dumb as to believe otherwise. Nor was she so certain of her answer that she wasn't going to put them on.

When he'd held her in the flat earlier, she'd wanted nothing more than to lie in a soft bed with him, naked skin against naked skin. She knew what awaited her when she did: heat and passion and physical pleasure so intense it would make her sob with joy. She wanted that again, even while it frightened her.

She wasn't afraid because she feared sex with Leo. She was afraid because she feared the truths she might have to admit to herself once he stripped her of her defenses. She turned to the last box with a little shiver of excitement dancing down her spine.

It contained a sequined dress in chili-pepper red. The dress was strapless, of course, and fitted through the bodice, hips and knees until it suddenly burst free in a gorgeous fantail. It was bold, far bolder than anything she'd ever worn in her life, with its blazing-hot color and sleek fit.

Her heart thrummed as she picked it up and went to stand in front of the mirror with it. Everyone would notice the woman who wore a dress like this. Could she bear the scrutiny right now?

Did it even matter? she asked herself a minute later. The press was already scrutinizing her. Since she'd started to appear in public with Leo, photographers had become a fixture in her life once more.

In the end, she decided to put the dress on. And the underwear. She left her hair long and loose, curling the ends so they fell in soft waves over her shoulder. A check of her reflection in the full-length cheval glass featured a woman she hardly recognized. A bright, sassy woman who walked into a room and owned it.

She'd never felt like she owned a room before. She'd been counting on her status after she'd married Alex to make her feel that way, but the truth was she should have learned the art long before. For herself alone.

A few minutes before eight, Leo arrived. He stood in the doorway with his hot coffee-colored gaze drifting over her and she felt as if an explosion had detonated inside her. He was resplendent in his custom-fit tuxedo. The white of his shirt contrasted sharply with his tanned skin and dark hair, making him seem even more devilish than he was. His sensual lips curved in a smile that whispered of sex and sin, and her heart went into a free fall.

She didn't even realize that she'd pressed her hand to her chest until he frowned.

"Are you feeling well?" he asked suddenly, coming into the room and taking her in his arms. "Is it the baby?"

"I'm fine," she managed. "I just felt light-headed for a moment."

And that was the truth. She'd taken one look at Leo and something inside her had shifted for the tiniest moment, taking her breath along with it.

"We can stay in," he said, looking concerned. "I'll order dinner up—"

"No, I'm fine. Really." She clutched his arm. "I want to go out. I didn't put this dress on for nothing."

He smiled, too, but there was worry in his eyes. "And a lovely dress it is, sweet Anna. You should always wear bold colors. They suit you."

She glanced down at the glaring red fabric. Count on Leo to see what she couldn't see for herself. When she'd looked in the mirror, she'd known he was right about the color. "This is a giant leap for me. I'm not accustomed to calling attention to myself."

"You should be," he said, his voice rough and soft all at once. Was that a kernel of need she heard? The idea thrilled her. "You are stunning, Anna. Marvelously stunning."

She laughed, but the sound was nervous, high. Could he tell? "Thank you for the dress. I would have never picked it."

But Leo had. Because he saw something in her that she was only just learning to see for herself. It warmed her, made her pulse kick again. She was prepared for it this time.

"But do you like it?" he asked softly.

"I do, actually. I feel quite special in it."

Leo's smile had the power to make her heart flutter. "Because you are special, Anna." He took her hand and kissed it. "Never doubt it."

The restaurant he took her to was very exclusive. He was greeted by a fawning maître d' and staff, and then they were shown to a table in an empty dining room. The room was exquisite, with deep mahogany paneling on the walls, a frescoed ceiling and crystal chandeliers. The single table was set with crystal wine and water glasses, heavy silver flatware and a profusion of cream roses in a silver vase at the center.

After they were seated and the maître d' walked away, Anna glanced around the empty room and then back at Leo. He lifted an eyebrow, as if waiting for the question he knew must be coming. She laughed, then pressed her hand to her mouth and tried not to. Nerves, she told herself.

He reached over and took her wrist gently, removing her hand so her laugh sprang free again.

"Leo," she said. "This is crazy! Did you buy the restaurant?"

His smile was genuine. Pleased. "No. But I did buy the night."

She shook her head. It was unreal. Romantic. "We could have eaten with other people."

"Not tonight. I wanted you to myself."

"You've had me to yourself nearly every day."

"Not the same," he replied. "It never lasts long enough. Tonight, however, we'll have as much time as we want."

"There are staff," she pointed out, feeling bubbly inside nevertheless. "They aren't going anywhere, I assume."

"No, and later there will be an orchestra."

She blinked. "An orchestra?"

"We've never danced, Anna. I want to hold you in my arms on a dance floor."

She looked down at the white napkin carefully folded across a charger plate bordered in tiny gold scrollwork. Her heart felt as if it would burst from her chest any minute. She was happy, happier than she'd been since the island, and it worried her. What if it all fell apart tomorrow?

"You might be disappointed," she said softly.

"I doubt that." His voice was strong, sure, as if he'd never doubted anything less in his life.

"What if I step on your toes?" she asked, trying to lighten up the moment. Because, for her, it was too intense. Her skin felt too tight, stretched thin over the weight of emotions boiling inside her.

"Can't happen," he said. "You spent years training to be a queen. Queens don't step on toes. Or, if they do, it's quite deliberate."

She laughed again. "So if I step on you, you will chalk it up to malicious intent?"

"Most definitely."

A bow-tied waiter appeared just then with wine for Leo and a nonalcoholic cocktail for her. They talked about small things once he was gone—the weather, the state of tourism in Amanti as compared to London—and then the food began to appear.

Anna found that she was starving for once, and she ate everything placed in front of her, whether it was a seared *fois gras* on a bed of baby greens, a grilled filet with béarnaise sauce or a truffle-stuffed mushroom. Everything was delicious.

After the meal was cleared away and dessert served, Leo placed a velvet box on the table. Anna put her fork down, her pulse skipping into full throttle.

"What is it?" she asked, unable to make herself reach for the small black box.

"I think you know, Anna."

"It's not necessary," she said, though it hurt to say it. She wanted a ring to be inside—

But she wanted the reasons to be real. Anna's breath shortened. Could that really be true? Did she want this to be real?

She did. Oh, God, she did. She wanted him to be marrying her because he wanted to, not because he had to.

Fickle, fickle Anna. This wasn't what she'd wanted when she'd come to London in the first place. Then, she'd only been thinking of her baby and protecting him or her from scandal. Protecting *them both* from scandal, if she were honest with herself. She'd wanted Leo's help, and she'd wanted to continue to play the martyr, the woman who needed no one or nothing to see her through life.

Now, she was realizing that she wanted so much more it frightened her.

"I think it is necessary." He pushed the box toward her.

She picked it up with trembling fingers and popped the top open. The ring was exquisite. A brilliant cut diamond of at least five carats in a platinum setting, surrounded by another two or three carats of smaller diamonds. The ring sparkled like fire in the candlelight, and she felt a pinprick of guilt and sadness. She'd pushed him into this, and she had no one to blame but herself if it wasn't real.

"Well?" he asked.

"It's beautiful," she said, her voice coming out far more hoarsely than she wanted it to.

Leo stood with a growl and took the ring from the box, which he tossed aside as if it were nothing. Then he put it on her finger and kissed her hand, his warm breath sending tiny fingers of sensation crawling down her spine.

When he tilted her head back and kissed her, she didn't resist. She opened to him, her heart filling with love and despair in equal measure.

Love.

She'd been denying it to herself, but she couldn't do so any longer. Anna's heart throbbed with pain and fear and so much love she wondered how she'd denied it for so long. She loved this man, had probably loved him since the moment on the island when he'd kissed her on the forehead instead of the mouth because he'd realized her first kiss should be special. He'd been so tender with her, so thoughtful and selfless. He'd always put her feelings first, and he'd urged her to be her own person without regard to what others wanted from her.

He hadn't done those things because he loved her, she knew that, but it was what made him the kind of man she could love. The man she *did* love.

Oh, God.

His mouth moved over hers so expertly, so hotly, that she wanted nothing more than to melt into him and forget everything but the two of them. He'd planned a romantic evening, given her a ring, but she reminded herself that he was simply doing what she had asked, playing a role she'd wanted him to play in order to protect the baby.

And she had no one but herself to blame. She was in love with this man, the father of her child, but he did not feel the same, no matter how beautifully he kissed her.

He lifted his head, his eyes glittering with need, and her heart squeezed with all she was feeling. With all she could not say.

"Damn the orchestra," he murmured, pulling her to her feet. "I'm through waiting."

Leo didn't take her back to his place. Not because he didn't want her in his space, but because it was Bobby's flat. And

Bobby had taken plenty of women there, both when he was married and when he wasn't. Hell, Leo suspected he still did, though not when Leo was in town.

To take Anna there would be wrong. Anna was not a bit of fluff. She was the mother of his child. His wife-to-be.

He took her back to the Crescent. The ride was silent, fraught with tension as they sat on opposite sides of the limousine. Leo did it to keep from tearing her dress off and taking her inside a car gliding through the London streets at night. He had no idea why she kept her distance. Perhaps for the same reason.

They rode the lift standing at opposite ends while the lift operator hummed and let passengers on and off. Leo wanted to kick everyone off and speed to the fifth floor, but instead he contented himself with watching Anna. She glanced up at him on occasion, her lovely face flushed. She licked her lips, and a spike of pain shot to his groin. He needed her so badly he was beginning to think he might embarrass himself once he was inside her.

When they arrived on the fifth floor, he swept her into his arms while she sighed and strode purposefully toward her door. He thought of fluffy puppies, of sunny fields of grass, of cows munching contentedly—anything but the woman in his arms. He was too completely aware of her. She was in his blood, his bones, and he wanted her utterly.

But he had to think of other things, or their night of bliss would become a minute or two of hurried coupling.

They reached the door and, with a swipe of the key card, were in.

The instant the door closed, her eager mouth fused to his. Leo groaned as he set her down and backed her against the door they'd just entered.

Her hands were on his tuxedo jacket, shoving it from his shoulders until he let it drop at his feet. Next she went for his belt. He found the zipper of her dress and slid it all the way down, pushing the garment down her lush breasts until he forced her to stop and step out of it before continuing with his trousers.

"Beautiful Anna," he said as he tossed the dress onto a chair. She stood there in the electric-blue underwear and heels he'd picked out for her, and she looked even more amazing than he'd dreamed she would. In spite of her protests, he turned her so he could view her lovely bottom in the thong panties. Her cheeks were bare, the thinnest slice of fabric disappearing between them before emerging again in a thin strap he wanted to tear apart with his teeth.

He dropped to his knees and worshipped that bare bottom with his mouth while she gasped. He'd never seen anything more beautiful than Anna's body. Her skin was golden, soft, and he wanted to touch it forever. Wanted to explore every inch of her while she moaned and sobbed and begged him to take her.

He needed her to beg him, he realized. He needed to know she wanted him as desperately as he wanted her.

"Leo," she gasped as his fingers slid beneath her panties and found the wet, hot center of her. He touched his mouth to the hollow of her back, slid his tongue up her spine and then nibbled her ear while his fingers found her most tender spot and stroked against the hot little ridge of flesh.

"Do you want me, Anna?"

She nodded, her eyes closed, her cheek pressed against the door.

"Tell me," he said.

"I want you. I want you so much."

He increased the pressure of his fingers as she began to moan. She shattered with a sharp cry, and then he was turning her, shoving those panties from her hips while she unsnapped his trousers and slid her hand beneath his underwear to wrap around his length.

She made a noise of approval. And then he was grasping her buttocks in his hands, lifting her against the door as his blood roared in his head. She wrapped her legs around him, knowing where he was going with this.

Another moment and he plunged into her as far as he could go. She took him greedily, her body so wet and ready it made him groan. The feelings washing over him were too much to process, so he shoved them down deep and concentrated on what he did best.

"Leo," she gasped as he slammed into her again and again. "Yes, yes, *yes...*"

He lost his mind. Lost what was left of it anyway. He drove into her as desperately and as precisely as he could manage. Had it ever felt this good? This right? Had he ever, ever wanted it to continue without end? Had he ever cared more for someone else's pleasure than his own? Of course he'd always made sure the women he bedded were happy, but had he *cared?*

When she flew apart, he knew. Her body gripped him hard, squeezed him as he thrust into her.

"Leo," she cried. "Leo!"

He gripped her harder, drove into her until he was spent, until he came in a hot rush that stole his breath. And then he swept her into his arms, took her to the plush queen bed in the adjoining room, and did it all over again.

Morning came too soon. Anna awoke slowly to the smell of coffee and hot food, her entire body feeling more languid and relaxed than it had in a very long time. She was boneless, a mass of satisfied nerve endings and raw emotions.

She turned over in the bed, encountered nothing but pillows and sheets. Leo had clearly gotten out of bed already.

Her heart turned over at the thought of him last night, of all that glorious single-minded male lust focused upon her lucky, *lucky* body.

He'd taken her with such animalistic passion against the door, and again in the bed, giving her no quarter at all, no mercy, as he drove her relentlessly toward shattering climax after shattering climax. But early this morning, in the hour after dawn, he'd made love to her much more tenderly, spinning pleasure up slowly and thoroughly until it crested like a high tide.

She'd loved every moment of it, craved it yet again, though it had only been a few hours. But hadn't that been the way on the island, as well? Warmth flooded her as she remembered.

Simply put, Leo Jackson was a drug she didn't want to quit.

Her drug of choice walked in then, carrying two cups of steaming liquid. He was wearing absolutely nothing, and her pulse skipped wildly, a trapped butterfly in a jar.

"Surely you didn't answer the door like that," she said evenly.

He grinned. "Of course not, darling. There was a towel. I seem to have lost it. No doubt to impress you."

"Lucky me."

He bent and kissed her, then handed her a coffee. "Lucky you indeed," he said. "That's decaf, by the way. With cream and sugar, the way you like it."

She took a sip, her lashes dropping over her eyes. He knew how she liked her coffee. It made her heart clench tight in her chest, but she told herself not to read more into it than it was. It was simply coffee, the way she liked it, and decaf because caffeine was bad for the baby. Nothing more, nothing less. He'd had coffee with her enough over the past few days to know what she wanted.

It was not a declaration of love.

Love.

Her stomach did a slow flip. The feeling was still so new, so raw, and sometimes it snuck up on her and grabbed her by the throat. She wanted to tell him, wanted to spill the words and ease the pain of keeping them locked up tight, but she was scared, too. Scared he wouldn't return the feeling, scared that he would look at her pitifully and say something noncommittal.

She couldn't stand it if he did. Better to be silent and hope he felt the same way than to speak and find out he didn't.

She reached out and touched the tattoo on his abdomen, traced the iridescent scales gently. His muscles clenched in response. It was a beautiful piece of art, seemingly alive in the soft light, but it must have hurt like hell when he'd had it done.

"Careful, or you'll wake the sleeping dragon," he said huskily.

"Oh, I think I can handle a dragon," she replied, arching one eyebrow.

He grinned at her. "Indeed you can. Dragon lady."

"Why did you get this?"

He shrugged as he settled on the bed beside her with his coffee. "A youthful decision, no doubt fueled by alcohol and bravado."

"You can't get a tattoo while drunk, Leo. No reputable studio will do it. And this is too fine not to have been done by a brilliant artist."

"No, I wasn't drunk, more's the pity since it hurt so damn much. But I believe I made a drunken wager that led to the tattoo."

"You could have said no," she pointed out.

"I made a bet, Anna. I could hardly renege."

Her heartbeat accelerated at the thought of him carrying on with something that he'd thought better of simply because he'd given his word. She didn't like to think of the implications to their situation now. Her pulse grew thick in her ears. "Do you always do what you promise, even if it turns out to be a bad idea?"

"I like to think I don't commit to things in the first place that are bad ideas. The tattoo is, as you say, beautiful. I don't regret it at all."

It was inevitable, however, that he must regret *some* things. Would she be one of them? She told herself to stop being fanciful, that tattoos weren't women, but she couldn't quite help it. She wore vulnerability like a second skin this morning. "But you do regret some of them in the end, I imagine."

He set the coffee down on the bedside table. "Who wouldn't? That's life, my darling."

She must have been frowning hard, because he leaned over and took her coffee cup away. Then he kissed her until she clung to him, lips and hands and body. Until desire flared to life inside her, hot little fingers of need caressing her and making her ache for him.

But instead of sliding her beneath him and making love to her again, he swung his long legs off the bed and stood. "Now come, you need to eat something. It's been a while since dinner."

Anna tried to push away the hurt throbbing through her at being rejected, though it wasn't *really* a rejection so much as a postponement. Still, it stung more than it ought when she was feeling so vulnerable.

She threw back the covers, determined to be strong, and reached for her robe. "You are the one who interrupted dessert," she reminded him.

"Did I? And here I thought I gave you a much more satisfying dessert."

Anna laughed as she tied the belt on her robe. "What arrogance," she teased lightly, though dread lay heavy on her heart. "Perhaps I would have preferred the cheesecake."

He stood there before her, one leg thrust indolently out to the side, his magnificent body still naked and rippling with muscle, and swept a hand from his shoulder to his groin as if to showcase the goods. "I am, you must admit, quite worth the interruption."

"I wouldn't dream of denying it," she said.

She left him getting dressed and walked over to the breakfast table. There were eggs, sausage, tomatoes and toast beneath the silver lids. Her folded newspapers lay on the table nearby, and she picked them up, wondering what silly thing the press had managed to say about her and Leo today. It was too much to hope they'd lost interest, of course. The Santina press had nothing else to do. The British tabloids were no better, though at least they filled their pages with plenty of celebrity gossip and WAG tales. Back home, she was front-page news. Here, it was a toss-up.

Not today, however, she discovered when she unfolded the first newssheet. The headline blared at her while her insides churned and a hot little flame began to lick at her.

She read it all the way through and then started again, until the moment Leo snatched the paper from her hand, swearing violently and long.

But it was too late. The words were already imprinted on her brain. How could they not be?

Lucky Leo's Luck Runs Out—The Jilted Bride Is Pregnant!

CHAPTER THIRTEEN

"I'M SORRY, Anna," Leo said, his voice throbbing with anger. "I had hoped we would have longer."

She was still trying to process it. "They took a picture. Of us kissing in front of Dr. Clemens's office. How did they know so soon? And why did they wait to use it?"

Leo swore again and raked a hand through his hair. He looked murderously, furiously angry. She, however, felt nothing.

Or, rather, she felt numb. That's what it was. She was perfectly numb.

It wasn't what she'd expected to feel. It wasn't what she'd felt when the pictures of Alex and Allegra had appeared, along with the headline proclaiming her a jilted bride. That had been embarrassing, no doubt. This, however…this was a violation. Of her life, of her baby's life.

Of Leo's life.

He came and gripped her shoulders, thrust his face into hers and forced her to look up at him. "It doesn't matter, Anna. We're getting married in five days. We're just going to have to deal with this sooner rather than later."

All her plans were wrecked. She'd wanted to marry so that by the time she began to show, the question of scandal would be dubious at best. Oh, sure, when the baby was born, anyone could count backward and figure it out.

But it would be months past, and she would be a married woman with a new baby.

It had been perfect. And now it lay in ruins around her like a pile of bricks that only a moment before the wrecking ball hit was a house.

"How did they figure it out so soon?" she repeated.

Leo's lips thinned. "I don't know, but I intend to find out."

She held up her hand, the ring sparkling and dazzling in the bright morning light. Last night, she'd felt so special and hopeful when he'd taken her to dinner in an empty restaurant and given her this ring. It was everything a romantic night out should be, except for the fact it was staged. Staged because the marriage was already planned.

But she hadn't cared, really, once he'd kissed her and brought her back here. He'd smashed every notion she'd had about how this marriage would go. He'd stripped her barriers, stripped her body, and forced his way into her soul. He was a part of her, in more ways than one, and she loved him. She'd actually had *hope* after last night that everything would turn out well. That she'd be happy, and that Leo would be happy with her.

Until she'd read the paper and realized their secret was out. No one would ever believe there was anything between them but an adherence to duty for the child's sake.

Did she care? Did it matter?

It shouldn't matter, but she found that it did. How could they ever be happy together if their marriage began under a dark cloud of suspicion and scandal? How could she ever be sure that Leo didn't resent her for the circumstance of their marriage?

As the next few days passed, the scandal grew. The usual made-up nonsense got twisted in with the truth, and everything got blown out of proportion. She refused to talk to reporters, as did Leo—so they made things up. They found witnesses, paid doormen and waitresses and coat-check girls, to say anything and everything outrageous and untrue.

Leo grew stony and distant. They had not spent the night together since the evening before the story broke. And, much to her dismay, pictures of their lovely evening together appeared in the papers. Taken with a telephoto lens through a window, someone had caught the moment when Leo had kissed her senseless before taking her back to the hotel.

Now, it was all about appearances, about making everyone think they were blissfully happy together when they were anything but. Leo still took her to dinner, to the theater, to corporate events he had to attend. Photographers lined up in droves outside the venues, the flashbulbs snapping and questions popping like automatic gunfire.

Anna said nothing. Leo ushered her through the gauntlet with either a firm hand on her back or gripping her hand in his. He made no comment, though he did once stop abruptly when a reporter asked him what it felt like to be trapped into marriage by a gold-digging foreigner.

Anna had wrapped her arm around his and urged him to keep walking. After a minute in which she'd felt the tension stringing through him like a bow drawn to the breaking point, he'd done as she asked and continued down the walkway.

Her parents called. They were shocked, outraged and so disappointed. And yet, when her mother had begun to berate her for her impulsive nature, her father had hissed out a curse. A moment later, there had been a heavy silence.

"Anna," her father had said into the phone while her mother started to cry in the background. "You are our daughter and we love you. If this man is not what you want, come home. We will take care of you."

She'd squeezed the phone in her hand. "I'm getting married, Papa. It's what I want."

"Ne," he had said solemnly. "Then we are happy."

She'd hung up then, feeling miserable because she'd put them through so much. And even more miserable that her marriage to Leo was now overshadowed by her pregnancy.

Or, to be fair, it had always been overshadowed by her pregnancy. But at least it had been between the two of them and not the whole world.

The evening before the civil ceremony was finally to take place, Leo had a business dinner in a penthouse suite overlooking the Thames. Anna accompanied him at his request, since there would be spouses and partners present.

As they entered the penthouse, all the chatter died and a dozen faces turned to them. The silence was awkward until a man suddenly came forward and shook Leo's hand, welcoming him to the gathering. The ice was broken and people behaved normally again, mingling in small groups and chatting, eventually coming together for a dinner that had Anna seated across the table and several spaces down from Leo.

She felt uncomfortable, isolated, and her eyes strayed to Leo. He laughed easily, talked to the people seated on either side of him. Anna made small talk with the old gentleman on her right. On her left, a woman pointedly ignored her, only engaging in polite small talk when it was absolutely necessary.

Anna felt the stares all night. It wasn't that these people were scandalized. She was pretty sure they weren't, being as wealthy and connected as they were. Some of them had no doubt been victims of the press in the past, as well.

No, it was the way they looked between her and Leo, no

doubt wondering if theirs was a marriage that would last. By now, everyone knew they'd been marooned on an island together. And everyone knew, clearly, they'd had sex.

Anna was pregnant, and Leo was stepping up to do the right thing. But, poor man, did he really want to be married to such an uptight woman as she? She was trying so hard, but she was still the woman she'd always been. She still liked her calendars and reminders and intricate plans. She felt grounded that way, and she wouldn't apologize for it.

But she'd allowed herself to wear color recently, and she'd even gone so far as to show a little bit of skin on her shoulders and arms. Leo had made her feel beautiful, and she'd felt confident enough to grow bolder in her choices. Tonight she'd chosen a pale pink sheath dress with tiny straps and a bolero jacket.

But she still wore her pearls and she still held her spine stiff and straight.

What a joke it had been to think she would have ever made a good queen. She didn't know how to relax, in spite of all her training. She was stiff, formal and uncomfortable when she believed people were scrutinizing her. As they would have done constantly had she married Alex.

She hid a yawn behind her hand and glanced at her watch. A quarter to eleven. Leo disengaged from the conversation he was having and came to her side as if he sensed her discomfort.

"Are you tired?"

"Yes. I want to go back to the hotel and go to bed," she said. *With you,* she silently added.

Leo made their excuses to the host and hostess, and then they were sitting in silence in the big limousine. Anna yawned again. She wanted him to hold his arm out, wanted to snuggle into the circle of his embrace and lay her head against his shoulder.

She wanted the warmth and happiness they'd had for that one night together. But it wasn't going to happen. Leo, it seemed, regretted their night. Whereas she thought of it as one of the best of her life. They'd almost been happy together. For the barest of moments, she'd thought they would make this marriage work.

That he would love her as she loved him.

Instead, he sat stony and cold and she was unable to break the silence between them. Unable to utter the correct words to make everything go back to the way it was when he'd taken her to dinner four nights ago and given her an engagement ring.

"It was a nice party," she said into the silence.

"Did you think so? I thought you were unhappy."

She colored in the dark, though he could not see it. "I wasn't unhappy."

He turned his head, and she could see the flash of his teeth. "You were. You hardly said anything tonight."

"That's not true," she replied. "I talked to those around me. The woman on my left at dinner was quite difficult, actually."

"Probably because we dated once, long ago."

Anna blinked. A sliver of anger uncoiled within her. And hurt. "Well, I should have guessed. Lucky Leo strikes again."

"Anna, I'm sorry."

"For what?" she said, trying to keep her voice light and gay when she felt anything but. Hurt and anger spun together in a vortex inside her, sucking her down with it. "You can't help that you've probably bedded half of London. Half of the *planet,* I should say."

"I'm sorry I didn't warn you when I saw her tonight. I wasn't pleased you were seated beside her, but whenever I looked in your direction, you seemed to be doing fine."

"My training, no doubt. I am a born diplomat." Hardly, but she wasn't admitting that particular failure to him tonight.

"It won't happen again, I assure you."

"How can you do that, Casanova? Are we to flee every dinner engagement where you've slept with someone present? I fear we'll never go anywhere."

He took her hand. She jumped at his touch. Her body began to melt, to need. Hot sparks flared to life in her belly, between her legs. It had been days since he'd touched her more than perfunctorily.

"You're nervous and upset. I understand. But let's just get through tomorrow, shall we? We have plenty of time to figure it out from there."

Get through tomorrow, get through tomorrow...

"Of course," she said, removing her hand from his lest she melt into a puddle of need and beg him to take her to bed and hold her close all night long.

He wanted to *get through tomorrow.* As if it were an ordeal to be endured. A sentence to be served. A penalty.

It hurt.

They reached the red awning of the Crescent and he helped her from the car. She deliberately took a step back when they were on the red carpet leading into the hotel. The flash of a bulb lit up the night, followed by another and another. Leo hurried her into the marble-and-glass lobby dotted with potted palms nearly two stories tall.

Anna disengaged from his embrace once they were out of sight of the photographers.

"Let's say good-night here," she said, needing to put space between them. Needing to think and plan and not *feel* so damn much whenever he was near. She could do this if she could only gain perspective.

He frowned. She thought he would say no, and then

he tipped his head. "Very well. I'll pick you up tomorrow morning at ten."

She waved a hand in the air as if it were a trifle. "There's no need, Leo. The registry bureau is in the opposite direction from your office. I'll meet you there at ten-thirty. It'll preserve the mystery, yes?"

His brows drew down. "The mystery?"

"If this were a church wedding, you wouldn't be allowed to see me in the dress before I walked down the aisle. Let's attempt to follow the form."

His frown didn't dissipate. But he acquiesced. "If that's what you wish. I'll send a car for you."

"Very well," she said.

And then she stepped up to him and pulled his head down to hers. She kissed him with all the pent-up passion she possessed, triumphing in the groan emanating from his throat. His tongue slid into her mouth, tangled with hers, and she almost believed it. Almost believed he needed her as much as she needed him.

But he didn't. Or at least not in the same way. She disengaged from the kiss, straightening her jacket, and bid him good-night.

He watched her get into the lift. The doors slid closed and she turned into the corner, pressing her fist to her mouth and willing herself not to cry.

It was all wrong. Once more, it was all wrong.

She wasn't coming. Leo stood in the hallway outside the registry office where they were to be married and processed the information he'd just been given. Anna had not shown up, according to the driver he'd sent over for her. A call to her mobile netted him nothing. Another call to the front desk, and he learned that she'd checked out more than two hours ago.

Rage was the first emotion that coursed through him, scouring his insides like sulfuric acid, eating away at him until he wanted to explode into action. But what sort of action? Punching something would do no good, no matter how exhilarating it might feel.

Despair was the second emotion to pummel him. Somehow, that was harder to deal with. She'd left him. Anna Constantinides, his beautiful uptight Greek with her pearls and her veneer of cool competence that he knew hid a passionate, fiery nature. Anna was molten, no matter how hard she tried not to be. All the buttoned-up clothing in the world couldn't hide that sizzling beauty of hers, no matter what she believed.

He stood in that hallway with people passing around him, going on with their lives and jobs, and he felt suddenly bereft. Empty. As if she'd taken the light with her when she'd gone. He didn't understand it. Why had she left? Why, when this marriage had been so important to her in the first place?

He'd always known she was doing it for reasons that had nothing to do with him. The knowledge that she could dismiss him so easily in her calculations had pricked his pride, but had he given her any reason to do otherwise? His greatest fear was being a horrible father. His second greatest was disappointing Anna.

Twice, she'd pushed him from her life. The first time, he'd been angry and disappointed. This time, he felt as if someone had punched him in the gut. Repeatedly.

He knew what he had to do, the only course of action that made sense.

He had to go after her. He had to stop her before she left. It was the only thing that would halt the agony inside him.

And say what to her, Leo?

His mind cast around for the right words. He had to tell

her that he *could* be a better person, that he *wanted* to be a father and a husband, and that he wanted her to give him that chance. That with her by his side, he knew he could do anything. He wasn't doomed to be his own father, wasn't doomed to a life of poor choices and empty relationships if he didn't choose to be.

Leo shot down the hallway, down two flights of stairs, and burst into the gloom of a rainy day. He didn't have time to wait for his driver to come around, so he hailed a cab. The trip to Heathrow took forever but he was finally there, finally bursting through the doors and sprinting for the British Airways counter to buy a ticket to Amanti. It was the only way to get through security to see her.

He strode straight to the VIP line and breezed through to the counter agent.

"I'm sorry, sir," the agent said when he told the man what he wanted. "But that flight is already on the taxiway."

"Then stop it."

"I'm afraid we can't do that, sir."

Leo wanted to haul the agent over the counter by his collar and demand he stop the plane, but he knew that was the surest way to spend a few days cooling off in a jail cell. Instead, he slammed a fist against the counter and went back out into the rain, hands thrust in his pockets, stomach churning with rage and pain. Eventually, he hailed a cab and had it take him back to Knightsbridge.

She'd left him. She'd bloody well left him standing at the metaphorical altar and run away at the last damn minute. Because she knew he didn't belong in her life. His relationships with women had always been about the physical, never the emotional. He was damaged when it came to knowing how to share the parts of him that went deeper than the surface.

But he'd tried. With her, he'd tried. And it hadn't been

good enough, had it? She'd seen through to the damaged parts of his soul and said, *No way.*

Leo didn't even bother drying off when he entered his father's apartment. He poured a glass of Scotch and slumped on the couch, raindrops sliding down his face and plopping onto his damp clothing.

Bobby found him that way hours later, still sitting, still staring at nothing. His clothes had dried, but they were now stiff and uncomfortable. He didn't care.

"What happened to you, boy?" his father demanded, coming over and taking the empty glass away.

Leo looked up, blinked. His eyes felt gritty, tired. "Got what I deserved," he said. "About time, too."

"What the hell are you talking about?"

"Anna. She left me."

Bobby thrust his lower lip out. "Mmm, I see." He perched on the edge of the table closest to Leo. "You love her?"

He'd been thinking about that for hours now. "Yeah, I think I do."

"Think? Or know?"

Leo rubbed a hand over his eyes, his forehead. "How do you ever know?" He knew he was asking the wrong man, not only because Bobby seemed to have an open-door policy on who he loved and how often, but also because Bobby had never yet offered him any advice of substance. But the lonely little boy inside him still wanted it to happen. Wanted his father to step up and be a father for once, not just another partner in crime.

Bobby blew out a breath and rubbed his hands on his knees. "You know because when she's gone it hurts deep down—" he put a fist to his torso, right below his rib cage "—right here. It hurts and it won't go away. No amount of alcohol can kill it. No amount of sex with other women can kill it. Nothing but time, if she won't take you back. And even then, it continues to burn."

Leo blinked. "Who did you feel that way about?" He was too surprised by what Bobby had just said not to ask the question.

Bobby leaned back, hands still on his legs. "Ah, well that's my secret to bear, isn't it? Suffice it to say I screwed up. But you can fix this, Leo. Go after her, tell her how you feel."

As if it were that easy. He'd tried that. It hadn't worked. Anna had left him without a word. She'd never given him the chance, and he was angry about it. Angry that he'd stood there in the airport and felt as if his world was crumbling from beneath his feet and there was nothing he could do about it.

"What if she doesn't care?"

That was the moment when Bobby said the most profound thing Leo would ever hear him say, even if they both lived another hundred years. "If she didn't care, I doubt she'd have left. Women don't run when they aren't scared of something. If all she wanted was your money or your name, she'd have said those vows faster than lightning. Trust me."

Bobby got up then and clamped a hand on Leo's shoulder. "I love you, Leo. I know I haven't always done right by you, but I love you. You'll be a terrific father, not because you had a great example to follow—and we both know you didn't—but because it's who you are inside. There's nothing you do that you don't excel at."

Leo felt tears pricking at the corners of his eyes. "Why haven't you said this before?"

It was…extraordinary. And just strange enough that he almost thought he must be dreaming.

Bobby shrugged. "Because I wasn't sure you'd welcome it. You're so damned independent—get that from your mother—and so competent that I feel a bit out of sorts with you."

"Out of sorts?"

"Hard to admit your kids know more than you do. If I opened my mouth and removed all doubt, would you ever respect me?" Bobby shook his head. "No, just seemed easier to spend time with you and hope you knew how proud you make me. I can't change the past, but I can let you know I'm here now. I've made mistakes, Leo, but I do love you."

Shame jabbed at Leo's conscience then. "When the story broke in the papers, I wondered for a moment if it was you who'd told them. Not on purpose, but inadvertently."

He knew better now, but his father had been the first flash of a thought. The guilt of it, however briefly it had entered his mind, ate at him, especially after what Bobby had just said.

His father shrugged again. "Of course you did. Who else would be most likely to get drunk and open his mouth?" Then he patted Leo. "I've gotten better about that. It wasn't me, but I don't blame you for thinking it could be."

Bobby started toward the elevator and Leo stood to watch him go. "Dad," he said when the doors opened and his father stepped inside.

Bobby turned, his finger on the button. There was so much Leo wanted to say, so much he wanted to know. This relationship was a work in progress and might always be. But it had just taken a step forward that he'd never expected and there was only one response needed.

"Thanks."

The other man smiled, and then the doors closed and he was gone.

CHAPTER FOURTEEN

"It seems as if I was wrong about you," a voice said from behind her. "You aren't a dragon lady at all."

Anna whirled, her toes catching in the sand, and nearly fell to her knees. Fortunately, she did not. The early-morning sun was behind him, silhouetting his body in a nimbus of light as he moved down the deserted beach toward her.

But was he a figment of her desperate imagination, or was he real?

"Leo?"

"Expecting someone else?" he said as he came to a stop a few short feet away.

Anna shook her head because no words would come out. It *was* him. And she could hardly believe he was here. She'd left London nearly a week ago, and she'd regretted it every moment since. As he'd implied, she'd been a coward. Hot emotion welled in her chest, her throat, aching to spill forth. But she swallowed it down and stood there, watching him as he watched her. Neither of them said a word for long moments.

And then he broke the silence.

"You left without saying goodbye." There was a hard edge to his voice that made her swallow the lump in her throat.

"I know. I'm sorry."

"That's all?"

"What else do you wish me to say?" she asked, her heart throbbing with hurt and love and passion for this man. He was here and she wanted to throw herself into his arms, sob and beg him to give her another chance.

"Why don't you explain why you thought it necessary to run away without at least telling me you no longer wanted to marry me."

Her heart ached so much. "I wanted to tell you," she said. "I started to tell you."

But every time she'd tried to initiate the phone call, dread had gripped her by the throat and refused to let go. She'd finally realized that the only way to release him from his promise was just to go.

"You should have."

She shook her head. "I couldn't. You would have insisted on going through with it anyway, and I didn't want to do that to you."

Leo growled. And then he shoved a hand through his hair and turned to look out at the whitecaps foaming on the surface of the sea as they broke toward shore. "*You* wanted the marriage, Anna. *You* asked me."

"And you always keep your promises, even when you know you'll regret it later!" she cried, suddenly unable to hold it in any longer. He turned toward her and she ducked her head, embarrassed. "I couldn't bear the thought that you would regret me."

He looked stunned. "That's what this is about? The fact I made a bet over a tattoo and went through with it?"

It sounded stupid when he put it that way. Embarrassment flooded her. "Of course it's not about the tattoo. It's about you being the sort of person who honors his promises."

"My God, Anna, you frustrate the hell out of me. You

wanted the marriage to protect the baby. What happened to change your mind? A bloody tattoo story?"

"Of course not," she said, stung. "I realized once the story broke that you were right. I did want the marriage for me, to protect *me.*" She dropped her gaze to the sand, studied the tiny whorls made by sand crabs in the night. "I'm ashamed of that."

She heard him move, and then he was gripping her shoulders and forcing her to look up at him. She felt like whimpering at his touch, but she bit the inside of her lip and kept quiet. She knew she was pitiful.

"Don't say that, Anna. You thought you were doing it for the baby. You *were* doing it for the baby. No one should have to endure the kind of stories you've had to over the past few months. You had every right to think of how our child would have been affected."

A tear trickled down her cheek and she dashed it away. "But I had no right to force changes into your life because of my problems with the press."

His grip tightened. "Anna, this baby is *ours.* I want to be there for him."

"Or her," she added automatically.

"Or her." He pulled her into his embrace suddenly, and she closed her eyes and breathed him in. His heart was thrumming hard and steady, and his skin was so hot beneath his clothes. Searing her. Making her want. She curled her fingers into his shirt and just held him. For a few moments, she could allow herself to enjoy this.

"When I told you about the stories surrounding my mother's affair with my father, and the subsequent stories when she died—I was wrong when I said they didn't affect me. Of course they did. I've been living with their impact all of my life. It's made me who I am, Anna."

She tilted her head back to look at him. "Oh, Leo, I'm sorry."

"I'm not," he said. "I like who I am. But I like who I am with you even better."

Her heart skipped a beat. "You're only trying to make me feel better for wanting to force you into marriage."

He sighed. "Don't you realize by now, sweet Anna, there's no forcing me to do anything I don't want to do? I agreed because I wanted this marriage. I still do."

Her knees were suddenly so weak that if he wasn't holding her tight, she'd have sunk to the ground. "I thought I was forcing you into something you didn't want to do. And I walked out without an explanation. How could you still want to marry me?"

"Isn't it obvious?" he said, teeth flashing white in his handsome face. His eyes were so hot and intense as they raked over her face, daring her to believe.

"I—I'm not sure it is."

He shook his head, but his smile never wavered. "I love you, Anna. I love our baby. I like who I am with you, and I want to spend the rest of my life with you. I want to see you grow big with our child, and I want to be there when he—or she—comes into this world. I want to bring you coffee every morning, and I want to make love to you as often as possible. I want to unbutton your high-necked shirts and make you wear colors more frequently. I want you in my life, and I want to marry you so you can't ever run away again."

The tears she'd been holding in sprang free, sliding hotly down her cheeks. She told herself to hold it together, but it was far easier said than done. She put her forehead against his shirt and sobbed while he held her tight.

When she finally managed to compose herself, she lifted her head to find him gazing at her tenderly. "I thought you didn't care," she said, her breath hitching. "I thought you must hate me for making you go through with a marriage you didn't want."

He looked stunned. "What on earth made you think that?"

"You grew so distant after the story broke. All I wanted was for you to hold me, but you wouldn't touch me." She sniffled. "You wouldn't spend the night with me again."

He squeezed her tighter to him. "I thought you were too upset, that you weren't resting. I knew if I were there, you definitely wouldn't rest. Because I couldn't keep my hands off you."

"You seem to have done a good enough job of it." Her voice sounded small, hurt. She dropped her gaze to his chest, to where she was still clutching him tight.

He swore softly. "I couldn't touch you, Anna. Not without wanting to make love to you. It was safer to keep my distance. I wanted you to rest. It was only four nights. We'd have been together on the fifth."

"But I didn't rest," she said, her fingers trembling as she smoothed the fabric of his shirt. "I tossed and turned because I thought everything was ruined between us. I loved you so desperately, and I thought you despised me."

"Look at me," he said, and she raised her gaze to his. His smile made her heart turn over in her chest. Soft, hopeful, full of tenderness. "You love me?"

She blinked, stunned at the question. "I thought it was obvious."

His laugh was broken. "You forget how good you are at the serene thing." He slid his fingers along her cheek, into her hair. And then he breathed a great sigh. "I'm a lucky, lucky man. And I plan to spend a great deal of time taking advantage of my good luck."

He dipped his head, his mouth claiming hers in a scorching kiss that could have melted ten-gauge steel. Warmth blossomed inside her, rolling through her like hot syrup. She was melting with need, with love.

"I need you, Anna. Come home with me. Marry me. Today."

It was everything she'd ever wanted, ever dreamed. Leo and her…and their baby. *Perfection. Bliss. Rightness.*

"Yes," she said. "Definitely, yes."

He groaned and squeezed her tight, as if he would never let go.

"Remind me," he said a few minutes later, between hot kisses to her lips, her throat, her cheeks, "to send Donna a thank-you note."

"Why is that?" she asked when he let her breathe again.

He lifted his head, his dark eyes glittering with heat. "She's the one who set the reporters on us."

A flash of anger rushed through her, but it was gone like a wisp of smoke on the breeze. How could she possibly be angry when she was so happy? "And that's a good thing because…?"

He grinned at her, and warmth filled her. "Because it opened our eyes to the truth."

And that, she realized, as Leo swept her into his arms and carried her back up the beach, was a very fortunate thing. Sex was fabulous. But love was better.

Fabulous sex *and* love? Bliss.

* * * * *

CAUGHT IN A STORM OF PASSION

LUCY RYDER

This book is dedicated to my niece and nephew, Cassandra and Sean Bassett, who are about to make me a great-aunt. I can't wait to meet the new addition to our awesomely crazy family. What a lucky kid to have you two as parents.

And also to my sister Jennifer Hargreaves, who needs a BIG hug and a lot of love and romance of her own. I love you, Jen.

CHAPTER ONE

Tuamotu Archipelago—South Pacific

DR. EVELYN CARMICHAEL squeezed her eyes shut, dug her fingernails into the armrests either side of her and thanked God for the harness strapped across her chest. The large seaplane slewed sideways in the storm that had appeared out of nowhere, just an hour out of Port Laurent. All she could think was, *I'm going to die... I'm going to die in the middle of the South Pacific and I've never had a halfway decent...well...that.*

A monster gust of wind hit the aircraft broadside, threatening to shake everything loose. Metal screamed under the assault, as though the agony of it was too much to bear in stoic silence. Eve could empathize. She was all too ready to start screaming herself. And she would if she had the presence of mind to do anything but sit wide-eyed with terror as the world around her went to hell.

A good thing too, since being frozen with terror kept her from freaking out. Because, frankly, she'd rather die than give the man beside her—the pilot from hell—the pleasure of seeing her fall apart.

She didn't look out the cockpit window and she didn't look sideways at the heathen turning the air blue. He was big and scary enough, without the palpable tension pouring off him between curses.

And, boy, were his curses inventive. Some she'd never heard before…others she never would have *thought*, let alone uttered. But they rolled off his tongue like they were best buddies.

Fortunately he seemed to have forgotten her in his battle with the aircraft and Mother Nature. Which suited her just fine. It meant he was too busy to witness her mental meltdown.

Again.

A few hours earlier she'd opened her eyes and realized she was lying on a rattan sofa with a big half-naked sea god looming over her. Wide shouldered and long legged, he'd filled the space with a toxic cocktail of masculine superiority and supreme sexual confidence. She'd hated him instantly.

Of course it had absolutely nothing to do with the unwelcome shiver of almost primal awareness his proximity had sent zinging through her veins, but rather the abrupt knowledge that he'd seen her at her most helpless.

And if there was one thing Eve hated it was being helpless.

Fine. It might also have had something to do with the way he'd made her feel—like she was awkward and gawky and thirteen again. Like she had to pretend she wasn't dressed in charity-shop rejects and the object of pity or derision.

She'd only had to look at him, leaning close and dripping water all over her, to know he'd put the *bad* in bad boy.

Fortunately for Eve she was no longer shy or geeky, and she'd never had a thing for bad boys. That had been her mother's weakness and one she'd vowed never to share. Besides, she was a thirty-year-old recently qualified OB-GYN specialist, on the brink of a promising career, and she'd learned early on that a cool look and a raised brow quickly dispelled any unwelcome ideas.

But this…this Neanderthal, with his hard body, cool

gray eyes and his soft cargoes worn in interesting places, had found her icy looks amusing. His eyebrow had arched with more mockery than she could ever hope to muster.

He'd promptly sent her blood pressure soaring into the stratosphere—and not just with aggravation. That, as far as Eve was concerned, was reason enough to hate him.

But none of that *really* mattered. Not when her entire life was flashing before her eyes—which were still squeezed tightly closed, to shut out the vision of her impending death.

"Just stay calm!" her pilot shouted above the roar of the storm and the screech of tortured metal.

"I *am* calm," she snarled, snapping her eyes open to glare at him. And she could have promptly kicked herself when he turned those disturbing slate-gray eyes her way and she got a little light-headed.

From jet lag, worry and exhaustion, she assured herself. Or maybe it was from all the testosterone that surrounded him like a thick toxic cloud. She was clearly allergic. All she needed was the antihistamine, hidden somewhere in her luggage, and she'd be fine.

Hopefully immune.

Oh, wait. Her suitcase was MIA. Along with her mind for even starting on this wild goose chase in the first place.

"Is that why you're whimpering?"

His mouth twitched and she was tempted to snarl at him again, maybe use her teeth. She'd never been a violent person, but she would make an exception with him. Unfortunately he was about as sensitive as a rock, and any biting on her part would in all probability be construed as interest.

"Just keep this flying boat in the air, Slick, and let me handle my own life flashes."

"We're going to be okay, I promise," he said. "Chris has never failed me, and I've flown in *much* worse."

She didn't know how that could be possible, but who the heck was she to judge? She could take or leave flying on a good day, and this certainly wasn't turning out to be one of them. Besides, after a lifetime of disappointments she never put much store in empty promises, and his promise to keep them safe was as about as empty as the sky had been a half-hour earlier.

"You named your seaplane Chris? So what's it short for? Christine? Crystal?" She smirked. "Christian?"

He sent her a *get real* look that questioned her intelligence before flicking the Saint Christopher medal hanging overhead with one long tanned finger.

"Saint Chris. We have an understanding."

She wished he had an understanding with the weather, instead of a piece of metal that had about as much magic as this flying boat.

The thought had only just formed when the world exploded in a blinding flash of blue-white light. She sucked in a terrified squeak and nearly scorched her lungs on white-hot sulfur an instant before sparks shot out of the control panel. They were almost instantly followed by ominous pop-popping sounds.

"Oh, great!"

"What?" Back ramrod straight, she turned huge eyes on her pilot. His face was grimmer than the Grim Reaper and the death grip he had on the joystick didn't fill her with a lot of confidence. *"What?"*

"Dammit, don't just sit there," he snapped, his hands flying over the instruments. "Grab the fire extinguisher."

"We're on fire?" Eve felt her mouth drop open. She stared at him in horror. *They were fifteen hundred feet above the sea, for God's sake*. They couldn't be on fire. She was *not* going to fry in a flying fireball.

"Flames are coming out the damn control panel, woman," he barked. "Of course we're on fire. *Now, get the extinguisher*."

"I thought you said we were going to be okay. You *promised*!" Eve could hear herself, but she was unable to move or keep the abject horror and panic from her voice.

She—who never panicked—was about to lose it.

"Dear God, we're going to die. I knew this was a bad idea. But did I listen?"

"We are *not* going to die. And I always keep my promises."

He caught her horrified gaze with his, and the burning intensity of his eyes was strangely hypnotizing.

"Always," he growled fervently. "Now, snap out of it and get the damn extinguisher."

In a daze, Eve fumbled for the buckle and wondered if it was such a good idea to leave her seat. Maybe the fire would go out on its own. Maybe he could smother it with his damn ego. Besides, her hands were shaking so badly it was several seconds before the mechanism gave and her safety harness snapped open.

She hadn't signed up for this, she told herself, struggling to hang on to her composure. It was all just a bad dream. She was supposed to be in London, sitting in a posh hotel, attending the Women and Birth conference. Actually she *had* been in London—for all of two hours—before catching the first flight out of Heathrow because her sister had left a message saying she'd met someone and was getting married.

Married! To a guy she'd only just met. In the South Pacific, for crying out loud. Had Amelia lost her mind? Had she learned nothing from their dysfunctional childhood?

There would be no marriage, Eve vowed fervently. At least not yet. Because if her sister *had* lost her mind, as the older twin it was up to Eve to help her find it again. Besides, Eve had a lifetime's experience of watching over her sweet, trusting sibling and she wasn't going to stop now. Especially with the kind of men Amelia seemed to attract. Men quick to take advantage of her naive and generous soul. Like the men parading through their mother's life.

Clearly being on a tropical island was messing with Amelia's mind just as it had their mother's, when she'd met and fallen head over heels in lust with their father. Just another man in a long line of users and abusers. All Eve had to do was fly out there, talk some sense into her twin and fly back to London in time for the last three days of the conference…preferably with her sister in tow. It would be just like their childhood. Just the two of them against the world.

Only now she might not make it to the conference. *Or* to Tukamumu to stop the wedding. Or was it Moratunga?

Oh, what the heck difference did it make, anyway? She wasn't going to make either of them because she was headed for a watery grave.

Feeling drunk in the violently pitching craft, she lurched upright and staggered to the fire extinguisher mounted behind the pilot's seat. Not an easy task in three-inch heels.

"Dammit, woman. Move!"

The words were delivered through clenched teeth, and Eve would have liked to tell him to stuff it. But what if he took her at her word and bailed out with the only working parachute? She didn't even want to consider what would happen then.

She yanked at the cylinder, shrieking as the plane took a nosedive. Lurching backward, she hit the cockpit wall and sent foam spraying everywhere.

Everywhere but the fire.

"What the seven levels of hell are you doing?" he bellowed, reaching back to grab a fistful of her silk blouse and yanking her upright.

She would have liked to tell him that he was manhandling two hundred dollars' worth of silk, but staying on her feet was more of a priority.

"The *fire*," he snarled, looking more scary than comical with foam in his hair and dripping off his nose and chin. "Aim the nozzle at the damn fire."

"Maybe you should keep the damn floor from moving," Eve snapped with extreme provocation, and slapped at the hand dangerously close to her breasts. Only it turned out to be a mistake when the floor abruptly tilted again and she tumbled into his lap—a tangle of arms, legs, nozzle and extinguisher.

Eve shrieked and attempted not to conk him on the head with the canister, because an unconscious pilot was something she wanted to avoid. At all costs. She whacked herself instead, instantly seeing stars and wondering if her life really was flashing before her eyes.

Dammit. It figured that she'd die in the arms of a man more interested in shoving her away than wrapping her close.

Yelping, she let the extinguisher go to slap a hand over the injury and thought, *Great—another bruise to go with the one I already have thanks to Mr. I'm-your-pilot, Chase.* There was a soft grunt, followed by a vicious oath, and the next thing she was being dumped on her ass. Through tearing eyes she saw him aim the nozzle at the controls with one hand while yanking at the yoke with the other. Within seconds the instruments were covered with a thick layer of foam.

The fire gave one last defiant fizzle before dying.

Kind of like her last relationship, she thought dazedly from her position on the floor. Actually, kind of like *all* her relationships, if she was being perfectly honest, because watching her mother flit from one man to the next had soured her when it came to love. She snorted. As if whatever her mother had had with her countless men had been *love*.

Relief, however, was short-lived, because no sooner had Chase tossed the canister aside than he wrapped both white-knuckled hands around the yoke, looked at the instruments now oozing white foam and cursed.

Again.

Eve didn't like the look on his face.

"Now what?"

His expression was taut and grim, his eyes narrowed in

fierce concentration. A muscle twitched in his lean, tanned cheek.

"Don't you dare tell me we're going down," she informed him tightly. "Because you'll have a hysterical female on your hands. And you do *not* want to see me hysterical."

He shot her a look that said she'd sailed past hysterical a half hour ago. She ignored him. They were going down. *She* knew it. *He* knew it. He was just too darn stubborn and macho to admit that Saint Chris had abandoned them.

She swallowed a sob.

And here she was in the prime of her life, on the verge of a promising career—the realization of all her dreams after years of hard work.

She had every right to be hysterical, darn it.

Grabbing the seat, she hauled herself up. He was back to ignoring her, wrestling with the controls and trying to bring the plane's nose up through sheer brute force.

And failing.

Oh, God, he was failing, and the nose was pointing down into what she knew would be a very unpleasant end. They might be in a seaplane, and not at the altitude of a commercial jet, but that would mean nothing when they hit the water at a sixty-degree angle. Besides, she'd watched all those seconds-from-disaster documentaries and knew there'd be no floating gently away from this.

Gulping, Eve watched in terrified fascination as the muscles in his arms and shoulders bunched and strained against his soft polo shirt and smooth, tanned flesh until she thought they'd burst right out of his skin.

"Buckle up," he snarled through clenched teeth. "It's going to get rough."

Eve felt her mouth drop open. More than it was already? A whimper bubbled up her throat and threatened to pop, along with her very tenuous hold on control. She was absolutely certain she could not handle rough.

They were going down.

"We're going to die."

"We are *not* going to die. I'm an excellent pilot," he said tightly, and the engines protested with an almost human scream.

"In case you haven't noticed, *Slick*," Eve yelped, almost as loudly as the engines as she fought with the safety harness that seemed to have taken on an evil life of its own, "this is not a storm for excellent pilots. It isn't even for creatures *meant* to fly. It's Armageddon. And if I die I'm going to kill you. Very. Very. Slowly."

"I have no intention of dying," he snapped, as though she'd insulted his manhood as well as his entire family tree. "And what kind of doctor are *you* to be threatening the man trying to save your delectable ass, anyway?"

He shook his head at her and reached out to snag his Saint Christopher, kissing it before he looped it around his neck.

Eve watched in fascination as the shiny silver disc disappeared into the neckline of his shirt, wondering at her brief flash of envy that Saint Chris got to be nestled close to his heat and strength.

Dammit. *She* wanted to be held and protected too.

Just this once.

"What *you* need is a little faith," he declared, just as the craft bucked and the engines gave an alarming splutter.

She swallowed another yelp, envy forgotten as she sank her nails into the armrests, wishing it was his hard thigh. She would like to put a few holes in his thick hide, despite the "delectable" quip. Besides, her "delectable ass," as he'd so gallantly put it, was in real danger of becoming shark bait.

"What I *need*," she snarled, "is for you to get us out of this storm. What I need is to find my sister and stop her from making the biggest mistake of her life." Her voice rose. "What I need is not to be thinking about meeting my maker without ever having had a screaming orgas— Well, never mind."

"What?" His gaze whipped to hers so fast she half expected his head to fly off his shoulders. After a moment his gaze dropped to her mouth. "A *what*?"

"Never mind," she squeaked, losing her famed cool just a little. "I am *not* discussing the fact that I'm nearly thirty-one years old and have never had an earth-shaking orgasm. Before I kick the bucket I'd like to have just one. *One!*" Her voice rose. "Is that too much to ask?"

"You… *What?*" He looked so stunned that if she hadn't been on the verge of a total meltdown she might have been flattered by his stunned disbelief. Or maybe insulted, since the disbelief was now edged with amusement. It didn't matter that at any other time she would have been mortified at having admitted anything so private. Especially to this heathen flyboy. But since she was going to die she guessed it didn't really matter. Dignity was the least of her problems.

"No. And now I'm *never* going to."

His answer was drowned out by another ear-splitting explosion and in the next instant the airplane lurched sideways and flipped, throwing her violently against the harness. Lights exploded inside her skull and she knew that this was it. She was going to die and she was never going to have that screaming orgasm.

And to think she could be safely in London, with a hundred eligible men…

CHAPTER TWO

Six hours earlier, Port Laurent, Tangaroa.

EVELYN PRACTICALLY FELL out of the cab as it came to a screeching halt in front of a squat building professing to be the offices of Tiki Sea & Air Charter Services. She'd flown halfway around the world, but the worst part of the journey by far had been the past five miles. Five miles of absolute white-knuckled terror in a cab that she was somewhat surprised to have survived.

Swaying in the intense midday heat, Eve clutched the side of the car and locked her wobbly knees against the urge to sink to the ground. The only thing stopping her was the knowledge that the road was hotter than the depths of hell and would fry anything on contact. If she didn't get somewhere air-conditioned soon the soles of her elegant heels weren't the only things in danger of vaporizing with a whimper.

She'd left Boston in freezing rain, landed at Heathrow in the middle of a snowstorm, and the smart little suit she'd bought to celebrate her new professional status was sticking to her skin as if she was a sealed gourmet snack. And, since her suitcase had been lost in transit, there was nothing in her overnight bag suitable for the current soaring temperatures and smothering humidity.

Fine. There was nothing in her suitcase either, but at

least she'd have something fresh to change into. She'd lost count of the time zones she'd crossed to get to... *Darn, where the heck was she?*

Blinking, she looked around, but that didn't help because she was in a daze of fatigue and jet lag and couldn't remember the name of the South Pacific island she'd just landed on.

Oh, boy... The South Pacific.

Her pulse picked up, her ears buzzed and a prickly heat erupted over her body. For an awful moment she thought she was going to pass out, and quickly sucked in the warm, moist air to clear her head.

Who'd have thought when she'd stepped off the plane at Heathrow and turned on her phone that instead of heading for the Women and Birth conference, as she'd been supposed to, she'd be getting back on a plane to fly off to Tuka-Tuka.

Or was it Moramumu?

She sighed.

She'd never even *heard* of the Society Islands, let alone a chain called the Tuamotu Archipelago. Which begged the question: what the heck was her doing down here? The last she'd heard Amelia had been singing at some fancy hotel in Hawaii.

"Lady, you sure you wanna be here?" the cab driver yelled over the music pumping from the boom box mounted on the dashboard. "There's a much better place on the other side of the marina."

"That's very kind of you," Eve said, hopefully masking her horror at the thought of getting back into that death trap for one mile more than was absolutely necessary. The guy flashed his gold teeth and cackled uproariously, making her think that maybe she hadn't been all that successful in hiding her dismay. But then she was about twenty-nine hours past exhausted and couldn't be expected to control anything more than the urge to weep. Or maybe scream.

And that was only because she was clenching her teeth hard enough to pulverize bone and enamel.

With a cheerfulness that Eve wished *she* felt—she was in the South Pacific, for heaven's sake—the driver wrestled her bag from the cab and dropped it at her feet, along with her heavy winter coat. Then he hopped back into his decrepit vehicle and took off like a lost soul out of hell, singing at the top of his lungs to the song blaring from his boom box.

Sucking in air so heavy with moisture she thought she might be forced to grow gills, Eve hoisted her bag and coat onto her shoulder. Clutching her laptop close, she headed across the road to the small building squatting like a smug hen in a bed of exotic flowers and dense vegetation.

Suddenly she had absolutely no idea what she was doing.

The wooden doors to Tiki Sea & Air were open, and Eve climbed the stone stairs to a wide wraparound porch decorated with hanging baskets exploding with exotic-looking flowers. The heady fragrance reminded her of the perfume counters at Bloomingdale's. Rich, lush and exotic.

Inhaling the humid air, Eve looked around and decided she must be dreaming—heck, she was exhausted enough. It was as if she'd stepped into a brochure advertising glamorous holiday destinations. But since she'd never taken a holiday, let alone been tempted to research one, she couldn't tell for certain.

Okay, that was a lie. She and her sister had used to dream all the time when they were kids about finding some exotic island where they'd live with their father and eat coconuts and fruit and maybe learn to catch fish. A place where they'd be safe and adored.

She snorted. *Yeah, right.* That had been so long ago it might have been someone else's dream. Before she'd stopped believing in fairy tales. Before she'd learned that if she wanted "safe and secure" she'd have to create it herself.

Swiping at a trickle of perspiration, she glanced over to

where an old man lay dozing on an old rattan sofa and experienced a moment of pure envy. She'd be willing to har-
vest her own kidney for a soft bed, clean sheets and about
twenty-four hours of oblivion.

Oh, yeah…and air-conditioning.

She groaned as sweat ran down her throat and disappeared between her breasts. Definitely air-conditioning.

Deciding that she didn't have the energy to fight the
old guy for sofa space, Eve headed for the open door and
stepped into an old French Colonial–style building that
looked about three decades past its sell-by date.

The room looked like something out of a movie. There
was a scattering of worn rattan furnishings, coconut fiber
mats dotting the floor and a large overhead fan that lazily
circulated the heavy air.

A large curved bamboo counter took up most of the far
end of the room, and behind that, through the open slatted
wooden French doors, Eve could see a back porch leading
down to a long, wide wooden dock. Bobbing on the in-
sanely bright turquoise water was a large white seaplane.
Beyond that she could see a headland and the open sea,
sparkling like a trillion jewels in the sun.

Approaching the counter, Eve peered over the scarred
surface, hoping to find someone who could help her. Other
than an empty mug, an overflowing wastebasket and about
a ton of boxes, the only sign of life was a quietly humming
computer and the soft *clunk*, *clunk*, *clunk* of the overhead
fan.

She glanced through another open doorway behind the
counter into a small messy office, but it too was deserted.

"Dammit," Eve muttered, huffing out an irritated breath.
"Where the heck *is* everyone?"

A loud, hoarse, *"Ia ora na e Maeva!"* had her jumping about a foot in the air. She looked around, wide-eyed,
for the owner of that raspy voice. But other than the loud

snoring coming from the old man on the front porch the building was quiet.

Quiet and deserted.

Wonderful. Now she was hearing voices on top of everything else.

Telling herself she wasn't losing her grip on reality, Eve dropped her belongings onto a nearby chair and headed for the open doors, determined to find the source of that raspy voice. And hopefully someone who could tell her where to find a pilot named Chase.

She stepped onto the back porch and was instantly blinded by the midday light. Heat rose from the dock and the large bay reflected sunlight like a laser show.

Resisting the urge to retreat inside the blessedly dim building, she lifted a hand to shade her eyes as the raspy voice yelled, *"Ia ora na e Maeva!"* in her ear.

Heart lurching with fright, she swung around, expecting a hatchet-wielding psycho, and found herself face-to-beak with a large bright blue-and-scarlet parrot perched on a tree stump, watching her with baleful eyes.

"Oh!" she said to the bird on an explosive exhalation of relief, and took a cautionary step out of range of the wicked-looking beak. "Hi. Do you know where I can find, um…Chase?"

The bird cocked its head and Eve sighed. Now she was talking to a bird. Which probably meant lack of sleep along with stress and panic was sending her right over the edge.

"Okay. How about your owner?"

The parrot ruffled its bright feathers.

"Anyone?"

"Squaaawk!"

"Fine," she said a little shortly. "I'll just go find him myself, then, shall I?"

"Ma-oo roo-roo ro-aa," the parrot crooned, and bobbed up and down.

"Yeah, you too," she muttered, heading for the porch

railing. She leaned over, looking past the abundant vegetation to follow where wide wooden planks led straight toward a fancy marina and the bustling business center. To her right it disappeared into the cluster of houses perched along the water's edge a couple hundred yards away.

Not a living thing stirred, everything having most likely locked itself away from the suffocating heat.

Feeling a little queasy, Eve sank onto the top step, expelling a weary breath just as a long, tanned arm appeared out of the water and slapped onto the dock.

Almost instantly another appeared, holding a string bag of fish. And then, with both large hands planted on the dock, the rest of him followed—all six foot plus of him— emerging from the bay like a sea god visiting lesser land mortals.

Eve's eyes widened and her mouth dropped open. Her eyes were locked on the gush of water lovingly tracing all that tanned masculine magnificence as it rushed south. *Waaaay* south.

She licked her parched lips, following the streams of water that cascaded over his wide chest and the almost perfect lines of his shoulders and biceps as though lovingly caressing the hard planes it traversed. Moving down spectacular pecs, racing over delineated abs toward the happy trail that disappeared into the waistband of his low-riding board shorts.

Eve sucked in a stunned breath—*holy molasses*—his legs were just as long and tanned and perfect as the rest of him. She blinked as the image wavered and wondered if she was hallucinating. But when he remained, bathed in sunlight that cast his ripped physique in bold relief, she sighed. One of those stupid girlie sighs that would have appalled her if she hadn't been on the very edge of exhaustion.

Wow…just wow!

Unaware of her fascinated gaze, the sea god shook his head like a dog, water flying off in all directions, before stooping to retrieve the string bag in one effortless move. He turned and headed up the dock toward her, his free hand wiping water from his face.

Eve knew the instant he saw her. His body stilled for just a heartbeat, and if her gaze hadn't been locked on him like a laser she would have missed that barely perceptible pause. Without breaking stride, he resumed that loose-hipped lope up the dock, his expression dark and hooded.

Feeling suddenly nervous, Eve rose to her feet and smoothed her hands down her skirt—whether to smooth out the wrinkles or to dry her damp palms, she wasn't sure. Almost instantly there was a loud buzzing in her head. Her vision swam alarmingly, and as if from down a long, hollow tunnel she heard herself say, "I'm Evelyn Carmichael and I'm looking…for…I'm looking for… Ch—"

If there was one thing Chase Gallagher hated more than the IRS, it was big-city career women with big-city attitudes. But even *he* had to admit that the sight of long shapely legs ending in a pair of elegant heels was sexy as hell, and something that he hadn't realized he'd missed.

And because he'd missed it he scowled down at the woman responsible for that unwelcome flash of yearning. He didn't miss the city, or the hectic hours and traffic, and he certainly didn't miss the big-city career attitude. Especially not the kind that made people put career before family. *Hell.* Career before *anything.* Except, of course, when something bigger and better came along.

He'd done that once and it had cost him more than a huge chunk of change.

So even though the sight of his visitor, all her prim tidiness beginning to fray at the edges, had sent his pulse ratcheting up a couple notches, he'd studied her coolly, determined to get rid of her as soon as possible. But that had been before she'd decided to sway on her feet and take a header into the ground, forcing him to leap forward and catch her before she fell.

Medium height, nice curvy body and scraped-back tawny hair that would probably glitter a hundred different colors in the sunlight—if she ever relaxed enough to let her hair down, he thought with a snort. Then a close-up of her face had him sucking in a shocked breath, because for one instant there he'd thought he was staring at his future sister-in-law.

But that was ridiculous, because not only had he left Amelia behind at the resort, with his brother, Jude, *this* woman had big-city impatience stamped all over her and none of Amelia's sunny sweetness.

This had to be Amelia's sister. The evil twin, he told himself as he slid one arm beneath her shoulders and the other beneath her knees.

Lifting her into his arms, Chase ascended the stairs, cursing his bad luck. He'd taken one look at the woman and recognized trouble.

And these days Chase Gallagher avoided trouble.

At least of the feminine variety.

He shook his head at the prim skirt, long-sleeved button-up shirt and nylon-clad legs. *Oh, yeah*—heat exhaustion just waiting to happen. If not for those things, this woman was a dead ringer for his brother's fiancée.

With the parrot leading the way in a flurry of feathers, Chase carried her into the waiting room and laid her down on the rattan sofa that had seen better days. He adjusted a cushion beneath her head and stood back.

He knew he had to do something. What, he didn't know. He knew only that the long-sleeved blouse was still buttoned at her wrists, and in this heat that was a sure-fire way to get heatstroke.

After a brief internal battle Chase cursed and reached out to slip the small buttons free, jolting as the parrot landed on his shoulder, crooning, *"Ia ora na e Maeva,"* in Chase's ear.

"Yeah, welcome to you too, buddy," he said in relief.

Ignoring the flashes of lace and silk was easier with the bird's talons digging into his shoulder, reminding him that tugging the damp shirt and camisole from her waistband was for medical purposes. And not for whatever his mind was suddenly conjuring up.

He shook his head as much at the woman as at himself. No wonder she'd passed out. She was dressed like a school librarian heading for Congress. And then he couldn't resist a little smile tugging reluctantly at his mouth.

Okay, maybe not a librarian, he thought, hurrying off to find water and a cloth. More like a sexy lawyer hoping to disguise herself as a librarian. He shook his head. No disguising all that creamy skin, or the curves beneath those prim clothes.

He sighed. The nylons would have to go. As would the blouse, or the under-thingy. But first he had to revive her and get some fluids down her throat.

She was moaning softly when he returned with a huge wad of paper toweling and an opened bottle of water. Tearing off a section of paper towel, he soaked it with cool water before wiping her clammy forehead.

The pulse at the base of her throat fluttered wildly; her breathing was rapid and shallow.

Great. Just great. Maybe he should just take her to the hospital and let them deal with her. Maybe he should just fly outta here and tell Amelia her sister hadn't shown.

Yeah, and maybe he wouldn't do *any* of those things, he thought as he envisioned the scene that would follow. He shuddered. Besides, the last thing he wanted was to see Amelia's big blue eyes shimmering with hurt and know he was the cause.

Soaking another handful of towels, he roughly bathed the woman's clammy skin, careful not to let his eyes wander to those tempting mounds of creamy flesh barely contained in silk and lace. If she suddenly woke up he didn't want to be caught eyeing the goodies.

First, she wasn't his type—*so not your type, Chase*—and second his mother had made sure her sons knew how to treat women with respect. Or else.

His mouth twisted as an unpleasant memory arose. Pity his ex-wife hadn't had the same upbringing. Maybe then she wouldn't have had a long-term affair with her boss and blamed Chase's job and his family for the alienation of her affection.

He snorted. *Yeah, right.* As if making mounds of cash trading stocks and bonds was remotely alienating. *He* was the one who should have sued the damn lawyer, but by the time he'd recovered from the shock of betrayal he'd realized he didn't care enough.

He'd survived the unpleasant discovery that his wife loved his money more than she'd loved him. But discovering that Avery had knowingly tried to pass off the Mercer Island shark's baby as his had been like a gut punch.

Fortunately he wasn't as stupid as he looked, and when he'd demanded a paternity test the whole ugly truth had come spewing out. What had really sickened him was the fact that whenever he'd previously brought up the subject of starting a family she'd always claimed that she wasn't ready, that a baby would ruin her career and her figure.

After that he'd left Seattle and moved out here to the islands. He still ran his brokering business, from what his brother called his "bunker"—a windowless, climate-controlled room that housed his huge bank of computers. It was from there that he kept in contact with the financial world and the rest of his Seattle-based family.

But his marriage was in the past and really not worth dwelling on. If he did, he might just dump Amelia's sister in the ocean, head off to his island retreat and pretend none of this had happened. But he really liked his almost sister-in-law, and he was fairly certain Jude wouldn't be happy if he ditched her twin.

In the meantime, what the hell was he supposed to do with an unconscious woman heading for heat exhaustion? Other than strip her and toss her in the bay, that is.

Shoving a hand through his hair, he was contemplating his options when she moaned again. His gaze whipped upward in time to see the long, lush fringe of her dark eyelashes flutter and then lift, exposing glassy eyes the exact color of the five-hundred-dollar bottle of single malt whiskey he kept for special occasions.

Holy—

Air whooshed from his lungs as if he'd been punched in the head. He'd only ever seen eyes like that once before. Twice, actually. Once on an ancient amber Viking ring he'd seen in a museum and the second time…his friend's eyes. But looking into Dr. Alain Broussard's eyes didn't normally leave him reeling like a drunken penguin.

Maybe *he* was the one in need of medical assistance.

She blinked and murmured a husky, "Hi," her expression so softly sensuous that for an instant Chase was startled. Okay, stunned. Because…*jeez*…that look had reached out and grabbed him in a place that hadn't been grabbed since his ex. Maybe even before.

In the next instant the sleepy expression cleared and any resemblance either to Amelia or Alain vanished. Soft and sensuous was replaced by razor-sharp intellect. And outrage.

"What…what the hell are you *doing*?" she demanded, the formerly husky voice full of indignation as she slapped at his hands, which had paused in the task of sponging her down.

Water dripped off the wad and soaked the silk camisole right over her left breast, drawing his fascinated gaze. She must have followed his eyes because she squeaked, shoved at his hand and lurched upright. Unfortunately he didn't move back fast enough, and her head smacked into his cheekbone with enough force to rattle his brain.

She gave an agonized yelp, slapped a hand to her head and sank back against the cushions, moaning as if he'd gutted her with a dull spoon.

Oh, wait—the groaning was coming from *him*.

"What the *hell*, lady?" he snarled, holding his cheek as he staggered backward and abruptly sat on the old rattan coffee table, which immediately groaned under his weight.

The move also knocked over the bottled water. He made a grab for it, only to have it sail through the air, spraying water in a wide arc. Most of it landed on her—soaking her already wet camisole. And...*oh, man*...rendering the thin silk almost transparent. Which he might have appreciated if she hadn't just tried to head butt him to death.

She made a kind of squeaking, gasping sound and he saw wide amber eyes glaring at him through a haze of pain. Realizing he was still holding a wad of damp paper towels, he slapped it over the lump already forming on his cheek.

"What...what the hell was that for?" he demanded, checking for blood.

"You...you..." she gasped, and then she turned an interesting shade of green. "Uh-oh." She gulped and slapped a palm over her mouth. A look of panic crossed her face. She sat up. "I think I'm... Oh!"

Understanding that garbled sentence, Chase surged to his feet, scooped her up and rushed down the short passage to the ladies' bathroom. He shoved the door open with his shoulder as she made horrifying gagging sounds.

"Hold on a sec—nearly there," he urged in panic, rushing into a stall and dumping her unceremoniously on her feet. In one smooth move he pushed her head over the toilet, with a firm hand on the back of her neck.

Unresisting, she sank to her knees, her body racked with a couple dozen dry heaves that made the sweat pop out across his forehead. He swallowed hard and retreated outside the stall. Just to give her some privacy, he told himself.

After a while there was silence, and when he heard a weak moan he stuck his head inside. She'd sagged against the wall, eyes closed as she wiped a limp wrist across her mouth. Tendrils of hair clung to her damp forehead and cheeks. She looked so miserable that Chase felt an unwelcome tug of empathy.

Dammit, he thought, shoving a hand through his hair. He didn't want to feel *anything*—let alone empathy. He'd get stupid and act like he had rescue issues, for God's sake—which, come to think of it, was how he'd met Avery.

Yeesh. What an idiot. He'd been a perfect mark. But he'd learnt a valuable lesson and he wasn't about to repeat his biggest mistake ever. Not now that he was older and wiser. Not now that he'd learned exactly how devious women could be.

Eyeing her pasty face with increasing concern, he crouched beside her. "You okay?"

"I'm...fine..." she rasped, and licked dry lips. "I just need a—"

"Another moment?" he supplied helpfully when her words ended abruptly. "A doctor?"

"Don't...don't be ridiculous," she scoffed huskily, planting one hand on the toilet and the other on his shoulder.

Her touch had him thinking bad thoughts, especially when his body stirred.

"I *am* a doctor." She tried to push herself to her feet but she was still weak and shaky and immediately slid back down.

He eyed her suspiciously as an unpleasant thought occurred to him. Fainting? Vomiting? It was exactly what had happened to Avery when—

"Are you pregnant?" he demanded abruptly.

Her head whipped up and her mouth dropped open. "What—? *No!*"

She looked so insulted that he should suggest such a thing that his breath escaped in a loud *whoosh*. He wasn't entirely sure why her reaction relieved him—for all he knew she could be lying. And boy did he have enough experience with *that*!

Slipping his hand beneath her armpit, he rose, drawing her to her feet. She instantly sagged against him, legs wobbly as a newborn calf. Instead of pushing her away he drew her closer, enjoying her soft, warm scent and the feel of her plump breasts against his naked chest.

Realizing what he was doing, he quickly backed out of the stall and led her to the counter, shoving her into a chair while he ripped paper towels from the dispenser. He gave the tap a vicious little twist and thrust the wad into the stream of water that appeared.

What the hell was that? Maybe the heat was affecting him too, because no way could he be attracted to her. Not only was she a big-city woman, she was almost his *sister*, for cripes' sake.

Well, her sister was. Which was the same thing. Wasn't it?

His breath whooshed out. *Hell.*

He turned to find her watching him with those solemn golden-syrup eyes and felt his gut clench with something hot and wild. Something along the lines of golden syrup and…and acres of soft naked skin.

The reaction shook him.

Realizing he was standing there like an idiot, he tore his gaze away, feeling the tips of his ears burn. She was the last person he wanted to feel anything for. Which just went to show that abstinence made people crazy.

Hoping to restore his IQ, he thrust the dripping mess of paper in her direction and eyed her out of the corner of his eyes.

"If you're a doctor, what the hell are you doing in the South Pacific dressed like…*that*?" He waved his arm, send-

ing drops of water flying. "That's an open invitation to dehydration and heat exhaustion."

She eyed the sodden mass for a couple beats before lifting her gaze, her expression rife with annoyance and maybe
her opinion of his medical skills.

It wasn't in the least complimentary. So why the hell did
Chase feel his lips twitch?

There was nothing amusing about this. Nothing at all.
And he certainly wasn't attracted to her. No way. She was
too uptight for his liking, and she literally vibrated with
exhaustion and impatience.

After a couple more beats she sighed and rose shakily
to her feet. Taking the towels from him, she sagged weakly
against the counter, where she dumped the sloppy mess and
reached for the dispenser.

"Maybe because I was on my way to a conference in
London when I got a very disturbing message about my
sister getting married to a man she's only just met. A loser
who's probably taking advantage of her right this minute.
And," she added, sending him a look in the mirror that
questioned the size of his brain, "in case you think everyone lives in perpetual summer, the northern hemisphere is
experiencing a season called *winter*. I left Boston in freezing rain and landed in a London blizzard."

"Well, *that*—" he gestured rudely to her once-snazzy
outfit, outraged by the nasty quip about his brother "—will
have to go, or you'll be fainting on me every five minutes."
Jude wasn't the kind of guy to take advantage of women,
more like the other way around.

She made a growling sound in the back of her throat
and her narrowed gaze snapped up to lock on his in the
mirror. Her expression didn't bode well for his continued
good health.

He barely managed to cover his grin with another frown.
Dammit. What the hell was wrong with him?

"I did not faint," she said slowly, precisely. As though he was a few bricks short of a wall.

He snorted, beginning to enjoy himself. "Could have fooled me."

Her eyes narrowed further. "I never faint. Anyway, why do *you* care? It's not like we're ever going to see each other again after I fly out of here."

Her tone suggested she couldn't wait for that moment, so he sighed and pushed away from the counter. Yeah, well, neither could he. But that wasn't about to happen.

For either of them.

His enjoyment abruptly vanished.

"Uh-huh?" he drawled, heading for the door, where he paused, turning to find an odd expression on her face as she watched him leave. "And how do you plan to fly out of here, Your Highness? Grow a pair of wings?"

"Don't be absurd. I'm looking for Chase…something or other." She frowned and lifted pale unsteady fingers to the bruise already forming on her forehead.

He tried not to feel guilty for putting it there as it had mostly been *her* fault. Besides, his eye was also swelling, and his cheek hurt like hell.

Her hand dropped to clutch the counter, as though she was a little dizzy. She sucked in a deep breath that just about gave him a heart attack as those creamy mounds of flesh rose above the lace-trimmed camisole. It was several seconds before he realized that while he was having some very racy thoughts, she was gaping at him with dawning horror.

"*You're* Chase, aren't you?"

For a long moment he stared at her with an odd feeling clenching his gut. It wasn't exactly fear. Because he wasn't afraid of anything. Not Chase Gallagher. Nuh-uh. No way. And certainly not of a city woman.

He snorted. Especially not *this* city woman, with her tawny hair, creamy skin and large whiskey eyes. She was going to be his brother's sister-in-law, for God's sake. Which made her practically family. And if there was one thing a Gallagher didn't do it was leave family—no matter what.

"Don't be too long," he ordered over his shoulder. "Our lunch should be here soon, and I need to load the cargo before we leave."

CHAPTER THREE

The crash site—Moratunga Island, one hundred miles north of Tukamumu.

CHASE BECAME AWARE of two things simultaneously. The wind and the pain. The former was slashing at his face along with needlelike rain, and the latter...*jeez*...was threatening to explode his brains all over the inside of his skull.

He gave a rough groan and fought the urge to empty his stomach. On the bright side, pain meant that he was alive. Which was good, he mused drowsily as he began drifting off into comforting darkness. Real good. Alive meant it had all been a bad dream...

He jerked awake, his heart lurching into a dead run as his gaze flew around the cockpit and he realized something was wrong with this picture. He instantly knew it was the wrong move when pain tore through his head and the smell of burnt plastic made him gag.

Fire!

The thought had him grabbing for his harness, which he released an instant before he realized he was hanging practically upside down.

The controls broke his fall, his left shoulder taking most of the impact before he slid to the floor in a groaning heap.

Holy freaking moly!

Chase lay dazed for a couple minutes, his shoulder radiating pain and fire, his head throbbing like an open wound. Finally his vision cleared enough to recognize that there was—*what the hell?*—vegetation growing inside his best girl.

Either he was hallucinating or—

The storm!

Oh, yeah.

He sucked in a breath when memories rushed back. The crash.

He'd crashed his plane.

Un-be-freaking-lievable.

Muttering curses about stupid storms that weren't supposed to change direction so fast, Chase grabbed his shoulder and sat up. His stomach instantly revolted and he froze. Okay. Note to self. No moving until the nightmare faded.

When it didn't, he sucked in a careful breath and blinked up into the darkness, wondering why there were two mannequins hanging a foot from his face. He knew for a fact there were no mannequins on the cargo manifest.

Then he realized that he was seeing double, and that he was looking at… What the heck was her name? He squinted past the pain and caught sight of a cascade of tawny gold hair a few feet away. His heart surged into his throat as he recognized… Amelia? Dammit, his brother was going to— *No, wait*. Not Amelia. *Evelyn*—Amelia's evil twin—and her arms, legs and hair were hanging limply from the harness.

"Eve…Evelyn?" he rasped, wondering how long he'd been out. A couple of minutes? Hours? Vaguely alarmed by her utter stillness, he cleared his throat and tried again. "Hey, Doc!"

Nothing. Not even the slightest of movements. He sucked in air, shoving down panic, and attempted to squelch the awful thought that came with the dread. His heart pounded. No, no, *no*! No way was the feisty doc—

"Eve! Wake up, *dammit*."

Head spinning, and nausea clawing its way into his throat, Chase hauled himself upright with his good arm. The world tilted, along with his stomach, and he braced himself between the chair and the controls until the urge to vomit settled. Not only did the thought of all that cool fire being extinguished leave a bitter taste of loss in his mouth, it filled him with a sudden hollow desolation he couldn't explain.

They'd only just *met*, for cripes' sake, and he didn't even like her. But she was his responsibility—not to mention his future sister-in-law, sort of—and the first thing he needed to do was check her vitals.

He fumbled beneath that thick curtain of tawny hair and searched for a pulse. When he found it, in the soft spot just beneath her jawline, his breath whooshed out with relief at the strong and steady rhythm.

She was alive.

With the realization dawning on him that they'd just cheated certain death, Chase reached into his shirt with unsteady hands. His fingers encountered the Saint Christopher and he pulled it out, pausing to give it a noisy, grateful kiss.

Thank God she was alive and breathing.

He was breathing too, which meant that when he checked her over for other injuries he got a little sidetracked by the sight of the long naked legs…all four of them…which any red-blooded man would have noticed. Two of the four feet were bare, and her ivory silk blouse had worked loose from her skirt, exposing a few inches of skin that suddenly seemed more erotic than if she was naked.

Which was just plain stupid. He lived in paradise, where women wore a heck of a lot less in public. Besides, he had way more important things to obsess about. Like the fact that she was still unconscious. Like the fact that he'd crashed his damn airplane…well, somewhere.

Hell! He couldn't believe it. He'd flown these waters for almost five years without a single incident.

Shoving unsteady fingers through his hair, Chase looked around and tried to come to terms with reality. It couldn't be a coincidence, he told himself wildly, that the day she'd practically thrown herself into his arms and then tried to head butt him to death, *this* had happened.

The woman was bad luck.

One he needed to avoid. Like a death plague.

Besides, she was uptight and anal—his *least* favorite type of woman. "The type of woman I moved thousands of miles to get away from," he informed the unconscious woman irritably. "The last thing I need complicating my life."

Even temporarily.

So why the hell was he so fascinated by her damn-your-hide attitude and glowing amber eyes?

Biting back a curse at his idiocy, Chase massaged his throbbing temple and ordered himself not to think about underwear. But the more he tried *not* to think about lace and silk, the more he recalled his first glimpse of her heart-shaped butt, encased in that tight soft green skirt, bent over the bathroom counter at Port Laurent.

It had sparked some pretty racy fantasies that had just about fried his brain. And before he'd known it his gaze had been sliding down a pair of spectacular legs more suited to a Vegas showgirl than a workaholic doctor.

He'd blamed it on testosterone and abstinence, of course.

And now possibly concussion—because the sedate little business suit would have looked perfectly respectable on anyone who didn't have enough curves to rival the Indy 500 race track.

Obviously living like a monk made a guy think about sex even when he'd just crashed his plane. Obviously he'd hit his head *really* hard. Maybe he even had brain damage. *Well...hell.*

Too bad Mother Nature had decided to have a little fun with him, he thought darkly, swiping at a trickle of something warm and sticky on his face. She'd fried the right engine and most of the electronics. And if that wasn't bad enough she'd made him look bad in front of this sexy, uptight doc after he'd promised her everything was going to be okay. But it wasn't okay, he thought morosely, looking at the vegetation invading the damaged cockpit. Not by a long shot.

Deciding to leave Dr. Eve where she was, until he'd made sure they weren't about to slide tail-first into an active volcano, Chase pulled himself upright. The move brought him closer. Closer to the intoxicating scent of woman… closer to temptation.

He quickly lurched out of reach, telling himself it was a good thing he was over women like her.

A *real* good thing.

Eve surfaced slowly, aware of a gang of vindictive road workers using power drills inside her skull. She frowned and tried to shift away from the excavation, but the move sent pain stabbing through her.

Oh…ow! What…what the—?

Carefully drawing in a shallow breath, she took stock, wondering where she was, why she couldn't remember… and why the heck someone was sitting on her chest. Then something cold and damp touched her head, right where it hurt. She gave a distressed moan and lifted her hand to swat feebly at the annoyance.

"G'way," she mumbled crossly, shivering when a trickle of cold water made its way down her throat.

"Keep still," a deep, familiar voice ordered, sending a bolt of something that felt like panic through her body.

Her eyes and mouth flew open, with the intention of giving him a piece of her mind, but the words froze in her throat when she found the hunky sea god close. Very close…and wet. As if she'd invaded his ocean kingdom and he was holding her hostage.

Yikes.

Every thought promptly flew right out of her head.

It was like déjà vu.

Or more like déjà dead.

She moaned softly on realizing that every part of her hurt. Even her eyes, which she narrowed against the light.

"Oh, great," she rasped hoarsely. "I should have known. I'm dead, and the pilot from hell isn't done torturing me."

A spark of amusement briefly lit his storm-gray eyes, along with a look of what couldn't possibly be concern and wild relief. Could it? And why hadn't she noticed before how long and thick his dark lashes were?

Annoyance replaced the amusement, momentarily distracting her from the wet cloth he pressed to her pounding head. She tried evading it, but he gently cradled her head and turned her toward him.

"Keep still," he muttered irritably. "I had to move you before I could check for internal injuries."

"Isn't that *my* line?" she rasped, gasping when he hit a particularly tender spot. *"Ouch!"* She grabbed his hand, her fingers barely fitting around the brawny wrist as she attempted to hold him off. And when she discovered that all she could do was cling weakly as he carefully dabbed the area, she grimaced.

Oh, yeah—and moaned. She could definitely moan too, she discovered—the low sound was slipping out without her permission. It was downright embarrassing. Besides, *she* was the doctor, dammit. Wasn't it *her* job to heal the injured?

"That…hurts…"

What didn't hurt was the oddly arousing sensation of crisp hair against her sensitive palm. It was more like a lifeline to something solid and safe. Then she noticed something dark and wet matting his thick hair, the pallor beneath his smoothly tanned skin, and her senses abruptly sharpened into medic mode.

With renewed determination she shoved his hand away and struggled into a sitting position, gasping and wheezing because her chest felt as if it was being crushed.

"What…what the heck have you done to me?" she rasped, wondering if this was what it felt like to have a coronary. If so, she suddenly had a wealth of sympathy for anyone who'd ever had one.

His startled, "Huh?" was followed by a growled, "I saved your ass, if that's what you mean…" accompanied by an injured scowl, as if she should be grateful that she ached everywhere. And she meant *everywhere*. "And just in case you forgot, *lady*, this is the second time in less than eight hours."

Eve ignored him and looked past his mile-wide shoulders and aggravated expression.

What she saw had her eyes widening in shock.

She gasped at the sight of the padded seats, twisted at odd angles, and the stuff strewn everywhere. There was also a large plastic sheet covering a jagged hole where the wall—fuselage?— used to be. Chase must have rigged it to block out the storm, but water still continued to pour in along the sides.

Then the truth dawned on her and her gaze snapped back to him, her mouth dropping open at the realization that they'd—

"Ohmigod, you crashed?"

Dull color crept up his neck and he snapped out an insulted, "I did no such thing. The storm—"

"We're upside down!" she interrupted, craning her head around his wide shoulders, slack-jawed as she studied the crazy angle of everything.

It made her feel off balance, because neither the floor nor the ceiling was where it should be.

Her gaze swung back to his, and when he opened his

mouth Eve sucked in a quick breath and accused, "You said everything was going to be okay."

A muscle twitched in his hard jaw and his expression darkened even more. "It *is*."

"You said you'd handle things."

"I *did*," he gritted out, his stormy gaze locking with hers so intently that Eve finally realized he wasn't as calm as she'd thought. And he looked...embarrassed, even.

They were barely hanging on to life and he was *embarrassed*? Typical alpha guy.

"How? In case you haven't noticed, you crashed your plane."

"No kidding?" he drawled, with a wealth of sarcasm that Eve thought was entirely unwarranted. "Congratulations, Miz Observant. In case *you* haven't figured it out, direct lightning strikes tend to fry electronics. So, yeah," he snarled, "we crashed. Happy?"

She sighed, recalling the sight of the seaplane, gleaming white and obviously well cared for as it bobbed gently on the bright blue waters of Port Laurent. "I'm sorry. It was a beautiful plane."

He grunted, looking even more dejected if that was possible.

She tried for a conciliatory tone. "Do you...um...know where we are?"

He was silent for a couple beats, then he flicked her a speculative glance, as though trying to decide how to tell her that they'd crashed on the back of a giant sea turtle—or maybe in the middle of a volcano.

"You mean other than in a wrecked plane?"

Something very close to panic edged its way into Eve's consciousness. He was looking at her with hooded gray eyes that had gone strangely wary. Conciliation went right out the window.

"You have no idea where we are, do you?"

"Well, not at the mo—"

"Oh. My. God." Her eyes widened and clung to his, in the vain hope that he was joking. "You don't!" she accused, the crushing feeling in her chest returning with a vengeance.

"Well, not *exactly*," he growled, flashing an unreadable glance in her direction. "But you're fine, aren't you? No broken bones or anything? Right?" He didn't even have the grace to look apologetic.

Eve's heart lurched into her throat, threatening to cut off her air. She gasped for breath and clutched at her chest, where her heart threatened to punch its way through her ribs.

She sucked in another painful breath. *This could not be happening.* She'd fallen asleep and was still having a nightmare about the South Pacific and a flyboy from hell. But that was okay. Any minute now she'd wake up and—

"Fine? You call this *fine*?" Her voice rose to a hysterical squeak. *"Oh, God."* Air whooshed in and out of her lungs a few times as she tried to calm herself, but she wasn't getting calmer—in fact her vision was graying at the edges. "I…think…I'm having…a heart attack."

"You're just hyperventilating," he said, with such masculine impatience she was tempted to whack him in the head. *Oh, wait.* He'd already been whacked in the head—which probably explained his abhorrent personality.

No, that wasn't true. He'd been like that before the crash.

"Take a deep breath before you faint again."

"I am *not* going to faint," she snapped, trying to calm her panicked breathing. *Oh, God, she was totally going to pass out.* "I just can't seem to…to take a deep…breath. My chest…feels…it feels like…you…punched…me."

"That's just bruising from the harness. Maybe you should let me check you out?" he offered helpfully. "Maybe you broke a few ribs."

"And maybe you should back the hell off," Eve wheezed,

slapping at the hand reaching out to help unbutton her silk blouse. "You just want to gawk at the goods."

Chase sat back with an exasperated huff. "Lady, I've already 'gawked at the goods,' as you so delicately put it," he announced.

When she narrowed her eyes on him, as though imagining taking a scalpel to his intestines, he gave a careless shrug. "If it makes you feel better, you're not my type. So I can be all professional without going insane with lust."

Eve growled, and when Chase ventured a glance at her face she was—*surprise, surprise*—glaring at him, her lush bottom lip caught between pearly white teeth.

He groaned silently. *Dammit.* Now was *not* the time to be noticing her mouth. She was mad. He was mad. And they both needed medical attention. And since she was the doctor—yeah, well, maybe he shouldn't think about her kissing anything better…

"But if you ask real nice…" he drawled, helping himself to a mouthful of bottled water and wishing it was expensive whiskey instead. Because, *man*, if there was ever a time for alcohol-induced mindlessness, it was now. "When we get outta here, I'll help you with that little problem you were screaming about earlier."

Large amber eyes blinked at him in confusion, and then he knew the instant she recalled what she'd been talking… *screaming*…about before they'd crashed. Her eyelashes flickered and her throat convulsed around an audible swallow. A faint blush crept into her cheeks.

Then her pink tongue sneaked out and slid over that bottom lip he was having such hot fantasies about and *he* was the one swallowing hard.

"Wh-what problem?" she rasped. "The only problem I have here is you." Her gaze slid around the interior of the cabin rather than look at him. "And the fact that you crashed your plane."

Ignoring her attempts to distract him, he held out the bottle and said, "Well…it was kinda hard to hear above all the hysteria, but I *think* you were babbling something about never having had a screaming orgasm."

She snatched the bottle on a strangled squeak of horror. "I most certainly did *not*." The blush had turned wild, staining her pale skin a rosy pink.

"You most certainly did," he said, enjoying himself enormously now that her attention had been diverted from his plane and her panic attack.

"Don't be ridiculous. I'm th-thirty. Of course I've had org—plenty of those."

He pointed at her. "See? You can't even say it." He swallowed a chuckle when she made a growling sound in her throat. "You're not my type, or anything, but I don't mind admitting it took everything I had just to concentrate on flying. Which, come to think of it, was probably why we crashed." His look turned accusatory. "So I guess it's *your* fault."

"You're…you're insane," she spluttered.

He hitched a shoulder. "Anyway, I thought…being fellow survivors and all…" He clenched his jaw on a chuckle at her expression and turned it into a cough. Her face was a mix of relief, outrage and stunned disbelief.

Priceless.

And almost worth crashing his baby.

Almost.

"Besides," he continued after clearing his throat, "not many guys get to be wrecked on a deserted tropical island with an exotic underwear model."

Her eyes widened and her fingers gave a convulsive jerk. Water shot up the plastic neck of the bottle, spilling all over her hand and down the front of her shirt. For about ten seconds she spluttered, her mouth opening and closing several times. She looked ready to toss the water in his face. Or maybe smack him on the head with it.

Considering he already had the mother of all headaches, he carefully edged out of reach.

"Better not waste that water," he warned, in case she gave in to temptation. "It's all we have."

Fighting the heat of embarrassment at being reminded of her temporary loss of control, Eve tugged nervously at her skirt and couldn't help thinking about the fact that she wasn't "his type."

Really? That's what you're focusing on?

"Lingerie," she said primly, wriggling around to pull at her narrow skirt. She didn't know why she cared. Let him look. There was absolutely no way she wanted this…this rude, obnoxious *heathen* thinking she was his type. Thinking that she *wanted* to be his type—even if she did get a hot flash every time his gaze dropped to her legs.

She didn't. Not even if he were the last man on earth.

"Huh?" The heathen gave her an odd look and she wondered for a mortifying moment if she'd spoken out loud.

"Lingerie—not underwear. Men wear underwear. There's a difference."

"Hmm…" he murmured, squinting at her chest as though he could see through her blouse.

She quickly glanced down and gave a sigh of relief when she saw that he couldn't.

"So you *do* model lingerie?"

Of course he knew she didn't. He was just baiting her. *The jerk.*

"Of course not," Eve snapped, rising irritably to the bait, anyway. "What gave you that idea?"

"You did."

"I think you hit your head," she said, eyeing his bruised, battered face and the wet gleam of blood matting his dark hair with sudden concern. But despite the obvious pain around his eyes he looked… *Oh, boy!* He looked good. Like an irreverent, roughed-up pirate, ready to raise hell.

Her belly quivered. A really *hot* hell-raising pirate, darn it.

His mouth quirked, as though he knew what she was thinking. "Maybe you should let me check it out for myself. For educational purposes, of course," he added innocently when she gave a muffled growl. "To show me the difference between lingerie and underwear."

Seeing the wicked gleam, she narrowed her eyes to dangerous slits. "You. Are. Evil," she said through clenched teeth, and shifted farther away from him—which wasn't far enough, given their cramped quarters. "And instead of focusing on my underwear you should be thinking about where we are and…and…" She sucked in a shaky breath as their situation hit her. "Oh, God, how we're going to be rescued."

He sent her a dirty look, as if she'd insulted his manhood, and gingerly lay down on the pile of towels he'd used to make a pallet. When he said nothing—even closed his eyes—Eve wondered if his head injury had affected his memory.

Fear crawled into her belly like a sly fox invading a chicken coop.

"What about the radio? Did you try the radio?"

He sighed. "Of *course* I tried the radio," he muttered irritably, without opening his eyes. "It's fried—like the rest of the electronics. And before you nag me about where we are, and how we're going to be rescued, all I can say is I don't know." His lids popped open and his dark eyes settled on her, oddly serious and hypnotic. "I checked earlier and all I can see is jungle. We crashed in a damn jungle." He sighed again. "But better than the sea, huh?"

After a short silence, during which she had no clue how to reply to such male logic, his expression lightened and he gave her an up-and-down look that lingered a little too long on her breasts.

"So," he said, deliberately changing the subject. "You're a GP?"

"No, I'm an OB-GYN."

"OB what?"

"OB-GYN. I specialize in pregnancy, birth and women's…um…reproduction organs."

He absorbed that silently while Eve felt the heat rise in her cheeks. She was a medical professional, for heaven's sake. There was absolutely no need to blush at the mention of reproduction and childbirth.

It was normal. Completely natural.

So why did it suddenly seem intimate and…and slightly indecent, discussing it with him?

"And you've *never* been a lingerie model?"

"No," she said with strained patience. "I've never been *any* kind of model. I've waited tables, cleaned motel rooms, and I did a stint at a doughnut shop and then a…" She stopped before she admitted that she'd also worked in an exclusive boutique, which was where she'd got her love of expensive lingerie. She could just imagine his reaction to *that*. "Well, never mind. Suffice it to say I've never had the slightest desire to parade around in my underwear."

With a little smile tugging the corner of his mouth, he studied her until her face grew hot. "Huh."

"What?"

He grunted an incomprehensible reply and returned his gaze somewhere over her head, as though disappointed by her answer. "I had this roomate in college who was specializing in gynecology," he admitted after a short silence. "He was this huge bear of a guy who couldn't ever seem to find clean socks, let alone know which end a baby was supposed to emerge from. You're nothing like him."

Unsure whether or not to be insulted, Eve rolled her eyes. "You went to college?" And then she could have kicked herself when his eyebrow rose up his forehead. She hadn't meant to sound insulting.

At least she didn't think so.

"Oh, yeah," he said sleepily, and Eve leaned closer to study the gash on his head. "Even managed to get a degree and everything."

"In what?" she murmured absently, more worried about his slurred speech and his pallor than the amount of blood. "How to raise hell while charming a girl out of her underwear?"

He chuckled tiredly. "Lingerie," he murmured, closing his eyes.

"What?"

"It's lingerie, remember?" And when she continued to stare at him in confusion he slurred, "You said so yourself. Men wear underwear."

Ignoring his babbling, she shook her head and focused on the important details. "If you have a degree, what are you doing flying tourists around the South Pacific in a flying boat?"

He tilted his head toward her and cracked open one laser-sharp gray eye. After a while he said, "It's a long, boring story."

When she just continued to look at him, he shrugged and shut his eye again.

"If you must know…"

He yawned, and Eve found herself holding her breath as if he was about to impart state secrets.

She had to lean forward to hear his murmured, "Keeps me in mai tais."

Her breath whooshed out in what she told herself *wasn't* disappointment, and she sat back to nibble uncertainly on her lip while considering what his head injury might mean. First, he was the only thing between her and an unknown, possibly hostile jungle. And second, despite the weird things those mocking gray eyes did to her control—like unravel it faster than line on a fishing reel—being in a jungle with a head injury was the last thing anyone wanted.

"I…um…" She cleared her throat and tucked her hair behind her ear. "I don't think you should close your eyes."

"I'm tired, and my head hurts like a bi— It hurts." He grunted, and she nearly smiled at his obvious attempt to clean up his language. "Hell, *everything* hurts."

She could sympathize. She was feeling every bruise, along with an adrenaline crash, and was all too willing to sink into a healing sleep herself. "I mean, I really don't think you should sleep."

Something in her tone must have registered, because his eyes popped open and he frowned at her. He sat up abruptly and looked around, as if he expected a horde of savages to be hiding behind the seats. "Why? What's wrong?"

"You have a head injury and you might be concussed."

"You have a head injury too," he pointed out reasonably, waving a hand in her direction, and she was somewhat taken aback that the mention of her head suddenly had it pounding like a heavy metal band.

"But…but I'm not concussed," she reasoned, fairly certain she wasn't—although she did have a splitting headache. Probably nothing a couple of painkillers and a bottle of water wouldn't fix. Oh, yeah, and about twelve hours' sleep.

"How do you know?" he demanded, sinking back onto the mound of towels with a groan. "You were out for a long time."

She digested that piece of information. "How long?"

"I don't know. A while."

Which meant he'd also been unconscious.

She looked around the cabin at the scattered debris. "Do you have a first-aid box?"

His mouth quirked, drawing her attention to the finely sculpted lips that did odd things to her insides. But then again it had been hours since she'd eaten, so she was probably just hungry.

"Strapped to the bulkhead behind you." He waited for

her to retrieve it before asking innocently, "We gonna play doctor, Doctor?"

She raised her eyebrows at him and opened the box, surprised to find it fully stocked with top-of-the-range supplies. More than adequate for a minor emergency—maybe even minor surgery.

"No," she said absently, mulling over another piece of the puzzle that was Chase Gallagher—the fact that he'd spared no expense on the seaplane he used to keep him in mai tais. "I'm going to do what I've been trained for."

She removed packaged swabs, antiseptic spray and some packaged adhesive strips from the steel box and placed them beside her.

"Should I be worried?"

Her gaze shot up and caught his smirk. "Worried?" she asked warily, not knowing how to handle him in his current mood. Scowling and cursing were easier to handle than this…this teasing and dangerously attractive man. Maybe the whack on the head had changed his personality. Or, worse, maybe the whack on *her* head had rendered her temporarily insane. "I'm an excellent doctor."

"A skull fracture is a far cry from childbirth and 'women's…um…reproduction organs,'" he said, perfectly mimicking her earlier words.

Her eyes narrowed and she contemplated doing a lobotomy on him, to take care of that personality change. "I wouldn't worry, if I were you," she drawled smoothly. "It's just big and hard."

The instant the words were out of her mouth she wished them back—especially when the wicked gleam turned to outright laughter. She sent him a dirty look that made him laugh even more, until she slapped a wad of alcohol swabs on his head.

Sucking in a sharp breath, he grabbed her wrist and eyed her warily. "Are you sure you're a doctor? You blush at the mention of reproduction and your bedside manner sucks."

"Newborns and their mothers are perfectly safe with me," she snapped. "It's just the *big* babies that need to watch out."

His mouth curled into a half-assed grin that she shouldn't have found appealing. *Oh, wow.*

"You're calling me a big baby?"

She shrugged, and a strange sensation moved through her at the sudden image of him as a little boy, his usually wicked gray eyes filled with hurt as his mother kissed his boo-boos.

Then he snorted derisively and she decided he'd probably emerged fully grown—with a sexy scowl.

Darn.

Now she was visualizing him wearing nothing *but* that sexy scowl.

A sigh escaped. She was obviously in need of medical attention herself if she was finding him—his *scowl*—sexy.

"Are you flirting with me, Dr. Carmichael?"

She rolled her eyes, and instantly regretted the move when pain stabbed behind her right eye, reminding her that she'd hit her head sometime during the crash—and also against his when they'd collided earlier. *Yeesh.* Maybe her injury was worse than she'd thought. A serious injury was the only explanation for imagining this…this sexy heathen as a vulnerable little boy. And then getting all mushy about it.

"Don't be ridiculous," she muttered, ducking her head and sliding her hands through his damp hair so she could examine his injury.

You were so flirting. The knowledge had her nipples tightening and her belly quivering with alarm, along with a renewed determination to ignore his bad-boy allure. She was *nothing* like her mother. *Nothing.* She'd hardly had a string of wild hookups that had resulted in not one but two unwanted pregnancies, along with heartbreak, cleared-out bank accounts and a few bruises. Besides, she'd worked since she was about thirteen and hadn't had the time.

"This is hardly the time or place."

There will be no time or place, Evelyn, she reminded herself firmly. *Bad boys are bad. Period.*

"You have something better to do?"

She sent him a long cool look. "You mean like checking for oozing brain matter?" She reached for more swabs. "I'd say there's little chance of that, Mr. Gallagher. You appear to have lost all yours."

CHAPTER FOUR

Oh, yeah, Chase thought moodily. He clearly *had* lost brain cells if the sensation of her fingers sliding though his hair was suddenly the most erotic thing he'd ever experienced.

He sighed, closed his eyes. *Great. Just freaking great.* Not only had he lost his plane, his mind had taken a hike too. The former was insured, but the latter… Well, he didn't know which one he'd miss the most.

He'd thought closing his eyes would shut her out, but he hadn't figured on the sensation of her fingers in his hair, or the heat and scent of her body invading his nostrils as she leaned close.

He found himself focusing on drawing in her wildly erotic scent and thought, *Aw, man, just my luck to want to jump Amelia's sister.* Which was not only wrong but strange, considering he'd never felt a lick of attraction for his future sister-in-law. But he wanted to yank Eve down, roll her beneath him and ravish her smart mouth.

She nibbled on a plump pink lip and he sucked in a sharp breath. Her forehead wrinkled at the sound, and when she dropped her gaze to his, they both froze.

The air sizzled and Chase's pulse leaped into an abrupt gallop. The next moment a crushing weight descended on his chest as the air inside the plane seemed to be sucked out. There one instant, then…*vhoop*…gone.

The moment stretched out and with each thundering

beat of his heart her pupils grew, until only a thin circle of shimmering amber remained. His skin hummed, his ears buzzed and all he could think about was letting himself drown in deepest, darkest velvet.

Before he realized what he was doing, he wrapped his fingers in her silk shirt and yanked her down. Instead of putting his mouth on her, like he wanted, swallowing her in one big, greedy gulp, he paused, holding her mouth barely a breath away from his.

She gave a strangled gasp.

His scalp literally crawled with the instinct to cover her mouth with his and swallow that soft sound—and any others she made. Along with more. A whole hell of a lot more.

For several long moments they remained frozen, eyes locked and mouths almost touching, floating in a silent world that contained nothing but heat, ragged breathing and a startling savage hunger.

Finally Chase realized that her huge eyes were dilated with wariness as much as with arousal. His gut clenched and his fingers tightened. *Dammit*, what the hell was wrong with him? He didn't usually grab women and practically force his kisses on them.

With a sound of disgust—mainly at himself—he gently nudged her backward, widening the gap between them. And hopefully removing temptation.

His jaw ached along with the rest of his body.

Looking a little shell-shocked, Evelyn lifted unsteady fingers to her mouth. She blinked at him, and then away, her breath as unsteady as his. He wanted to curse himself for putting that wary look in her eyes. Then again, better wariness than the hot, dark need that was a lit match to his.

She opened her mouth, then shut it again, her brow wrinkling in irritation as much as confusion.

"What the hell was that?" she rasped, sounding as if she'd chewed on glass.

He grunted out a mirthless laugh. "Damned if I know."

And when he felt his neck heat he rolled onto his side, presenting her with his back.

After a lengthy silence, she cleared her throat. "I'm not finished dressing your head wound," she said briskly, but Chase could feel her eyes boring holes in his back.

"I'm fine," he muttered.

He would not apologize. It was her fault, anyway. For looking at him with those shimmering eyes. Yeah, and nibbling on that plump lip. He was a guy who'd been on the sex wagon for a while. She was smart. She should know better than to tempt a starving man.

"If I need any doctoring," he practically snarled, "I'll let you know. Right now I'm tired. So…good night."

There was a moment of stunned silence, then Chase heard her moving around, muttering to herself about giving grumpy flyboys a lobotomy to improve their personalities.

But his personality was fine. Or it had been until she'd swooned into his life. Maybe it was *her* attitude that needed adjusting. Didn't she know that men were attracted to soft, feminine women? Women who didn't hike their eyebrows and look at a man like he was a delinquent in need of disciplining. Women who didn't treat a man as if he was a moron for crashing his seaplane.

He snorted silently. If that was true, then why the hell did he find her smart mouth and sharp wit so darn…*sexy*?

Heart hammering, Eve gaped at the ragged path Chase's seaplane had cleared through the jungle before coming to rest at a drunken angle about fifty yards in. One wing and a pontoon had broken right off, leaving the bulk of the battered plane half-buried in thick tropical vegetation and tilted at an impossible angle.

The sight had her sucking in air and locking her knees against the urge to sink to the ground.

How did I not feel this happening?
How did we manage to walk away from this?

The last thing she remembered was the seaplane flipping upside down and a scream tearing from her throat. She'd been convinced she was going to die.

And then... She inhaled and exhaled noisily, until her heart rate settled and the black dots swimming behind her eyes disappeared. Then she recalled waking up to a wet, half-naked sea god bending over her—for the second time in less than twelve hours.

The whole thing seemed...surreal, somehow. As though it had happened to someone else. As though she'd opened her eyes to find herself in someone else's nightmare.

This morning she'd woken to the sounds of shrieks and squawks, convinced that hostile animals had invaded her bedroom. But she'd been in a wrecked seaplane.

Nowhere near the sea.

For a long moment she'd lain absolutely still, absorbing the shock, because she'd kind of hoped that it had all been a bad dream.

No such luck.

Now, smoothing the hair off her face with trembling fingers, Eve looked everywhere but at the crumpled plane. It was past dawn and the sky—what she could see of it—was lavender and a wild orange-red that reminded her of that childhood saying about a red sky in the morning being a sailor's warning.

She gave a soft snort. It would have been *really* great if she'd had that warning yesterday morning, on her stopover at Oahu. Maybe she would have been prepared for the coming disaster. Maybe she could have avoided it altogether by turning around and heading back to London.

She let out a sigh and looked around.

Speaking of disasters...where the heck was Chase?

For a couple of really intense moments she'd thought he'd ditched her, but then she'd remembered how he'd treated her the night before. Impatience mixed with baffled tenderness. It had been a novel, if uncomfortable experience. Especially as she'd always had to be the strong one. For her mother, her grandmother...Amelia. It had been kind of nice to let someone else be strong for once.

Just briefly, she reminded herself quickly. Because life had taught her that she couldn't rely on people. When she did, they either left or died on her.

After the heat and intensity of that weird almost-kiss she'd escaped outside, hoping to get her emotions under control before she faced him again. But she needn't have worried. By the time she'd returned he was fast asleep. With nothing to do, she'd swallowed a couple of pain meds and stretched out beside him—and had been asleep within minutes.

She'd woken once, to find herself snuggled against a large warm body as though she'd sought his heat, and when she'd bolted upright—*horrified*—he'd muttered irritably and tugged her back down, yanking her against him.

They'd had a brief tug-of-war that he'd won by throwing one heavy leg over her and growling at her to go to sleep. She'd finally succumbed, wrapped in delicious heat and feeling strangely relaxed and contented.

If she hadn't been so exhausted she might have had the presence of mind to freak out. Or maybe slip from his embrace. But she hadn't. And she hadn't been disappointed when she'd awakened to find herself alone either.

Well, not much.

Keeping a sharp lookout for snakes and spiders—because *everyone* knew there were serpents, even of the two-legged variety, in paradise—she took care of her morning business before setting off toward the beach. She bravely ignored all the strange rustling coming from the dense undergrowth and hurried as fast as her bare feet and stiff muscles could carry her.

She was acutely aware of the ridiculous picture she must make, picking her way through broken branches, jagged plant stems and squishy ground cover dressed in a rumpled green pencil skirt and a cream silk blouse, clutching a pair of strappy high heels.

With all her scrapes and bruises, she probably looked like an advertisement for domestic abuse.

Or—*yikes*—the morning after a *very* rough night before.

She rolled her eyes. So much for her professional image, she thought—which, come to think of it, had tanked just about the time she'd landed in paradise.

And met him, of course.

He was clearly bad luck. And she was done with bad luck. *Soooo done.* From now on her life was going to be charmed. Or she'd have something to say about it.

By the time she emerged from the trees to step onto soft, cool sand, tinted pink in the early-morning light and littered with storm debris, Eve was huffing, perspiring and wondering when the heck she'd let herself get so out of shape. Although it might have something to do with the dark bruises across her chest and belly, or the many hours since her last decent meal.

Thinking about food made her stomach growl, although she'd rather have a long hot soak in scented bubbles. Scented bubbles up to her neck, surrounded by candles, a bottle of wine. Oh…and a hot bronzed sea god to massage her aching body.

Inhaling the amazingly cool and fresh morning air, she looked up—and promptly froze. Because the sea god had stepped out of her vision into the flesh— She blinked. He was emerging from the turquoise water. Her eyes widened. He was…he was…*naked.*

Ohmigod! He *so* was naked. Her breath escaped in a stuttered whoosh. Gloriously naked. From the top of his seal-dark wet hair to his big tanned feet and everything— she meant *everything*—in between. And—she gulped— there certainly was a *lot* of "in-between."

She must have made a sound, because he stopped shaking water from his hair and lifted his head, stormy eyes zeroing in on her with laser-point accuracy.

Eve's gaze flew upward and her mind came to a screeching halt.

For a long, breathless moment they stared at each other, the memory of last night like a blaze across the fifteen feet separating them. Finally an arrogant dark brow rose up his bruised forehead, galvanizing Eve into action.

She squeaked out an *"Oh!"* slapped a hand over her eyes in delayed reaction and half spun away, aware that her entire body had gone hot because she'd been caught eyeing his package. The image had been burned onto her retina—her brain—for all time.

An amused baritone drawled, "Enjoying the view?" and Eve could have kicked herself for reacting like a ninth grader caught in the boys' locker room.

"What—what the heck are you d-doing?" she squeaked, stalling for time. She peeked at him through the gaps in her fingers and admired—professionally, of course—the wide shoulders, the clearly defined but not overly bulky deltoids, biceps, pectorals, the eight-…*eight?*…pack and the deep vee arrowing down to—

"Taking an early-morning swim." He interrupted her awestruck mental anatomy list, scooping up his shirt with which he proceeded to dry himself off—totally unconcerned with his nudity.

She squeezed her eyes closed and waved her hand in his direction, thinking if she looked like that she'd probably be unconcerned too. Because…

Whoa.

"But you're…" She snapped her mouth shut at the sudden realization that she was acting like a scandalized old maid and not a medical practitioner who'd seen her share of naked bodies. "I mean your head. You're, um…concussed."

He snorted, as though he knew she hadn't been referring to his head injury. "It's fine. In fact I feel great."

Well, he certainly *looked* great. And would probably feel great too. Especially if she—

There was a rustle of fabric and then his amused voice drawled, "It's safe now, Dr. Prim. You can look."

Eve's eyes snapped open to find him barely a foot away, looking all cool and damp and...and *amused*, darn him. But *safe* was hardly a word she'd use in connection with this sexy, grumpy pilot. Especially on a storm-ravaged beach with that dark, dangerous aura surrounding his half-naked form and making him look like he belonged in this wild, deserted place.

Then she looked closer and caught the way he held himself, held his head and shoulders. Stiffly and carefully—as though it hurt to move.

"You're lying," she accused, relieved to be reminded of her profession. Relieved because now she could focus on something other than all that masculine awesomeness.

Stepping closer, she reached up to cup his head so she could examine his eyes. He froze, as though her touch surprised him, and for a moment it surprised her too. But then she told herself that they'd survived a terrifying ordeal and even slept together. What she was doing was in a professional capacity, and not...definitely *not* because of a sudden overwhelming need to touch him.

He looked tired, she thought, and he was trying to hide his pain. Her sigh was an exhalation of exasperation. Men made really sucky patients—which was one of the reasons she'd gone into obstetrics and gynecology.

The other had been personal. Her grandmother, Isadora, had been a midwife, and Eve had often been called on to help. Sometimes, like the night her mother had died giving birth to her second set of twins, things had gone bad, and the remembered helplessness had motivated her in the long, hard years of studying medicine and holding down three jobs.

She held up three fingers.

"How many?"

His hooded gaze remained locked on hers and Eve's heart gave a funny little stutter in her chest at the smoldering intensity turning his gray eyes smoky. He wrapped a large hand around hers, trapping her fingers in warmth. The little stutter became a wild tumble that she felt clear to the soles of her feet. The next thing she knew her nipples had tightened into painful points.

Her knees wobbled. She sucked in a shocked breath and her mouth promptly went dry. That had been…unexpected, to say the least. And totally unwelcome, she told herself firmly, nervously sliding her tongue over her bottom lip as she tried to tug her hand free. His grip was gentle, unbreakable, and short of an embarrassing tussle, she wasn't going anywhere.

His thumb set up a hypnotizing caress. "If I tell you where it hurts," he murmured, his gaze dropping to her mouth, "will you kiss it better?"

Her stunned "What…?" ended in a muffled *oomph* when he used his possession of her hand to yank her against him. Right up against that awesome naked chest covered in bruises.

"How 'bout we start here?" he growled roughly, and before Eve could react he swooped down and closed his mouth over hers.

Her eyes widened in shock. There was nothing tentative or gentle about the move. In fact if she'd had the ability to think she might have said it was forceful and more than a little heated. As though he'd been compelled to give in to some wild, dark impulse and blamed her for it.

She made a soft sound of protest, which he promptly swallowed, and when she tried to jerk away, his hands speared into her hair, wrapping around her head to hold her captive as he set about totally overpowering her senses. He didn't ask permission or even coax. He just *took*, blasting through her defenses with his mouth and tongue, consuming all thoughts of resistance along with her breath.

Dizzy, Eve clutched at the nearest surface and found smooth, warm masculine flesh beneath her hands. But that was okay. More than okay, actually.

In the guise of needing something solid to hold on to, she did what she *really* wanted to do.

It took her hands only a few seconds to explore his abdomen, glorying in the way the steely muscles twitched and rippled beneath her touch. And then she became lost in the mindless haze of his kisses, unaware that she was greedily and possessively exploring acres of smooth warm flesh with her hands while her mouth answered the demand of his.

She'd never experienced anything remotely like it. He sucked her in like a level-five twister, until she sagged against him, all control over her limbs forgotten.

One arm snaked around her waist, anchoring her against him as he whipped her up and sent her senses spinning into an endless moment of shocking heat and erotic need. A need she'd never before experienced.

The kiss seemed to last forever, and when he finally released her mouth to suck in air, she wheezed, "That's… that's not how you k-kiss anything…um…better." She was shocked that anything remotely coherent had emerged from her mouth. Even more shocked that the mere touch of a man's mouth could leave her feeling so…*changed*.

His dark brow rose up his forehead and his eyes glittered with humor—and something imminently incendiary—as though no one had dared question his technique before.

But, Eve noted with satisfaction, his heart was pounding beneath her hand…the hand currently smoothing over hard pectoral muscles covered in warm taut skin. The other was curled into the waistband of his cargoes, against taut, satiny-smooth skin—as if she'd needed to hold on to something or risk falling at his feet like a boneless blob.

"Oh, yeah?"

"No," she said, wondering why she wasn't getting as far away from him as possible.

She didn't even like him, for heaven's sake, and that kiss couldn't have been further from her idea of romantic than if he'd hauled back and slugged her. It had been too intense— an assault on her senses. It had left her breathless, dazed, which might have something to do with the fact that when she moved her hand just a fraction to the left she abruptly froze when she realized exactly what she was touching.

Oh, boy. It looked like he'd dressed in a hurry and forgotten his underwear.

Her breath hitched and her senses swam—which was probably why she did what she did next.

Sliding her free hand up to cup his jaw, she eased up the length of his body on her toes and pressed against this evidence of his reaction to their little experiment.

"*This* is how you do it," she murmured huskily, and with her eyes locked on his she very carefully touched her mouth to the heavy bruise on his shoulder, before moving to his jaw, covered in a sexy two-day stubble and a dark bruise. The delicious rasp against her lips sent a shudder of pure sensation racing over her flesh, making her skin prickle and each tiny hair lift…as if straining to be closer still.

Her lips curved against his jaw and his hands, warm and heavy at her hips, clenched almost convulsively, as though he fought the need to crush her against him.

The heat in his now-stormy eyes blazed hot and bright. Her belly clenched with nerves and something that felt very much like…excitement?

No. Her eyelids fluttered and she froze. *No getting excited, Evelyn. This isn't some adolescent make-out session that you can control or laugh off.*

He was a fully grown man, with over a foot and a hundred pounds on her. There was no controlling *him*—or the way he made her body react.

Her breath shuddered out against his skin and he turned his head. A sound—deep and rough and thrilling—emerged from his throat. "Don't stop there," he growled softly, his sculpted lips brushing hers and making them tingle.

Oh, yeah. Definitely time to stop.

"I…um…" She slid her hands to his shoulders and tried to ease away, but his grip on her hips tightened, holding her firmly against him. Right there, against all that delicious…um…hardness.

She sucked in a sharp breath, going still. The scent of warm aroused man had her eyes literally rolling back in her head. Suddenly the sheer size of him had her fighting two opposing instincts. One was to press closer and offer her mouth—heck, offer *everything*—the other…to escape.

She knew instinctively which one she should choose.

As though he knew what she was thinking Chase gave a low chuckle, the sound rumbling through his chest and sending delicious vibrations rolling through her body.

"Chicken, Doc?"

She swallowed. "D-don't be ridiculous." *More like terrified.* "I…I just think the lesson is over, that's all," she croaked, wedging her hands between their bodies and sucking in a shaky breath when her palms accidentally rasped against his tight male nipples. "I can see you're all better now."

"Liar," he crooned, shifting his hips closer, so the part he pressed against her belly was big and hard and… Eve's breath whooshed out.

And nothing.

Not feeling a thing here.

Her eyes widened. And not *there* either.

"I'm now in pain somewhere else," he murmured against her ear. "Wanna know where?"

Her gasp of outrage was muffled by his soft laughter and he allowed her to shove him away.

"You…you…" she stuttered, wanting to kick herself for rising to his bait. *"Jerk."* Wanting to kick *him* for making it so darn tempting.

"I meant my elbow," he said mildly, folding his arms across his wide chest and exposing another bruise. His eyebrow rose. "What did you *think* I meant?" The move made his biceps and deltoids bulge in a way that almost had her drooling.

No. No drooling.

And no touching after that last comment either.

"Besides, isn't a kiss supposed to cure everything?" he continued, when it was clear she wasn't going to reply.

"No," she snapped, tucking her hands into her armpits before they ignored her brain. "Not everything."

Not anything.

Because now she was in pain too. The kind of pain she'd read about but never experienced. The kind of pain she'd give anything not to feel. Certainly not with him.

"Uh-huh?" He sounded skeptical.

"Well, for one thing," she muttered, massaging the ache in her temple, "it won't cure your enormous ego."

He laughed and bent to pick up his damp shirt, which he held out to her with such a wicked look that her clothes nearly melted right off her body.

Deeply suspicious, she stared at it as though it might bite her, because it suddenly reminded her of the apple incident in the Garden of Eden. *Yeah, and look how that turned out.*

"What's that for?"

"I thought you might like a quick swim."

Instantly a vision of him joining her in the cool, clear water popped front and center into her head. A renewed surge of heat stained her cheeks—and blazed elsewhere when she realized that in her vision they were both naked and wet as seals.

She took a stumbling step backward, her hand flying up

to clutch the lapels of her blouse as though she was afraid he might offer to help her strip.

"But…but…shouldn't we be finding a way to get off this island?"

He shook his head as if she was hopeless and tossed his shirt at her. She barely caught it before it smacked her in the face.

"Doc, Doc, Doc…" He sighed, gesturing with his hand. "How often does anyone wake up to *this*? Besides," he added when she opened her mouth to argue, "I'm hungry. I'm going to find food. Go enjoy your swim. I promise not to peek."

Eve held the shirt to her front, as though it would provide an adequate shield against him. Against all that smooth, warm masculine skin. Against the urge to invite him to join her.

She pressed her lips together and he grinned before turning to head up the beach. "Suit yourself. Water's great, by the way," he called over his shoulder. "Might even cool you down."

Hah! As if.

Eve watched him disappear and thought it unlikely—especially as somewhere in the center of her body a fire raged, heating her up from the inside out.

It would take a lot to douse that.

Eve turned and eyed the crystal-clear water with sudden longing. It had been a couple of days since she'd taken more than a quick shower. Surely it wouldn't hurt to face the prospect of them being stranded on a deserted island, fresh and alert?

Casting around for a safe place to strip, she spied a secluded area and headed over to it. *Hmm…* She thoughtfully studied the area between some rock outcroppings. It made a perfect little cove, sheltered on both sides.

She cast a quick look over her shoulder at the empty beach and the line of thick jungle vegetation. Maybe if

she undressed behind the rocks and slipped into the water
there she wouldn't be seen. And if she saw someone coming—*fine, saw him coming*—she'd be able to scramble out
and dress before he saw her.

Maybe.

She struggled mentally for about three seconds, before
tossing his shirt onto the sand and quickly stripping out of
her skirt and blouse. She was just about to wade into the
water when she impulsively reached behind her to unfas-
ten her bra. Before she could change her mind she shed it,
along with the tiny matching cream and green lace panties, and added them to the growing pile.

Naked, Eve quickly waded into the water, her heart hammering at her daring. But then the water hit her midthigh
and—*oh, God*—it felt amazing.

For just a moment her recent application for a new job
in DC, her plans to start a new life there, seemed a million light years away. For just an instant she wondered
what it must be like to live in this Garden of Eden, where
life was simple.

Then she shook off her fanciful thoughts. Life was never
simple, and this was nothing more than an amazing inter-
lude. A harmless fantasy just like she and Amelia used to
have as children.

And if the big male figure in her childhood fantasies
had been replaced by someone infinitely more real—and
more dangerous—she shrugged it off as delayed shock
from surviving an air crash.

Her world, her life, was back in the States. All she had
to do was find a way back to it.

CHAPTER FIVE

CHASE WENT OFF in search of food. He found bananas, a few small ripe papaya and some goji berries, and was wrapping his find in a banana leaf when an ear-piercing scream shattered the peace. The echo of it had barely registered when Chase dropped his bounty and tore through the vegetation toward the beach.

Damn, damn, *damn*. He shouldn't have left her alone. He should have ignored his promise not to look. He should have stayed…stood guard, done something. But, no. He had to go and make a stupid promise and now—*oh, God*—was she being attacked by a shark? Stung by box jellyfish? Or, worse, kidnapped by pirates?

Exploding onto the beach with a blood-curdling yell, he plowed to a halt in a shower of wet sand at the sight of the scene before him. His mouth dropped open more in shock than in an effort to fill his lungs with air after that mad dash.

A naked Eve—*and, boy, was that ironic*—stood with her back to him, facing the tiny cove and clutching his shirt to her front. He was momentarily distracted by the sight of her long slender back, heart-shaped bottom and endless Vegas showgirl legs before he realized she was facing a boatload of locals, all gaping at her as though she'd just been beamed down from the mothership.

The instant they saw him their attention swung his way,

and for a couple of beats they all seemed frozen in a tab-
leau that might have been comical if not for the fact that
his heart was pounding and his breath was sawing in an
out of his lungs.

Relieved that there wasn't a drop of blood in sight, he
lifted his arm in greeting, realizing that they hadn't crashed
onto a deserted island at all. And that she hadn't opened
an artery and didn't require CPR...although he probably
wouldn't have minded *that* so much.

Ambling down to the water's edge, Chase spied some
pieces of frothy lace that resembled sea foam and paused
to scoop them up. He shoved them into his pocket before
rescuing her blouse and skirt.

Eve must have sensed him behind her, and she cast a
wide-eyed, panic-filled glance over her shoulder as though
she expected a rear attack. When she saw him eyeing her
naked rear, she gave a distressed bleat and slapped a hand
over her bottom.

Covering absolutely nothing.

He arched a brow at her and held out her clothes, which
she snatched as she scurried crab-like behind him, careful not to flash her very excellent rear at the newcomers.

Using his body as a shield, she wheezed out, "Ohmigod,
ohmigod, ohmigod! Some protector you are. How *could
you*?"

Confused about why she was mad at *him*, he said,
"Huh?" and tried to turn around. But she squealed and
whacked his shoulder. He shook his head and faced forward. *Women*.

A couple men had hopped into the shallow water and
were pulling the boat closer to shore. Chase took a step
forward to help but was abruptly stopped when she curled
a hand into his waistband and yanked him back, growling,
"Move one inch and die," in his ear.

He might have laughed if the feel of her knuckles pressing into the small of his back hadn't threatened to blow the

top of his head right off. Goose bumps broke out across his skin and a shudder of pure lust zinged in all directions, turning him into one big electromagnetic generator. Or some kind of generator. Because he was suddenly harder than he'd ever been in his life. A breath away from ravishing Eve in paradise.

In clear view of a curious audience.

Shocked by the force of his reaction, he stuttered, "Wha-at?" wondering if the crash had caused permanent brain damage after all.

"Where the hell is my underwear?" she hissed from behind him, and Chase tried not to imagine her struggling to put on silk over wet skin. Wet naked skin.

His mouth curved with appreciation.

"Really?" he demanded out the corner of his mouth. "You're going to worry about that *now*?"

"What—what do you mean?"

He snorted and folded his arms across his chest. "What do you think I mean? This is a remote South Pacific island. You have to be on the lookout for pirates and human traffickers."

"Wha-a-a-at?" she squeaked behind him, and he nearly laughed at her gullibility.

But she'd cleaved herself to his back as though trying to get inside his skin. Instantly his entire being perked up, every hair covering his body standing straight up and saluting the sun. He promptly lost his train of thought.

And, *dammit*, his body hair wasn't the only thing saluting the sun.

He sucked in a shuddery breath. *Not now, Gallagher. Not ever. Not with her.*

"Chase Gallagher, is that you?"

Chase blinked to uncross his eyes and spotted Teiki Manea, a teacher whose wife had nearly lost her baby in the last stages of pregnancy a year ago. Chase had just dropped off a couple of tourists when Teiki had arrived, looking like a wild man, threatening to sink Chase's plane unless he flew them to the hospital in Rikirua.

Chase lifted his hands in a gesture of surrender. "Teiki? Don't tell me your wife's in labor again?"

The islander gave a booming laugh and charged up the beach to wrap his big arms around Chase. Chase returned the back slap—which was more of a pounding—and decided things could be worse. A lot worse.

The big islander's grin was quick and white. "And what if she is, *mon ami*?"

Chase shrugged. "The storm managed what you couldn't. My plane's wrecked."

"That was you?" Teiki demanded, stepping back to study the bruised and battered duo. "We heard something during the storm last night but—"

"Hey, don't sweat," Chase interrupted, knowing full well that a search party would have been dispatched immediately if it had been possible. "We're both fine."

Teiki snorted and peered around Chase to where Eve was zipping up her skirt. "You're uglier than ever," he said, smiling charmingly at Eve. "But your lady sure is fine."

Chase shook his head and laughed. He was about to tell Teiki that Eve wasn't his lady when she stepped around him and aimed a blinding smile at the islander. A smile that literally stole Chase's breath—along with his damn amusement.

What the—?

He gaped at her, captivated by the genuine laughter that transformed her from attractive to, well…stunning. And then, abruptly realizing he was standing there with his mouth hanging open, Chase snapped it shut and scowled at the way she beamed at Teiki—as though he'd just saved her from a fate worse than death.

So what the hell was Chase? Fish fungus?

"Teiki, this is Dr. Carmichael from the US." He practically bit out each word and folded his arms across his chest in case he gave in to the primitive impulses of a male defending his territory. Eve Carmichael wasn't his to defend. "She's visiting her sister on Tukamumu."

Eve flashed him a confused look, as though she couldn't understand his abrupt testiness. Heck, he was just as confused. Why the hell did he care that she didn't see him as her hero? He didn't. Besides, he was no hero, and frankly he was done rescuing women in distress.

Done, he repeated irritably. Just in case his thick skull hadn't got the message the first time.

"A doctor?" Teiki demanded, looking even more pleased—and impressed. "Kanaloa must have heard our prayers. Dr. Tahuru is having a hard time coping with all the injuries from last night's storm." He looked up into the sky and shrugged. "The next one's going to be even worse."

"Next one?" Eve said, looking up into the sky.

Chase could understand her confusion. It was crystal clear, as if last night's storm hadn't occurred.

"You can tell by looking at the sky?" she asked.

Teiki chuckled. "Well, the elders can," he said with a wink. "But my brother-in-law runs the local met station."

"Oh, I'm s-sorry," Eve stuttered, heat rising into her cheeks. "I didn't mean—"

"No worries, Doctor." Teiki laughed, gently patting her shoulder with a huge hand. "We take as much pride in our island's unspoilt beauty as we do in our hospital, school and met center." He shrugged. "If we want to compete with tourist destinations like Tahiti, Bora Bora and—" he winked at Chase, confusing Eve "—Tukamumu, then we have to be able to track storms and stay connected to the outside world. Which reminds me—" He gestured to the boat. "Why don't we take you to the resort so you can get cleaned up and rested? You must be starving. I'd open my home, but we had to take in family whose houses were damaged in the storm."

Chase wanted to refuse. Why, he had no idea. He *was*

starving. *And* he was overjoyed that they were on an inhabited island. That way he could contact his brother and get out of here sooner rather than later. That way he could make Eve someone else's responsibility.

That way he could salvage what was left of his freaking mind.

"That's a great idea," he said, shoving his hands in his pockets. His fingers touched something soft and flimsy and in a moment of confusion he nearly whipped it out, recalling at the last instant that he'd pocketed her underwear.

No. *Lingerie.*

The word conjured up an image of her wearing nothing but those pieces of silk and lace. Gulping, he pulled his hand out as though he'd been bitten and shoved his fingers through his hair, feeling—*what the hell?*—rattled.

"Why don't you…um…go ahead, Doc?" he stuttered, wondering when he'd turned into an awkward adolescent.

The thought panicked him and he suddenly couldn't get away fast enough. Besides, the break would keep him from doing something dumb. Like kissing her again.

Or worse.

She blinked at him as if he was abandoning her to a volcano-worshipping hostile tribe and he had to steel himself against making promises he couldn't keep. Promises he sure as hell didn't *want* to keep.

"What about you?"

"I need to salvage my cargo." He turned to Teiki. "Can you send the boat back for me?"

"I can do one better," the teacher announced, and gestured to the men waiting beside the boat. "Timéo and Bradley can take the doctor to the resort and return with a second boat. The rest of us will help with your cargo."

For some reason that she couldn't explain, Eve experienced a moment of panic at the thought of leaving Chase. But the sexy pirate who'd sucked the breath from her lungs just a half hour before had been replaced by a distant stranger, reminiscent of the man she'd met yesterday.

And so, because he seemed almost eager to be rid of her, Eve allowed Timéo to guide her to the boat. She watched as Chase held an intense discussion with Teiki, then disappeared into the trees without so much as a glance in her direction.

She wanted to pretend she didn't care, but when the big islander sent her an encouraging wave and headed up the beach after Chase, she felt lost. Which was just ridiculous. She wasn't lost. Just the opposite.

They'd just been rescued, for heaven's sake.

Besides, she was a big girl. She'd been taking care of herself—and everyone else—for a long time. There was absolutely no need to feel abandoned just because her sexy, grumpy pilot had left her with strangers.

Okay, he was essentially a stranger himself, and he was definitely not *hers*. But somehow he'd become...*more*. Which was somewhat alarming. As alarming as her childish feelings of abandonment.

Timéo must have sensed her distress, because he smiled reassuringly while Bradley pushed them away from the beach and jumped into the boat.

The engine puttered to life and they were soon heading out of the small cove and up the coast. The two men chatted quietly, leaving Eve feeling confused and disoriented about everything that had happened: the storm, the crash, their rescue...the—

Oh, no. Nope. Absolutely not. She was not going to think about the ki—*that*.

Besides, too much had happened in such a short space of time, leaving Eve reeling at the speed with which her life was changing...*she* was changing.

Worst of all, her life back home abruptly seemed like something she'd only read about.

Feeling a little freaked, she wrapped her arms around

herself and wondered if there was something on these islands that messed with people's minds, making them forget about their pasts. Making them think they'd finally arrived in Nirvana.

A light, balmy breeze brushed against her damp skin, sending an army of goose bumps swarming across her flesh. It reminded her that she'd had to dress in a hurry and that her pilot was walking around with her underwear in his pocket.

It also reminded her that the instant he'd realized they were being rescued he hadn't been able to wait to get rid of her. But she wouldn't think about that. Not now, she decided, gazing up at the island's jagged volcanic peaks that stretched into the sky and seemed to snatch clouds out of thin air.

Maybe later, when she'd recovered her mind.

After she'd found her sister, stopped her from making a huge mistake with some island bum and returned to her life.

Yep. Good plan.

She sighed. *Only* plan.

All too soon the boat was rounding a lushly vegetated headland. Eve noticed isolated bungalows hidden amid exotic jungle foliage that looked like something out of a honeymoon catalogue for the rich and famous.

Further up, the main resort grew out of the jungle, looking picturesque and strangely as if it had been part of the wild surroundings for centuries. The closer they got to the dock, the more people she could pick out—clearing storm debris, shoring up damaged buildings and carting away what looked like a ton of driftwood.

Seeing the destruction reminded her of Teiki's promise of another storm.

She turned to the islander steering the boat. "Is there really another storm on the way?" she asked as Bradley made for a long wooden dock jutting about fifty yards out into the bay.

He cut the engine, nodding at the thin line of clouds on the far horizon. "It's expected to reach us by midafternoon—maybe sooner."

Timéo leaped onto the jetty even before the boat gently bumped against the row of tires above the waterline and held out his hand to Eve. "I will accompany you to the resort," he said shyly. "Mr. Gallagher would like you to be comfortable."

Eve grabbed his hand and stepped onto the sturdy wooden planks, thinking that what "Mr. Gallagher" really wanted was to be rid of her.

Pushing aside that unwelcome thought, Eve thanked Bradley for his help and followed him along the wooden jetty. She was starving. She wanted a bath—and coffee—in the worst way possible and she didn't need a big strong man to get it for her.

She couldn't help noticing the curious glances she received as they made their way into the hotel, and wondered if she looked as bad as she imagined.

Timéo approached the front desk and a young woman looked up, her dark eyes widening when she caught sight of Eve.

Okay, so that certainly answered her question. The woman's expression didn't do much for her feminine pride, but there wasn't a lot she could do about it. She had no change of clothes, no money and—*dammit*, she thought, trying not to squirm—no underwear.

The receptionist sent her a smile of sympathy and nodded at whatever Timéo had said. He finally turned to Eve.

"Kimiki is my cousin." He smiled reassuringly. "She will take good care of you."

Eve reached out and touched his arm. "Thank you for your help."

"It was no trouble at all, Doctor," he replied with a flash of white teeth. "We are happy you are safe. *Ia ora na e Maeva.*"

Then he turned and, with a wave, disappeared the way they had come, leaving Eve standing barefoot and a little dazed in the resort lobby.

It wasn't until she was finally alone in a spacious bathroom and caught sight of herself in the full-length mirror that she realized just how bad she looked.

Her mouth dropped open. *Yikes*. No wonder Chase had been so eager to get rid of her. She looked like something the sea had discarded along with all the other storm debris, while *he'd* just looked pirate hot.

She sighed. Her clothes were wrinkled and stained, her hair a damp, tangled mess, and she was covered in enough scrapes and bruises to make her look like—her mouth twisted at the irony—an air-crash survivor.

Quickly shedding her skirt and blouse, Eve stepped into the shower stall and turned on the water, groaning with appreciation when it hit her skin, hot and incredibly soothing.

Maybe there wasn't a bath, she told herself, but the shower—virtually open to the jungle and pouring hot, steaming water over her aching body—was the next best thing.

It was, she thought lifting her face, heaven. And for the first time since she'd opened her eyes in Port Laurent yesterday she felt like things were going to be okay.

All she needed was hot coffee and a huge breakfast, along with a couple hours' sleep, and she'd be able to face anything.

Chase let himself into the suite and moved toward the shutters, intending to open them and let in the bright morning light.

He needed a shower, clean clothes, food and sleep. Not necessarily in that order.

It wasn't until he had his hand on the shutter that he realized he wasn't alone. His head whipped around so fast he was momentarily dizzy. The instant his vision cleared his jaw dropped and he found himself gaping, his brain disconnected from the rest of his body.

The covers on the huge bed had been shoved aside. And there…in the middle…a *naked* Eve lay on her stomach, head turned away, her long, curvy form only partially covered by a snowy sheet.

Holy snickerdoodles!

Realizing he was staring—and possibly drooling—Chase snapped his mouth shut and shook his head. Then he heard something rattle and thought maybe his eyes had popped out and were rolling around on the floor somewhere.

He blinked a few times and when the vision remained, felt as though someone had sneaked up and punched him in the chest. His feet took him closer to the bed as his gaze swept up one long leg, uncovered right up to the sweet, familiar curve of a naked buttock.

He'd only had a quick glimpse of her on the beach, but now he let his greedy gaze take a more leisurely cruise over all that pale silky skin.

Honey-gold hair spilled across the pillow in a luxurious cloud and there, beneath her upraised arm, he could see the plump curve of one breast.

And suddenly, despite his exhaustion and pounding headache, his mouth watered. A dangerous interest stirred. An interest he didn't want to feel.

He instructed himself to leave, but the warm, smooth creamy skin that invited a man's touch was barely an arm's length away, tempting and even more dangerous to his health than a bed full of live rattlesnakes.

Shoving a hand through his hair, Chase grimly turned away. There was no way he could stay in the room and not think— He grunted softly, his mouth twisting dryly. Yeah, *those* kinds of thoughts. Thoughts better left unthought. Especially about a woman soon to be his brother's sister-in-law.

But it was already too late. He'd seen more than he should and less than he wanted. And now that was *all* he could think about.

Determined to do the right thing, Chase reached for the in-house phone and dialed the desk to request another suite. A minute later he carefully replaced the handset and scowled at the phone as if it had reared up and bitten him.

Great. Not even a storage closet available. He sighed. Unsurprising, really. It was peak tourist season, and whatever empty rooms they'd had were filled with guests from the bay units damaged in last night's storm. According to the receptionist, they'd been lucky to get this suite.

He eyed the huge comfortable bed—*and its occupant*—and sighed. *Yeah. Real lucky.*

But that was okay. He'd just pretend Eve was his ex and any spark of interest would be snuffed out. *Phfft.* Gone. Just like that.

So, yeah, they could share a bed. And he'd keep his hands—all his body parts—to himself.

No problem.

Absolutely no *problemo.*

CHAPTER SIX

FEET STUCK IN the bathroom doorway, Chase rubbed a towel over his dripping hair and glared at the naked woman sprawled across the bed. Completely oblivious to his misery.

The back of his skull tightened and he muttered a few choice curses.

So he had a problem. A number of problems, actually, the least of which was his wrecked plane. Nor was it that during his call to his brother, Jude, had made him promise not to reveal Amelia's little secret. Well, two secrets, actually—and neither of them could be termed "little" by any stretch of the imagination.

He'd had no problem agreeing because it wasn't his place to discuss family stuff that had nothing to do with him. And, frankly, his loyalty was to Jude and not to some woman he'd only just met.

He sighed. But that was for later. Right now his most pressing problem was asleep and taking up a good portion of the bed.

Okay. Bad idea, he realized, when his body decided to ignore the directive from his brain. Absolutely *not* going to think about long lengths of naked thigh. If he did it might be what finally made him cry like a girl, and he hadn't cried since the third grade, when Becca Thompson had bloodied his nose for using her waist-length pigtail as a paintbrush.

Sighing, he tossed the wet towel over his shoulder and moved into the room, heading for that tempting cloud of cool white. He was too damn tired and sore to care about *where* he crashed right now—no pun intended—as long as he crashed. Besides, he thought morosely as he probed the angry bruise covering his left shoulder, he deserved it after the past twenty-four hours.

Just minutes ago he'd caught sight of himself in the bathroom mirror and nearly laughed out loud at his reflection. It was no wonder people had given him a wide berth. He looked like he'd taken brawling to new heights—against an entire biker gang.

Yawning, he thrust a hand through his damp hair and contemplated his limited choices.

One: sleep on the floor. Two: shove the sexy doctor onto the floor and take the bed. Or three…

He snorted when he realized what he was doing. When the heck had he turned into such a wimp that he was running scared from a *woman*? A cool, I'm-all-professional one at that? Huffing out an irritated grunt, he decided the bed was big enough for them both. Besides, he was exhausted. Too exhausted to do anything his mind was conjuring up.

Maybe.

Tightening the knot on the towel around his waist, Chase took a determined step toward the bed and tried not to feel as though he was heading straight into a storm. And that this one might cost him more than his plane.

Persistent ringing penetrated Eve's sleep-fogged brain. Groaning softly, she groggily ran through her list of patients who could be in labor and came up empty.

She tried to reach for the phone but something warm and heavy had her pinned to the bed, and by the time she realized it was a body the ringing had stopped.

For a couple of seconds she freaked out, trying to remember who was in bed with her. Because drunken one-night stands had never been her thing and she hadn't had a relationship in a long time. A *very* long time. Not since the beginning of her specialist residency, in fact.

Frankly, she hadn't had the time or the energy.

There was, however, something familiar about the big body she was vacuum sealed against. Which was alarming enough, as she wasn't on intimate terms with any—

Memory returned between one heartbeat and the next and she recalled in vivid detail that not very long ago she'd awakened in a crashed plane in this exact same position. Only now she was—they were—*naked*.

Her eyes slammed open and she sucked in a shocked breath when she took in her position. She'd rolled right across the bed onto the side that had been unoccupied when she'd stretched out to consider her next step. The side that was currently occupied by—she squinted at the tanned chest and the eight-pack—her sexy, grumpy pilot.

She swallowed a whimper when she realized that that wasn't even the worst of it. She'd practically draped herself all over his delicious *naked* body as though she was a heat-seeking missile and he the center of the sun.

What the heck was he doing in her bed? And, more importantly, *what the heck was* she *doing snuggling up to a guy who island-hopped in the South Pacific to keep him in mai tais?*

Carefully, without moving a muscle, or even breathing, she took stock. Chase was on his back, his big body relaxed in sleep, dark silky hair falling in a tousled tumble across his forehead. And she... Well, she'd curled into his big body, one leg thrown over his, her head tucked under his chin. Her left hand was low on his belly, disturbingly close to... Well, never mind where. It had no business being there. As if she was staking her claim. As if her hand was accustomed to wandering into dangerous territory.

It wasn't. *She* wasn't. She had no interest in Chase Gallagher, or his big...*gulp*...ego, despite the fact that her body appeared to want to be close to his. His body appeared to want that too, as a muscled arm was wrapped around her and his big calloused hand was cupped possessively over one butt cheek.

And *darn* if her belly didn't give a quiver of interest and then promptly melt. She squeezed her eyes closed. No melting. Melting was bad.

Carefully expelling her breath, Eve began to ease away, but at the first movement his muscles tightened, rippling like a large hungry cat whose coveted meal was about to escape.

She stilled and waited a couple of seconds. When his breathing remained slow and steady she carefully lifted her head...to find his sleepy gaze locked on her.

Her heart gave one hard kick against her ribs before taking off like a frightened rabbit, sending blood pinging through her veins.

Making her dizzy. Snatching her breath.

Deciding that a good offence was the best defense, Eve accused, "You're in my bed."

A dark eyebrow arched as he took in her position, on his side of the bed...with her hand still close to ground zero. Ground zero that was in the process of waking up too.

Her eyes bugged. She gave an alarmed little squeak and tried to jerk away, but his grip tightened. And before she could demand to know what the heck he was doing or apologize for her body's behavior—*whatever!*—he'd flipped her over onto her back and was looming over her as if he intended making a meal of her.

The hard thigh between hers pinned her to the bed, bringing his ground zero terrifyingly close to hers.

Shocked by the ease with which he'd accomplished the move, Eve gaped up into his hard, handsome face. For a long moment his gray gaze was hot and fierce, then his attention dropped to her mouth, where it lingered a moment before traveling south to where her breasts, naked and tingling, were squashed up against all his sculpted magnificence.

His lips curled and, helplessly, Eve looked too. She nearly combusted on the spot.

After a breathless pause, his eyes burned a path from her breasts, up her throat and back to her mouth, setting fire to every nerve ending along the way. And when he dipped his head to trace a scorching path across her cheek to the corner of her mouth, she could do nothing more than suck in a sharp breath and wait for his next move.

His low chuckle had her every hair follicle tingling with excitement. She wanted to smack him for finding this amusing. It wasn't. She didn't want to feel this out of control, this desperate—not with him.

His smiling mouth skimmed hers, leaving her lips tingling with anticipation and frustration as he moved on, nipping at her chin, dipping to scrape his teeth along the tendon in her neck, before heading for the curve joining her neck and shoulder.

Expecting the same tantalizing, barely there torture, Eve felt her entire body jolt when his mouth opened and sucked her flesh into his hot mouth. And to her absolute horror a whimper escaped from her throat. Even worse, her nipples tightened into diamond-hard buds that he wouldn't be able to help but notice. Her belly flooded with a languid liquid heat that made her shudder and squeeze her thighs around his.

He must have liked that, because he groaned and pressed his thigh tighter, higher against her core.

Another shudder and a rush of liquid heat. She gasped. "Chase…" Oh, God. Was that *her* sounding so husky and… and needy? She wasn't. Or she wasn't normally. But something about Chase Gallagher brought out the worst in her. Made her want things she hadn't thought about in a long time. Made her yearn for the touch of another human being.

Okay—fine. A man. He made her yearn for the touch of

a man. But not him. Never him. He was too forceful, too demanding. Like now, as he dropped his head to nip at her breasts, demanding a response. And, *God*, her body was all too eager to give it to him, arching up as a low moan tore loose from somewhere deep in her belly.

He lifted his head. Tension crackled in the air between them as the hell-fire heat of his gaze burned into hers.

Holy cow. No one had ever looked at her with such naked *lust* before. It was wildly exciting and totally unnerving. So unnerving that when he murmured, "Do you want me to stop?" Eve opened her mouth and babbled, "No. *Yes!* I don't know..." before she could stop herself.

His chuckle was a dark, thrilling sound in the dim room, sending anticipation streaking across her skin and a bone-deep need vibrating in her core—along with a rush of mortification.

Way to sound sophisticated, Evelyn.

His next words, "Why don't I help you make up your mind?" were whispered against her skin, giving her a full-body flush.

She bit her lip to prevent an, *Oh, yes, please!* from escaping, because she had a feeling it wouldn't take much on his part to get her to agree. First because her body was already in full agreement, and second...second she was an inch away from climaxing. All from the touch of his mouth and the sound of his voice.

Well, that's just embarrassing. As was the impatient way her body moved against his. If she hadn't been half out of her mind with the way sensations zipped through her she might have been mortified that she was begging.

He lifted his head and their gazes held for a long, breathless beat. His hands smoothed circles of heat on her hip, then her thigh, moved up to her waist...and finally her ribs. His thumb flicked out to tease the bottom curve of her breast, drawing it into a tight, painful mound of need and entreaty.

Eve sucked in a breath, only just managing to stop a whimper from emerging—because if he'd meant his caresses to soothe he'd totally miscalculated. *Big-time*. All they had done was electrify her skin until even the most delicate touch made her want to scream.

Then finally...*oh, God, finally*...he leaned forward and opened his mouth over hers in a kiss as hot as it was hungry. And when she murmured into his mouth he deepened the kiss, his tongue sliding in to stroke hers.

Teasing was clearly over. *Thank God*.

She'd thought their kiss earlier today had been pretty darn hot, but it was nothing compared to this...this invasion of her senses. There was nothing playful about the way he just moved in and sucked the breath from her lungs, along with the rapidly fading notion that she should resist.

That she *could* resist.

You should at least try.

He was everything she didn't want in a man. He was too big, too bold...too *everything*. Including too good at making her forget what it was she was supposed to be doing.

Which was... *Oh, yeah*. She was supposed to be resisting, pushing him away. Escaping while she could still think.

Obeying the directive from her brain, her arms came up. But instead of pushing, they pulled him in, sliding their palms flat up his wide back to his shoulders. From there they headed up his strong neck and—*look at that!*—totally without her consent tunneled into his thick silky hair.

It was Chase's turn to shudder as her nails scraped against his scalp, his body jerking against hers. The realization that she had as much power over him as he had over her was a little overwhelming. And wildly exciting. Especially when she tried it again and he growled—a low, thrilling sound that had her going damp in secret places.

Her eyes fluttered closed and she let herself drift in the moment, enjoying the way his mouth felt plundering hers, his taste, the way each kiss fed the next and then another, until she was moaning and clinging to him—moving urgently against him in desperation.

She felt overwhelmed, soaking up his heat, his taste. His hard, hot thigh was sliding between hers and setting aflame nerve endings she'd hadn't realized existed.

He finally abandoned her mouth to slide his lips down her throat and lick the hollow at its base before moving on. Her breasts tingled in anticipation, the nipples hardening into tight little buds of eagerness.

But, *dammit*, instead of taking them in his mouth he merely skimmed the inside curve of her cleavage before heading south once more, smiling at her moan of frustration.

His tongue painted her skin with heated swipes, dipping into her shallow belly button and soothing the small pain he'd created by gently nipping at her hip with his teeth.

Goose bumps erupted and the muscles deep in her belly clenched against the urge to explode.

"Chase…" she moaned, unsure of what she'd been about to say because he'd robbed her of the ability to think, to do anything but feel. And, boy, she was feeling a whole heck of a lot—including excitement and heat. And something along the lines of—*ohmigod!* He nudged her legs apart and his mouth headed…right into dangerous territory.

Just when she thought she might die if he didn't put his mouth on her the phone began ringing again, the sound an unwelcome jangle in the heated silence.

Eve jolted like she'd been shot. Chase froze, his grip on her tightening. Their eyes met down the length of her body, and when she saw his mouth barely an inch from… *yikes!*…it abruptly dawned on her what he'd been about to do. What she been on the verge of *letting* him do.

With a squeak of embarrassment Eve lurched upwards, slamming her legs together.

Eyes blazing molten heat, Chase stretched out a long

arm to snatch up the phone, the movement vibrating with barely leashed violence.

"Yeah?" he growled, and Eve felt a moment's empathy for whoever was at the other end. But then his eyes sharpened and cleared. "The doctor? She's an…" His eyebrows rose in query. "Obstetrician?" When she silently nodded, he said, "A doctor's a doctor, right? All right, I'll tell her."

He listened for another few moments before sitting up and replacing the receiver with studied casualness. With his back to her, he shoved both hands through his hair and expelled his breath on a ragged laugh, clearly wondering what the heck they'd both been thinking.

They hadn't been thinking, Eve admitted, that was the problem. He'd put his mouth on her and she'd lost brain cells. Brain cells she could scarcely afford to lose—especially to a huge mistake. And this…them…would be a mistake. At least it would be for her.

She wasn't a one-night stand kind of woman, and he… Well, for all she knew he most likely wasn't anything else.

Furthermore, she didn't know all that much about him. Other than that he was a sexy, grumpy pilot, mourning the loss of his seaplane like it was his best friend, and that he kissed like he really knew his way around a woman's body. Oh, and he looked good in a pair of cargoes—*really* good—which was difficult for *anyone* to pull off.

Realizing she was lying there naked and exposed, Eve snatched the sheet and yanked it up to her chin, waging an internal battle about whether she was relieved or disappointed they'd been interrupted.

Then he glanced over his shoulder at her. Definitely relieved. Especially as the eyes that had been smoky with heat just a few moments ago were now cool and unreadable. As though his mouth *hadn't* been an inch from her…

Her belly clenched and embarrassment heated her cheeks, because he clearly hadn't been as affected by what had almost happened. Sucking in a shaky breath, she tried to look relaxed—as though it had been nothing. As though she did this all time when in fact it rarely happened. Obviously he was a lot more experienced at this sort of thing than she was.

On the other hand, she wasn't blind. And when he rose and headed for the bathroom she got an eyeful of the erection he was sporting. It drew a muffled gasp and a hot flash, because...*wow*...the man had heft—and girth.

She gave a silent snort. Okay, so maybe he hadn't been as unaffected as she'd thought. Because that erection certainly wasn't *"nothing."*

And neither was the wild leap of her pulse at the sight of him in all his glorious nakedness.

But that could just be relief, she hastily assured herself. Relief that she'd escaped before she'd made the biggest mistake of her life with a man she barely knew.

He was opinionated, rude and irascible, and he liked having fun at her expense. She was obviously suffering from low blood sugar and an overload of potent pheromones if she was lusting after someone who was happy flying around the South Pacific just because it kept him in fancy cocktails.

But, boy, his body was hard—brawny and aggressive in a way that made a woman stick out her chest and reach for her lipgloss. It vibrated with barely leashed violence— testament to the fact that his blood was probably 90 percent testosterone.

She'd learned early on that alpha males couldn't be trusted. And it was as clear as the tanned skin on his tight buns that he was alpha from the top of his sleep-mussed dark hair to his big, brawny feet.

Face it, she told herself firmly, *there's nothing to get all worked up about.*

He was just a guy. An annoying one at that.

Not attractive at all.

Eve snorted and rolled her eyes.

Who the heck was she kidding? He was magnificent. All hard planes and rippling muscles. Every inch of him gorgeous and tempting…begging to be touched…licked.

But not by her, she reminded herself firmly.

Nope. He was definitely not the man for her.

He turned suddenly, catching her in the act of ogling his sexy body. His chuckle was a low rumble in the quiet room. He was obviously amused to be the object of her lustful glances.

Heat and mortification flooded her. *Darn*. What the heck *was* it about this man that made her act like a silly blushing adolescent? It had to stop. Right now.

Tucking the sheet beneath her armpits, she licked her lips and inched her way to the opposite edge of the bed.

Time to start acting like an adult, Evelyn.

"Who was on the…uh…phone?"

Chase casually snagged a towel off the bed, and when he'd wrapped it around his narrow waist and tucked in the ends she sighed with relief. Now maybe she could think.

"Front desk. One of the guests is suffering from stomach pains and her husband is asking for a doctor."

"Isn't there a clinic on the island?"

"There is. But apparently she's almost doubled over in pain, and since you're closer he wondered if you'd have a look at her." He glanced toward the window. "Her husband doesn't want to travel into town if it's something minor. Not with the next storm practically on our doorstep."

"Do they know I'm a gynecologist?"

"They do now. But you studied medicine before you specialized, right? A stomach ache should be child's play."

Hardly child's play if it was a symptom of something serious…

Nibbling on her lip, Eve felt her mind race as she sorted through the reasons anyone might have severe stomach pain. "Does she have abdominal bloating or swelling? Leg pain? Pelvic pain before her menstrual cycle? Painful inter-course? Breast tenderness? Nausea…vomiting?"

There was a short silence, and when she looked up it was to see Chase staring at her like she was asking if he had a foot fungus.

Her brow wrinkled. "What?"

He shook his head, looking a little panicked. As if he'd been trapped with a crazy person and was casting around for an escape.

He exhaled noisily. "You don't really expect me to an-swer that, do you?" He huffed out a disbelieving laugh. "Firstly, what guy asks any woman about painful sex? And menstrual cycles…?" He looked like he'd swallowed some-thing bad. "You're *kidding*, right?"

Eve sighed. She might have been crazy to start this wild goose chase, but when it came to medicine she was clear-headed and focused, often to the point of obsession. She sometimes forgot nonmedical guys got a little weird when it came to "women's problems."

"I just thought—"

"Well, you thought wrong," he interrupted hastily, look-ing like he was thinking about bolting, and she paused to enjoy the mental picture of him streaking through the hotel in just his towel. "Believe me when I say those are things I never discuss. *Ever*." He shuddered. When she just stared at him, he demanded, "Well?"

"Well, what?"

"Go and do…whatever it is women doctors do. And please ask someone else those questions."

Eve hid a smile and finally looked down at herself. "I can hardly go out wearing a sheet," she pointed out. "My clothes are wrecked and—" She blushed. "And you…um… stole my underwear."

Relieved not to be talking about periods and painful inter-course with the woman he'd almost had sex with, Chase tilted his head and studied her. Wrapped in a sheet and looking all flushed and flustered, like she'd just been ravished, she was one big temptation he didn't need.

Another minute and he would have been buried deep inside her body—which clearly meant he should be grateful they'd been interrupted. Especially as he hadn't given a thought to protection.

That thought was enough to scare him rigid.

Okay, he amended, looking down at the tented towel. Maybe not rigid… But he had been an eager participant, and didn't know whether to thank the concierge or beat the hell out of him for interrupting what would most certainly have been a spectacular ravishing.

Besides, he reminded himself, she wasn't his type and he clearly wasn't hers.

Good. Great. They were both not each other's type.

Message received.

"I don't know," he said, scratching his jaw. "I think it suits you."

Eve rolled her eyes, obviously relieved to change the subject. "Please. I look like I'm dressed for a sorority toga party."

Chase's mouth curved at the vision that popped into his head. "Yeah," he said, recalling the toga parties he'd attended in his sophomore year that had all but descended into debauchery. "Looks great."

She cast a disbelieving look at herself. "Great?"

Suddenly the idea of anyone seeing Eve walking out of the suite looking like an ancient Roman delicacy made his brow furrow in displeasure. She was right, he decided. She needed clothes. Preferably a sack that covered her from head to toe.

Yeah, and he was an idiot.

"You didn't happen to…um—" She broke off, looking away, clearly embarrassed.

Intrigued, Chase studied her closely and decided he

liked seeing her flustered. She was softer and a lot less the sophisticated professional. Very appealing. And also very bad. Especially bad were the ideas it gave him.

She was still staring at him. He had no idea what she'd been saying, so he went with, "What?"

She grimaced. "Find my bags? In the wreckage, I mean?"

He opened his mouth to admit that he hadn't even given it a thought but, "I thought you didn't have a change of clothes with you?" emerged instead.

"I don't. I need my wallet to…um…pay for a few things from the hotel boutique."

He shrugged. "Don't worry about it. The company will pay for anything you need. Just charge it to the room."

"I'd rather pay for it myself," Ms. Independence countered primly. "Besides, I need my passport and airline tickets." She lifted her head, glowing amber eyes beseeching now. "Please tell me you found my bags. I…I need my phone. I need to get home."

"I thought you needed to stop your sister from making a huge mistake by marrying some loser she's only just met?" he said a little sarcastically.

"Well, yes…" she said, looking confused by his sarcasm. "But after that I intend going back to London. I'm supposed to be at a medical conference. I'm also waiting for a DC medical center to let me know about a position I applied for."

Chase rubbed his hands over his face and shook his head. "Nope," he said with a head shake. "We didn't find anything."

Eve sucked in an audible breath, looking like she was on the verge of a full-blown panic attack, so he hitched one shoulder helplessly.

"We crashed in a really dense part of the island," he explained. "It could take days…weeks…to search the area and you'd still probably never find anything. It's so humid out here that the jungle reclaims everything in a matter of days.

"So…" She sucked in another deep breath, struggling to stay calm. "You're telling me I'm stuck here in…the middle of the South Pacific…indefinitely? Without a passport or a way to get home?"

He mentally cursed his lack of foresight. "That about covers it. You can use my computer on Tukamumu to contact the embassy. But I need to warn you that life…official life, that is…moves at a different pace out here."

She paled and looked a little sick, and again he cursed himself—because the loss of her passport meant she was going to be around awhile. Which abruptly seemed like the worst thing that could happen.

For him at least.

He studied the picture she made, sitting there all soft and sexy, nibbling on that wide, plump bottom lip, and recalled something Jude had said about Amelia's childhood.

It had been bad. Bad enough that from an early age Eve had taken on the role of caregiver and protector—all the while working herself through high school and then med school.

Yet here she was; looking young and fresh and as untouched as a schoolgirl. No sign of that backbone of steel.

He thrust an unsteady hand through his hair. You had to admire the hell out of someone with that much grit. But accompanying his admiration was the realization that he was in trouble.

Biiiiig trouble.

Sexy, silky woman trouble. From her tawny hair and golden-syrup eyes to her small, elegant feet.

Oh, yeah. He was screwed.

CHAPTER SEVEN

EVE FOLLOWED A uniformed employee across the patio, shocked to see that while she'd been sleeping—and crawling all over a certain sexy pilot—an ominous bank of clouds had swept across the sea toward them, dispelling this morning's image of a forgotten Eden.

Trouble, it seemed, was a lot closer than the horizon.

Wind gusted in from the bay, setting the palms and banana trees rustling an urgent warning of the oncoming storm. It had turned the sea an eerie gunmetal gray, far removed from the clear, calm turquoise of this morning.

Despite the fact that it wasn't cold, Eve shivered. The sight of those towering black clouds and flashes of lightning brought back memories of the crash and...well, stuff she'd rather not think about.

Like being stranded without money or her passport.

Much better to think about— *Oh, boy.* A flush moved through her until she thought she was probably glowing like a luminescent glowstick in the early gloom.

Okay, maybe not. Maybe she should think instead of the reason she was on this very vulnerable piece of volcanic rock, stuck in the middle of the Pacific instead of in London.

Amelia.

Who'd most likely expected her yesterday and was probably thinking the worst right about now. That Eve was shark bait.

And Eve was thinking about a tanned eight-pack, long, muscular legs and tight buns, instead of a way to reach her sister.

She was certain that she just needed to hear Amelia's voice and all those unwelcome emotions would disappear. Clearly she wasn't the only twin susceptible to tropical islands. Maybe she just needed a healthy dose of reality. Like…like those clouds, for one. Another thought hit her and she groaned. Or maybe it was something more basic. Something along the lines of the potent cocktail of testosterone and pheromones that surrounded Chase Gallagher like a toxic cloud of doom and made her misbehave.

Staying away from him would be the smart thing to do. And Eve had always done the smart thing.

Always.

Feeling very unprofessional, in a brightly colored muu-muu—the island version of a sarong—silk panties and a pair of flip flops, Eve waited while the porter knocked on a suite door.

A man in his mid-thirties answered and did a double-take when he saw her. Had he expected someone older? More professional-looking? Someone not covered in bruises?

"Hi," he said, looking a little frazzled. "I'm…uh…Mark. Are you…?"

"Hello, Mark. My name is Dr. Eve Carmichael. How can I help you?"

"I…I don't know what's wrong with my…uh…wife, Raina," he explained hurriedly. "She's in a lot of pain. We thought that by this morning it would be okay, but it's worse. *She's* worse." A muffled groan came from behind him and he cast a haunted look over his shoulder. "Oh, God, I don't know what to—"

"Why don't you let me come in?" Eve interrupted gently.

He hesitated another moment, his gaze taking in her casual attire and her bruises, before taking a step back. "You're really a doctor?" When Eve just looked at him he shoved a hand through his rumpled hair. "I honestly don't know what I was expecting. The concierge was using words like *rongoa* and *tohunga*, and I kind of assumed…"

He gave an embarrassed laugh and closed the door behind her. Eve frowned and studied him with assessing eyes, wondering if he'd been drinking or taking recreational drugs.

"Rongoa? Tohunga?" Eve shook her head in confusion at the unfamiliar words. "I'm sorry, I don't know what that means."

He led the way through the suite. "Apparently it's a kind of healer. A *tohunga* is a specialist, or something."

He hovered in the bedroom doorway and Eve had to brush past him.

"We're smack-dab in the middle of the South Pacific," he said on a loud whoosh of air. "Thousands of miles from the nearest city. I half expected a medicine man to arrive at our door."

"Oh, I don't think they have those anymore," Eve said drily.

The young woman curled on the bed was pale, her lovely features twisted in pain and slick with perspiration.

"Hi," Eve said, gently taking Raina's wrist and unerringly finding her pulse. "I'm a doctor. An OB-GYN specialist, actually."

"Really?" Mark said, skepticism written all over his smooth handsome face. "You're a little young, aren't you? And you look…" He gestured to her battered face and the bruises covering the rest of her.

"We were forced to land in the storm," she murmured absently. "It was a little rough."

He snorted. "I'd say more than 'a little rough.' Maybe you should sue the airline?"

Eve looked up to see if he was serious. He was. "The airline and the pilot weren't at fault," she said mildly, even though the pilot *was* responsible for at least two of her bruises. The hickey on her neck and the first bump on her head. "Lightning struck the engine."

Without waiting for him to reply, she turned back to her patient.

"Are you pregnant?"

"Pregnant?" Mark burst out, horrified.

A flash of something indefinable crossed the young woman's face and she hurriedly shook her head, lowering her eyes. Eve caught the quick flash of tears and sent Mark a speculative look across her shoulder.

He looked appalled. And green.

"You never said anything about being pregnant, Raina," he accused angrily. "If you had I never would have—" He stopped abruptly when he realized both Eve and Raina were gaping at him, stunned by his outburst.

Tears sparkled in Raina's eyes. "I'm not—I promise. It's something else. It's got to be."

Without taking her eyes off Mark, Eve asked quietly, "Would you feel better if Mark left the room while I examine you?"

The young woman bit her lip and nodded, carefully avoiding looking at her husband. After a short, tension-filled moment Mark sighed and left, closing the door behind him. Once he'd left Eve gently probed the young woman's abdomen, noting her soft cry of pain.

"Now that your husband has gone," Eve said quietly as she continued her examination, "I'm going to ask you why you don't want him to know you're pregnant."

Raina sucked in a sharp breath and shook her head. "I'm not," she rasped, looking distressed. "I *can't* be."

"Raina—"

"Look, Mark isn't my husband," she confessed in a low voice, her gaze sliding away from Eve's. "He's my b-boss."

She gave a muffled sob. "My *m-married* boss. I can't…
He'll f-fire me. Besides, I c-couldn't be. It's not possible. I
thought…I thought it might be my appendix?"

Eve was continuing with her examination. "Tell me why
it's not possible?" she asked gently.

Raina went on to explain that she'd been spotting for a
few days, and experiencing the lower abdominal and back
pain which she assured Eve was normal for the first couple
of days of her cycle.

On further probing Eve discovered that the pain had
started in her right side and moved to the left, until her
pelvic area was very painful, making it hard for her to
walk upright, which was why she'd thought it was her appendix. She was nauseous, exhausted and kept needing
the bathroom.

Eve then posed the same questions to her that she'd
asked Chase, and by the time she was finished with her
examination she was convinced it wasn't dysmenorrhea,
appendicitis, kidney stones or even ovarian cysts.

If she was right, the woman would likely need surgery.
Very soon. Especially if the bleeding worsened and she
went into shock.

Eve smoothed Raina's hair off her clammy forehead. "I
don't want you to worry," she said firmly. "We're going to
take good care of you."

She rose and left the room. This was a procedure that
needed a team of physicians, preferably in a sterile environment. Raina needed a hospital.

She found a pale Mark waiting nervously in the small
lounge, slugging back three fingers of whiskey while he
paced. Ignoring his signs of extreme agitation, she explained that further tests were needed and that Raina
needed to go to the hospital immediately.

"She's pregnant, isn't she?" he demanded a little wildly.
"Dammit, I *knew* it. I should have—"

"I need to run a few tests to confirm my diagnosis," Eve

interrupted coolly. "And I can only do that at a hospital. It's imperative that we go immediately."

He shoved his hand in his hair, looking really rattled beneath the anger. "But... But..."

"Look," she said firmly, trying not to judge his attitude, which she suspected was more about not getting caught by his wife than ensuring his mistress received proper medical attention. "If we don't get Raina to the nearest hospital— and this island has one," she informed him briskly, "she could die." She waited for the news to sink in before adding, "I'm sure you don't want that to happen to your *wife*."

He turned red. "She's not my...um..." His breath escaped in a loud whoosh when Eve's eyebrow rose up her forehead. "No," he said, avoiding her level gaze. "I don't want that to happen."

"Good. Then I suggest you phone the concierge and request a car. We don't have a moment to lose."

The wind had picked up, sending trees and palms bending at impossible angles. Eve glanced worriedly at the black clouds barreling toward them and sucked in a nervous breath when a powerful gust hit the car broadside.

She'd never seen anything as angry and scary as those towering, boiling columns, and couldn't help wondering what was heading their way.

Nothing good—that was for certain.

Was the shiver of premonition sliding down her spine due to the storm—or something else?

Fortunately the driver didn't waste time, racing along the deserted roads toward town. Eve didn't know if he was aware of their urgency or just wanted to get home before the storm broke.

She wouldn't blame him if it was the latter. After yesterday's experience she wanted to be somewhere safe too. Like in London. Or Washington. Even if they were knee-deep in snow.

The hotel must have called ahead. A couple of orderlies waited at Emergency, rushing out with a wheelchair. Eve introduced herself and was surprised when the men traded significant glances.

"Is something wrong?" she asked as she and Mark helped Raina out of the car.

"Oh, no," the older man said quickly. "We heard how you and Mr. Chase crashed in last night's storm."

"Oh?"

The younger of the two blushed and Eve wondered what else they'd heard, and if it had anything to do with her introduction to the islanders. When Eve had been caught swimming naked by a boatful of gaping men.

"Yeah," he said with a wide smile. "Teiki said that Lono and Kanaloa must have brought you here for a purpose."

"Lono? Kanaloa?" she asked, keeping a hard hold on Mark as she followed them into the clinic. He was strung tighter than chicken wire. The muscled arm in her grip vibrated with a tension that she suspected was a desire to bolt at the first opportunity.

"Polynesian deities," a smooth voice cut in, and Eve turned as a middle-aged woman approached.

She was dressed in a lab coat, with a stethoscope around her neck, and her brisk no-nonsense attitude identified her as a doctor. She couldn't be anything else. Not with that quietly efficient yet unmistakably authoritative aura.

Eve stepped forward and offered her hand. "You must be Dr. Tahuru."

The older woman smiled and clasped Eve's in a firm handshake. "And you're the specialist the storm brought to our island."

Eve felt herself flush under the woman's amused scrutiny. She let out a breathless laugh. "You heard about the crash?" *And possibly about how they'd been found.*

Dr. Tahuru grinned, her sharp eyes assessing first Eve

and then Raina. "We're a small community. News travels fast."

She instructed an orderly to take the patient and her husband to a nearby exam room before turning to Eve.

"Have you examined her, Dr. Carmichael?"

"I did, yes," she admitted. "At the…the husband's request."

"And?"

"I suspect an ectopic pregnancy, but you'll need to run a few tests."

Dr. Tahuru sucked in a sharp breath and cast a worried look out the ER door. "I'm a general practitioner," she explained. "And this is a very small facility. Any serious cases are usually sent to Rangiroa or Raitea."

"I'm afraid she doesn't have time for that," Eve said quietly. "If I'm right, she's going to need surgery tonight."

Dr. Tahuru narrowed her eyes and quietly studied Eve, obviously weighing her up. Eve knew what she saw. Dressed in a sarong and flip-flops, and without make-up, she looked like a teenager.

She held her breath. The last thing she wanted was to offend the woman, or the island's customs, and appear as though she wanted to take over, so she waited, holding the doctor's gaze with quiet intensity.

Working in a large city hospital had the benefit of letting her encounter a host of unusual cases, but she'd never done laparoscopies or performed a laparotomy in anything but a well-equipped OR. Or without an attending anesthetist.

A laparoscopy was less invasive, but the question here was, did the tiny facility have the equipment?

After a couple of beats Dr. Tahuru gave a decisive nod. "Very well, Dr. Carmichael, let's find you some scrubs."

Ninety minutes later Eve and Jasmine Tahuru scrubbed up as they discussed the procedure. The HCG test and sonogram had come back positive. Raina Ellis was pregnant, and the fetus was growing in the right fallopian tube.

Given her symptoms, Eve suspected the young woman didn't have time for any more tests. At the last check her BP had dropped and she'd complained of shoulder pain, which meant the fallopian tube had ruptured and was leaking blood into her abdomen. If she was lucky it wouldn't be a serious tear and Eve wouldn't have to remove the entire fallopian.

Entering the tiny OR through the scrub room door, Eve glanced around and felt a moment's apprehension that was tinged with excitement. She usually felt both just before surgery, but this time her apprehension resulted from the knowledge that the room only contained the basics.

Which meant they'd have to operate.

Her excitement, she admitted silently, was caused by the notion that she'd have to rely on her skills without the aid of high-tech equipment.

Raina was already on the table, anxiously waiting. She gave a low sob when she saw Eve in a surgical gown, her eyes filling with tears as the seriousness of her situation finally registered. Her grip was fierce when Eve took her hand.

"Hey," Eve said with a reassuring smile. "You're going to be fine, I promise. Dr. Tahuru has been running this hospital for almost as long as you've been alive. She's probably seen just about everything. You're in good hands, I promise."

"I still can't believe I'm pregnant. How did I not know?"

Eve continued prepping her while Jasmine fitted electrode discs to Raina's upper chest. "Many women have periods during pregnancy," she said gently. "It's not uncommon." She waited a couple of beats while the young woman processed that, before saying quietly, "But maybe you should think about making a few changes when you get home. You owe it to yourself."

A look of unhappiness crossed Raina's face and she bit her lip before saying in a low, fierce voice, "You're right. I do." She blinked away her tears. "I finally realized he's just been stringing me along. I'd heard rumors, but I thought... He made me feel so...special." She sniffed miserably as she faced the truth. "He really has no intention of leaving his wife, does he?"

"I can't say," Eve responded reluctantly. Frankly, judging by Mark's reaction to her diagnosis, he probably wouldn't. "But you deserve a man willing to commit fully."

Raina inhaled shakily. "You'll be here, though. Won't you?"

Eve smiled and applied a saturation probe to her finger, listening as the quiet beeping filled the room. "I'm not going anywhere," she assured her, lifting her head to catch the other doctor's level look. "Let's finish getting you prepped. When you wake up you can start making those plans."

Eve waited until Raina Ellis was under before lifting her scalpel. "We'll have to be quick," she told Dr. Tahuru. "Even with a light anesthetic we can't keep her under too long without an anesthetist."

"Florine will watch her vitals." She paused while Eve nodded at the veteran nurse. "Ready when you are, Doctor."

Eve sucked in a deep breath, lifted her mask into place and said a quick prayer. She was aiming for a quick in-and-out procedure, and as she made the first transverse incision along the bikini line she said, "The main concern here is to stop any hemorrhaging and remove all traces of trophoblastic cells." She paused as Dr. Tahuru mopped the welling blood. "We don't want them reattaching and growing again."

She gently exposed the tube and waited while Dr. Tahuru applied clamps to either side of the gestational sac.

Jasmine peered closer. "What's that? About four, five weeks?"

"Hmm…" Eve murmured, carefully examining the ovary and uterus for signs of trauma. She gave a quick sigh of relief. They were intact. She gently exposed the sac to evaluate the area of attachment. "Looks about right. Fortunately the rupture is close to the attachment site. We should be able to dislodge it with minimal damage."

Thirty minutes later, and after a hair-raising incident during which they'd thought they wouldn't be able to stop the bleeding without removing the entire fallopian tube, Eve released the suture ligature she'd applied a few minutes earlier and held her breath.

When no new blood appeared she exhaled loudly, and waited while Jasmine flushed the tube. She then carefully placed a few microsutures along the rupture to keep the edges together and began closing her up.

"What about scarring along the tube?" Jasmine asked, injecting antibiotics into a bag of Ringer's lactate solution and closing off the port dispensing the anesthetic. "Won't that narrow it?"

"That is a concern," Eve murmured, working a suture with quick, efficient hands. "She'll have to visit her gynecologist when she gets home. A laparoscopy will determine if there is any scarring that could cause future egg implantation. If that happens they will most likely remove the tube completely. I'm hoping that won't be necessary."

Eve completed the final suture and checked Raina's vitals. It had been forty minutes.

"Neatly done, Doctor," Jasmine said. "Why don't you tell the 'husband' while I finish up here?"

Her dark eyes gleamed over the top of her mask when Eve groaned.

"I think it'll be better coming from you."

Mark had made enough noise earlier about "backwoods hospitals and incompetent medical staff" that she understood Jasmine's sentiments.

Eve shook her head. "It'd be better coming from a man, you mean," she said drily. "He's obviously one of *those*."

"Those?"

"You know—those men who think woman are good for only one thing."

"We get that all the time," the older woman agreed. "Some men still haven't entered the twenty-first century."

Especially as there were still women willing to let them continue with their antiquated beliefs. Her mother had always looked for men who would take care of her.

Yeah. And look how *that* had turned out. Knocked up and abandoned—not once, but twice.

Sighing, Eve stepped away from the table and stripped off the double-layered latex gloves. She dropped them into the disposal bin on her way to the door. She was accustomed to dealing with rude next of kin. She didn't like it, but she understood that some people reacted to fear and stress by being obnoxious.

And Mark had been as obnoxious as they came. He was certainly handsome, but Eve didn't understand the appeal. At least not beyond the first five minutes.

She found him pacing the small private waiting room. He spotted her immediately and headed over, looking like he was working on an internal storm to rival the one brewing outside.

Eve had opened her mouth to tell him he was heading for a stroke and should learn to relax when the irony hit her. She sucked in a shocked breath instead. Here she was, the queen of stress, about to advise someone to relax. When the heck had *that* happened? She lifted her hand to the bump on her forehead and frowned. Maybe she really did have brain damage.

"I've been here three hours and no one will tell me what the hell is going on!" Mark snapped, scowling at her as though he was accustomed to intimidating everyone he perceived as inferior. "What kind of hospital is this, anyway? It doesn't have a cafeteria or even a vending machine, for God's sake. And no one speaks any English."

Eve ignored his outburst. She could understand his agitation, if not his prejudice. And plenty of people on the island spoke English if you didn't treat them with arrogant superiority.

"The procedure went well," she said calmly, determined to be civil. Even if it cost her. And it did cost her—especially when his eyes sharpened at her words.

"She's no longer pregnant?"

Eve ground her teeth together. No matter how much she might want to, punching him in the mouth wasn't the answer. Mark wasn't one of her mother's boyfriends, and this wasn't *her* drama. Even if it brought back memories from her childhood. Bad memories of constant fighting and unwelcome attention from her mother's man du jour, especially after she and Amelia reached puberty.

"No," she said quietly. "She's no longer pregnant."

He stared at her for a couple of beats, as though struggling to absorb the news. Then naked relief filled his eyes and he choked out a rusty laugh. "Oh, thank God!" he burst out, shoving shaking fingers through his already rumpled hair. He caught Eve's expression and froze. "I mean…I don't… You can't know—"

"As soon as the weather clears Raina will be moved to a larger medical facility." She coolly interrupted his babbling. "It will be a few days before she can fly home."

"I don't *have* a few days," he said, his relief turning into a frown. "I need to get home."

Eve struggled not to let her contempt or her temper show. It was hard not to judge a man who willingly left his wife in order to have a romantic tryst in the South Pacific with his mistress and then abandoned her among strangers when he had no more use for her.

But when he gave a long exhalation and had the grace

to look uncomfortable Eve realized she hadn't been successful in concealing her feelings.

"You know."

She didn't pretend to misunderstand.

"Your relationship with Raina isn't my concern," she said coolly. "Her health and recovery is." She was silent for a few moments before adding quietly, "She needs emotional as well as physical recovery time, Mr. Greenway. I hope you do the right thing."

Without waiting for his reply she turned and left, heading back to the OR at a fast clip.

Jasmine looked up when she shoved open the door, her eyebrows rising up her forehead at the sight of Eve's face. "I take it that didn't go well?"

"He's…he's an ass," Eve snarled, having too much respect for the older woman to say exactly what she thought of Mark Greenway. "Do you know he was so relieved she's no longer pregnant that he didn't even ask how she is? Or if he could see her?"

Jasmine patted her arm. "He *is* an insensitive ass," she agreed. "But not all men are so quick to abandon their responsibility once the fun is over."

Eve just sighed, not wanting to upset the other woman by disagreeing. Of course she knew that not all men were alike. She just hadn't had personal experience with any other kind.

It always made her think that maybe there was something wrong with her. With her family. Maybe the Carmichael women were cursed—destined always to choose the wrong kind of man. The kind who would abandon them once their fun wasn't so much fun anymore.

But not Eve. She would rather be alone than find herself as the "other woman." No man, she reminded herself firmly, was worth the utter devastation that they left behind.

She just had to convince her sister of that.

CHAPTER EIGHT

EVE BECAME AWARE of the roaring sounds beyond the hospital walls. Something heavy thudded against the building and she jumped, flashing a nervous look toward the door when windows and shutters rattled violently.

The lights flickered. It sounded like all hell had broken loose.

Jasmine, placing instruments in sterilization trays, sent Eve a reassuring glance. "Wind," she explained. "Sounds like a one-fifty."

Eve didn't reply, thinking it sounded like an out-of-control freight train barreling toward them. Everything rattled and banged, and when there was an ominous creak overhead she half expected the roof to go flying off into the night.

Since there was little chance of her making it back to the resort, she might as well be useful.

"Do you need help?"

Stripping off her surgical gown, Jasmine lifted her head to smile at Eve.

"You offering?"

"If you'll have me."

"Then, yes," the older woman said decisively, shrugging into a lab coat. "I just received news that rescuers are bringing in casualties. Apparently a few yachts in the marina found their way into some sitting rooms along the waterfront. From what I hear we need all the help we can get—although I doubt there'll be too many gynecological cases."

Eve grinned, relieved to have something to do. "I'm sure I can remember my ER training."

Jasmine's dark eyes gleamed with amusement. "It's a bit like sex." She laughed. "You never forget how."

Considering how long *that* had been for Eve, she was afraid she *had* forgotten. Oh, not working in the ER. She could probably do *that* in her sleep.

Just as they stepped through the doors to the ER the world outside lit up for a brief instant and then exploded, the resounding boom shaking the building. One second they had lights—the next it was pitch-black.

Eve froze, seeing a whole lot of nothing. Worse, she wasn't familiar with the layout of the hospital and was afraid she'd fall over something or—*oh, God*—someone if she so much as breathed.

There was a moment of utter silence, then the disembodied voice of Jasmine Tahuru muttered a heartfelt, "Dammit."

Eve reached out tentatively and hissed her relief when her hand encountered cool plaster. Carefully edging closer to the wall, she pressed back against it. All the better to face whatever came her way.

There was muted murmuring and footsteps, and then a loud clatter, followed by cursing. The resultant laughter was a little nervous, but it served to cut the thick tension.

"For heaven's sake, everyone, stay where you are until I find some lamps," Jasmine ordered loudly. "We have enough casualties coming in without adding anymore."

Something clicked close by, and a thin beam of light sliced through the inky blackness.

Eve watched as the blade-thin beam moved away. There was the sound of a door opening and the beam disappeared, swallowed by the dark.

She felt utterly alone.

And kind of spooked by the sounds of breathing.

It was creepy—especially when jagged flashes of lightning lit up her surroundings for a split second. She heard a collective sucking-in of breath, as though everyone was waiting for the resultant boom.

It soon came—accompanied by a prickling sensation on the back of her neck. Goose bumps broke out and she sucked in a calming breath, wondering why she felt so on edge. Almost as though she knew something was about to hap—

And then…*there*…behind her…came a stealthy scrape of a shoe on linoleum, the brush of fabric. Heart surging into her throat, she spun around, wishing she had one of those big-ass syringes, or maybe a scalpel—and abruptly come up against a hard wall of muscle.

At that moment lightning flashed briefly, and the huge shadow looming over her had her reacting instinctively. Okay, so it might also have been leftover memories of her childhood—bumping into her mother's men in the middle of the night—or watching too many horror movies, but she gave a strangled gasp and lurched backward, intending to escape.

Hard hands shot out, closing over her upper arms and keeping her from falling on her ass. The next instant a hard, warm body had the same grateful ass pressed up against the wall—along with every other part of her.

With a startled squeak she instinctively brought her knee up—before she recognized the body preventing her from sliding to the floor. Fortunately he reacted just as swiftly, and twisted to prevent a ground-zero touchdown. Her knee grazed his thigh instead.

A pained grunt and a muffled "Dammit…" filled her ears as a warm, familiar masculine scent filled her head.

She sagged in relief. After a couple beats he released her shoulders to flatten his hands against the wall beside her head. Probably to keep himself from wrapping them around her throat.

It would have been a little alarming to be so attuned to someone she'd only known two days if her relief hadn't rendered her so weak.

"Chase?"

His head dipped and the rasp of his stubble scraped the side of her face, setting in motion a full-body shiver that tightened her nipples and sent heat arrowing into secret places. Secret places that hadn't seen any action in forever and were still humming with unfulfilled tension.

His voice was a rough slide of sin and irritation against her tightly strung nerves.

"Expecting someone else?"

She huffed out a nervous laugh, unaware that she was clutching his shirt in tight fists. "I wasn't expecting *any-one*," she lied breathlessly. "And certainly not sneaking up on me."

He gave a soft snort against her neck, as if he suspected she was lying. The feel of his warm breath on her skin had goose bumps marching across her flesh and heading for parts unknown.

Almost as if he knew what he was doing to her, Chase dipped his head and licked her ear. "I wasn't sneaking," he murmured, blowing on the wet spot. It drew a little gasp of pleasure from her throat and sent her nipples into a frantic happy dance of anticipation. "For a city girl, you're certainly oblivious to your surroundings."

"What's that supposed to mean?"

"It means you should be aware of people sneaking up on you."

"I thought you weren't."

"Is that why you tried to knee me in the nuts?"

Her head swam. She really had no intention of discussing his…nuts. "Why are we having this conversation?"

"Maybe I'm trying to distract you from freaking out."

"I'm not freaking out," she whispered defensively.

His voice was a low, amused rumble against the pulse in her neck. "Is that why your heart is pounding?"

Her heart was pounding because he was so damn close she couldn't breathe. Close enough that an idea wouldn't be able to pass between them—although her body was getting *plenty* of ideas. And, *dammit*, he was close enough that she was an inch away from burying her nose in his throat and inhaling his amazing scent.

"My heart is pounding because one minute I was alone and the next you were there. I thought you were a hatchet-wielding psycho."

"Who says I'm not?" he murmured, sliding his big hands to her waist. "Maybe I'm a serial killer who terrorizes the islands, flying off to the next stop before I'm caught."

Her snicker turned into a gasp when he spread his fingers to span her torso, sending heated shivers spreading throughout her body. She recalled in perfect detail the way they'd felt on her naked skin—rough and exciting. She felt a shudder move through her and bit her lip against the moan rising up her throat.

"Then—" she gasped "—I…I g-guess I should w-warn you that I have a b-black belt." *Really? She was stuttering now?* "So…so maybe you should b-back off," she growled a little fiercely. "Before I…before I—"

He gave a low, sexy chuckle and slid his hand beneath her scrubs top to rasp erotically against her belly. She jolted and nearly melted into a puddle at his feet. Darn, but the man had magical hands.

"Before you what?" he murmured, nuzzling the sensitive spot just beneath her ear. She licked her lips and tried to focus on their conversation, wondering why her muscles weren't obeying the command from her brain to shove him away. "Before I…um…"

What the heck were they talking about?

"Before you rip off my clothes?" he murmured helpfully,

chuckling when she gulped noisily. "Have your wicked way with my sexy body?"

She gave a strangled snort, but her body was happy to comply with his suggestion. And to make matters worse a little voice in the back of her mind begged, *Oh, yes. Can we? Please.*

"I was thinking more along the lines of drawing blood," she said breathlessly. "You know—check for tropical diseases? I hear there are some pretty rare ones that can wreck your…um…well, your love life."

"You're a little bloodthirsty, you know that?" he murmured, not sounding particularly perturbed by her threat. "But my love life?" He chuckled. "It's just fine. Wanna check it out, Doc?"

She was on the verge of saying, *No, thank you,* when the lights flickered and an amused voice filled the heated silence.

"Wow," Jasmine Tahuru said dryly. "Maybe we should hit the lights again. No telling who'll show up next time."

For a breathless beat Eve's eyes collided with Chase's. There was something in the look he sent her that had the backs of her knees sweating—and a hot ball of something that felt very much like panic cramping her stomach.

Where was a good earthquake when you needed one? Or lightning and thunder, for that matter? And what the heck had happened to her self-control?

"So," she gulped through a tight throat, facing their audience while trying to pretend she *hadn't* been about to be kissed senseless. "What would you like me to do first?"

She smoothed her hair off her face with shaking hands, painfully aware of Chase standing behind her. It seemed even the air molecules separating them were supercharged with heat, sizzling with a primal awareness she'd never experienced.

The shocking truth was that he only had to come near her and every strand of her DNA went berserk.

"I'm putting you in charge," Jasmine said briskly. "Until I find out what's wrong with the generator."

"I'll deal with the generator," Chase said, sounding amused. "Sounds like you'll have enough on your hands soon."

His words had no sooner emerged than the ER door banged open, bringing in both the storm and their first casualties.

"I hope you're good with your hands," Jasmine said striding forward. "It can be a little temperamental."

"I'm *very* good with my hands," Chase assured her, but he looked at Eve. The heat almost had her brand-new panties melting off her body.

Jasmine snorted. "I'll just bet you are."

Rattled, Eve was about to join her when one of those large fists grabbed her scrubs top and pulled her back against him. The contact lasted only a brief second, but the sensation of his hard chest echoed through her body like a howl in the Grand Canyon.

Eve sent a wild-eyed look over her shoulder at him, thinking she'd likely be safer out there. In the storm.

"Don't go anywhere," he growled. "*Especially* not out there."

"You are not the boss of me," she managed, over a tight, dry-as-desert throat. "Besides, what about you?"

"I'm a big boy," he said shortly, and turned on his heel. "I can handle myself."

Oh, yeah, Eve thought, watching his broad back disappear around the corner. He certainly was. A big boy, that was. But she was a big girl too, she reminded herself fiercely. She could handle anything as well as him—if not better.

Couldn't she?

Abruptly aware of a little niggle of doubt, she promptly squared her shoulders. Of course she could. She'd handled med school, three jobs *and* her needy family. If she could do

all that without breaking a sweat she could handle one su-
persexy grumpy pilot with her hands tied behind her back.

No sweat.

Chase was glad to have something to do. Hospitals gave
him the willies and he usually did everything and anything
to stay out of them.

He was also rattled by what had just happened. Or
what he'd allowed to happen…in a crowded ER and with
a woman he wasn't sure he even liked.

He'd clearly lost his mind, because he just had to be near
her and when he was, his body took over. That had never
happened before. Not even with his ex.

Dr. Tahuru's son Henri, a civil engineering student helping out during his vacation, took him to the building that
housed the generator. For an hour the two of them tinkered
and sweated in the torchlight, managing—briefly—to re-
suscitate the generator by banging on the motor with a
wrench. It didn't fix the problem but it did make Chase
feel better. Marginally.

Finally he opened the fuel line and found it clogged with
dirt. *Yep*. No wonder it sounded like an asthmatic, geriatric
smoker with a heart problem.

This necessitated a full inspection of the motor, which he
did by taking it apart. It was antiquated, to say the least, and
looked like it hadn't had a good service in years. The cooling and exhaust system was clogged with dust and debris.

Chase cleaned the filter, surprised that it hadn't seized
years ago. He also opened and cleaned the piston shafts,
sending Henri to look for lubricant.

After replacing the spark plugs and flushing the fuel
line he put everything back together, waiting with bated
breath as Henri flipped the switch.

The generator gave a couple pathetic shudders before it
kicked in and settled to a noisy humming. After a few tense
seconds the lights flickered, brightened and finally held.

The two men shared a grin and a fist bump before securing the building and dashing back through the torrential rain. Chase headed back to the tiny ER and watched the controlled chaos for a while, marveling at the sight of Dr. Eve Carmichael in her element.

And she *was* in her element, even though she looked nothing like the snooty, well-groomed big-city professional who'd swooned at his feet two days ago.

Dressed in light blue scrubs accessorized with a stethoscope, and with her hair escaping a high ponytail, she looked both capable and somewhat rumpled. It was a look he found he liked. It made her appear younger...softer... and when she looked up and their eyes locked across the room that glowing amber gaze felt like a one-two blow to the chest.

Whoa! he thought. He wasn't sure if it was the sharp intelligence or the flash of vulnerability that had made his head reel and his chest ache.

Dammit. Did she know that he was genetically incapable of resisting vulnerability? Cool, remote and uptight he could resist. But she'd had to go and change on him. Becoming warm, soft and vulnerable.

He scoffed at himself. He was imagining things. There was nothing helpless about this fancy specialist from Boston.

Turning away, he shoved shaking hands through his hair. "Hey."

At the softly spoken word right behind him, he glanced over his shoulder into her serious eyes. And *damn* if she wasn't suddenly the most beautiful women he'd ever seen. Even bruised and battered, and dressed in baggy scrubs, she took his breath away.

"Hey," he said back lamely, unable to think of a single smart-ass comment. Her eyes were strangely intent, running over him as if she expected to see new injuries.

"You okay?"

Unable to tear his gaze from hers, he lifted a hand to scratch his jaw. He'd shaved hours ago and the sound rasped into the awkward silence. "Yeah—you?"

She blinked, clearly startled by the question, and Chase had to wonder if anyone ever took the time to ask her if *she* was okay.

She angled her head, looking amused. "Of course I'm okay. I'm always okay."

Arching his eyebrow, he said softly, "Always?" And when the smooth skin between her brows wrinkled in confusion he had to fold his arms across his chest to keep from reaching out to smooth it away. "Well…" he mused. "Just yesterday you were afraid you'd die before you had a screaming orgasm. You definitely weren't okay then."

Wild color surged beneath her skin and right before his eyes she became all flustered annoyance, heading for uptight. And, although he welcomed that flash of irritation, he wondered at the constant need he had to nudge her off balance.

"I can't believe you brought that up," she accused, spinning away. Laughing, he grabbed her scrub top and drew her back against him when she would have stomped off.

Yeah, well, the only reason he'd brought it up was to divert her from those soft looks of concern. Concern he didn't know what to do with. It made his chest ache and the back of his skull tighten.

But, hey, imagine that… It had worked. He was diverted. She was diverted. Mission accomplished.

With a growl, she wrenched herself free and he let her go, his gaze dropping to that world-class ass as she hurried off. Unfortunately it was hidden beneath the baggy scrubs, but that didn't stop his mind wandering into dangerous territory.

He'd had a narrow escape earlier and he assured himself that he wasn't thinking about getting another up-close-and-personal view of that part of her anatomy. Or any other part.

It had been a mistake. Besides, she was only here to mess up his brother's life. He had no intention of letting her mess up *his*. Been there, done that. He just wished certain parts of his damn anatomy would receive the message too.

CHAPTER NINE

IT WAS NEARLY two in the morning when Chase let himself into the hotel suite. He was wet, steaming mad and, he had to admit, struggling to remain calm. Especially when he found the suite empty and no sign that she'd been there.

There was also no sign that anyone *else* had been there either. With her.

Hissing out air through his clenched teeth, he shoved his hands through his dripping hair, thoroughly disgusted with himself.

His marriage had been over a long time and he'd been over it even longer. But he clearly wasn't over himself. Because the combination of mad panic and disgust had left him with a ball of fire in his gut and a tight, hollow sensation in his chest. It reminded him of a time in his life he wanted to forget and cranked up his irritation into the red zone. He'd left that life far behind, and in the five years he'd been in the South Pacific not once had he experienced that gnawing, angry helplessness.

Until *she'd* dropped into his life, with her tawny hair and 100-percent-proof whiskey gaze, turning his carefully constructed life upside-freaking-down. It was no wonder he was stomping around like an idiot without GPS.

After leaving her in the ER he'd joined the rescue effort and spent the next few hours helping out. At least until the wind had dropped to thirty knots and the island had no longer been in danger of being blown away. It was still pouring with rain like a rerun of Noah's flood, but they'd finally managed to evacuate everyone from the marina.

With nothing to do but wait for morning he'd returned to the hospital, filthy, elated, and sporting a few more scrapes and bruises than he'd had that morning. Along with his elation there had been an odd impatience to see a certain sexy doctor, with visions of escorting her back to the hotel and—

Yeah. Fine. So the *and* had been a little X-rated. Sue him. He was a guy on the edge and the thought of that *and* had had him steam-drying in seconds. That was until he'd found out that Jasmine Tahuru had sent Henri to take her back to the hotel over an hour earlier—and hadn't returned.

His blood had promptly turned to ice as he'd imagined all kinds of scenarios. Okay, so he wasn't exactly proud of that first scenario—of Eve and the young student locked in passion—but then an even worse image of a giant wave swallowing them whole, or Henri crashing into a downed tree, had popped front and center, sending dread slicing through him.

He'd torn out of the hospital as though his ass was on fire. But hadn't come across a crashed vehicle. Or signs that a car had gone off the cliff either. And then a slow boil had started in his gut. He'd told himself he'd find her fast asleep in their bed—alone—and that he'd laugh at his stupid-ass thoughts.

Only now, he realized, checking out the empty bathroom, he was the one alone.

Uh-huh. Story of his life.

He glared at the empty bed for so long a puddle of rainwater formed around his feet and he swung away, a sound of disgust finding its way past his lips.

What the hell had he expected? Her waiting in the bed? Candlelight flickering across her soft naked skin? Her smiling softly as she waited for him to join her?

He snorted rudely at his own lame imagination and

then a sound outside the door had him spinning around. It banged open, revealing Eve backing into the room and nudging the door closed with her hip. She turned, and instead of seeing her arms wrapped around the young stud—*yeah, yeah, he was an idiot*—he saw they were filled with a tray piled high with food and an open bottle of wine.

He knew the instant she saw him. She came to an abrupt halt, a loud gasp escaping her lips. "*Ohmigod!* Chase?"

Her eyes widened to dinner plates. He opened his mouth and took a step toward her, but she gave a gasping squeak and backed up, bumping into the entrance hall table.

Dishes rattled loudly and began to topple. Acting on instinct, he grabbed the tray just as it began to slip from her shaky grasp.

Well, hell. "Yeah, it's me," he all but snarled. "Who the hell *else* would it be?"

She slapped a hand to her chest and gasped. "*Dammit.* You have *got* to stop *doing* that." Her wide eyes took him in with one sweeping look, as if to make sure it really was him, then she sagged against the table, eyes closed, her breath whooshing in and out like she was practicing for the labor ward.

After she had her breathing under control she opened her eyes to glare at him. "What…what the heck were you doing? Steam-drying? You scared the bejesus out of me."

He was steaming, all right, and about to blow a gasket. But for a minute longer he just stared at her, drinking in her rumpled, flushed appearance. The anger warred with relief at seeing her unharmed, and it made him feel a little sick—and a lot unbalanced.

He wondered inanely if he'd finally cracked.

Yeah. No way was he answering that question.

He was just about to shove her up against the nearest wall when he realized he was still holding the tray. Casting his gaze around irritably, he gave a muttered curse and dumped the whole lot on the floor, catching the wine at the last instant.

Still crouched, he caught movement out of the corner of his eye and looked up to see her edging along the wall, watching him like he was a large and hungry predator about to pounce.

Yeah, well. He *felt* like pouncing. And there'd be no avoiding him. Not this time.

She froze, looking like a deer caught in the headlights— a realization that had dark satisfaction adding to the volatile mix of emotions making him a little crazy.

Smart move, lady.

For a long moment they remained frozen, until she expelled air in a long hiss of annoyance.

Feeling more than a little annoyed himself, he rose and stepped closer. Okay, he *stalked*, and he had the satisfaction of seeing her blink uncertainly at him. And when he pushed her a little roughly up against the wall and caged her between his arms she gaped up at him like he'd grown two heads.

Yeah, well, that's what you get for acting crazy.

"What—what are you doing?"

He leaned forward and cursed the warm, heady scent hijacking his senses. His head spun. Whether it was from the smell of the food on the tray or her, he wasn't sure, but it ratcheted his annoyance factor up a couple hundred notches.

"Do you *know* what I've just been through?" he grated softly in her ear.

She nudged him back to check him over, and when she made a low sound of concern he knew she'd found his new scrapes and bruises. But he didn't want her concern, *dammit*. He wanted—

"You're hurt?" She interrupted his thoughts with soft words and soft hands cupping his face. "Why didn't you say something?"

Grinding his back teeth together, he ignored the urge to rub his face against her soft palms.

What a sap.

"Forget about that," he growled impatiently. "I'm fine." *Uh-huh.* "I thought…" He hissed out a breath and the words rasped through the heated silence. "I thought I told you not to leave the hospital."

Oh, yeah. That should go down well with Ms. Independence.

She instantly stiffened, sucking in a furious breath. Her shove was no longer a nudge, and the light of battle was sparking a golden fire in her eyes. Being the ass he was, he decided he liked it. *A lot.*

Hoping to annoy her further, he crowded her between the wall, the hall table and his body, and was rewarded by a soft growl and a hard shove.

Oh, yeah, that's more like it, he thought with a savage grin. *Bring it on, lady. Let's rumble.*

"I don't answer to *you*, you arrogant ass," she hissed furiously, reminding him that he was mad about something too.

Oh, right.

"I went back to the hospital," he gritted through clenched teeth. "And when Dr. Tahuru said you'd left hours ago with Henri I couldn't help imagining him losing control and driving you both off a damn cliff."

Okay, so he'd imagined other stuff too, but he didn't have to tell her that. He was stupid, but not *that* stupid.

She instantly stilled, and the tension thickened until he could have practically hacked at it with a broadsword. He dipped his head to see her eyes and found that potent whiskey gaze an inch away from his, confused and wary. She slowly slid a pacifying hand up his abs to his chest and patted him.

Like he needed *soothing*, for God's sake.

His muscles turned to stone, rippling beneath her long

fingers and warm palm. And *damn* if it didn't soothe and electrify him all at once.

"I'm sorry you were worried," she said carefully. "But, as you can see, I'm fine." A shoulder hitched helplessly. "I was starving, so we raided the kitchen."

"We...?"

"Me and Henri. His uncle is the chef here."

Exhaling explosively, Chase dropped his forehead to the wall beside hers and wondered idly if *everyone* on this damn island was related. It was a stupid thing to think in the circumstances, but with his body resting against her trembling form he needed a moment.

Oh, wait. That was *him. He* was the idiot trembling like a little kid after a terrifying nightmare.

Disgusted with himself, he pushed away from the wall and turned, shoving a hand through his wet hair. Droplets of water scattered everywhere.

What the hell was wrong with him? It wasn't like he *wanted* to be responsible for her. He didn't. He was *relieved.* Relieved she didn't expect more from him than a way to reach her sister.

Which was fine. *So freaking damn fine.*

Rattled by his internal chaos, he turned back to find her eyes locked on him, wary and a little confused. *Yeah, well, join the club.* He was confused too.

He'd clearly lost his mind.

Realizing he needed to put a little distance between them before he did something stupid, he moved away.

"So where *is* young Henri?"

In the pause he could practically hear her eyebrows rising up her forehead. "Eating ice cream, probably."

He gave a snort and sent a look over his shoulder. She'd folded her arms beneath her breasts and her narrow-eyed look told him louder than words that he was an idiot.

His mouth twisted. *Tell me something I don't know, lady.*

With an irritated sound in the back of her throat she tried

to move—shove past him—but he wasn't ready to let her go so he just shifted, neatly blocking her escape. And nearly smiled when she stopped abruptly with a loud exhalation.

"Look," she said.

She was getting annoyed again—and why he found that hot, he didn't know. But he was hanging on to his sanity by his last nerve and couldn't be held responsible for his actions.

"I'm sorry you were worried," she said with exaggerated politeness, "but I've been taking care of myself for a long time. Besides—" she shrugged "—you'd disappeared, and I didn't think you'd care what I did."

"Why the hell wouldn't I care?" he demanded, feeling a little insulted by this slur on his character.

Her quick look of surprise left a crease of confusion between her brows. As though she wasn't used to anyone caring.

Scowling, he lifted a hand to rub at the sudden ache in his chest. An ache that had appeared at the notion that she didn't expect anyone to care. Then again, maybe he was having a mild coronary. Maybe he should get her to check him out.

She was a doctor, wasn't she?

His gaze swept over the damp, rumpled scrubs, molded to her very fine body.

Yep. Good idea.

And an even better idea would be to do it naked.

He reached over his head, grabbed a handful of the wet cotton between his shoulders and yanked the shirt over his head. Then he kicked off his sneakers and reached for his jeans.

"What are you doing?"

A glance in her direction caught her shocked gaze locked on his fingers. She was wildly flushed. A dangerous heat gathered low in his belly. A heat that had been growing steadily since she'd passed out at his feet. It would have been all the more precarious because of his dangerous mood if he hadn't begun to enjoy himself.

What that said about him, he didn't know. Or particularly care. There was only one thing on his mind.

Okay, two.

One: get naked.

Two: get Eve naked.

Things would get pretty interesting from there.

"I'm taking off my clothes."

Her eyes widened at the sound of his zipper filling the tense silence. She looked a little panicked. "I... You... *What?*" She gulped. "Aren't you um...hungry?"

He paused to study her in the low lamplight, taking in her heightened color and the tight nipples pressing against the thin damp cotton of her scrubs top. Her fascinated gaze was sliding all over his chest, arrowing down to his gaping jeans as though she couldn't make up her mind what she wanted to lick first.

His lips twitched. "Oh, yeah..." he drawled softly. He had several ideas about where she could start. "I'm starved."

Her eyes jerked upward and, on seeing his expression, narrowed to slits. She growled. Actually growled. And since he couldn't help himself, he smirked.

"Chase—" she began, trying to sound firm and patient, as though about to explain to a preadolescent why he couldn't smoke weed.

"Eve?" he mocked softly.

Rolling her eyes, she made a wild gesture with her arm. "What is...this?"

"This?"

"Yeah...*this.*"

He raised an eyebrow. "You're...wet," he murmured silkily, coming to a stop barely an inch away.

She gaped at him, her face flushing bright red. "I'm... *wha-a-at?*"

Suppressing a chuckle at her misinterpretation of his words, he leaned close. "Yep. And you need to undress."

"I...no...I do not," she spluttered, gripping the scrubs top between her breasts.

"Uh-huh. You can't shower in your clothes."

She paused, narrowed her eyes. "Shower...?"

His mouth twitched at the wary expression that turned hunted when he leaned closer. "Yeah," he murmured in her ear. "Sh-o-w-er." He let that sink in as he straightened. "What did you think I meant?"

"Um...nothing..."

He grinned and settled his hands on her hips. She jumped, tensing even more when he gripped her scrubs top and began to lift it up her torso. Squirming, she slapped at his hands, so he transferred them to her soft skin instead.

"S-stop that," she gasped, wriggling, her breath catching as his palms slid up her sides. "I mean...um..."

He bent his knees to look her in the eye. "You have something to say, Doctor?"

She tried to appear unconcerned as she continued to tug on his hands. "This is a...a mistake."

"I beg to differ."

"It *is*," she insisted, practically shooting his blood pressure through the top of his head when she nibbled nervously on her lip.

He wanted to do that, dammit. He had plans to do it—as well as nibble on other very delicious parts of her anatomy.

"Angry sex is *always* a mistake."

He froze. "Angry...?" He gaped at her, insulted that she would think him capable of that. He nearly stepped away, but one look at her face told him she was as aroused as he was.

He pressed his thigh into the notch of her thighs. She sucked in a sharp breath, and by the way her pupils dilated he knew it wasn't just because his jeans were cold and wet.

"This is I-want-to-jump-your-bones sex," he explained

with a growl. "This is if-I-don't-have-you-now-I'm-going-to-explode sex."

She looked like she didn't know whether to be flattered or insulted. "So…you're not angry?"

He pressed his erection against her. "Does this feel like I'm angry?"

She made a sound in the back of her throat—kind of a mix between a squeak and a husky laugh that shouldn't have been sexy but was.

"Chase."

"Eve." He said it with a smile in his voice. But his amusement faded when he saw the look in her eye. Kind of aroused and terrified all at once. "Dammit," he cursed, moving back a couple inches. "I'm not angry and I won't hurt you. Tell me you know that?"

She rolled her eyes. "I know that. It's just…"

"Just what?

She gave a huge sigh and muttered something beneath her breath. Her gaze slid away, not quite meeting his.

He cocked an eyebrow, wondering if he'd heard right. "What was that?"

Color stained her cheekbones. "It's been a long time," she repeated loudly, looking flustered.

"A long time?" he echoed distractedly, momentarily pre-occupied with her mouth. Especially when she licked her lip and left it shiny and damp. His mouth watered.

Oh, man.

"Since…what?"

She huffed out an incredulous laugh and gave him a hard shove. Her death look was answer enough.

"That's okay," he said, laughing at her. Laughing at him-self. "I think I remember enough for both of us." Then he whipped her top over her head and tossed it somewhere behind him, not caring where it landed.

Beneath the scrubs top was a teeny-tiny crop top. And no bra. As evidenced by the way thin, tight fabric molded to her full, naked breasts. Breasts, he discovered as his breath whooshed out, that were either cold or really…*really* happy to see him.

Seeing the direction of his gaze, Eve gave a mortified squeak and slapped her hands over her breasts.

"Didn't you want to…um…shower?" she asked desperately.

His lips twitched, but she was too busy sliding her gaze over his chest like he was a five-course meal to notice. "Uh-huh." He was only interested in dessert.

"But…but I'm starving."

"Yeah…" he breathed, his fingers caressing her naked shoulders, and he was gratified to see goosebumps erupting beneath his touch. Holding her gaze, he drawled, "Me too."

"S-stop that," she gasped, waving her arm desperately. "Maybe what you n-need is a c-cold shower. A *really* cold shower."

He grinned and caught her flapping hand to lace his fingers with hers. "Nuh-uh," he said firmly, dropping his gaze to the tight nipples clearly outlined in damp white cotton. "There'll be no cold showers tonight." He turned to the bathroom and tugged on her hand. "What you need is a steaming…*hot*…experience."

She gulped. "S-steaming?" She looked a bit dazed, a lot aroused. "Hot?"

"Uh-huh." He nodded, eyeing the shower stall to gauge if they would both fit. He was a big guy, and he took up a lot of room, but since he didn't intend to let her get too far away from him he reckoned they'd manage just fine.

He pulled her all the way into the bathroom and closed the door, barring her escape. Then he slid his hands around her hips and shoved both scrub pants and panties down her legs.

Her eyes, slumberous and dark as old gold, shimmered in the soft light. And when she just looked at him, once more sending his blood pressure shooting through the top of his head, he took her hand and put it on his shoulder.

She leaned on him as he helped her step out of her clothing. Then, rising to his feet, he swept the little crop top over her head, leaving her naked.

Oh, man. She was hotter than a bushel of jalapeños.

Conscious only of the storm brewing inside the bathroom, Chase and Eve silently regarded each other, each waiting for the other to make the next move.

Deciding it would have to be him, Chase reached behind her, opened the stall and flipped on the water. The abrupt sound was startling in the heated silence. A silence that cocooned them in intimacy, isolating them from the rest of the world. It was just them. Here. Now.

By tomorrow he would have her out of his system and he could go back to his peaceful life.

He opened his mouth to tell her that he wasn't interested in anything more than one night when she beat him to it, cupping his face in her hands.

"I'm leaving," she said, so intently that he paused, confused. And, he had to admit, shocked.

"What? *Now?*"

She gave a low, husky laugh and his IQ shrank another hundred points. "Soon," she said much to his relief. "I just want you to know that…that…"

"That what?"

Her gaze caught and held his. "That this is a one-time thing. Brought on by…circumstances."

He tried not to feel offended, since he'd been thinking the same thing, and just said, "You mean the result of adrenaline and sharing something intense, like surviving a plane crash?"

A strange emotion flittered across her face too fast for Chase to identify. "Yes, something like that."

He held her gaze for a moment longer and then decided

not to waste any more time arguing. "Are we finished talking now?"

She blinked at him, then huffed out a surprised laugh. "Yes. We're finished talking."

Her breathing was ragged and uneven, and it was a moment before he realized that his was too. With relief and renewed lust.

Thank God she's not planning on leaving right now, nor expecting anything beyond sunrise.

Her hands wandered over his damp flesh to the waistband of his jeans and he forgot to think.

"So, then, why are you still dressed?"

"Maybe…" he rasped hoarsely, feeling her touch like a brush of living fire across his skin. "Maybe you should do something about it."

After a long moment her eyes dropped past his mouth and moved down his tight throat before sliding hungrily over his chest to where his jeans gaped.

At her sharply inhaled breath he looked down and realized he was so big and hard—bigger and harder than he'd ever been—that his erection was pushing the zip and plackets aside.

His chuckle was a rusty sound, low in his throat. "Looks like I'm just as happy as you."

"Me?"

"Oh, yeah." He brushed the backs of his fingers against one tight nipple and nearly combusted at her soft murmur of hunger.

In that instant any control he might have had vanished.

With a growl of impatience he tugged her to him, shuddering when her soft breasts and hard nipples flattened against his chest. The contact made a mockery of his famed control and he turned, backing her into the stall, covering her gasp with his mouth as he followed her in.

The kiss instantly heated, and before it sucked him under

he remembered to reach behind him and fumble the door closed.

The next few minutes were a battle of hands and mouths and tongues. Chase was so hard it was painful. Especially when she wriggled against him like she couldn't get close enough. His eyes literally crossed in his head and his knees buckled.

Before he could regain control of his legs—or his mind—Eve had pushed him to the built-in seat and climbed into his lap. Her soft wet heat pressed against his erection and he just about shot off into space.

Cursing, and breathing like a steam engine chugging up a mountain pass, he grabbed her hips and held her away from ground zero—before he exploded and things ended before they'd even had a chance to begin. Besides, he had plans that would hopefully take the rest of the night to fulfil…

CHAPTER TEN

TAKING ADVANTAGE OF the space he'd made between their bodies, Eve reached down and stroked him through the opening of his wet jeans. When she couldn't quite reach all of him—*ohmigod, he was huge*—she slid off his lap and tugged him to his feet, her hands impatient as she shoved the denim over his hips.

"Wait…" Chase chuckled, catching her wrists and tucking them into the small of her back. *"Wait!"* he gasped, his eyes nearly rolling back in his head when the movement arched her back, so her breasts thrust upward and her belly brushed his blue steeler.

She wriggled closer, reveling in the wild look that flashed through his stormy eyes.

"*God*, Eve. What's…the…rush?"

What's the rush? He was the rush. *This* was the rush. And she was afraid that if they stopped for even a second she'd combust and it would all be over and she'd never get to feel him inside her.

And she needed this…*him*. Really, *really* badly.

Ignoring his rough, barely incomprehensible words, she growled, "You're overdressed," and sank her teeth into the hard muscle of his shoulder.

He hissed out a soft curse and, taking advantage of his distraction, she managed to free one hand—which she used to touch him…finally touch all that long, thick, silky hardness.

"*Dammit*, woman," he ground out, capturing her hand and roughly shoving her up against the wall, where he held her captive. Breathing heavily, he muttered, "At this rate I'll last about two seconds."

Eve licked her lips and lifted her hungry gaze from his open jeans. His smoky eyes burned hellfire bright, and the sheer naked lust in them had her inner muscles clenching convulsively.

Oh, boy. Talk about lasting only two seconds… *Yeesh.* She was a heartbeat away from coming herself. Right. Out. Of. Her. Skin. And he hadn't even touched her good parts yet.

Shocked by the storm of sensation whipping through her, Eve squeezed her eyes tightly closed and at the same time squeezed her inner thighs together. The move only made an explosive orgasm more imminent. She gave a low moan and froze, breathing hard.

With her hands held captive beside her head, hard cold tile at her back and heat pumping off him in waves, Eve felt like a willing sacrifice to the volcano gods. Then, because the waiting was driving her out of her mind, she rocked her hips into him.

And because it felt so darn good she moaned in the back of her throat and did it again.

"Stop," he gritted through clenched teeth.

But when he didn't move away she gave a slow little cat smile and did it again and again, until he growled out a guttural curse and abruptly pushed away.

Feeling light-headed and weak-kneed, Eve watched as Chase shoved the wet denim down to his feet in one violent move. Finally kicking his jeans aside, he straightened and stared at her, a wild, hungry male intent on his next meal.

Eve, determined to feast on him too, pushed away from the wall and stepped into his space. Surprised by her bold move, he stumbled back until his shoulders met resistance. Elated at having *him* backed against the wall for once, Eve grabbed the soap and finally put her hands on his sculpted eight-pack.

Unfortunately he hadn't been caught *that* off-guard. He grunted. "Oh, no, you don't," he said, swiping water from his eyes with one big hand and the soap from her with the other. "If we're going to play all night, *I* get to go first."

Actually, it was Eve who got to go first…then second… and *ohmigod*… By which time she was squeaky clean and limp as a noodle.

Chase quickly soaped and rinsed himself before hitting the controls. The water was abruptly shut off, leaving her wheezing and panting in the sudden silence. Good thing he was wheezing and panting too—for an entirely different reason. She smirked, hungrily eyeing his erection.

Before she could recover he was tugging her out of the shower and wrapping her in a huge fluffy towel.

"Dammit," she murmured weakly, sagging against his wide, damp chest. "I wanted to do that!"

"What? Get the towel?"

His lips twitched, and if she'd been compos mentis she might have interpreted his look as loaded with amused affection.

His next words, "Make yourself come three times?" had her lifting a limp hand to swat at him.

"No," she wheezed. "I wanted to make you lose control."

Through sleepy eyes she saw his mouth curve, and she got a hot flash just remembering where that mouth had been and—*oh, my*—what it was capable of doing.

The hot flash turned into a spark and then—*wow, look at that!*—she was suddenly raring to go for round four.

And considering she'd had the edge taken off—*three times!*—being the one in control sounded like an excellent plan.

She waited until he'd tossed her onto the bed and followed her down, a condom between his teeth.

Quick as a flash she hooked her leg around his and shoved at his shoulder, rolling them both over until she was leaning over him, straddling his hips. At his shocked expression, she smirked down from her lofty height, and then took advantage of his surprise at finding himself on his back to pluck the small foil packet from between his teeth.

Instead of getting all grumpy and alpha, Chase grinned up at her, his eyes gleaming like polished silver between dark spiky lashes. As though amused by her bid for dominance, he stacked his hands under his head like he was relaxing on a South Pacific beach.

We'll see about that, flyboy.

"We gonna play doctor, Doctor?"

His lazy drawl was deep and amused, but Eve was pleased to discover that his heart was pounding beneath her palm like it wanted to leap into her hand.

Ha. He clearly wasn't nearly as cocky as he pretended.

Her gaze dropped to his erection and she did a quick reassessment. *Okaaaay*, so that wasn't quite true. She smirked. He was *very* cocky. And getting cockier the longer she studied him.

She licked her lips, grinning when a low, rough groan emerged from low in his throat. It sounded like the ragged sound of a man on the very edge of control. A control she wanted to shatter.

"No," she murmured gleefully. "We're going to play another kind of game altogether."

His mouth quirked even as his eyes darkened. "Do your worst, Doctor," he invited smugly.

And Eve did.

Eyeing his ripped chest and shoulders, she reached out and drew a teasing line from the center of his chest down the middle of his torso with her fingernail. He hissed out a curse and arched into her caress, jaw tight, muscles straining.

Distracted from her enjoyment at seeing his smug expression fade, Eve thought that he was even more beautiful like this: features tight, eyes glittering and the low lamplight etching his muscles in stark relief.

There were six hundred and forty muscles in the human body and his were...*awesome*. She knew the names of every muscle and she wanted to lick each one as she named it.

Leaning forward, she licked one pectoral and then the other. And then, because the size of his arms fascinated her, she moved there next, muttering each name an instant before she licked first his deltoid, then his tricep, followed by his bicep. Each muscle was rock hard and quivering beneath smooth, damp skin, and tasted so yummy she just had to open her mouth and...bite.

He reacted like he'd been shot. With a savage growl he surged up and quick as lightning reversed their positions. Shocked by the speed at which the tables had been turned, Eve gaped up at him.

"Dammit," she complained breathlessly, fighting the urge to rock into the narrow hips snug between her open thighs. "I...was...*busy*."

His grunted words, "Later...you can play later," sounded almost incomprehensible. He was breathing like he'd just swum around the entire island—underwater. After a few harshly sucked in breaths he confessed, "I'm about two seconds from launching."

Snickering, she gave in to the urge and rocked her hips, watching with fascination as the tendons in his neck stood out in stark relief. His breath whooshed out on a muttered string of curses. But before she could revel in her small victory, Chase had ripped open the packet and protected them with unsteady fingers.

Suitably...uh...suited up, he locked his fierce gaze with hers, laced their fingers beside her head and in one smooth, hard move, thrust home.

Eve felt her eyes roll back in her head. Her breath caught

and her back arched off the bed. *Oh, God.* He was huge, and despite her readiness the sudden invasion—after long abstinence—sent a tiny pinch of pain shooting through her.

He must have felt the small involuntary reaction and he froze. "Sorry," he ground out in her ear. "Just gimme a sec and I'll make it good, I promise."

But Eve was already melting, already feeling more "good" than she'd ever felt in her life. Her inner muscles rippled as they adjusted to his size and he gave a low, rough laugh.

He lifted his head. Blazing gray eyes seemed to see straight through to her soul. Before she could think to panic and hide, he breathed, "Oh, yeah. Just…like…that."

Dizzy with the heated sensations radiating out from her core, Eve brought her knees up to bracket his hips. And… *oh, man*…the movement forced him deeper than anyone had gone before. With lights exploding behind her eyes, it also forced a low wail to her lips.

With a rough laughing groan Chase began to move, his big, brawny body tense and trembling, every one of those muscles she suddenly couldn't remember the name of, straining.

Things got a little out of control then. He dipped his head and kissed her with all the pent-up hunger that had been building over the past few days. And with little thought to the emotions she'd been suppressing for what seemed like a lifetime, Eve responded as though she'd been starving for the taste of him.

His body began to move…over hers…in hers…with a stamina she might have found impressive if she'd been capable of thought. Even though she was desperate to retain some part of herself aloof, Chase drove her right out of her mind.

It was a short trip to the edge of oblivion and beyond. Clutching him with both arms and legs as she leaped right off the edge, she was vaguely aware of Chase following, his breath escaping in a long, low ragged moan of completion.

Chase awoke wrapped in woman. And for a few sleepy seconds he enjoyed the feel of soft feminine flesh pressed against his body. Since his divorce he'd had a few casual hookups, but he'd never, *ever* fallen asleep afterwards. Falling asleep signified an intimacy he didn't want or need.

Not again—and certainly not with a woman who was set to wreck his brother's life. A woman who, by her own admission, was just passing through, and who, much like a comet, would burn anyone in her path. Especially someone caught up in her fiery beauty.

And he *was* caught up, he admitted, as his skin prickled and heated. He was caught up in a giant fist of need that demanded he take her again. And then maybe again. Because, instead of slaking his thirst, the past five hours had made him hungrier than ever. If he didn't have her again— right now—he would explode.

It was that realization that had his heart pounding and his skin breaking out in a cold sweat. Not panic, he hastily assured himself as he eased away from her soft, feminine warmth, but a very strong sense of self-preservation.

Besides, they'd both said that it was a one-time thing. Well, *she* had. But if she hadn't brought it up, he would have. He didn't intend on letting a woman twist him into knots ever again. Leaving now, while she was soft and warm with sleep, was the kindest thing. For both of them.

Yep. Good thinking. Let's go with kind.

He carefully slid off the bed, ignoring the faint sounds of protest from behind him. He froze, racking his brains for an excuse to give her if she woke and demanded to know where he was going. But when her breathing settled again into those soft snuffling sounds he found so damn sexy Chase's breath escaped in a silent whoosh.

Leaving kept things from becoming awkward—kept

things light and uncomplicated. It also kept him from doing something supremely dumb. Like forgetting himself. Like sliding back under her bewitching spell. Like maybe thinking there was something more than one hot night in paradise.

But there wasn't. Could never be. She was like the storm, sweeping through his life and wreaking havoc.

Quickly gathering his duffel bag and his other belongings, Chase headed for the bathroom. Just before he quietly closed the door he caught sight of her snuggling into his pillow, as though seeking his warmth. He paused a moment to take in all those long lovely lines one last time, greedily.

He pulled on his clothes in the dark, knowing exactly why Adam had taken a bite of that apple. If the biblical Eve had had half the fire and sensuality of Evelyn Carmichael, Adam's fate had been sealed the instant he'd looked into her come-sin-with-me eyes.

Heck, Chase had willingly sinned, knowing it was a mistake. He had no idea what it was about her that turned him into a lust-struck idiot, but he wasn't stupid enough to hang around until she crushed his heart.

Shoving everything into the duffel, Chase quietly headed for the nearest exit, eager to get the hell out before he gave in to impulses that would cost him a lot more than a wrecked seaplane.

A price Chase was unwilling to pay.

Eve woke from what could only be described as a dead sleep to find that she was sprawled across the bed in a boneless, satisfied heap.

Naked.

Naked? Alarmed, she lifted her head—*where was her pillow?*—and discovered through bleary eyes and a curtain of tangled hair that she was alone.

Oh, thank God...

But what the heck had hit her? Then she remembered.

Oh, yeah. Chase Gallagher.

Her head plopped weakly back onto the bed and she lay still as the dead until she recalled in high definition exactly how her bones had gone missing.

Chase Gallagher.

She shivered. Sexy, grumpy flyboy had surprised her with his amazing hands...and mouth...and moves—some she'd never heard of, let alone experienced. But when she caught herself grinning and drooling like a crazy person, she groaned and rolled over, blinking in the bright light flooding the room.

Maybe now *wasn't* the time to be thinking of the creative ways he'd used his tongue, but, *boy*... Eve whooshed out a shuddery breath as her body heated and melted. The man certainly knew how to kiss.

Stunned by the events of the night—by what she'd done—Eve lay unmoving until she was startled from her rapidly escalating panic by a knock at the door. Her heart jerked like she'd been given a jolt from a defibrillator and she jackknifed off the bed. The last thing she needed was Chase catching her lying around naked with a stunned, speechless look on her face. He was smug enough about his sexual prowess without her advertising how thoroughly she'd been ravished.

The movement set all of her six hundred and forty muscles protesting. And her head spinning. *Holy cow.* She felt like she'd fallen off a cliff and caught every rock on the way down.

The knock came again, and with a hasty "Coming..." she fumbled around wildly for the sheet, finally locating it—along with all the other bedding—on the other side of the room. How they had got way over there boggled her sleep-deprived mind.

Wrapping herself in soft cotton, she stumbled to the door and was surprised to find a tray containing coffee—

thank you, God—a plate of exotic fruit and a selection of pastries. And a long flat box...

She looked up to thank the hotel employee but found herself alone. Securing the sheet, she lifted the tray and nudged the box into the suite with her foot, bumping the door closed. The suite appeared empty and she wondered idly—okay, not so idly, she admitted sheepishly—where Chase was.

She took everything back to the bed and poured herself a cup of black coffee. With caffeine finally pumping through her system, she lifted the lid off the box. She didn't know what she expected to find, but hidden beneath a cloud of tissue paper was a wraparound dress in soft green, silk underwear—*no, lingerie*, she recalled absently—a pair of strappy sandals in the same soft green, sunglasses, a hairbrush, a collection of cosmetics from a well-known French company and a designer handbag.

She gawked at the contents, all clearly of the highest quality.

What the heck...?

No note?

Oh, yeah, there it was, she realized, spying a folded piece of paper. She fumbled nervously as she opened it, feeling like a swarm of kamikaze humming birds were dive-bombing her insides.

There was no name scrawled at the bottom to identify the sender, but Eve knew it was Chase. Somehow that bold, illegible scrawl could only belong to the sexy flyboy.

One by one the humming birds turned to lead as she scanned the contents. She had to read it three times before the hastily scrawled words finally registered.

Hitched a ride to Port Laurent—business with insurance co. Bill already settled. Al will take you to Tukamumu. Enjoy.

Enjoy? That was it?

The question was, "enjoy" what? Breakfast? The goodie box? Seeing her sister? Being abandoned? What?

No *Dear Eve.* No *Love, Chase.* No *Thanks for the memorable one-night stand, I'll never forget you.* No *That was amazing. Let's hook up again.* No *Goodbye, have a nice life.*

Blinking away the sudden prick of tears, Eve swallowed the dry lump of humiliation lodged in her throat.

First of all: *What the heck had she expected?*

Second: *Who was Al?*

And third…

Eve froze when it occurred to her that she'd just been spectacularly dumped. In a scrawled, curt-to-the-point-of-rude note. After the most exciting, *hottest* night of her life.

With a strangled whimper she slapped a hand over her mouth. Oh, God—she'd been dumped. In the middle of the South Pacific. With no money, no passport, no air tickets and no clothes. Except for the ones in the box, of course. Designer lables Chase had most likely paid for.

She wondered a little hysterically if he'd chosen the accessories and cosmetics himself.

Trying not to feel like a hooker who'd been paid for services rendered, Eve shoved everything aside and rose. With a hand pressed to the queasy feeling in her belly, she stared unseeingly out the large window; heart pounding and tears burning the back of her tight throat.

Please tell me I haven't just become my mother.

Finally black spots began dancing in front of her eyes and she wondered if she was about to pass out from humiliation. When her chest began to hurt she realized she was holding her breath, and expelled it in one long, shuddery sigh.

Dammit. She was a thirty-year-old professional woman. A medical specialist, for heaven's sake. She was not a frightened ten-year-old, panicking because she'd been abandoned once again with strangers. Besides, even then she'd squared her shoulders and done what was necessary to protect her sister.

But she was alone now—*oh, God, she was alone*—because her twin had found someone else to love. From here on out it would no longer be Eve and Amelia against the world. Just…Eve.

Shoving shaking hands through her tangled hair, she worked on calming her breathing. She didn't have time to stress about the sudden feeling of abandonment, or the growing anger and disgust aimed right at herself. Not only was it childish and ridiculous, she had more pressing problems. Like replacing her passport and credit cards while being thousands of miles from home. And she really, *really* needed to pay Chase back—if only to salvage her ragged pride.

He must have dropped a couple thousand dollars at least, she thought a little hysterically. And that wasn't counting the luxurious accommodation.

An arbitrary thought occurred to her.

How on earth could a pilot who jaunted around the South Seas because it kept him in mai tais afford designer labels? Especially with his main source of income a tangled mess of twisted metal.

Unfortunately, before she could solve the mystery that was Chase Gallagher, the in-house telephone rang. Thinking that maybe he hadn't left without at least a *so long*, Eve shoved aside her disturbing thoughts and answered.

A soft, feminine voice said, "Dr. Carmichael, this is Kimiki from the front desk. The pilot is here to collect you."

Shoulders sagging, Eve assured herself it was fatigue making her throat burn and not disappointment.

She was lying through her teeth. She *was* disappointed. Stupidly, ridiculously disappointed.

And suddenly on the verge of a panic attack at the thought of getting into another aircraft.

"What? *Already?*" She cast around frantically for luggage she didn't have and remembered at the last instant that she was still wearing a sheet. "I…" She gulped, and then managed a strangled, "Never mind. Tell him I'll be out in twenty minutes. Oh, and, Kimiki? Can you please call Dr. Tahuru and find out how the hotel guest I treated yesterday is?"

"Word is she's recovering just fine," Kimiki assured her. "Mr. Chase flew them out early this morning."

"O-oh?" she stuttered with surprise, her fear of boarding another aircraft fading for a moment. "He f-flew them out? Himself?"

"Yes," Kimiki replied. "He bought one of the small seaplanes the resort uses for island tours and left before seven."

He…*bought*? Her mouth dropped open.

"I—I s-see." *Yeah, she saw about as well as she could digest that particular piece of information. Which was… not at all!*

Thoughts whirling, Eve thanked Kimiki and replaced the receiver. Stunned, she sat staring into space as she absorbed the news until one thing became clear. Chase Gallagher had been in such a hurry to get off the island that he'd bought the first available transport out.

Bought?

Who the heck did *that?* Or, more importantly, *who could* afford *to do that?*

Had he left because he'd thought she would make a scene? Cling? Or—her stomach clenched into a hot ball of humiliation—had he left because he didn't want to see her again?

For some reason that last notion felt like a slap in the face. Stupid, considering she'd made it clear that *she* was leaving, implying—no, *insisting*—that it was a one-time thing. Only now she felt sick to her stomach. Because whatever had happened last night felt anything *but* a one-time thing. And also because she suddenly knew how her mother had felt every time the latest man had walked away without looking back.

Determined to reach her usual aloof state, and to ignore her growing self-directed anger, Eve squared her shoulders and headed for the bathroom. She wasn't her mother. She wouldn't fall to pieces and go on a wild spending and drinking spree, and she darned well wouldn't be returning home with a broken heart or having a string of wild affairs to help her get over this one.

She was strong—far stronger than anyone gave her credit for. She was a survivor, and she had survived worse things than being dumped after the best night of her life.

So, even though it felt like the worst personal betrayal, she dressed in the clothes, armed herself with the make-up he'd provided and left the room without a backward glance.

Her South Seas adventure, it seemed, was over. The sun was shining and the island was once again bathed in that otherworldly light and a soft, balmy breeze.

Everything was as it should be.

Everything except...*her.*

But she'd be fine. She *was* fine, she informed herself, swallowing back the hot burn of angry tears. It had been a really rough few days, but it was time to get back to the real reason she was there. Amelia. Once she'd handled that with her usual calm competence she'd be out of here, home, and getting on with her life.

By the time Eve walked into Reception it was empty. Kimiki smiled when she saw her—probably because for the first time Eve didn't look like a castaway survivor. She'd also managed to conceal most of the bruises and her pale terror at the thought of getting on another seaplane.

She knew she looked poised and together, and she thanked her childhood for teaching her to mask her feelings. It was sheer grit and pride that had her following Kimiki's directions to the terrace, where she found the pilot sharing a cozy coffee with the elegant concierge, Sylvie Armand.

"Ah," Sylvie said, rising to her feet with a welcoming smile. "Here's your girl now."

Eve might have thought it an odd thing for someone to say about a stranger if she hadn't been distracted by the way the older woman leaned forward and, with her hand on the man's shoulder, kissed his tanned cheek before walking away.

Looks like I'm not the only one with a thing for flyboys, Eve thought with a sympathetic grimace.

Not that she had a *thing* for Chase, she hastily assured herself. *No freaking way.* That would just be downright emotional suicide. Besides, even if there *had* been a "thing" between them, it was most definitely over.

The pilot rose and shoved his chair back so quickly it nearly toppled over. Cursing softly, he turned and caught it one-handed, his gaze seeking hers. Eve had a brief impression of a fit, tall, youthful-looking man in his fifties before their eyes met. Dismissing the weird skin prickle down the back of her neck as wild imagination and raw nerves at the thought of having to board a seaplane, she thrust out her hand.

"I'm Evelyn Carmichael," she said coolly, to cover her nerves. "Sorry to keep you waiting."

The man's strangely hopeful expression faded to disappointment, almost as though he'd expected her to…what? Recognize him? But that was ridiculous, considering that, other than finding his amber eyes oddly familiar, she'd never seen him before.

His large hand engulfed hers. "Alain Broussard," he murmured, his gaze intent on her face, as though memorizing her features. "I'm very pleased to meet you, Evie."

Evie? The eerie skin prickle occurred again and Eve slid her hand free, feeling more and more freaked out.

What the heck was going on here?

Seeing her expression, he shoved his hands into his pockets. "Forgive me for being familiar," he murmured sheepishly. "Your sister calls you Evie all the time, and I feel as though I know you."

"Th-that's all right. Evie is…um…fine," she murmured politely as a really awful thought occurred to her. There was only one reason her sister would share personal stuff with this man.

Her blood froze.

Oh, God, please, no.

"Are you…? Is she—?" She stopped abruptly and huffed out an embarrassed laugh, feeling unaccountably flustered and horrified.

She'd always known Amelia had daddy issues, but this was ridiculous. The man was old enough to be their *father*, for God's sake. Besides, how did you ask an almost middle-aged man if he was your sister's fiancé without being rude?

Suddenly very glad she'd dropped everything to make this crazy trip, Eve shoved aside her own problems. It was glaringly obvious that Amelia needed her—if only to prevent her from making a really, *really* bad mistake.

Mentally squaring her shoulders, she sent him a narrow-eyed *I've-got-your-number* look and was surprised to see his amber eyes gleaming with an amused affection mixed with yearning.

Affection? Yearning?

What the hell was going on?

"Why don't we talk on the flight to Tukamumu?" he suggested gently. "I know how eager Amelia is to see you."

After a short pause Eve nodded, her stomach cramping, her heart doing somersaults in her chest. So intent was she on her own nerves that she jolted when he settled a hand in the small of her back. Maybe it was only a gallant gesture on his part, but the feel of his warm hand startled and disturbed her.

He must have felt her instinctive withdrawal, because

he dropped his hand immediately and put a little distance between them.

"I know what you're thinking," Alain said quietly, and when Eve looked across her shoulder, she again caught a glimpse of that odd yearning.

But, she reminded herself firmly, his problems weren't hers. *Sheesh*, she had more than enough of her own to deal with. First, she had to get on a seaplane and survive the flight to Tukamumu without freaking out. And second, there was no way in hell she was letting her sister marry a man old enough to be their father.

"I doubt it," she said coolly, struggling against the almost overwhelming urge to escape. But where to? They were on an island, for God's sake. And he had the only transport out.

He must have sensed her turmoil and decided not to press the issue, because once they were in the air he kept his comments to the scenery. Which Eve appreciated as it kept her from hyperventilating.

Fortunately they were soon flying low over a handful of small, densely vegetated islands clustered near a much larger volcanic island. Most of them were connected by long narrow spits of sand edged with delicate lacy surf. Surrounding the islands was a much larger spit of sand, much like a natural moat, that seemed to embrace the little cluster of islands.

It was…*wow*…stunningly beautiful, and it simply boggled her mind to think her sister would call this place home.

"Tukamumu," her pilot yelled, grinning when he saw her stunned expression. "The island closest to it on the leeward side is Rangi-ura—the resort."

She probably looked like she'd been whacked in the head, but she didn't care. Never—not even in her wildest dreams—could she have dreamed up such a pristine setting. Little wonder her sister had fallen under its spell. It was like something out of a romance novel.

"And that island there?" she asked, pointing to the smaller, rockier island farthest away from the main island.

"That's Matariki—privately owned. If you look carefully you can see the house."

Eyes narrowed against the bright sunlight, Eve could just make out a sprawling structure, practically built into the steep jungle-covered terrain. Winding stone steps led down from a wide wooden deck to a pristine beach and a wooden jetty.

"Someone actually *lives* there?" It was like something out of a movie. Not quite real. People in her world didn't own islands in the Pacific. In fact she'd never even met anyone who owned a holiday home in Martha's Vineyard or Cape Cod, let alone a private island.

He nodded, and she was distracted from the odd look he sent her by their low approach over a crystal-clear lagoon. He banked the seaplane and headed straight for the section of beach a short distance from what she guessed from the thatch umbrellas and deck chairs was the hotel grounds.

Eve spotted the house immediately. Set back from the beach, it was surrounded by a lush green lawn and thick jungle foliage. A woman appeared almost at once, and began running awkwardly across the grass toward the beach.

It took Eve only a second to identify her twin. And, despite the wild relief and joy, she was shocked speechless by the sight of her.

Because not only was she waddling like a duck she was—

"*Ohmigod.* She's…*pregnant*?"

CHAPTER ELEVEN

OBLIVIOUS TO THE fact that her voice had risen to a shocked shriek, Eve gaped through the cockpit window at the enthusiastically waving figure.

She finally turned to glare at the man beside her, almost incoherent with stunned fury that he'd taken advantage of a much younger woman desperate for love and affection.

"She's...*pregnant*?"

Alain maneuvered the plane close to the shore before killing the engines. Something in her expression and tone must have registered. "I told her you needed to be prepared. But—" he shrugged helplessly "—she wanted to surprise you."

Eve's jaw flexed as she ground her teeth together. Oh, she was surprised, all right. Try also shocked—*and devastated*—because her sister looked like she was about to pop.

And she hadn't even told her.

Over the years they'd shared everything. First words, first teeth, first steps. They'd confided in each other about dates and their first sexual encounters, for heaven's sake. How could Amelia keep something like this—something so *huge* and life changing—from her? And be with a man old enough to be her father!

Was Eve so removed from her sister's life that Amelia hadn't thought she would want to *know*? Want to share in the joy and anticipation of a child?

Fortunately there wasn't time for her burgeoning emotional crisis, because Alain was unbuckling her from her seat and guiding her to the exit. And before she knew it Amelia was throwing herself at Eve and clutching her close—as close as she could get with her huge belly—as if Eve was the last survivor of a nuclear holocaust.

"Oh, thank God you're safe," she whispered hoarsely in Eve's ear. "I thought…I thought… Oh, *darn*," she sobbed, giving Eve a fierce hug before moving back a few inches. Her huge blue eyes sparkled with tears as she greedily took in Eve's cleverly disguised bruises. "Look at me, bawling all over you, and you're the one who should be bawling."

She sniffed and laughed at the same time. Probably at Eve's expression. Which was most likely blank with shock…and anguish—because there was no doubt that she was hurt. Deeply hurt by her twin's secrets.

"Looks like a fiancé isn't the only thing you've been keeping from me," Eve said quietly, reaching out to brush the tears from her sister's cheeks. They'd been born only minutes apart, but she'd always felt like a much older sibling. Caring for Amelia, shielding her from their circumstances, had become a habit that was hard to break.

An indecipherable expression flashed across Amelia's face, leaving her flushed and glowing—and looking like a kid caught pilfering cookies. But she was radiant with health and contentment.

Eve closed her eyes on the rush of emotions, most of which she couldn't identify, and suddenly she felt like an outsider. No longer the most important person in her sister's life.

Unaware of Eve's emotional turmoil, Amelia gave a strangled sob. "I know—and I'm sorry, *really* sorry. It's just that…" She bit her lip and sent the man behind Eve a look filled with guilt, apprehension and stubbornness.

Eve glanced over her shoulder and caught the look of gentle reproof the pilot aimed at her twin. "You should have told her, Lia," he said. "Hitting her with everything at once isn't fair."

Amelia—*Lia?*—flashed Eve a worried look, and chewed on her thumbnail. "I know, Dad. I'm sorry. But she wouldn't have come if I'd told her."

Wait… *What?* Eve froze, her eyes darting between her sister and the pilot, widening with shocked disbelief. Her first thought was, *Thank God he's not her fiancé*, the second… *"D-Dad?"*

She shook her head, as though to clear the sudden buzzing in her ears. A buzzing that got louder the longer her head whipped between the two of them. She was giving herself whiplash, but…*what the hell?*

"What the hell do you mean… *Dad?*" she demanded, gaping at her sister as her world abruptly tilted, suddenly wavered and dipped before her eyes—even when she blinked rapidly to clear them.

"If this is a joke," she rasped, "it isn't… It's—" She lifted a hand to her fuzzy head, feeling abruptly light-headed.

Alarmed, Alain stepped toward her, and in that instant the sun caught his eyes and she—*oh, damn*—she sucked in a wobbly breath and swayed. She really needed to sit down. Because the vague sense of familiarity she'd experienced earlier struck her again—with the force of a level-five hurricane.

Those eyes were…*hers.* Exactly like hers.

Her shocked denial emerged as a strangled gurgle and she stumbled backward…away from those reaching hands. Away from the appalling truth.

Her last thought was, *Will this nightmare never end?*

Eve opened her eyes and wondered if she was right back where she'd started, with a sexy sea god leaning over her as she lay on an old rattan sofa in the waiting room at Tiki Sea & Air.

She half expected a hoarse voice to call out a guttural, *Ia ora na e Maeva*, but then she blinked her surroundings into focus and realized that the worried sea god wasn't her sexy, grumpy pilot but a younger, sweeter version, with soft brown eyes. There was enough resemblance to have her jolting—as if her internal balance had been thrown for a crazy loop.

Pressing a shaky hand to her queasy stomach, she squeaked when tearful, *pregnant* Amelia shoved him roughly aside. Before she could utter a protesting gasp her twin had thrown herself at her and was sobbing into her neck, her huge beachball belly cutting off her air.

The younger version of Chase—*ohmigod, she'd told Chase she'd come to stop her sister from marrying a loser*—sent Eve an apologetic grimace and gently pried Amelia's death grip from around Eve's neck.

"Lia, sweetheart, you're crushing her," he murmured soothingly, and when Amelia just gave another loud sob he said more firmly, "She's starting to go blue."

With a ragged laugh Amelia abruptly let go and plopped down on the floor beside the sofa—which, Eve finally realized, wasn't old at all and was luxurious and comfortable. As was the large, airy room they were in.

Before she could take in the rest of the decor her gaze came to a screeching halt, locking on to the fourth person in the room. Alain… *Al*…Broussard. The pilot. Her…*father*?

I'm hallucinating. There must be some flower blooming around here with hallucinogenic properties, or the coffee I had this morning was spiked.

An awkward silence followed, during which everyone watched Eve staring silently at the older man as though they expected her to…what? Start yelling? Freak out? *Believe me, I'm too stunned to resort to tantrums.* But freaking out was a distinct possibility. And her head felt like it was about to explode.

Chase's brother finally rubbed his white face, looking as shaky as she felt. "I think this calls for a drink."

"I'll help," Alain murmured, and that odd yearning was back in his eyes as he gazed at Eve. Eyes so much like hers it was freaky—and too much for her to process.

Once they were alone, Eve continued to stare at the empty doorway, not wanting to deal with any more surprises. But since she couldn't escape, because she was on another island—*yay!*—she sighed and sat up, swinging her legs off the couch.

She lifted a shaky hand to her head and breathed carefully until the urge to lie down faded. Her sister was waiting not so patiently for her to say something. But…what was there to say? Okay, *fine.* She had *plenty* to say, darn it. She just didn't trust herself to voice any of it. Not until she'd recovered her brain.

And, she decided, staring down at her bare feet and wondering idly what had happened to her new sandals, not until she'd made her sister suffer just a little.

Her head was pounding and she wished almost desperately she could rewind the clock. Back to the previous night…the past three days…when she and Chase—

Her thoughts abruptly halted as the truth blindsided her like a blow to the temple. *Chase. Ohmigod.* And then humiliation—and a healthy dose of fury—filled her. He'd known. *Had* to have known about…about— Oh, yeah, she thought, catching sight of her sister's huge belly, *that*.

Of course he knew. You couldn't see Amelia and *not* know. Why hadn't he told her? Warned her? Especially after— She buried her face in her hands to hide from the memory that he hadn't said a word about anything, had let her ramble on about leaving as soon as she'd stopped her sister from marrying someone she barely knew.

She gave a silent snort. Seemed like her sister and Chase's brother knew each other pretty damn *well*.

"Are you really mad?"

Amelia's tearful voice wobbled into the thick silence, bringing Eve's whirling thoughts to a screeching halt. Slowly turning her head, she glimpsed her sister's fearful, hopeful expression through the gaps in her fingers. It was a reminder that Amelia was waiting for her to say something.

She sighed. "I came here to stop you from marrying a man you barely know," she admitted, her words scraping over a raw, tight throat. She inhaled and exhaled a few times to calm herself, before dropping her hands and looking—*really* looking—at her twin for the first time. "Only to find you pregnant, looking like you're about to pop, and already *living* with this guy you 'barely know.' And your... *father*? What the hell...?"

"*Our* father."

"You don't know that." Eve sighed, massaging her aching temples.

"I *do* know, Evie," Amelia argued gently. "All your life you've felt different because your eyes are...*weird*. Your word, not mine," she spluttered with a laugh, when Eve narrowed her "weird" eyes at her. "They were different from the rest of us and it bothered you. But when I saw Alain— *Dad*—I knew. Besides, what are the chances that two unrelated people have the exact same eyes—the exact same shape, the exact same color?" Without waiting for Eve to comment, Amelia continued, almost bubbling over with excitement. "And guess what else you inherited?"

"The urge to strangle you?" Eve asked dryly, not yet willing to forgive her twin.

Laughter bubbled up Amelia's throat as she hugged her and then planted a noisy kiss on Eve's knee. "No, silly." She grinned, excitement bringing back the joy that always seemed to light her up from the inside. A joy Eve would do anything to protect. "He's a doctor too. A military medic, actually. He was stationed in Hawaii, when he and Mom met. He runs the small clinic in town now."

A military medic? That *was* a surprise—and it kind of explained Eve's affinity for medicine.

"You were determined to track down your father even when I told you not to waste your time and money on all those investigators? Most of whom took your money and produced nothing but dead ends. And what for? A man who abandoned our mother when she found out she was pregnant?"

"He's *your* father too," Amelia pointed out sharply. Then, as though unable to help herself, she babbled on, looking beyond excited. "And he didn't even know she was pregnant, Evie. Mom lied. He was redeployed before she even found out. He didn't know about us."

"A likely story," Eve said wearily, shoving her hair off her face. But mentally she recalled all the other lies her mother had told—to them, to her countless men. It was just like Chloe to manipulate everyone into feeling sorry for her.

"It's true. And the best thing is we can be a family now...a *real* family. Just like we always dreamed. I can't wait till you get to know him, Evie. He's wonderful. Everyone adores him."

Eve refrained from pointing out that they'd *always* had a family—each other.

"What about your fiancé?"

"Jude?" She giggled, flushing wildly. "We met in Hawaii. He was attending some hoteliers' conference and I was singing in that hotel nightclub when he came in. It was just like Mom said. Eyes meeting across a crowded room and—*wham!* Love at first sight."

Not wanting to upset Amelia by pointing out where "love at first sight" had got her mother, Eve said, "So what are you doing here?"

"He owns it. Well Chase does but Jude does all the managing...and stuff," Amelia admitted, blithely unaware of the shock her words caused Eve.

First a seaplane and now a resort?

"So, I guess I can't talk you into going back home?"

"What? *No!*" Amelia looked horrified at the suggestion. "I love Jude more than anything. He's my soul mate. Besides, Dad's here too. We…" She placed a protective hand over her belly. "We're a family now. I'm never going back."

Eve noticed *she* hadn't been included and tried to swallow the hurt. But Amelia must have seen her expression, and with a twin's instinct she grabbed Eve's hand and squeezed.

"You know I love you, Evie. I'll always love you. You're my twin. My best friend. But I can't go back. Not even for you. But I want you to stay…and not just for the wedding." When Eve opened her mouth to remind her of her job, Amelia hastily added, "At least until after the birth. I always wanted you to be there when my baby was born. Nothing has changed."

Yet everything *had* changed, but rather than remind her twin, she sighed instead. Ignoring everything but the mention of her baby, Eve sent her sister a wry look. "You *do* know you're carrying twins, right?"

Amelia's attempt to look surprised was ruined by the secret little smile tugging at her mouth. "How can you tell?"

"Well," Eve snorted, "other than the fact that you look about twelve months pregnant?"

Amelia pouted, then burst out laughing. "Yeah…" She grinned. "Other than that."

Placing her fingers on her sister's wrist, Eve checked her pulse. "I'm a qualified OB-GYN, remember? Twins are more likely to have twins. Besides, no one can be *that* pregnant with just one infant. Unless you swallowed a beach ball?" she observed with sisterly candor.

Amelia just smiled serenely, taking Eve's hand and placing it on her baby bump. She looked happier and more content than Eve could ever remember seeing her. Clearly the island, being in love and being pregnant agreed with her.

"No beach ball," Amelia murmured dreamily. "Just two perfect little girls, lying side by side." She looked at Eve, her eyes sparkling with unshed tears. "Just like us."

Suddenly the hard belly bulged beneath Eve's hand. She identified a knee, then a foot, as the infant kicked at her hand in greeting. She couldn't prevent a misty laugh from emerging.

She was going to be an aunt.

And soon, if she read the signs correctly.

"Hi, baby," she said softly, gently massaging the restless infant until it quieted.

Eyes locked on Eve's face, Amelia sucked in a wobbly breath. "I'm scared, Evie," she admitted softly, "but I can't wait to meet them. I'm going to be the best mom, I promise."

Enormously moved by a flood of intense emotion, Eve swallowed hard and took her twin's face between her palms. They hadn't had the best role model.

She studied Amelia carefully before saying softly, "I know you are, darling." She leaned forward and kissed her twin's forehead. "Seems like you found your happily-ever-after, after all."

And you don't really need me anymore.

"Yes." Amelia sighed blissfully and placed her hands over Eve's. "And you will too, Evie, I just know it." She turned her head and kissed Eve's palm, her mischievous glance peeking from beneath her lashes. "Maybe it will be sooner than you think too. There's a local custom that says if you meet someone the moment just before the sun sinks into the sea, you're destined to be together."

Eve rolled her eyes and slid her hands free. "Right. And the tooth fairy really took our teeth when we were six."

They shared a laugh at the memory of Eve hiding her tooth until Amelia's had come out, so they could put them under their pillows together.

She sobered. She was genuinely happy for Amelia, despite her misgivings. Misgivings, she admitted, that came from their difficult childhood and their mother's death during a birth gone wrong.

Eve had learnt the hard way that things often went wrong even with the best care. And, with just a military medic in attendance, Eve worried that history would once again repeat itself for Amelia. She didn't want to lose another person she loved.

"You look disgustingly healthy," she observed. "How are you really?"

"Oh, I'm wonderful." Amelia beamed. "Now that you're here, everything's perfect."

One evening a week later Eve murmured her excuses and rose from the dinner table. She needed to escape. All the loving looks between Amelia and Jude, the talk of babies, weddings and family, were giving her a headache.

Or that was what she told herself. The truth was harder to swallow. She was jealous—and ashamed of it. Although why she should be envious of her sister's happiness, Eve didn't know. Protecting Amelia had always been her first priority and nothing had changed. She was so darn grateful her twin had found the stability she'd always craved.

Besides, she had her entire future ahead of her. She'd finally accessed her messages and heard that she'd been offered the OB-GYN fellowship in Washington. Exactly what she'd worked so hard for, for so long.

So why hadn't she accepted? Why had she said she needed a few days to think it over? And why did the thought of returning leave her feeling depressed?

It was everything she'd ever wanted.

Wasn't it?

Of course it was, she told herself firmly, changing direction and heading for the beach instead of the veranda as she'd initially planned. She needed to be alone to sort through the wild pendulum swings of emotion that had her happy and excited one minute, filled with dread the next and then feeling a yawning emptiness a minute after that.

If she didn't know better she would think she was pregnant. She wasn't, and it frankly irritated her to think that her plans were coming together and all she could think about was—

Yeah. Dumb, dumb, dumb.

Sighing, she brought her mind back from straying in dangerous directions and kicked off her sandals, pausing a moment to enjoy the warm silky sand beneath her feet before wading into the shallows. Cool, crystal-clear water instantly rushed over her feet as though eager to welcome her.

Over the past week she'd been frustratingly unsuccessful in not thinking about Chase. She'd even dreamed about him. Several times. So often, in fact, that she'd started thinking there must be something in the air that had drugged her with a lust spell.

She'd kept herself busy taking care of her sister and spending a few hours each day with Alain—*she still couldn't think of him as her father*—at the small clinic. It had been…*nice.* The clinic more than her father, although she was getting to know him and had to admit she was glad her sister had tracked him down.

And yet despite the circumstances—or maybe because of them, she admitted wryly—she felt utterly alone.

She sighed. It was time to go home. Back to her life, her work. Where she wouldn't have time to obsess about things she couldn't change and wasn't certain she would even if she could.

Wrapping her arms around herself, she stared at the giant fiery ball hovering lazily on the far horizon and came to a difficult decision. She would accept the Washington position tonight because, as beautiful and tranquil as the island was, her sister no longer needed her. And since that was the case… Well, there was nothing keeping her here.

Nothing at all.

CHAPTER TWELVE

AT THE SIGHT of the lone figure standing motionless at the water's edge, Chase came to an abrupt stop. A gauzy calf-length dress billowed around the lithe feminine form, teased by the gentle evening breeze. He knew instinctively who it was. His body had recognized her long before his brain caught up.

Eve.

Shoving his hands in the pockets of his ratty jeans, he looked his fill. The deepening glow of the setting sun high-lighted the curvy body beneath the gossamer fabric. Even as his heart pounded and his body stirred, the unbearable loneliness surrounding her made his chest ache.

He exhaled in a long, silent curse. *Damn*. He didn't want to feel this way. Although exactly what he *did* feel wasn't clear. He knew only that the sight of her made him want to tackle her down onto the sand and have his merry way with her. One night hadn't been nearly enough to get her out of his system. But, after the way he'd left, she'd probably knee him in the nuts if he so much as looked sideways at her.

He snorted. Big deal. So he was a mess. He would just become *un*messed. He'd done it before.

But then again... He'd been so sure that when he saw her again all the conflicting emotions he'd practically fallen over himself to escape would turn out to be nothing more than lust for a beautiful woman. Oh, yeah—and the memory of spectacular sex.

Because the sex *had* been spectacular, he admitted. One-of-a-kind spectacular. The kind you waited your entire life to experience. The kind you wanted to keep having until the raging urgency cooled. Or until someone left. Because she *would* leave—and soon, if what his brother said was true. She'd received that offer from some fancy DC medical facility and would leave as soon as her new passport arrived.

Or sooner if she really wanted.

He'd returned to the crash site and found her laptop and purse. Instead of forwarding them he'd taken them back to Port Laurent without saying a word to anyone.

He didn't have a specific reason for keeping it to himself—at least none that made sense. One thing he *did* know was that having her hadn't cooled his jets. It had just made the ache deeper, the need sharper. It had also made him question the strange restlessness he'd been experiencing lately.

And now that he was standing here, witnessing the stark loneliness surrounding her, he saw the restlessness for what it was.

It was loneliness.

He was lonely. And it was all her fault.

He'd been sane and happy, bouncing around the South Pacific in his plane, free as a bird and doing exactly what pleased him. It had taken surviving an air crash with a mouthy, stressed-out doctor with soft ivory skin and amber-gold eyes for him to realize what he was missing.

He was missing…*connection*. Yeah, that was what it was. A connection with someone other than family. A personal and intimate connection.

And if he thought he could find it anywhere else he'd leave a vapor trail across the South Pacific.

Yet here he was, heart pounding, palms sweating, because he had feelings for a woman who couldn't wait to leave her own vapor trail. Feelings that left him unable to sleep, tied up in so many knots his sanity had begun to unravel—one *get real* look, one *you're an idiot* smile, one feminine snort and an eye roll at a time.

If he didn't know any better he would say… He would think he was in l—

Wait…*what*? He sucked in a shocked breath and slapped a hand over where his heart had stopped in his chest. *Love?* He staggered and thrust out the hand not clutching his chest, grabbed hold of the closest tree.

Could he be in…? *No way! No freaking way.* He was just having a coronary. Yep, that was what it was. He was just… *Oh, man.*

He gaped at the woman responsible for his mental melt-down and the truth hit him with all the subtlety of a sledge-hammer.

Well, hell. Wasn't that just great? he thought on a surge of resentment. He was in freaking love with a woman so wrong for him she might have been from another planet. And when a little voice in his head snickered—*Look at Mr. I'm-too-cool-to-fall-for-that-again…cut off at the knees by the woman least likely to stick around*—he sagged against the tree, knees wobbly, blood roaring through his head.

No wonder… No damn wonder he felt like he was los-ing his grip, he thought on a fresh surge of resentment. He'd lost his head along with his heart—to a woman who couldn't wait to be thousands of miles away. But there was no doubt—no doubt at all—that he was… He was— His breath whooshed out. He was in…*love*?

Breathing heavily, he glared at Eve, standing in para-dise as though she *hadn't* stolen his heart along with his mind. And before he knew it his feet were taking him to-ward her, as though obeying some command that certainly hadn't come from his brain.

But now that he was moving he'd just go down there and give her a piece of his mind, he thought furiously. How dared she make him crazy? Who did she think she was, coming here to paradise and messing with his carefree life?

She stiffened the instant he came up beside her, clearly seething with her own jumble of conflicting emotions and thoughts.

"Go away," she said, turning away as though she couldn't bear to look at him. That stung, but he figured he deserved it for sneaking out like he had, so he let it go. What he couldn't let go was her—not without a fight.

"This is your fault, you know," he growled when she began to move away.

Her purposeful stride halted and after a couple beats she turned, her face shadowed by the approaching night. But Chase knew she was staring at him as though he'd lost his mind.

"My fault? *My fault?*" Her voice rose with disbelief, interrupting his mental litany of the things she was guilty of. Now that she was looking right at him he noticed the anger glinting in her golden-brown eyes.

That surprised him—okay, only surprised him a little— because she'd been the one to put a moratorium on their... on sex. But then she was a woman. He should have known she would change her mind. *Had* she changed her mind?

"You said one night only," he pointed out, sounding like a petulant kid. "I was just giving you what you wanted."

"You don't know what I want, Mr. Gallagher. How could you? You didn't stick around long enough to find out."

Yeah, well, he hadn't wanted to get kicked in the teeth either. But he couldn't very well say that, so he racked his brain for something to say and finally came up with, "I hear you're spending time with your father?"

The instant the words emerged he knew it was the wrong thing to say.

Her head whipped around and in the gathering darkness he saw her jaw clench and her eyes narrow. "Really?" she drawled coolly. "We're going to talk about *this*? About my *father*? A man you knew about but didn't see fit to mention? Or how about the fact that your brother got my sister pregnant—with twins?"

In the half-light their eyes met and held. A primal awareness snaked down his spine and he opened his mouth to say... He didn't have a freaking clue. Because all he could think about was grabbing her and kissing the hell out of her.

When he remained silent she sighed and her shoulders sagged. Almost immediately they straightened again—that backbone of steel he admired, stiffening her resolve.

"You know what? Never mind. It doesn't matter because I'm leaving."

His gut clenched. "Leaving?"

"Tomorrow. Maybe the day after."

Without waiting for his response she turned and walked away. Instinctively he reached out and caught her hand, wrapping his fingers around her delicate wrist.

"Just like that?" he demanded, feeling her pulse jitter beneath his touch. "You'd leave your sister? Your twin and her babies? They're your *nieces*, for God's sake. And what about your father? What about—?"

She yanked at her arm and rounded on him, her eyes spitting angry fire, her body vibrating with barely leashed fury.

"What *about* him?" she demanded, her voice tight with an emotion that went way beyond anger. "He's a stranger—a man I never knew existed until a week ago. A man who didn't give a damn about the woman he'd knocked up even enough to leave a forwarding address."

She sucked in a couple shaky breaths before continuing, her voice low and raw.

"I had to take care of them. *All* of them. My mother, my sister and then my grandmother. Because beautiful, talented and vivacious Chloe was too busy looking for the next exciting man, the next dream job, the next adventure. She didn't care that her children were hungry and wearing clothes rejected by welfare. Or that her mother was too sick to manage two jobs as well as two little kids." Her breath hitched. "Was he there to protect us when my mother's men sneaked into our bedroom at night?"

Shocked to his soul, Chase could only stare at her while her ragged breathing tore at something deep inside. "Did they...? Did you...?" He couldn't voice the awful, terrible things he was thinking.

"No," Eve said, so quietly that he had to strain to hear her above the quiet *shush-shush* of the waves that lapped at their feet. "But not for want of trying. I fought and screamed bloody blue murder until my mother roused herself enough to kick him out. And then I learnt to defend myself—and Amelia. It didn't stop, of course, but our neighbor, Mrs. Friedman, was a kind old lady. When things got bad she'd let Amelia and me sneak in through the fire escape."

"Eve—"

"It doesn't matter," Eve said wearily. "Not anymore. I vowed to make something of myself and I have. Besides, Amelia doesn't need me anymore. She has her happily-ever-after. She has Jude and the babies." Her voice hitched again and she gestured to the island. "She finally has the home, the family, she always wanted."

Chase caught sight of the glitter in her eyes and his throat ached. He clenched his jaw against the urge to wrap her close and promise she'd never be alone. Because hearing about what she'd had to go through, the strength and courage of a little girl determined to protect her twin... God, how could he *not* love her? How could he not want to offer her anything she wanted...everything she deserved?

"And you, Eve?" he demanded quietly. "What do *you* want?"

After a short pause she turned away, and a soft, "Nothing..." came to him on the warm breeze.

Before he could blurt out all the dumb things whirling

around in his head he heard a shout. They turned as one as Jude came tearing down the beach.

"Eve!" Jude gasped, looking white and wild-eyed. "Come quickly. It's…it's Lia."

CHAPTER THIRTEEN

HEART LURCHING INTO her throat, Eve lifted her dress above her knees and took off up the beach toward the house. Her sister had looked tired and pale all day, and despite her protestations that she was fine Eve had made her rest. Her blood pressure, which had been a little high, had come right back down after her rest, but she'd complained of a nagging backache.

She was almost thirty-four weeks pregnant—about the time most twin births occurred—and lower back pain was normal. It was also right about the time in her second pregnancy that their mother had died. And although her mother hadn't had the kind of care Jude had insisted on for Amelia, things—bad things—could still happen.

Jude had spared no expense in having a high-tech nursery-cum-birthing-room installed, along with two incubators, oxygen tanks and a fully equipped emergency trauma kit. Just in case.

Clearly Jude could afford to pamper his family.

With the brothers on her heels, Eve tore across the grass and up the stairs, bursting into the house with a frantic, "Amelia, where are you?"

"We're in here," their father called frantically from the family room, just as a scream tore through the silence.

Eve changed direction, surging into the room to find him kneeling beside the hunched figure of her twin. The dark stain surrounding her confirmed Eve's worst fears. Amelia's water had broken.

"What happened?"

"She got up from the table and…and suddenly clutched her belly." Jude gulped at her shoulder, looking pale and shaky.

Alain was pale too, and she noted the faintest tremble in the hand he used to smooth back her sister's hair. He'd probably spent his entire military career caring for men, and didn't know a thing about birthing premature twins. Besides, when it was someone you cared about stress levels rose up the wazoo.

"Jude, help me get Amelia to the nursery," she ordered briskly, dropping to her haunches beside her sister to check her pulse. "Chase, go to the nursery, plug in the incubators and get the sterile units ready. I'll also need an old clean T-shirt and a pair of shorts. Dad, prep the emergency tactical kit. We might need it."

For a couple of beats everyone froze, including Amelia, who was hunched over, clutching her belly. They all stared at Eve as though she'd grown horns and spikes down the length of her back.

She frowned at their stunned expressions. "What?" she demanded. "Am I going too fast? Fine, I'll talk slower. Jude, help—"

"No," Amelia panted, grabbing Eve's hand in a painful grip that became crushing as the contraction reached its peak. "You…you…called…him…Dad."

Eve frowned, concern for her sister uppermost in her mind. Especially as Amelia's pulse was racing—a sure sign that something was wrong.

"Who?" she asked absently as Alain and Chase disappeared.

"Da-a-ad!" Amelia wailed as another contraction seized her. "You…you called him Dad."

"Don't be ridiculous," she denied absently, looking to her brother-in-law-to-be. "Jude. *Now!*"

Jude jumped at the order, seeming to come out of his trance. Within seconds he and Eve had Amelia up, practically carrying her out the living room.

"Don't touch anything until you've all scrubbed up," she ordered on entering the nursery. She helped Amelia onto her side. "Draw your legs up to your belly, sweetie. It'll be more comfortable while I get suited up, and you won't be tempted to push." She looked at Jude, who was standing there as though someone had hit him in the head. "Don't leave her. She's going to be focused on the pain, so you'll have to breathe with her."

He sucked in a shaky breath, looking around wildly. "I...uh...I don't think I can do this."

She stepped forward just as Amelia gave another hair-raising wail and squeezed his arm. "You can," she said in a low, firm tone, her gaze holding his until his eyes cleared. "It's going to get a little rough on her and she's going to need you to be strong. Besides, I'm here. Doing all the easy stuff."

After a short pause he sucked in a deep breath and nodded. "All right. Where...um...do you want me?"

"Just help her breathe. I'm going to wash up."

Without waiting for him to obey, Eve turned away and stripped out of the dress she was wearing, reaching for the shorts and T-shirt Chase handed over.

It was clear from the size of them that he'd raided his brother's wardrobe, but she didn't have time to find anything that fitted. Besides, he was looking a little stunned. Kind of like when she'd blurted out all her old childhood issues. Issues she would have sworn she'd been over for a long time.

Clearly she wasn't.

But she didn't have time to revisit her childhood, she mused, rushing over to the basin to scrub up. It was over and done and she wasn't that vulnerable, scared little kid anymore. She was a medical professional, about to deliver premature twins.

Her sister's babies.

The thought jolted her, but she firmed her jaw, turning and shrugging into the sterile gown her father held ready. By the time she was suited up Chase was edging out the door, looking alarmed and like he was wishing he was a thousand miles away.

But he wasn't. He'd chosen tonight to reappear, after eight days of silence, so he might as well be useful.

"I'm going to need you," she said, locking gazes with him and brushing aside her embarrassment at her earlier outburst.

His mouth dropped open. "I...uh...*wha-a-t*?"

"All hands on deck," she insisted briskly, trying not to smile at his hunted expression.

He swallowed. "What about Jude and...and Al?"

"They'll soon be pretty busy and won't be able to help this end."

He paled. "This...? Oh, no. No way in hell I can do... *that*."

Eve sighed and did a mental eye roll. "Do you fix your own planes?"

Surprise and confusion crossed his face. "What does that have to do with anything?"

"Think of it as fixing an engine."

He gaped at her. "You're joking, right? I can handle grease. I just can't handle bloo— *Holy hell!*" He shoved shaking hands through his hair, looking a little wild-eyed. "Why is she screaming like that? Is she dying?"

"No, she isn't." Eve reached for the pressure cuff. "Jude, bring Amelia to the edge of the bed and get behind her. She'll need you to support her shoulders," she ordered, dropping to her knees at the bottom of the bed, where Alain had already placed a sheet of plastic. "Don't let her lie flat. Dad, where's the fetal monitor?"

She turned back to find Chase still hovering in the doorway.

Her gaze caught and held his. "Can I count on you?"

His eyes darkened to a mysterious stormy gray, their depths swirling with intensity. After a weighty pause, he nodded. "Always."

For some odd reason a shiver worked its way up Eve's spine. She held his gaze for another beat before nodding. "Good," she rasped, her throat strangely tight, before abruptly turning away—because now wasn't the time to think about its significance. "Then bring that chux pad and help me get it under her."

By the time Alain had fitted the fetal monitor, the pressure cuff was inflated and beeping out its reading. It was a little high, she noted, but not dangerously so.

Amelia suddenly sucked in a sharp breath and Eve saw her body arch as a powerful contraction gripped her. "Breathe through it," she advised calmly. "Breathe, sweetie, but try not to push."

Amelia cried out and grabbed a fistful of Jude's shirt.

"I…need…to push!" she yelled, panting.

"Not yet," Eve said firmly, looking up into her sister's wild eyes between her propped knees. "I see a baby's shoulder and I'm going to have to reposition her."

Amelia gave another long wail that would have raised the hair on her neck if Eve hadn't been used to the sounds of labor. Amelia grabbed both Jude's forearms and Eve caught his pained grimace as Amelia squeezed until her knuckles whitened. The man was likely to have bruises later.

"Jude," Eve said, catching his attention. "I need you to keep her calm while I move the baby." She waited until his glassy eyes cleared. "Can you do that?"

He looked shell-shocked. "Uh…yeah…sure. Calm… got it."

Amelia started sobbing, her words an almost incoherent wail as she kept saying over and over that she couldn't do it, that she'd changed her mind.

She sounded so terrified that Eve reached up to squeeze her knee. "You can do this, sweetie. Just relax for a minute while I reposition her. After that she'll slide right out, okay?" She looked at her father, who was frowning at the fetal monitor. "Alain...Dad?"

He turned his head and Eve could see the fear and concern he was trying to hide. Without changing her expression she quickly noted that one baby's heart rate was rising, way above one-forty.

"Can you feel for the baby's other shoulder and bottom while I work on easing her around?"

"Piece of cake," he said, placing his large, capable hands on her sister's hard belly.

It wasn't a piece of cake, but Eve was grateful for his cheerfulness, knowing it would calm her sister.

"Eve, what's happening? Is everything all right?" Jude demanded, his voice a little higher than normal. He was sweating, and his breathing was almost as ragged as Amelia's. The hand he lifted to smooth Amelia's hair off her damp face was unsteady.

"Everything's fine," she assured him, with a calmness she told herself was real. "Just keep doing what you're doing. And for God's sake, Amelia, don't push until I tell you to."

Amelia made a growling sound in the back of her throat that Eve might have found amusing at any other time. She gently inserted two fingers beneath the baby's left shoulder and carefully pushed until it disappeared. Then she felt around until she'd identified the back of the neck and the head, supporting both as she cautiously eased the infant into a better position. Within seconds the head appeared.

"Thank God." She huffed out her relief, soothing her sister as another contraction gripped her. "You're doing great," she soothed quietly. "Not long now and you can push."

When Amelia screamed and arched her back Jude leaned forward, fisting a hand in Eve's T-shirt. He yanked her upwards. "It's killing her! *Do* something!"

Without a beat she shrugged him off, her attention on the sight of the head emerging. "Get it together, Jude," she ordered quietly. "She needs to know she can count on you."

"She can… She does… Oh, God. We're not doing *this* again." He grabbed Eve again and shook her. "Do you hear me? We…are…*not*…doing…this…again!"

"Hey, bro…" Chase suddenly appeared beside her. He pried Jude's fingers off her. "They heard you in Honolulu. Chill. Get a grip, man. Eve knows what she's doing. Let her do it."

She sent Chase a quick look of gratitude, faintly amused by his fierceness. "It's okay," she murmured, transferring her attention to Jude. He was a wreck, so she smiled encouragingly at him. "Fathers tend to get a little intense. It's allowed."

Helpless tears swam in his soft brown eyes and for a moment hers got a little misty too.

She inhaled. "We're doing this now," she said, transferring her gaze to her sister's sweat-slicked face. "Amelia. You can push on the next contr— Oh, yes. Just like that. Another one. Nearly there…"

The baby's head suddenly cleared, face downward, one shoulder still wedged tight. She gently supported the tiny head and neck.

"Breathe through the next one for just a sec…" When the tension lessened, she eased the left shoulder free. "That's great," she murmured, and took the heated towel her father handed her. "Just one more push and you'll be holding your baby. What are we calling her?"

"Is—Isabella," Amelia gasped.

The rest of the infant slid out into her waiting hands.

"I've got her," she said in triumph, her gaze flying up to connect with her twin's for a second. "Isabella. And she's beautiful."

The baby gave a muffled squawk, then let out a lusty cry, her little fists waving at the indignity she had just experienced. Eve gave a wobbly laugh as a collective sigh of relief followed. With her sister laughing and crying, and panting with exertion, Eve dried the baby as Alain applied a plastic clip to the umbilical cord and then cut it.

She swopped the wet towel for the dry one that Chase held out. Their eyes connected for an instant. She froze, and the room and its occupants went *whoosh*, leaving just the two of them floating in a vacuum. The only thing keeping her from drifting away was the invisible link between their locked gazes.

Ears buzzing, heart pounding, Eve felt a tingle skate across her skin. As though something profound and earth-shattering had just occurred. And then for one blinding instant her mind cleared—and she staggered.

Oh, God. She'd gone and done the unthinkable. She'd committed emotional suicide.

She shook her head to clear the unwelcome thought, but the truth remained—a neon light blazing in the darkness.

She gone and fallen for a sexy, grumpy flyboy with commitment issues. But that wasn't just ridiculous...it was impossible. No one could fall in love in less than a fortnight—well, three days, actually.

It was... It was... She blinked rapidly to clear her vision. *Dammit.* It was true. This...this madness could only mean one thing.

She was in love with Chase Gallagher.

He must have seen something in her face, because he stepped forward, his gaze filled with concern.

That "something" might very well have been horror... and panic...because not only did he not love her back, he'd *bought* a plane to get the hell away from her.

* * *

Chase's heart leaped into his throat. One minute Eve had been staring at him as though he was the only person in the room, the next her expression had turned stunned—as though something earth-shattering had just occurred to her.

And by look on her face it had filled her with horror.

He reached out, catching her shoulders as she stumbled back a step. Was there something wrong with her? With the baby? Or was it Amelia?

His eyes flashed to his brother's fiancée and he saw she was moaning again, her back arched off the bed. She was also chanting.

"Oh, God, oh, God, make it stop."

He shook Eve and she abruptly came out of her trance.

"What's wrong?" she demanded, instinctively cradling the now quiet infant.

"I was about to ask you the same thing—" he began, but she wasn't listening, swinging around as Alain interrupted quietly.

"Uh…Evelyn, darling, I think we have a problem.'

"Here," she said, thrusting the tiny bundle at Chase.

His arms automatically closed around the baby, but he was shocked speechless that she would trust him with a fragile newborn.

Heart pounding, knees knocking, Chase stared down at the tiny face with its big eyes, cute little nose and rosebud mouth. What the hell was he supposed to do with a fragile scrap of life that weighed as much as a kitten? Didn't Eve know that he'd never held a baby in his life? What if he dropped her? What if he—?

"Keep her warm," she ordered. "And keep an eye on her breathing and her color."

"But…"

"She needs to stay nice and pink."

"Wait!" he said a little frantically. "I—"

"Busy here, Chase," she said impatiently, already focusing on the problem.

Chase noticed immediately that there was blood. *Oh, man.* He gulped when Amelia arched her back again and gave the kind of scream that sounded like fingernails scraping down a chalkboard. It echoed in his head as his eyes were drawn to the blood... He blinked and felt his world tilt. A lot of blood.

"Man up," she snapped, taking in his abrupt loss of color. "Isabella needs you. *I* need you."

Without waiting for him to respond—and he couldn't anyway...not with his stomach sitting in his throat—Eve turned away, issuing orders in a quiet, firm voice.

He stumbled backward until his shoulder hit the wall. Through the buzzing in his ears he heard her say something that sounded like placental abruption. Then she began ordering Al around in a way that calmed him even as his stress levels rose through the freaking roof.

Something was wrong.

He didn't want to know what his brother was going through, but he knew that whatever it was, it was bad. Almost blindly, he gazed down at the tiny girl in his arms. "If your guardian angel is close, kid, I think you'd better start praying. You gotta be strong, sweet Belle. Your mama needs you. Your sister needs you."

She blinked up at him and for an instant he thought that maybe she'd understood him, because her little forehead creased, her eyes locked on his. But that was impossible. Babies couldn't see clearly. At least that was what he'd heard.

Everything happened really quickly then. And despite his squeamish stomach, Chase couldn't keep his eyes off Eve, off the way she handled the crisis—calmly, clearly the one in charge.

Alain administered an injection almost directly into Amelia's stomach that had Chase's own giving a greasy roll. As he watched, Eve prepped Amelia's belly with a swab of some brownish fluid. And then—*oh, man*... His head spun. He was going to pass right out, and then they'd have two crises on their hands. He sucked in a steadying breath and cradled the baby closer, as though to protect her from what was happening a short distance away.

Eve probed the distended belly and with one careful line of the scalpel opened Amelia up. He saw blood welling through the new incision and Amelia's cries echoed through the buzzing in his head. Before he could bellow at Eve to stop before she injured the baby, Eve's hands had slipped in—*oh, God*—and then...and then... He blinked... *Oh, wow. Look at that!* She gently eased the tiny head out, still covered with a membrane.

With a few deft moves Eve ruptured the membrane, accepted the suction thingy Alain held out and she cleared the baby's nose and mouth. Then she was lifting the tiny little body out into the world.

He was stunned and awed by what had taken less than a minute.

"Go," Alain said, quickly wrapping the baby in a towel as Eve applied a clip and severed the umbilical cord. "I'll deal with things here. Get that baby with us. Her twin needs her."

It was then that Chase realized the little body had been limp and mottled before being bundled up. His heart lurched in his chest as his eyes followed Eve's progress across the room. He felt like the room was pressing in on him as she placed the baby on a soft warmer, her body shielding the rest of the room from what she was doing.

For long tense minutes he waited, holding his breath. And just when he thought the little girl in his arms, scarcely an hour old, was going to experience a devastating loss, a thin wail broke the tense silence.

His legs gave way then, and the next minute he realized

he was sitting on the floor, staring at his niece and blinking back tears of joy and relief.

"Thank God," he murmured, dropping a gentle kiss on
the baby's soft head and murmuring a word of thanks.
"Those prayers worked, kiddo. She's okay. Your sister's
okay. And your Aunt Eve—she's the best. She's made sure
your little sister's gonna be just fine." He lifted his head,
addressing his next words to Eve. "She's going to be okay,
isn't she?"

Eve turned to him, her smile a bit wobbly. Her golden
eyes shone with joy and love and a wild, deep relief. She
blinked back tears and gave a watery laugh. "Shc's going
to be just fine."

In that moment Chase realized she was everything he'd
ever wanted. If only—

Hell, no. He was going to make her listen, keep her here.
Even if he had to steal her new passport too.

CHAPTER FOURTEEN

Eve placed a pink and squalling Anastasia on Amelia's chest and bent down to kiss her cheek. Her twin looked up then, and in a brief telling moment all their love and shared history passed between them.

"Congratulations, Mom. You did great."

"Oh, my gosh—she's beautiful," Amelia said, looking exhausted but elated. "Where's her sister? I want to hold them both."

"She's right here," Chase said, stepping close to the bed.

In Eve's opinion he appeared a little reluctant to relinquish his precious armful. She thought back to earlier, when he'd looked like she'd handed him a box full of live grenades. Now he was wearing an expression of such stunned love, awe and heartbreak that she instinctively reached out to him.

Realizing what she was doing, she dropped her hand and turned away. She didn't need to burden him with her feelings, she thought. Besides, this was about Amelia and Jude—not her.

Alain, finishing the wound closure, looked up at that moment. He must have caught her staring at Chase, because he said quietly, "You're in love with him."

Her head whipped up, an automatic denial on her lips. "No, I—"

But Alain was gazing at her with his own brand of love and heartbreak, and her heart squeezed again.

"It doesn't matter," she murmured. "I'm leaving soon. Besides, he doesn't love me back."

"Are you so sure of that, Evie?" he asked gently, reaching out to touch an unsteady hand to her shoulder. "Are you so afraid you're unlovable?" He shook his head. "You're not, sweetheart. You just have to let people in—let them love you."

Instead of replying she just shook her head, suddenly eager to be alone. *Did* she think she was unlovable? *Did* she shut people out because of her past?

"Go meet your granddaughters, Dad. But only for a few minutes. They need to go into the incubators for a while. Especially the little one."

For a long moment he seemed conflicted, and Eve thought he meant to push her. His gaze searched hers, then he nodded and turned away—but not before he murmured, "We need to talk, Evelyn, and soon."

Eager to escape the emotionally charged moment, Eve swallowed the lump in her throat and moved off to tidy up, clearing away the debris so the new family could bond in a fresh, clean environment. Thankfully her part of the drama was over, she thought, gathering up the soiled linen and towels before quietly slipping out of the room.

At the door she looked back and drew in a long, shuddery breath as the scene hit her like a sharp blow to the heart. Her head swam and her knees buckled as something she'd been ignoring struck her with a sudden blinding clarity.

Everything that meant anything to her was right there in that room. Her twin and the man she had chosen to love, their new twin daughters, her father and—

Yes, and Chase too. Because she loved him. More than she would have thought possible. But the question was…

could she make herself vulnerable to him? Could she trust that he wouldn't leave her?

She honestly didn't know. And the knowledge had her taking that step away, even as her brain greedily stored away the image of him sharing in the joy of new life. It was one of those moments that would be seared into her memory for all time. A moment that, if a person was open to it, redefined their life.

It was a moment of new life, new beginnings and second chances. Because everyone deserved a second chance, didn't they? Even her father. Because he *was* her father. She knew that—just as she knew she'd been unfair earlier.

He wasn't to blame. Just as Chase wasn't to blame for her fear of rejection when all he'd done was what she'd said she wanted. A one-off thing. Nothing more.

But, knowing what she did now, how could she leave all this behind? How could she walk away from everything she'd always thought only her sister yearned for?

A family.

Her eyes locked unerringly on Chase and her heart clenched. The big question she should be asking herself was how could she stay, knowing he didn't...couldn't... love her back?

Pressing an unsteady hand to the ache filling the center of her chest, Eve quietly left the room. She needed a minute to herself. A minute to shore up the wall around her heart. Because, despite what she so desperately yearned for, it wasn't to be.

And maybe it never had been.

Chase found her in the same spot, the same pose as before. It was like déjà vu. Only this time, instead of the glowing sun, a huge moon illuminated the small private beach, gilding the sand, the water and the woman in glowing silver.

For a moment it staggered him, had him sucking in a sharp breath at the depth of his feelings for her. The woman of his dreams, the woman of his heart, stood apart—isolated and alone.

"Why are you out here?" he asked quietly as he came up beside her. "They need you."

She jolted, as though he'd surprised her, and turned away, murmuring something that sounded like, "No. They don't. Not anymore."

He opened his mouth and caught a flash of something sparkling on her cheek, her lashes.

Tears?

"You're crying?"

She gave a husky laugh that reached out and grabbed him by the throat.

"Don't b-be ridiculous. What's there to cry about?"

He took her shoulders, turned her toward him. "That's what I'd like to know," he murmured, reaching up to catch another tear, sparkling like a tiny diamond on her thick lashes.

She irritably brushed his hand away, wrapping her arms protectively around her body as she put a little distance between them. Was she protecting herself from her emotions…or him?

"It…it got a bit tense there for a minute," she admitted on a ragged sigh, rubbing her upper arms briskly. "I thought we might lose her."

"Hey," he said gently, moving close, careful not to touch her. Especially as she vibrated with enough tension that he was afraid one wrong move would shatter her fragile control. "You were awesome. Amazingly calm when everyone else was panicking." He sucked in an unsteady breath at the memory. "Although I have to admit it totally grossed me out, and if I hadn't been holding Belle I most probably would have hit the floor horizontally."

Eve gave a watery laugh and then, in a move that surprised the hell out of him, she dropped her forehead onto his chest and sobbed as if her heart was breaking.

For an instant he panicked. Had he said the wrong thing? *Aw, man...*

"Hey...hey," he crooned, instinctively wrapping his arms around her, pulling her in, tucking her head beneath his chin. He felt as if he was finally home—that *she* was home. Right where she belonged.

So he held her, let her cry. Knowing he could do nothing else.

A minute stretched to two, but he was in no hurry to let her go. He'd walked away once, but he wouldn't let her scare him off now. Not again. Besides, he had to show her somehow that she could count on him. Always.

"Eve... Eve... Eve..." he murmured softly, dropping a soft kiss on her head. "It's okay—everything's fine. The babies are fine. Amelia is glowing. And you'd swear that Jude—he's standing there smiling like an idiot, like he did it all himself. But you know what, babe? They need you there, celebrating with them—not out here, crying like your heart is breaking."

She stiffened, and then in an abrupt move shoved him away. He caught her wrist as she turned.

"Don't go," he urged, and his own heart squeezed in his chest, because he had a bad feeling she was gearing up to walk away. He'd seen her expression when she'd left the room and he knew, just *knew*, she was leaving.

"Why?" she asked quietly, her voice emotionless, her eyes dark and remote.

Chase's mind went abruptly blank.

"I...I..."

Misinterpreting his hesitation, Eve tried to break free, but Chase tightened his grip. He wasn't letting go. Not until he'd—

"Because...they...they need you, Eve. Amelia...the girls...your father."

There was a buzzing sound in his head and his panic ratcheted up a couple million notches when he saw the expressions chasing each other across her face. Anguish, desolation, grief. And then…right there…that backbone of steel, straightening with pride. He could feel her slipping away.

"And I…I n-n…" His throat closed but he forced the words out before he blinked and she disappeared. "I need… I need…" He took a couple ragged breaths and ended with, "I-need-you-too," in a breathless rush.

For long, tense moments Eve's gaze remained steady on his, then a quiet "Why?" drifted across the couple of feet that separated them.

He blinked. "Why?"

"Yes. Why?" Her voice was curiously emotionless. "Why should I stay when everything I've worked for is in DC?"

Panic moved through him like an oily snake, slithering and burrowing deep. "Because…because everything you care about is here. Isn't it? Besides…" He shrugged. "I need you."

For long moments she simply stared at him, until finally she blinked and turned away, hurt battling with the desperate hope in her eyes.

"I can't," she said, drawing into herself, away from him.

Chase's heart sank as she slid free from his hold. Feeling his own hands shake, he shoved them in his pockets.

"You can't?" he muttered, swallowing the last of his hope. And with it came a rising anger. Here he was, offering her everything, and all she could say was, *I can't.* "What the hell does that even *mean*?" he demanded. "You can't *what*? Stay? Love me? Need me? *What?* What the hell can't you do, Eve?"

She turned on him then, her eyes flashing with anger and a deep, deep fear. "It's not enough." And then, more quietly. "It's not enough."

"Not…*enough*?" His jaw clenched. "I offer you everything and it's…not enough?"

Her body stilled in the process of turning away. Her eyes were dark and unreadable. "What do you mean by *everything*, Chase? How can you say that and then leave?"

"Who says I'm leaving?"

"You *did* leave," Eve pointed out in a sharp reminder, and when he arched his brow she snapped, "Oh, don't look at me like that. You even bought an aircraft so you could escape." Eve was gratified to see him wince. "Really? Who *does* that?"

"An idiot," Chase muttered, and when she gave a strangled laugh, he lost his battle with his temper. He grabbed her, shook her. "An idiot in love—that's who. Why the hell do you think I didn't tell you about your passport? Why the hell do you think—?"

He stopped abruptly when he realized what he'd admitted. He let her go and shoved his hands through his hair, wondering if he could go back a couple of minutes. To when he hadn't shoved a foot in his mouth.

She blinked rapidly looking stunned. "You... My... what?"

He sighed. "Yeah. I found it," he admitted quietly. "I found it and I kept it."

Her eyes widened. "What...? Why?"

Chase turned away with an awkward laugh. "Hell, I don't know." Then he sighed and swung back, his resolve hardening. When had he become such a coward? *When you fell in love—that's when.* "Yes, I do," he countered harshly. "I was married before, did I tell you that? No?" He gave a harsh laugh. "Yeah, well I was. And it was a huge mistake. From the beginning. I promised myself I would never let a woman hurt me the way she did, and I haven't. Until you.

"It was easy to walk away from Lauren because looking back I never really loved her, not like..." He drew air into his lungs and shoved unsteady hands through his hair. "The truth is I kept your passport because I didn't want you to leave. I kept it because…because… Dammit, I didn't know it then, but I love you."

"What—what did you say?"

"I couldn't just let you walk away—" he began, but she reached up and covered his mouth with trembling fingers.

"Not that…" She gulped. "Before."

"What?" he demanded around her fingers. "That I love—?" He stopped when disbelief and desperate hope battled with the automatic denial in her eyes. "Yeah." He smiled, tension easing in his chest, his shoulders. "Yeah, I do. I love you, Eve, although I don't know why. You're uptight and mouthy and you don't know how to relax. You like to argue…"

He gave a soft laugh when her eyes narrowed. He covered her hand with his and tugged her against him. When her body melted against his, he smiled and planted a gentle kiss on her fingers.

"But I found I like it, *really* like it, when you're mouthy. Especially when you—"

Eve reached up and gently silenced him with a kiss, and with their lips still touching she breathed, "I'm scared."

"Yeah, me too—"

"No." Her voice hitched as she pressed her forehead against his cheek. "I'm really…*really* scared."

Chase felt an enormous relief flood though him. His fiery, fierce Eve was afraid. But that was okay. He was too. Afraid that he wouldn't be enough.

"I need you, Eve, more than I've needed anyone. And I think… I think you need me too."

She tensed for a fraction of a second, then her arms slid around him and she clung.

"It's too soon," she murmured against his throat, and a shudder of pure need flowed through him.

He shook his head. "No, it's not. I waited a long time for you, Dr. Carmichael, and I'm not letting you go."

"It's impossible," she said fretfully. "Two people don't fall in love in a fortnight. That's…r-ridiculous."

His heart stopped, then began a slow slog through his body. Had he heard her correctly? "*Two* people, Eve?"

She froze for a couple of heartbeats and then she tried to move away, but he tightened his arms around her.

"No. *No*. I…I just meant that it isn't possible for anyone to fall in love so fast."

"You have no idea," he admitted softly, and when she made a distressed sound in her throat he chuckled, pressing a kiss against her forehead. "Yep," he murmured. "Right about the time you opened your eyes and called me the pilot from hell."

Her head shot up and she gaped at him. "But…but…" she spluttered. "That's crazy. You didn't even *like* me."

"Maybe not." He chuckled. "But I *wanted* you like crazy. I still do. But you have to say it first."

She stilled. He saw her throat convulse before she turned her gaze to the huge rising moon. It dazzled him, that silvery glow that turned her amber eyes luminous.

"It must be the moon," she murmured.

He gaped at her. "The moon? What does the moon have to do with anything?"

"Seems I'm crazy too," she murmured, lifting her face. She brushed her lips against his. "Crazy about a sexy, grumpy pilot who crashed his seaplane in paradise."

He spluttered out a laugh. "Grumpy? You're calling me grumpy?"

"You forgot sexy," she murmured, sucking his lip into her mouth and then giving it a little nip.

He murmured something and caught her mouth in a punishing kiss. When they were both breathless, he broke it off and leaned his forehead against her.

"I'm crazy about you, Eve, and when you leave here I'm coming with you."

"You can't. This is your home." She gasped, taking his face between her palms. "I couldn't expect—"

"I can work—live—anywhere," he interrupted gently. "I just can't live without *you*."

"Why me?"

"You're it for me, Eve, and where you go, I go."

"What…what are you saying, Chase?"

Chase's smile turned tender. "I'm saying you're my everything. I'm saying I want to be your everything too."

For an instant she squeezed her eyes closed, and when she opened them again they sparkled with unshed tears. "You are. Don't you know that you are? That's why I was terrified," she admitted. "Terrified it was all just me."

"It's not. Never again. And if you still want to go to Washington—well, I'll just have to tag along."

"It doesn't have to be DC," she assured him gently. "It isn't the only city with great hospitals."

"No," he said. "It's not. In fact there's a great clinic right here on the island that needs another doctor. Or you could apply in Seattle, it's where I'm from and where my parents live, but I can run my business from anywhere in the world. All I need is a computer and internet access."

"You need a computer and internet access to fly a seaplane?"

Chase snorted. "Nope. I run an online brokerage firm, which is great because wherever you go I go." He cupped her face. "Anyone would be crazy not to snap you up in an instant, Eve. You know that, don't you?"

"I love you, Chase. It doesn't matter where I go. I just… I really want to be *your* everything too."

"Then let's go."

Her eyes widened. "What? Now?"

Chase laughed and turned her toward the house, suddenly lighter and happier than he could remember being. He tucked her against his side and pressed a kiss to her forehead, reveling in the way she pressed close.

"Later. I'll show you later how crazy I am about you. But right now Jude is opening a bottle of champagne. Right now I have to go ask your dad's permission."

"Wha-at?" she spluttered on a laugh, and he paused to snatch the lighthearted sound with his mouth.

"Yeah. It's what the guy does," he murmured when they were both breathing hard. "He asks the girl's dad's permission. I want to do this right, Eve, because…this feels right. *We* feel right."

"Yes," Eve said, smiling up at him and looking so beautiful she took his breath away. She took his hand, lacing their fingers together. "Yes, we do."

* * * * *

LET'S TALK
Romance

For exclusive extracts, competitions
and special offers, find us online:

facebook.com/millsandboon

@MillsandBoon

@MillsandBoonUK

Get in touch on 01413 063232

For all the latest titles coming soon, visit
millsandboon.co.uk/nextmonth